AS SHE THR— —— ——
THE STREET STALLS IN THE ENT-
RANCE TO VINE COURT, SHE WAS
AWARE THAT THE MEN GAZED
AFTER HER, ADMIRING HER TRIM
FRAME IN THE JAUNTY BLUE JACKET
AND SKIRT, THE NEATLY TURNED
ANKLE IN THE LITTLE BUTTON
BOOTS.

But she was a fantasy, the kind of woman they
pretended to want, but in reality they feared.
Fortunata never flirted; she preferred to talk
about politics. While younger women than she
were cementing relationships on the front
doorsteps of their narrow little houses under
watchful parental eyes, Fortunata would be leaning over the back gate, where Papa and his
friends discussed Italian politics ...

ABOUT THE AUTHOR

Among other things, Lilie Ferrari was a waitress in the South of France and a teacher in California before gaining a Master's degree in French literature, writing a thesis about Flaubert and suicide. She then went on to more cheerful work at the British Film Institute, where she worked in the Television Unit, taking particular interest in popular dramas and soap operas. From there she went to the BBC, script-editing *Eastenders*. Currently a full-time script writer for television, she has recently moved to Essex, where she lives with her partner. She has one son and at forty-four is a reluctant grandmother. *Fortunata* is her first novel and was inspired by the history of her own immigrant family.

LILIE FERRARI

FORTUNATA

A SIGNET BOOK

PENGUIN BOOKS

Published by the Penguin Group
Penguin Books Ltd, 27 Wrights Lane, London W8 5TZ, England
Penguin Books USA Inc., 375 Hudson Street, New York, New York 10014, USA
Penguin Books Australia Ltd, Ringwood, Victoria, Australia
Penguin Books Canada Ltd, 10 Alcorn Avenue, Toronto, Ontario, Canada M4V 3B2
Penguin Books (NZ) Ltd, 182–190 Wairau Road, Auckland 10, New Zealand

Penguin Books Ltd, Registered Offices: Harmondsworth, Middlesex, England

First published by Michael Joseph 1993
Published in Penguin Books 1994
1 3 5 7 9 10 8 6 4 2

Printed in England by Clays Ltd, St Ives plc

For Colin, with love and thanks

PROLOGUE

Nemi, Italy, 1920

S ERAFINA WAS ROLLING, rolling, down the steep hillside towards the lake, in a trance, arms folded across her chest, bumping down the dry grassy slopes, hearing faintly the cries of Guido and Violetta as they rolled down somewhere close by. Then gradually as the incline softened and straightened itself, her progress slowed and she became aware again of the bright sun overhead, the smell of the strawberries by the lake, the gurgling and giggling of Violetta.

For a moment she lay there, panting, face down, aware of her heart pounding, her chest heaving. Then she pulled herself up and peered around. Guido had stopped below her – she could see his legs sprawled out beyond a patch of gorse. And Violetta was sprawled nearby, panting and gazing, wide-eyed, at the sun.

'Let's do it again!' Guido was shouting below. 'Let's go back to the top!'

'Can't! I'm puffed out!' Serafina was firm. She usually got her own way. 'Let's go down to the lake. Come on, Violetta.' She scrambled to her feet, went over and pulled her friend up.

They had come so far down the hill that the strawberry fields no longer looked like lattice work, as they did from the village wall, where their descent had started. Here, the perfectly symmetrical squares were revealed to be tangled rows of strawberry plants supported by sticks, the strawberries not yet ripe, but pale and hairy. The children skirted the edge of the rows, having learned, like all the children in the village, that these fruits truly were forbidden. These were the lifeblood of the strawberry farmers in the village, and Santa Maria could not protect you if you were caught interfering with the precious crop. Even later in the year

1

when the hills were turning golden and the autumn sun burnished the village rooftops and the strawberries were huge and succulent, the sweet smell pervading the lake where the women washed the clothes and the children splashed in the shallows, no one would stray near the precious crop. The village of Nemi was poor; it could not afford to lose one strawberry.

Serafina flung herself down in the long dry grass by the water's edge, and Violetta, as usual, immediately did the same. Guido wandered away, swishing the grass with a thin stick, to paddle in the shallows, lost in his own thoughts.

'They were shouting again last night.' Violetta was squinting thoughtfully at the sun through her fingers.

'I know. I could hear them at the bottom of the steps, near the church.'

'Do you know what it's about?'

Serafina shrugged. 'Mamma told me it's to do with men being angry about the unionists.'

'What's the unionists?'

Serafina didn't know. 'Come on! Let's push Guido in the water!'

Quietly they crept up behind him, tiptoeing on bare feet across the hot mud at the lake's edge. Guido had scratched his name, in large shaky letters, on the surface of the mud and was now carefully writing the date, 'JUNIO, 1920'. As the stick carefully completed the 'o', they pounced, shoving him, screaming, closer and closer to the water.

'Let go! I'll tell Mamma! I'll tell Father Antonio!' Guido struggled desperately and the two girls giggled with pleasure as he writhed, helpless in their grip.

'Father Antonio won't listen to you! He told Mamma that you still haven't learned your letters – so into the water with you!' They hurled him, screaming, into the shallows. He landed with an ignominious squelch in the mud, looked shocked for a second, then rose, furious.

'That's done it now – I'll push you both down the well and tell Mamma that the Devil came to take you away for pushing me around. I'll tell Father Antonio that I saw you kissing old Ladrone, the beggar, right on his lips! I'll tell your mamma, Serafina, that you took your dress off – right off – in front of Ladrone and asked him – to – to kiss you *there*!'

2

Squealing with horror, the two girls clasped hands and began to run back up the hill towards the village, the threats of Guido echoing behind them.

'I'll tell Roberto Nuncio that you want to marry him! I'll break the head off your doll, Violetta! I'll tell your grandmother you cursed the Virgin, Serafina!'

Gradually his voice began to fade, and they slowed their pace, dawdling up the last incline, pausing to pick a flower, or to gaze back down at the lake and the tiny gesticulating figure of Violetta's brother, silhouetted against the glittering waters of the lake, beyond the strawberry fields. At last they reached the wall at the edge of the village, and clambered over it, back into the world. Serafina gazed wistfully back over the precipice, and paused.

'Wouldn't it be good if we could build a little house down by the lake,' she mused aloud, 'and live there *forever*?'

A familiar voice interrupted her thoughts. '—And who would clean in this house? and who would make you supper?' It was Serafina's grandmother, leaning on her stick, holding on to the wall for support, 'You pair of lazy good-for-nothings never help your own mothers in the house – how would you manage in a house of your own?' They ran to help her turn and retrace her steps along the road back to the village, still grumbling. She was very old, and Violetta and Serafina thought she was very wise. As they trotted impatiently alongside the old woman, Violetta asked, 'But when will we get a house of our own, Nonna Florio? Do we get one when we marry?'

The grandmother paused for a moment, in the cool shadow of the church wall, and smiled down at the small solemn girl. 'You will have a house sooner than you want, *ma bella* Violetta.' She touched the girl's soft cheek, 'With a face like yours, the village boys will be queuing up for you. You, however—' Grandmother turned to Serafina, and studied her snub nose, direct brown eyes and stubborn chin. 'You're a different story, 'Fina. Our Heavenly Father alone knows what will become of you. But I have a feeling you won't be producing babies in Nemi, like Letta here. I don't know why, but I feel it in my bones.'

Serafina shrugged, trying not to mind. 'I don't care. I don't want babies. I want to be very rich and wear jewels. I want to wear . . . a long pink dress, with a blue sash, and a beautiful blue cloak with stars on it – gold stars that glitter.' Grandmother looked down at the small figure stomping along the cobblestones, head defiantly erect. Serafina had just described the clothes on the statue of Our Lady in the niche to one side of the main altar in the church. Nonna's eyes brimmed with tears. Perhaps that was it: perhaps Serafina's destiny would lead her to the Church, and to wearing the nun's habit – a bride of Christ. She studied the proud little figure stomping crossly ahead. It was difficult to imagine Serafina with the calm smile of a nun, the accepting nature that life in the convent required. She sighed; no, 'Fina as a nun was a most unlikely idea.

'Hurry, Nonna!' called Serafina, 'I'm starving!'

Starving, starving, thought the grandmother, we are all starving slowly here. At least if 'Fina were sent to the convent she would eat. Here in Nemi, the children were always hungry; there was never enough food. Half of the young women in the village didn't even know how to make gnocchi, because there had never been enough potatoes for them to get into the habit of making it. Imagine! They lived now on an endless diet of polenta and bread, with an occasional vegetable grown down by the lake, too small or too hard to be sold at the market. There were no fat people in Nemi, not even the priest.

'*Ciao*, Nonna Florio!' Violetta was disappearing down a dark alley to the back entrance of her parents' home. The grandmother paused for a moment, leaning against the wall, preparing herself for the climb up to the Florios' house. Serafina came back and took her arm. 'Lean on me, Nonna, I'll help you.' Together they toiled up the steep steps, past the small dark windows of the village houses piled one on top of each other on the edge of the hill.

Maria was waiting in the doorway for them, her face drawn and tired. 'At last!' She turned back inside to the tiny little room where they would eat. 'Where have you been, 'Fina? I told you not to go far, and poor Nonna had to go and find you – you will tell Father when you go to confession that you've been thoughtless.' Her face bore the same characteristics as her daughter's: the same snub nose and strong chin, and their similar personalities meant many disagreements in

4

the small cramped house. Grandmother saw her role as peace-maker between the two, and as usual, she intervened. 'It's all right, Maria – I enjoyed the walk. But your mother is right, 'Fina – you shouldn't have gone all the way down to the lake – if you hadn't come back when you did you wouldn't have had any food.'

Serafina ignored all this, and sat down at the table. 'What's to eat?'

Her face fell, as her mother produced the same small hard loaf they had begun at breakfast.

'I know – I'm sorry. There's the bread and I made some *zucchine* soup. That's all.'

'Where's Papa?'

'I suppose he's still working. I don't know. He can eat when he comes home, he told me this morning we shouldn't wait for him.' Grandmother looked sharply at her daughter-in-law. Giuseppe was at a meeting, trying to persuade some of the casual farm labourers to join the unionists. Their eyes met across the table, and Maria shrugged. Grandmother understood. Better not to tell a child – she might accidentally tell the wrong person what her father's affiliations were . . . and there had been stories of recriminations in Pavona and Cecchina, even as close as Ariccia. There was no saying if the anti-unionists would bother with a little village like Nemi, but Maria was right to be careful.

Silently, the two women chewed on the bread, dipping it into the small bowls of soup to soften it, and only half-listening to Serafina's chatter. They were both tired, worn out by the blinding heat of the day, the endless toil to find food, keep their few clothes clean, keep the little dark house free from the interminable layers of dust that descended onto every stick of furniture, every surface, every day. If they had not been so tired, the two women might have been depressed by the awful unending vista of struggle and poverty that stretched both behind and in front of them, but the terrible fatigue of having worked hard and then having stopped work had set in, and they were both content to eat silently, resting their aching limbs, and envying little Serafina her energy and evident enjoyment of life. Such was the way of children: able to find pleasure even in the grimmest of situations. Not that Serafina didn't understand their plight; but of course everyone in the village was poor, all her friends were as hungry as she was. It was hard for her to feel deprived.

Her mother sighed. 'Time for bed, 'Fina.' The stubborn chin went up.

'I want to wait for Papa.'

'Well, you can't. I don't know how long he'll be, and when he does come in he'll be very tired and he won't want to listen to your chatter.'

'Yes, he will! He likes listening to me, he told me!'

Grandmother listened anxiously, knowing the tell-tale signs of a prospective argument which could rage for what seemed a very long time.

An unusual noise made the three of them pause, and look up. A strange mechanical thumping sound. The argument was immediately forgotten. Maria and her mother-in-law exchanged frightened glances.

Serafina's heart missed a beat. Something bad, something terrible, was coming down the main street of the village. She could tell from her mother's face. Without a word the three rushed towards the door.

''Fina! No!' Her mother tried to pull her back, but she was too late. Wrenching herself out of her mother's grasp, Serafina raced down the steep hill towards the main street. The clanking was the sound of men with weapons, marching. Around the corner they came, men she did not recognise, wearing a kind of uniform, blue and dusty, cold-faced men, staring straight ahead. Behind them trundled a small lorry, smoke belching from its rusting exhaust, two men standing upright in the trailer, guns glinting. Serafina had reached the bottom of the hill. She pushed her way through the silent crowd of villagers, as the lorry clattered to a halt in front of her. The men (only about a dozen in all, she realised) stopped marching in a disorganised straggle and turned towards the villagers. One, big and unshaven, stepped forward and gestured towards the dilapidated truck. The two men inside nodded, jumped down and went to the back of the vehicle, from whence they dragged three figures. The three, hands and ankles tied, tumbled into a heap on the cobblestones.

'Papa!' Serafina leapt forward, but was hurled brutally back against the legs of the onlookers by the unshaven leader of the marching men. A murmur went through the crowd.

Hands held Serafina firmly by the shoulders, preventing her from rushing back to challenge her assailant.

'No, Serafina, no . . . You mustn't!' The familiar voice of Pino, the father of Violetta and Guido, hissed urgently in her ear. 'You'll only make things worse for your papa. Do nothing, nothing!'

What happened next was a nightmare slowly unfolding, unreal, distant, yet somehow immediate and terrible. Pino clutched Serafina's shoulders in a vice-like grip and moaned softly to himself. Serafina watched, frozen, as her father and the two other men from the village were hauled to their feet, grabbed by the throat from behind and pressed against the side of the lorry. Only then did she see the blood caked in their hair, the cut lips, the smashed cheeks.

'Papa!' she whimpered. But now she clutched Pino's leg and turned away.

'Cowards . . . you're all cowards,' a woman in the crowd muttered. 'How long will this go on . . .?' She was silenced by one of the men in blue, who stepped forward and menaced her with his rifle.

'Shut up, you old fool, if you know what's best for you and your children.' He surveyed the crowd grimly. 'Watch with care,' he said to them. 'Take note. Remember. This is only the beginning. We don't take kindly to peasant groups organising themselves.' The villagers shrank together, trying not to look at the three village men choking and struggling in the grip of the strangers. The man with the gun jumped on to the running board of the lorry and surveyed the terrified crowd.

'So the men of Nemi thought they would join a union, thought they'd be part of some great socialist organisation . . . We've come to explain things properly to you. There is no organised movement of socialist peasants. It's a lie, invented by troublemakers in Rome. There are only petty dictatorships here in Latium. There are only a few men who want to control all the work in the area!'

The villagers began to murmur again. A boy ran forward, suddenly heroic, shouting, 'It's a lie! Damned *squadristi*! *Fascisti*! Leave us alone!' One of the men grabbed him and lifted him as easily as if he were a small sack of flour, and threw him on to the back of the truck. The man on the running

7

board tightened his grip on the rifle he was holding. 'I'm losing patience!' he shouted. 'Even your children's heads are filled with poison! Look—' He held out a blackened hand, one of its fingers missing, as if in explanation. 'We fought for you people. Our comrades died for you. We want a great Italy again! We want the peasants to have power and land! Do you want to spend your lives ploughing other people's fields, planting other people's crops, watching your families starve?'

Pino's grip tightened on Serafina's shoulder. 'What are you saying?' he yelled, his voice inexplicably hoarse. 'You think we enjoy starving?'

The man shrugged. 'I'm bored with this argument. This is the last time we'll tell you. The Fasci di Combattimento is offering you a new life – get rid of the labour leagues, and you'll get jobs, leases, you might even get a smallholding of your own. Think of it, you would be farmers yourselves!'

Serafina's father, blood streaming down his face, struggled and choked his defiance. 'It's not true! You all know what the *squadristi* are like! Is this freedom? Beating up honest men—' He was silenced with a blow from the rifle butt. Pino held Serafina tighter.

'No, 'Fina, no. They may kill him if you interfere now,' he muttered.

The man on the truck had produced a huge stone flagon and he held it aloft. The crowd groaned and quivered.

'Yes!' he yelled, 'you know what this is! When children blaspheme, we make them swallow castor oil to purge them. You – you're all children! Your socialism is a blasphemy! We want no more of it!'

This was the catalyst. The villagers surged forward, no longer able to contain their anger. Serafina was thrown to the ground, aware only of a forest of legs and feet, swirling dust, hoarse cries and the crack of knuckles meeting flesh. As she clambered to her feet, a man fell groaning with a great crash close by. Women screamed, a yelping dog tore past, panic-stricken and dragging its broken leg, the bone sticking out through the flesh at a grotesque angle. Suddenly Serafina felt herself firmly lifted up and carried to the far wall. It was her mother, a great smudge of dust on her cheek, black curls damp on her forehead, her eyes wide with fear.

''Fina, stay there, for the love of God!'

8

She pushed Serafina to the ground in the shadows, and disappeared as swiftly as she had come into the mêlée. For what seemed like an age Serafina watched, shaking and open-mouthed, as the villagers fought the intruders. But it was no use, Pino and the others could not prevent the hideous humili-ation as the three men, Giuseppe Florio among them, were dragged back on to the lorry in full view of the entire village and forced to drink the castor oil, gagging and choking, the grease drenching their clothes. They will die, thought Sera-fina, they will die of shame. Another figure was on the lorry, struggling with the man who had held the jug. Caught off-guard and with one hand still clutching his prisoner, the man ducked vainly trying to ward off the pounding fists of his assailant. Another *squadristo* leapt on board and joined in the struggle. Serafina gazed up at the three figures fighting grimly and silently above her, and at the moment when she realised that one of them was her mother, the two men suddenly hurled their attacker off the truck with such force that she hit the wall with an almighty crack, and then slumped to the ground.

Serafina gazed at her mother's body, crumpled and twisted like a discarded doll. Silly Mamma, she thought insanely, always telling me to stay out of trouble, now look what you've done ... Faintly she was aware of the lorry's engine starting up; of the lorry racing away in a blast of hot air; of villagers giving chase, shouting; of a crowd around the greasy, groaning figures of the three men, their faces creased in agony.

Serafina crept to her mother's side. Mamma's face looked surprised and cross, her eyes gazing unseeingly at a little procession of ants making its way over the cobbles, inches away. Serafina cuddled up to her mother for comfort.

'Brave Mamma, brave Mamma, *bravissima* Mamma,' she cooed, gently arranging a black curl on the tired forehead. She was still singing a song of praise to her mamma's courage when, later, she was gently lifted up and taken away.

The lake looked the same, Serafina thought. The sun still dappled the water, the occasional fish still rippled the surface. Far away on the opposite shore a small figure dived from a rock, a sight Serafina had witnessed so often that it seemed as much a part of the landscape as the sky and the dry earth.

Today Serafina gazed across the water as if for the first time. You must remember this day, you must remember it for the rest of your life, a voice inside her head was commanding her.

'You must not forget.' It was Grandmother, not inside her head at all, but by her side, gazing at the lake, her old, lined face streaked with tears. 'When your life is troubled, remember the lake, and remember your home, Nemi. No matter what happens, they will be here forever. Long after we are all dead and buried, the water will still be here, the church bell will still call everyone to Mass, the houses will still be up there on the side of the hill in the sunshine.'

'It will all be here,' Serafina echoed, not really understanding, but wanting to comfort Nonna, who had turned, crying, to watch the men of the village cover the coffin of Maria Florio with earth. The villagers were moving away now, the funeral service over, crossing themselves, their faces stony with grief, the women's shawl-covered heads bowed, the men stiff and angry still, impotent and silent.

Papa stood watching the men as they worked, holding his cap in his brown peasant's hands, immobile. In the graveyard, other graves had proper headstones, small cases with family relics and candles burning, even the occasional blurred and faded photograph. But the Florios had no money, so Giuseppe had made his dead wife's coffin himself, using wood from the back of Mamma's dresser, and an old table. Serafina had stood in the back yard watching as he hammered each nail carefully, his face impassive. He might just as well have been mending a chair or hammering a leg back on to Nonna's old bed, as he often did.

No one explained what had happened on that terrible day when the men had come to Nemi with their lorry and their guns and had tortured Papa and killed Mamma. No one seemed to speak of it. All Serafina knew was that Mamma had gone to heaven, she was sitting with Santa Maria the Blessed Virgin, wearing a gold dress and great white wings with golden tips on the feathers and a halo. And a cloak of stars. Mamma had gone to heaven and had left everyone behind in pieces. Papa had become cold-faced and silent. Nonna Florio had suddenly become a very old woman, all of life behind her and nothing ahead. Serafina didn't understand any of it. Why had God taken Mamma for Himself and left them all so unhappy? She had asked Father Antonio this as they walked slowly behind the coffin up the hill to the graveyard, but he had blushed inexplicably, and turned his face away.

Now it was all over. Only Papa remained by the fresh grave, staring down at it. And Nonna, her body bent, sobbing, her hand heavy on Serafina's curls.

Serafina, clutching her grandmother's hand and gazing at the lake, knew that Nonna was right. Nothing mattered – the anxious faces of the villagers, even the adults stumbling over their words, at a loss in the face of such a cruel and pointless death, embarrassed by the agony of Giuseppe Florio, nonplussed by Serafina's stoicism and Nonna's collapse. One day they would lie alongside Mamma – she shuddered at the thought – cold and white-faced in their shrouds, buried in the hillside cemetery. On that day, when the Florio tomb was sealed forever, the lake and the houses, the sunshine, the glittering water, the cobbled streets – they would remain. She squeezed Nonna's hand and smiled up at her, reassuringly.

'When we are all gone, Nemi will still be here, Nonna. And Mamma and I will be spirits together, we'll look down from heaven and we'll be able to see fishes in the lake, and when the strawberries are ready, and when the figs are ripe—' Nonna's lips quivered ominously. '—And – and – you'll be with us, Nonna,' Serafina added hurriedly. 'We'll all be together in heaven, all of us.'

The old woman lowered herself painfully on to the ground into a hunched, sitting position, and reached for something hidden in the folds of her apron.

It was a small, brightly coloured object, about eight inches high, partly hidden by her gnarled fingers as she turned it continuously in her hands.

'What's that?' Serafina was curious. 'Is it a doll?'

'No, *cara mia*. It is not a doll.' Nonna's fingers slowly opened, to reveal a small statue of the Virgin Mary. Serafina gasped at its beauty.

'It's like a jewel!' she breathed. Nonna allowed her to lift it, and Serafina held it gingerly aloft, enraptured. The plaster figure was indeed the most lovely thing she had ever seen. Its robes were almost identical to those of the Virgin in Nemi church; the same soft pink dress, the pale blue sash, the

11

blue-black cloak studded with gold stars. But the face! Serafina gazed entranced at the finely moulded, delicate features. The eyes, dark and heavily lidded, gazed impassively and steadily into the distance; the mouth, a delicate rose pink, was soft and full; the cheeks were pale with just a hint of a flush on the high cheekbones. Serafina's fingers traced the fine features, touched the tiny chin, and then followed the curve of an elbow and the scrolled edge of the cloak of stars. The Virgin's hands were clasped in prayer, and over one arm dangled an enormous gold rosary, the jewels on the cross picked out in reds and greens. Peeping from the hem of the pink robe were two perfect feet, each decorated with a fully blown golden rose. The Virgin stood on a small grey rock, with a trickle of blue painted onto a grooved section of plaster at the front, evidently representing a small spring.

'That's the source of life,' said Nonna, pointing. 'It means she will always be where there is life.'

'Like now.' Serafina carefully placed the statue on the grass in front of her. 'Is it your statue, Nonna? Where does it come from?'

'It doesn't matter where it comes from, 'Fina, only where it goes. It was made by my grandfather in the Lucca valley where my father was born.' She sighed. 'Papa just never wanted to make statues, so when he left the village, my grandfather gave him this statue of Our Lady. He told him to pass it on, in the hope that one of his descendants might have the gift. Papa came to Nemi to be a farmer, and he gave me the statue.' Nonna gently touched the small plaster figure. 'I never had the gift, neither does your papa.'

Serafina was suddenly excited. 'You think I have?'

Nonna Florio shook her head. 'No, I don't think so. I think the gift has disappeared. Perhaps it only lives in Lucca. But I promised my papa that I would pass the statue on. My life is almost over, 'Fina, and yours is just beginning. Take the statue, pass it on when you're ready. But in the meantime, take comfort from Our Lady. She means life, she says that the world keeps turning even when we believe it has stopped for us. Take the statue, pray for me often, pray for your mother—'

Grandmother was sobbing, her face in her apron. Serafina picked up the statue again and gazed at it. She thought the

12

face reminded her of someone. She narrowed her eyes, to make the face more blurred, less distinct. Yes, of course! It was Mamma! Nonna's old grandfather had made a statue, all those years ago, of someone who hadn't been born yet, of the woman his great-grandson would marry! Serafina sat bolt upright, her heart pounding. It was magic. It was the magic of Our Lady. She was here to give comfort, to remind Serafina of her mother's dear face, so suddenly lost, so swiftly and horribly taken away. Then, at last, the tears began to flow. Clutching the painted figurine which suddenly and powerfully had become the focus for her feelings, Serafina wept, sobbing out loud.

Giuseppe Florio watched his daughter's grief, and made a decision of immense proportions. Nonna reached out and enfolded her in the black stuff of her dress, and together they rocked back and forth, the Virgin still held tightly in Serafina's hand, their cries echoing across the lake and fading away as Serafina's father strode decisively down the hill and back to the village.

CHAPTER ONE

Little Italy, London 1920

FORTUNATA VIALLI STRUGGLED the length of the crowded tram and managed to get down the stairs just as the Vine Hill stop lurched into view. Trying to hold her hat on, lift the hem of her skirt free of the steps and keep hold of her shopping basket, she was so busy negotiating the running board and the steep drop to the pavement that she hardly noticed the appreciative stares from the male occupants of the tram.

A freckle-faced man in a flat cap nudged his companion. 'I wouldn't mind that one in place of the wife, Joe!'

The red-haired youth seated next to him gave a wide grin. 'Forget it, Sean. That one I've earmarked for meself.'

Fortunata, safely on the pavement, was vaguely aware of two grinning faces as the tram rattled away. That red-haired Irish fool again. She shrugged as she descended the steps into The Hill. The Irish were a breed apart – rough, loud, drunken layabouts. It was hard to believe they shared the same religion with the Italians. Fortunata couldn't imagine the Pope bestowing his blessing on such a collection of ne'er-do-wells. Mamma was even afraid of the Irish – she would never leave the crowded streets of Little Italy and stray into the corners of Clerkenwell where the Irish lodging houses and drinking parlours were. Fortunata sighed. But her mother would probably even prefer to see her daughter married to an Irishman than not married at all. Fortunata, at twenty-five, was considered shockingly old to be without a husband. The despair of her parents, Fortunata's beauty and intelligence had been her shortcoming. The Italian boys had always been intimidated by both – they wanted strong, childbearing wives who didn't argue. Fortunata's deceptively fragile frame and delicate features were to be admired, certainly, but coupled with her quick tongue and sharp wit, she wasn't the ideal Italian wife. A couple of suitors had come forward in the past, but Fortunata had politely refused their offers of marriage, explaining that her life was far too busy to incorporate the duties of a wife and mother. These pronouncements had been received with amazement by the suitors, derision in the local community, and fury by her father. And Fortunata knew that her father's patience was swiftly running out . . .

As she threaded her way past the street stalls in the entrance to Vine Court, she was aware that the men gazed after her, admiring her trim frame in the jaunty blue jacket and skirt, the neatly turned ankle in the little button boots. But she was a fantasy, the kind of woman they pretended to want, but in reality they feared. Fortunata never flirted; she preferred to talk about politics. While younger women than she were cementing relationships on the front doorsteps of their narrow little houses under watchful parental eyes, Fortunata would be leaning over the back gate, where Papa and his friends discussed Italian politics, poring over a well-thumbed and out-of-date copy of *Popolo d'Italia* and arguing about Giolitti, Mussolini, Nitti. The other young women had never heard of these men who struggled for control of their distant homeland. They felt there was something unfeminine and aggressive about Fortunata's voice drifting across the alleyways as she interrupted a neighbour complaining about the Liberals.

'No, listen, Signor Rocca; Albertini may have said that the Socialists deserved a beating, but that isn't a position he can hold for long. He'll lose the support of the people, and I can't see him aligning himself with the *squadristi* when he realises what thugs they are . . .'

The men would laugh dismissively and, when old Bruno Vialli wasn't paying attention to his daughter they would eye her pert breasts and narrow waist regretfully, wishing Fortunata had more interest in sex and less in the fortunes of her parents' native land. They were glad their own daughters were not like Fortunata. She would end up in some kind of trouble, they predicted to each other when old Vialli was out of earshot. She was a troublemaker, that one. Bruno should have sent her to a convent if she didn't want to marry. After all, what use was she, arguing about men's business instead of making some man happy?

'Fortunata, *ciao*! How are the rich folk today?' one of the stallholders called to her as she passed.

She stopped and grinned at him. '*Ciao*, Giorgio.' She picked up one of the tomatoes from the front of the stall and fingered it, mock-disapproving. 'Still selling substandard goods, Giorgio? I should report you to the *Federazione* . . .' The man laughed and slapped her wrist playfully. In spite of himself, he liked Fortunata.

'Bad girl! You'll drive my customers away. Is it busy in the West End?'

Fortunata worked in a small but exclusive dress shop in Bond Street. Her face reflected her loathing of both the place and the work. 'If you mean are the rich still throwing their money away, then the answer is yes.' She leaned conspiratorially over the vegetables. 'A woman came into the salon today and spent more on an ostrich evening cloak than I earn in a year.'

The stallholder shrugged. Typical Fortunata. Other girls would have described the cloak longingly, dreaming of one day wearing such finery themselves. Not Fortunata, she only ever saw injustice wherever she saw wealth.

Giorgio's wife, rocking a baby in her arms nearby, sighed. 'An ostrich evening cloak!' Fortunata looked at her despairingly, but bit her lip.

'Such is life, Fortunata,' Giorgio sighed. '*Que sera . . .*'

'No, Giorgio.' She threw the tomato back to him, 'We can change things if we want. We don't have to accept —' But a customer had appeared and he was no longer listening. His wife jiggled the baby a little in her arms and tutted as she watched Fortunata's departing figure, head erect and determined. She was an odd creature, that was certain; but what a marvellous hat! She watched Fortunata go, torn between disdain and envy.

'Money, always money,' Fortunata murmured, continuing her journey home towards Grape Street. She turned the corner from Vine Hill into the side street where she lived, nodding at neighbours as she passed. Italians spent as many hours as possible outside, leaning over their gates (if they had them), or chatting in back yards. The old women would take their chairs and place them in little groups on the pavement, from where they would watch the children playing and talk

17

sentimentally about Italy. She waved at a young girl flirting on the pavement with an ice-cream seller.

'*Buona sera*, Valentina!' she called. The girl smiled and waved back, but as Fortunata passed she heard the young man murmur something disparaging and heard Valentina's answering peal of laughter echoing over the cobblestones.

Fortunata's mouth tightened a little. Silly young Valentina Moruzzi, she was laughing now, but soon she would marry one of the young men who flirted with her after work, and then she would have a baby, then another, then another . . . Soon she would look tired and haggard, a young woman made old too early. Then she too would dream of ostrich evening cloaks and escape, like Giorgio's wife. But it would be too late . . .

'Fortunata! *Buona sera!*' She had almost fallen over a group of men on the pavement, so engrossed had she been in her thoughts. They were acquaintances of Papa's, *figurinai* like him from Lucca, covered in plaster dust from the statues they made, now relaxing in the street after a long day. Some were gathered furtively round an upturned crate, keeping one eye out for the police as they threw dice for money. Others were playing an impromptu game of football with their small sons, the air filled with their cries of triumph and groans of despair.

They all paused for a moment and watched Fortunata's progress, grinning and nudging each other as she passed, but always respectful. This was, after all, the daughter of Bruno Vialli, their friend and *compaisano*.

Down a side alley some women were cooking over a makeshift outdoor oven, and the smell of spicy sausage meat wafted temptingly on the breeze, mingling with the powerful scent of vanilla emanating from the Castagnos' back yard, where the entire family worked, churning ice-cream.

Fortunata threaded her way past the children playing with hoops, past the old women talking, past the young girls already giggling in pairs on their doorsteps, or, if already '*promessi*', arm-in-arm with their fiancés. She knew, even as she nodded and smiled at them that they thought her odd. A virgin at twenty-five! She had heard the young men jokingly refer to her as 'the Madonna of Grape Street'. I don't care, she told herself as she arrived at the Vialli house and let herself in, I don't care. I won't marry just to stop tongues wagging.

'Mamma!' she called in the dark hallway. 'Are you there?'

'In the kitchen, *cara mia*.'

Lucia Vialli, a thin, spare woman with a deceptively cross expression permanently etched on her face, was kneading dough on the scrubbed table top. Fortunata kissed the proffered floury cheek, deposited her shopping basket and unpinned her hat.

'That Irish boy was on the tram again.' She ran her fingers through the black curls pinned into a bun, so that the tendrils escaped and tumbled to her shoulders. 'I swear he waits at the tram stop in Oxford Street until he sees me come along.'

'Pshaw! Take no notice. They're all wastrels, the Irish.'

'Perhaps not all of them . . .' Fortunata looked thoughtful for a moment. 'I heard him arguing with his friends the other day about home rule in Ireland. He's at least got a brain.'

Fortunata's mother wiped an arm across her forehead, leaving another streak of flour. 'Oh, I see.' She gave her daughter a sharp look. 'He talks about politics and you get interested.' She hammered at the dough with renewed vigour. 'You haven't forgotten about this evening, have you?'

'This evening?'

'Don't pretend! You know perfectly well!' Lucia gazed in complete exasperation at the mischievous face of her daughter.

'You promised me, Fortunata!'

'I know, I know. You want me to visit the Viazzanis and parade myself in front of their awful sons.'

'I want you to take one of Papa's new statuettes to Signora Viazzani. I promised her I would send you this evening. I promised her, Fortunata.'

'You know how I feel about the Viazzani brothers, Mamma.' Fortunata's mouth shaped itself into a mock pout, 'Federico is an idiot and Antonio is as vain as a peacock. Signora Viazzani will make us sit in the parlour and drink tea. Federico will make sheep's eyes at me and Antonio will be desperate to leave because he thinks I'm an old maid. Why do you do it, Mamma?' Fortunata's amused tone disguised the annoyance she felt. She loathed the way her mother arranged these outings so that Fortunata could be paraded before prospective husbands. She had learned, however, that it was easier to co-operate; that way her parents could keep up the

19

pretence that their only daughter was as marriageable as all the other Italian girls; that way they didn't have to face the fact that most women of Fortunata's age were already married with several children clinging to their skirts.

Lucia thumped the dough ferociously. 'I told Signora Viazzani you would be there after supper.'

'Very well, Mamma.'

'And I have laid out your pink dress. You can wear it with the velvet cape. And I'll hear no more objections from you, my girl, until you're married and off my hands! The Viazzanis are good boys . . . But then so were the others you refused.' She turned the dough again with an angry thud.

Fortunata bit her lip. The humiliation of it! Dressed up like a Christmas tree and paraded in front of those dolts, no better than a brood mare at a horse sale! And she had a new Futurist pamphlet she wanted to read before the meeting tomorrow . . .

At eight o'clock, Fortunata was excused the dishes and, wrapped in her best blue cape with Papa's statue in a small brown parcel under one arm, stepped out under a darkening autumn sky. The streets of Little Italy were still alive with activity. Women hung out of windows calling to each other, interrupting their conversations to placate crying babies or reprimand wandering toddlers. Groups of men strolled together to sit in the cafés where they could drink wine and argue and imagine for a moment that they were back in Naples or Florence. The tradesmen had packed away their benches until the morning, and now sat smoking their curved reed pipes and frowning at the descending gloom, trying to predict tomorrow's weather. One thing was for certain: they would not see the brilliant sun that shone over Italy here, on this grey little island.

Fortunata hurried along Cowcross Street towards the great cathedral-like arches of Smithfield market, away from the Hill, and into virtually unknown territory. Like most Italians, she never felt comfortable outside 'il quartiere Italiano' or 'The Hill', as they usually called it. She felt doubly anxious walking these unfamiliar, silent streets alone.

A group of men lounging against the wall outside the Duke of York eyed her appreciatively, admiring the narrow ankles revealed beneath the pink hobble skirt, the flashing dark eyes, the cascade of curls escaping from the jaunty hat with the bronze feathers. Fortunata tossed her head and quickened her step as she turned into St John Street. If she cut her hair, as she longed to do, perhaps the men would leave her alone. But her mother had absolutely forbidden it. Short hair was for 'flappers' – flighty, immoral girls who had got out of control as a result of the war. That was not the Italian way. Italian girls, even rebellious ones like Fortunata, did not cut their hair.

Not for the first time she railed inwardly at a God who had seen fit to give her a woman's body. If only I were a man, she thought for the hundredth time, how much I could do, how much I could learn! She drifted into a daydream which involved her maiden speech (as a man, of course) in the House of Commons, in which she (or was it he?) spoke eloquently and fluently on 'The Italian Question' (for there was always an Italian Question, it seemed), and even Lloyd George applauded.

She sighed wistfully as the dream faded. She had been aware, even as a child, that the world seemed to be divided into those who could, and those who could not. The first word she remembered hearing had been 'NO!'. At first it had seemed to her that it was merely a question of her sex; that if you were a boy, all doors were opened to you. You chose a wife, you inherited Papa's trade and then his home, and then you made your own destiny. Girls, she quickly learned, must wait and hope and above all, be silent and obedient. But then as the years passed, she had seen other divisions – the rich and the poor, the sick and the well, the weak and the strong. And she had realised, finally, that it was not just a question of being born a man. There were greater inequalities to battle against. She had seen the haughty rich in the West End, she had seen the downtrodden poor in the slums of Clerkenwell. She had heard of the clinics in Switzerland where the daughters of the wealthy went to recover from tuberculosis, and she had seen for herself the charity hospitals, overcrowded and smelling of despair, where the factory girls died for lack of medicine. Every day her tram passed the imposing mansions of Mayfair, with their high-ceilinged, elegant rooms, and every night the same tram brought her home to the huddled tenements of Little Italy, where families slept six to a room. That was why she had become a socialist.

'Now there's a beauty, and no mistake!'

Fortunata was shaken out of her reverie by two unsteady figures blocking her way on the pavement.

'And if it isn't that little Neapolitan girl we see'd on the tram, Sean!' It was the grinning Irishman with the red hair, slightly the worse for drink, his eyes sparkling at the sight of Fortunata and the prospect of a little sport.

'Let me pass,' Fortunata was obliged to stop. She forced her voice to sound calm, although something was telling her that she might be in danger. 'Let me pass, please.'

'Letta — mee-a — passa please!' The other man in the flat cap mimicked her accent in a sing-song voice, lurching towards her. Fortunata pulled away from the smell of beer wafting from his breath onto her face.

'I heard that the Irish have no manners,' she flashed at them, 'and now I see that it's true. No—' she cried as the older and drunker man grabbed at her arm, 'Let me go!'

Now the younger man pushed his companion aside, smiling down at Fortunata. She stared back at him, defiant, her heart pounding, praying he wouldn't see how she trembled.

'Have you no better manners than your friend here?' she demanded, forgetting all her mother's advice about never tangling with the Irish.

'I do indeed, girl. When sober, I have perfect manners. Unfortunately —' his eyes, large and surprisingly blue, twinkled out at her from the sandy, freckled face — 'unfortunately I'm far from sober.'

'I can see that. Now let me pass.' She went to push him aside, but he grabbed her wrists and held her, trapped. She realised for the first time how tall he was as she gazed up at him, furious at her helplessness.

'You great Irish peasant!' she hissed, 'let me go before I call a policeman!'

He pulled her towards him as easily as if she weighed nothing and was not struggling like a bird caught in a trap.

'Give me a kiss, girl, and I'll let you pass.'

'I will not! How dare you, you—'

'The name's Joe O'Connell. And I predict that you'll be Mrs O'Connell before the year's out, if I have my way.'

'I'd rather be in hell first!'

His grip tightened and he frowned. 'That's blasphemy, Fortunata, you bad girl—'

Suddenly, all was chaos. Before Fortunata had even formed the question 'how does he know my name?' in her head, a figure had appeared from behind the two Irishmen, and had pulled the large, freckle-faced man so abruptly away that he had released his hold on Fortunata. With a cry of shock she stumbled against the wall and almost fell into a doorway, her feet just missing a child or an animal curled up asleep there, in the dark.

'*Dio stra maledissa!*' She heard the interloper curse under his breath as he swung the Irishman round to deliver a blow in the general direction of his jaw. Drunk as he was, the flat-capped companion lurched between the two men, caught the punch on his shoulder and crashed to the ground.

This is it, Fortunata thought, her heart pounding. Now one will stab the other and then the Irish will come in gangs and fight on the Hill and it will go on all winter again.

There was a strange moment of surprised silence, as if all the participants in this drama were absorbing the implications of what had happened.

Then the red-haired Irishman threw back his head and laughed. It was a wonderful sound to Fortunata, that deep and throaty guffaw; the genuine happy bellow of a truly carefree man. He helped his stunned friend to his feet, and grinned at Fortunata, ignoring the panting figure of the man who had intervened.

'Your friend is absolutely right to upbraid a couple of fellas when they're slightly the worse for drink and showing their ill manners to a lady.' He gave her a mock bow. 'Beggin' your pardon, Fortunata. A bit of harmless horseplay badly timed.'

'There would never be a good time for your kind of horseplay,' Fortunata said, breathless and haughty. 'And don't you dare speak to me again, you vulgar, idle *briccone!*'

He shrugged as he turned away, still supporting his stunned friend. 'I don't know what it means, but it sounds beautiful when you say it!'

And they were gone, heading away in the direction of The White Bear further up the road, no doubt to get even more intoxicated, Fortunata thought disapprovingly.

Still flustered, she turned to her rescuer, who had retreated to the shadows of the doorway, and was bent over whatever it was that lay sleeping there, an indistinguishable bundle of rags which stirred and groaned. Staring at the figure in the shadows, she had the faint impression of a wiry body belonging to a once strong man who had not eaten properly in a long time. His clothes had the grey, greasy look of a traveller's, and he was unshaven. What struck her most was his absolute stillness, as he stood watching her, evidently waiting for her to speak; and with her customary vigour she did.

'How dare you interfere like that!' she rounded on him. 'I'm not some damsel in distress out of a fairy tale, waiting to be rescued by a hero! I was dealing with those stupid Irish by myself, and now you've made me look a complete fool, like a helpless young girl! You could have been the cause of another round of gang fights, and I would have got the blame – another black mark against me, more muttering in the street whenever I pass by! I'll thank you to keep your nose out of a girl's business in future!' – and Fortunata strode off, a vivid picture in pink and blue, the gold feathers on her hat bobbing angrily.

Her anger gradually subsided as she walked. She had been, she realised, very unfair to the unknown man who had intervened. If she had been any other girl, she would have needed someone's help; he wasn't to know that he had chanced upon the one young Italian woman who would be insulted by a man's interference! But she would never even know who he was, let alone have an opportunity to apologise for her brusqueness. She thanked God that the Irishman, Joe O'Connell, had a sense of humour, even when drunk. Heaven knows what would have happened if he had reacted differently, or if his companion had really been hurt when he fell ... She pondered on the red-haired young man, allowing herself to remember the directness of his blue eyes, the grip on her wrists like steel, the sense of a powerful presence that just for a moment had threatened to undermine her usual self-protective poise. Then with a little shudder, she shook the thought away. He was a vile street thug. A pity, really, that the Italian traveller hadn't punched him to the ground – that way he wouldn't be so cocky. As it was, she was sure that come Monday morning, Joe O'Connell would be grinning at her again from his seat on the tram, that same knowing twinkle in his eyes.

She was approaching the street where the Viazzanis lodged on the second floor of a small tenement building. The ground floor housed the cramped workshop of Signor Oriani the clockmaker and mender, its small window crammed with clocks awaiting repair, the panes dark with city grime. The main door of the building, which Fortunata had to lean against with all her might to open, was scratched and scarred by the knives of passing street urchins. The dank hallway echoed to the frustrated sounds of too many families crammed into too few rooms, and the smell of cooked cabbage pervaded the air. Glumly, Fortunata climbed the stairs to keep her unwanted appointment.

Signora Viazzani had ushered Fortunata into the narrow front room where her two sons awaited their visitor. As usual Federico, calf-like, hovered at Fortunata's elbow, offering another biscuit, more tea, murmuring about the weather, tongue-tied and clumsy in the presence of a woman.

Fortunata tried not to dislike his long, eager face with its aquiline nose and narrow mouth. Federico meant well, but he was so dreary. She sat glumly on the lumpy settee and smiled bleakly at Signora Viazzani, as Federico handed her a teacup with trembling hand, slopping liquid into the saucer.

'Mamma says she hopes you will be pleased with the statue,' she said politely.

'How could I be otherwise?' Signora Viazzani gushed. 'Your father is such an artist! All his statues are little works of art!' Antonio, the younger son, suppressed a snort of mirth and choked on his biscuit. Fortunata turned to glare at him as he squirmed by the window, desperate to leave.

'You have something to say, Antonio?' she asked him sharply.

Signora Viazzani looked anxious. 'Antonio! Don't fidget! Fetch Fortunata another biscuit.'

Fortunata shook her head hastily, as the plate was proffered. 'No, really, signora . . .'

Antonio smiled at her and she returned his stare coldly. He was considered handsome by the girls on the Hill – a real catch, they would say, hopeful. But Fortunata despised his dandy-like appearance, his empty boasting. Theirs was a

25

mutual dislike. He had no interest in this opinionated oddity, however pretty. She would not make a good wife. He also had the uneasy feeling that somehow this Vialli girl knew more than the other local girls, that her sharp eyes had seen him lurking in places where he should not be, talking to people he should not know. He glowered at her from his place by the window. She sipped her tea and looked away, her face contemptuous.

When the chimes of the watchmaker's clocks suddenly all struck nine at once, Antonio had leapt to his feet and offered to accompany Fortunata back to Grape Street. She had accepted graciously, knowing that Antonio had ulterior motives rather than good manners. He was anxious to meet his gambling '*baloche*' companions who would be hanging about on the street corners of the Hill, at the doorway of the betting shop on Saffron Hill or drinking at their favourite bar in Eyre Street. Thus, by nine o'clock the ordeal was mercifully over and Fortunata emerged, feeling lighter of heart. The entire visit had lasted less than an hour, but to Fortunata it had seemed like an eternity.

Now she and Antonio were heading back towards the Hill along Cowcross Street. The evening shadows were deeper now, and passers-by hurrying home appeared suddenly out of the gloom like ghosts and then were gone.

Antonio was boasting. 'I shan't be living here much longer.' He swatted imaginary opponents with his silver-topped cane as he strode along, resplendent in a red waistcoat and matching cravat.

'Where are you going, Antonio?' Fortunata feigned interest as she strained to keep pace with her dashing companion, inwardly cursing the restriction of her fashionably tight skirt.

He slid her a sideways, furtive glance. 'I can't say. It's still top secret.'

'Don't tell me,' she was sarcastic, 'the Sabini Gang is going to set you up with a racecourse of your own.'

Antonio blanched. 'Ssh! Don't even joke about these people! They mean business!'

Fortunata shrugged. The gangster racecourse mobs and their silly vendettas didn't interest her at all. They were heading along Farringdon Road, where trams rattled and clanged on their way to Kings Cross or in the opposite direction

26

towards Blackfriars. This was not a beautiful part of London. There were few trees, and the buildings were old, squat and crammed together in a disorganised hotch potch of factories, shops and tenements. But this was the edge of the Italians' familiar world, the triangle of Little Italy, bordered by Rosebery Avenue, Clerkenwell Road and Farringdon Road, and dominated by the Church of St Peter, built by the first Italian immigrants in Clerkenwell more than fifty years earlier.

Within this magical triangle another Italy had sprung up, managing somehow to capture all the energy and colour of *la patria* in spite of the grey English climate – or so Fortunata believed, even though she had never actually been to Italy herself. Here, as she and Antonio threaded their way back into the heart of the Hill, were the colourful fruit and vegetable stalls, the tiny delicatessens stuffed with salami and a hundred different cheeses; here were the cafés where the men drank cappuccino and argued politics until the small hours. As they passed, the old men called out and waved, grinning as they registered this well-turned-out couple. So now it was young Viazzani's turn to make sheep's eyes at the Vialli girl, was it? Antonio, aware of the talk, scowled and passed on, but Fortunata waved back gaily and called greetings to her father's friends. She liked to annoy Antonio, he was such a puffed-up popinjay, far too mindful of the opinions of others.

They passed the Summers Street bakery with its wonderful aromas that wafted into the confessionals of St Peter's early every morning to distract penitent souls. They could hear the Ruffoni brothers singing as they banged and kneaded the dough ready for baking.

'Poor idiots,' Antonio remarked. 'All that work for a few shillings!'

'At least their shillings are honestly earned,' Fortunata said drily. Antonio shot her a sideways glance and said nothing, stepping disdainfully over a puddle. A brightly coloured parrot squawked suddenly, making Antonio jump, eyeing them beadily from its cage in a shop window. Antonio brushed the mud splashes from his trousers and swore richly in Italian, forgetting his manners not for the first time, and Fortunata laughed, her heart lifting. This place, these people – this was her home, where she belonged, no matter how infuriating, no matter how imprisoning. Here, the grey, insular world of the British seemed a distant, foreign thing. Here everyone spoke in Italian – indeed some of the older inhabitants could not speak English at all and rarely ventured from the Hill, preferring to preserve the illusion that this was a corner of Naples or Rome. Even the children at the Italian School, required to speak English in class, would burst into Italian the moment they reached the playground, with much clamour and a clear sense of release, so that the few English children who attended would feel uneasy, like tourists without a phrase book.

It was true that there were now Italians living all over London; and indeed the Italian Quarter itself had spread beyond the triangle into the surrounding streets of Clerkenwell, Finsbury and St Pancras. But for all Italians in London, the Hill was their heart and soul, where they married their sons and daughters, celebrated saint days, fought long-standing vendettas and confessed their sins, comfortably sealed off from the mysteries of the British. For Fortunata, born in the little house in Grape Street, it was the centre of her universe. So Antonio's announcement that he intended to leave was destined for a frosty response.

'And what could you do anywhere else, pray tell? You're a waiter at the Café Royal, aren't you? Surely that's good pay . . .'

Antonio raised a superior eyebrow. 'It might be good pay for a waiter. I don't intend to be a waiter for very much longer. There's big money to be made in Brighton.'

Fortunata stopped abruptly and glared at him. 'Brighton! So it is to do with racing! You're a fool, Antonio. That's a dangerous game. Those men shoot each other when they quarrel. Stay away from them.'

'That's women's talk.' This remark, intended as it was to inflame Fortunata into stalking away in a temper, hit its target with complete accuracy.

'Imbecile! See if I care when they carry your coffin into St Peter's! Stupid boy, playing stupid boys' games!'

Antonio's wry laughter followed her as she strode away along Clerkenwell Road and disappeared down Vine Hill. He grinned, twirled his cane, and turned towards the betting shop.

Crossly, Fortunata let herself into the house.

'Mamma,' she called, 'I'm home! I've just had a ridiculous argument with that stupid Viazzani – oh!' She had entered the kitchen and was surprised to see a visitor sitting in her father's chair by the stove. Her father was perched on the edge of the table, smoking his pipe, and her mother was looking pleased with herself and pouring tea.

'Fortunata, come and meet our guest. Come in, come in!' Her father beckoned impatiently, as she stood, open-mouthed, on the threshold.

The man stood up politely.

'This is Giuseppe Florio, a *compaisano*. Giuseppe, this is my daughter, Fortunata.' The man stepped forward and gave an odd formal bow.

'How do you do, Signorina Fortunata.' He raised his eyes to meet hers. It's him, she thought, the man who hit Joe O'Connell's friend, the man I shouted at.

'Where are your manners, child?' Lucia glared crossly at her daughter. 'You could at least welcome our guest. He's come all the way from Nemi, near Rome.'

'Welcome to the Hill,' stammered Fortunata, blushing. Would he reveal that they had already met? If he told her parents that she had been arguing with the Irish, she would never hear the last of it. His face revealed nothing at all, as he appraised her slowly.

'Thank you, signorina.' They stared at each other, both expressionless. Only the flush on Fortunata's cheeks revealed that she was not as calm as she appeared.

'Get a chair, Fortunata – here's some tea. Giuseppe is telling us about his journey here.' Obediently Fortunata pulled a chair nearer the stove and took the proffered teacup. The stranger spoke in a low, exhausted voice, describing how he had walked from Rome into France, travelling down the coast of the Mediterranean doing whatever work he could find. Eventually in Marseille he met the first mate of a battered vessel carrying sugar to England, who was persuaded that he needed an Italian cook on board.

'We landed in Yarmouth,' his eyes were on the floor as he quietly recounted his story, 'and I worked in a fish factory for several weeks so that we would have the money to get a train to London.'

'We?' Fortunata was curious.

His eyes flickered upwards and met hers. 'My daughter, Serafina, is with me.'

'She's asleep in your bed, Fortunata. The poor *bambina* was exhausted. More tea, Giuseppe?'

Fortunata's father leant forward eagerly, 'Tell us about the situation at home when you left – how long ago was it?'

'Eight weeks.' From his tone it was clear that this had been an eternity.

'No, Bruno – before you start on your endless politics, I want to hear about Lucca. Have you any news of Lucca?'

Giuseppe looked apologetic. 'As I told you, I was born in Nemi. My mother was from Lucca. But I can remember some of the things she told me . . .' His brow creased as he tried to remember. Then his face lit up. 'There was a scandal about a priest, Father Guido, who ran the monastery in the Upper Valley—'

'Yes, yes! I've heard about it! Tell me what you know!'

Fortunata's father made a sharp, cross sound at the prospect of what sounded to him like 'women's talk'. As Lucia and Giuseppe talked, he gestured to his daughter. 'Go and get that bottle of Benedictine from the cupboard, Fortunata. This occasion calls for more than just tea – a *compaisano* appearing in London out of the blue!'

Fortunata fetched the Benedictine and four tiny glasses. As she poured the golden liquid carefully, she asked her father under her breath, 'How is he a *compaisano*?'

Giuseppe heard this. He looked at her mildly as she handed him the glass. 'My mother knew your father's father, in Lucca,' he explained. 'When I left Nemi, my mother gave me your address. You are the only people I know in this country.'

Fortunata's father had had enough of this small talk. 'Tell me –' he had already drunk the strong, sticky liqueur and was pouring himself another – 'tell me about the unionist activity in your area – was it crushed?'

Giuseppe sat stiffly upright in his chair and told the Vialli family about that terrible day in July when the *squadristi* came, how his beloved wife was left dead in the street, how he had been beaten and tortured, how little Serafina had watched her universe crumble and had hardly spoken since.

When he had finished, there was silence. Fortunata, usually

so restive, had not moved a muscle while Giuseppe told his story.

Her glass of Benedictine sat untouched on the table beside her, and her eyes were fixed on the man in her father's chair, taking in his broad brow, wide-set brown eyes and gentle mouth. He had the dark weather-beaten skin of a peasant who has spent most of his life in the fields, and the thick blue-black hair of a Southern Italian. But it was not his looks that hypnotised Fortunata. There was something magnetic about his stillness and the calm clear voice recounting his awful story. It was as if he were telling a folk tale, one that he knew by heart, but from which he had distanced himself because of its unpleasant nature.

The silence that followed was broken by the murmuring of a prayer from Lucia and the flutter of her hand as she genu-flected.

'May God protect her soul,' she sighed, tearful. It was not clear whether Lucia referred to the dead Maria's soul, or to that of her traumatised child, but Fortunata and her father followed suit and crossed themselves, 'Amen.'

'It is over. I must think of Serafina now,' Giuseppe said. 'First I must make a life for us here, and then perhaps I can work to change things in Italy.'

'Change?' Bruno leaned forward again, eager. 'What do you mean?'

Giuseppe began to talk about his hopes for a change in his homeland since the resignation of Premier Nitti in June. 'Giovanni Giolitti seems to be for the socialists. We hope he'll stop the village raids and weaken the *fascisti*. It is too late for me and my family, but there are others still in serious danger.'

Unusually, Fortunata appeared not to be listening to the political debate that ensued. After a few moments she rose from her chair and went to light the paraffin lamp she would take upstairs with her. Dutifully kissing her parents, she nodded at Giuseppe and left the room. She mounted the stairs slowly, clutching her hat, in a daze. It had been a surprising evening. Her emotions were in turmoil – whether from her brush with Joe O'Connell, her argument with Antonio Viaz-zani, or her odd encounter with Giuseppe Florio, she didn't know.

31

She slipped quietly into the little back bedroom where she slept, and went to sit at her dressing table, suddenly exhausted. Gazing at her reflection in the soft gold glow of the lamp, she felt an odd tremor of fear about the future.

'*Santa Maria!*' a breathless voice whispered behind her, and with a start Fortunata turned to see a little girl sitting bolt upright in her bed, staring at her with the same strangely wide-set eyes as the man downstairs. She was looking at Fortunata with an expression of both terror and joy, and clutching something to her chest. She held the object out with a sudden involuntary gesture.

'*Guarda! Santa Maria, guarda!*' Fortunata's face softened as she approached the bed, unaware of the effect her pink-robed, blue-caped figure was making in the half gloom. Gently she took the object from the trembling, outstretched hand, and looked at it. It was a statuette. She touched it, wonderingly, and looked again at the small quivering child gazing up at her, wide-eyed. Fortunata understood.

'*Cara mia*,' she sat down on the edge of the bed, 'little girl, I'm not the Blessed Virgin, I'm flesh and blood, I'm real. You poor little soul. Come here!' She held out her arms and was surprised at the speed with which the child scrambled into her embrace. Fortunata enfolded the sobbing Serafina in the soft velvet of her cape and rocked her gently back and forth, caressing the damp black curls, surprised at the sob rising in her own throat.

'It's all right, little girl, it's all right. You're safe now. You're home.'

CHAPTER TWO

1922

SERAFINA BECAME AWARE, through her sleep, that a shadow had fallen over the bed. She was curled up next to the warmth of Fortunata and far too sleepy and comfortable to wake up. She had insisted on sleeping in Fortunata's bed ever since that memorable night two years ago when the glorious beauty of Fortunata had appeared in the gaslight, her hair shining like a halo, her face clear and bright like a Madonna. Serafina had adored her from that moment, and while she occasionally felt a pang of guilt about Papa curled up uncomfortably on a camp bed in the Viallis' kitchen, her lonely, anxious soul needed Fortunata's warmth. Her father's pain and homesickness shut Serafina out, and while she still loved him dearly, instinct told her to seek recovery elsewhere.

She half-opened one eye. Fortunata was asleep on her back, her mouth slightly parted, her breathing soft and even. Her long black hair trailed over the pillow and one arm was flung above her head. Serafina looked up. Standing silently over the bed was Papa, dressed and ready to leave for work. She remembered then. Papa was going away again to work on the roads. She wouldn't see him for a long while. The last time he went away he had been to Scotland, and the time before that to somewhere called Yorkshire. To her surprise, Papa was gazing not at her, but at Fortunata, with a strange expression on his face.

'Papa!' she whispered. He started, and signalled to her not to make a noise. Silently, he leaned over and kissed her on the forehead.

'*Carissima* . . .' he murmured. '*Ti amo*, Serafina. Be a good girl.' And he was gone without a backward glance.

Serafina yawned, stretched, and then snuggled back into

the crook of Fortunata's arm. She would have liked to stay there forever, so warm and snug and safe. It was just like it had been sometimes with Mamma, when Serafina had a night-mare and trotted to her parents' bed, secure in the knowledge that Mamma would chase the badness and fear away. She turned to look at Fortunata and saw that she was awake, her large brown eyes fixed on the door.

'Fortunata?'

Fortunata turned her head and smiled. 'Good morning, little mouse. Did you sleep well?'

'Papa woke me to say goodbye.'

'I know.' Fortunata sat up on one elbow, her cheeks still flushed from sleep. 'You'll miss him, won't you?'

Serafina nodded. 'He goes for such a long time. But he says he must work.'

Fortunata sighed, a faraway look in her eyes. 'And so he must.' She flung back the blankets. 'And so must I.'

Serafina groaned. 'But it's Sunday, Fortunata! Surely not today!'

'I don't mean the shop.' A door closed quietly somewhere below them in the house. Fortunata went to the tiny dormer window, pulled the curtain aside and peered out, craning her neck so that she could see down Grape Street. Footsteps faded away on the pavement outside.

'Aren't you going to Mass? Lucia will be cross.'

'I'll go to the eight o'clock.' She turned away from the window, 'Do you want to come with me to Soho?'

Serafina's eyes shone, 'Oh, yes *please*!' The grim prospect of a day spent with Lucia in a dull round of Sunday visits to relatives and old ladies dissolved into the endless possibilities for adventure offered by a day with Fortunata. Life with Fortunata was never dull.

Downstairs, it had been difficult to get away. Nonna Lucia, already in her Sunday dress ready to entertain the friends who always visited after Mass, had begun a muttered argument with Fortunata over the breakfast table. Serafina did not really understand why Fortunata and Nonna Lucia were so angry. It was something to do with Valentina Moruzzi, who had died last week. Serafina was in the same class at school as Valen-tina's sister Maddalena, so she knew that Valentina had died tragically young, at sixteen, from a mysterious illness. Maddalena Moruzzi still wept every day, loudly and profusely, isolated from the other children by grief. Serafina watched her tears coldly. What did Maddalena know about being sad? She had only lost her sister, not her mamma.

Now Nonna Lucia muttered to herself over the dishes, inflamed by some provocative remark of her daughter's. Fortunata had said a mysterious word that Serafina did not understand, but Nonna Lucia had become almost purple with rage, blustering, 'Not in front of the *bambina*! Have you no shame? No modesty? *Madonna mia!* On a Sunday!'

Fortunata had shouted, 'Why don't you want to hear the truth, any of you? You know as well as I do why Valentina died!' and she had said the word again. Abortion. Serafina supposed it was an illness. Why on earth was it so important, this abortion that had been the death of Valentina Moruzzi?

She and Fortunata left the house early, the day slightly soured by the argument. Nonna Lucia would not say goodbye to Fortunata, and Fortunata had slammed the front door rather hard . . .

By nine o'clock they had walked from St Peter's to Rosebery Avenue and were boarding a tram for the West End, both resplendent in their 'Sunday best'. Mass was over too soon for Serafina, who loved St Peter's Church. Compared to the little church in Nemi, St Peter's was a cathedral, a glittering palace, crammed with dazzling objects. There were enormous Madonnas, their soulful eyes gazing to the heavens, their pale drooping hands caressing infant Christs that were larger than even the largest doll Serafina had ever seen (in the window of Hamley's toy shop in the West End, the previous Christmas). Serafina always lit a candle for Mamma at the statue of Our Lady of Mount Carmel, because she had gold roses on her slender plaster feet, just like the statue Nonna had give her so long ago in Nemi. She would kneel before the flickering candles and, gazing up at the benign face of Our Lady, she would remember Nonna telling her that the statue meant Life. And, turning to see the smiling face of Fortunata, Serafina knew that Life was indeed here, with her. For hadn't Nonna died soon after they left the village? She had given the statue away and so the life had drained out of her, and had come here, to this dark and rainy country, and to Serafina.

They alighted from the tram on Oxford Street and made

their way through the narrow back streets of Soho. Fortunata walked rather too fast, still fuming over the argument with her mother, and Serafina had almost to run to keep up with her, clinging to her hand and panting a little. As they walked, Fortunata's anger gradually subsided. Here was another part of London she loved, because it was full of Italians.

'Listen, 'Fina!' she said, as they passed a café where two boys argued over a mop and bucket, '*Piemontesi* — they're from Piemonte!'

Although Serafina now understood English, Fortunata knew that her heart still warmed to the sound of her native tongue, spoken in this grey place with such odd accents. Serafina didn't know it, but the men arguing politics in café doorways, the women hurrying to St Patrick's church in Soho Square for Mass, were from all corners of Italy. Thus in a few streets in Soho she could hear the flat guttural sounds of Sicilian villagers, the soft musical accent of Northern Italy, and the harder, sharper edge of the Roman dialect. Added to this was a new and more exotic accent, acquired by the second generation: a strange combination of lilting Latin and the coarse nasal whine of Cockney, combined in a language that was almost Italian, but not quite.

'Why do you not speak English like the others?' Serafina was fond of asking Fortunata.

Fortunata would grin and shrug, very Italian. 'I had to learn to talk posh, because of the shop,' she would say, and then, pushing her chin in the air she would mimic the upper-class ladies who condescended to her in the dress shop. 'Good mornin', gel,' she would say, in a strangled parody of the Home Counties. 'Hurry along, young woman! I wish a yahd of thet dee-laight-ful butter muslin for mai hat!' Then she would scowl at the memory. 'I hate the English,' she would say.

'Why?' the child would ask, and Fortunata would look at her, surprised by the question, since to her the answer was obvious.

'Why? Because they hate us, of course. They hate all foreigners.'

This never failed to puzzle Serafina. For surely Fortunata was English? She had been born in the house in Grape Street, Serafina knew that because Nonna Lucia was always describing the terrible birth, which had taken place in the front bedroom amid much wailing, agony and bloodshed, and had done terrible things to something inside Nonna called her womb. However Serafina did not dare suggest to Fortunata the possibility that she might be English; this would have seemed insulting.

A woman called to them from the doorway of a restaurant, as they passed down Dean Street.

'Fortunata, *buon giorno!* Are you still working on *Il Comento*?' They paused on the pavement.

'Why else would I come to Soho on my one day off, Elena?' Fortunata laughed, and the other woman smiled down at Serafina. 'So this is the child! Wait there—' She disappeared into the darkness of the restaurant for a moment, calling, 'I'm sure I can find something to welcome her to Soho!'

She reappeared, and handed Serafina a peppermint. 'Here, *bambina*,' she said, 'you'll need some solace if you're to spend all morning with this madwoman!' Her affectionate smile at Fortunata belied her words. Serafina crunched the mint, pleased.

'I hear they put you on the editorial committee,' Elena said to her friend. *Il Comento* was a radical newspaper with an editorial stance very close to Fortunata's heart.

'Yes, and Maria Williams is too. Two women!' They both seemed peculiarly delighted by this thought. Serafina watched them as she munched her peppermint.

'Maria said someone's coming to talk to you about what's going on in Ireland,' Elena was saying. 'She went past about an hour ago.'

'An hour!' Fortunata was aghast. She grabbed Serafina's hand. 'Come on, we're late!' and calling goodbye to Elena, she hurried Serafina away and down to the next street corner. Serafina, clinging to Fortunata's hand, gazed around her with interest.

They were now in Old Compton Street, the heart of Soho, where the delicious smells of other continents wafted from the upstairs windows – coffee, newly baked croissants, hot chocolate. The many nations of Soho were having a late breakfast as Fortunata and Serafina arrived at King Bomba, the great glass-fronted grocers. Serafina stood gaping at the mountain of goods heaped there inside the shop. Baskets full

37

of eggs stood next to bins of crusty grissini on the counter, gleaming jars of caramelle jostled for space on the crowded shelves with great greasy vats of black olives, bags of dried peas and lentils; and swathes of salsiccie hung like huge bloody fingers from hooks in the ceiling.

Fortunata waved to someone sweeping in the shop and then led the protesting Serafina to a door at the side of the entrance. It was unlatched, and they went inside.

Serafina stomped crossly up the stairs behind Fortunata. 'Why can't we go through the shop?' she wanted to know.

Fortunata's rich laugh floated up the stairs in the gloom. She had recovered now from the argument with her mother. 'So you can nag me for cioccolato, you little imp? Certainly not! We're here to work! Chocolate may come later . . .' She paused at the top, turning to smile at Serafina. 'You be a good mouse while I work, and then we'll go to La Perla for lunch.'

How beautiful she is, Serafina thought for the hundredth time. She followed Fortunata into a large sunlit room, heaped with books and papers. Two men, one old and one young, were standing by the window looking down into the street, smoking and talking quietly. A young serious-faced boy in rimless spectacles sat at the table shuffling papers. In a corner an angry-looking woman with a severe haircut was stabbing at a typewriter with one finger and saying 'Damn!' under her breath, every so often.

'Fortunata!' The older man by the window came over, with a welcoming smile.

'*Buon giorno*, Signor Recchioni,' Fortunata responded to his welcome, with an outstretched hand, which he took and clasped warmly.

'And who is this?' He gazed down sternly at Serafina, who returned his look, fearless. If Fortunata liked him, then he would be kind to her.

'*Buon giorno, signore.* I am Serafina Florio, from Nemi.' Solemnly, she shook his hand.

'Welcome, Serafina. Are you as blessed as your name implies?'

Fortunata squeezed Serafina's hand. 'This is the little girl I told you about, *signore*, the one whose mamma was killed by the *squadristi*.'

'*Mamma mia!*' The man knelt down before Serafina, his kind eyes brimming. 'And her papa is Giuseppe Florio . . . a living symbol of the struggle.'

Serafina recognised the pity in his voice; it always appeared when people were told what had happened to Mamma. It was often useful.

'May I have some chocolate?' she asked hopefully. Signor Recchioni, who was the owner of the shop downstairs, laughed out loud, and stood up again.

'A true Italian, always ready to seize the moment! Yes, indeed, Serafina, you shall have some chocolate soon. For the moment . . .' he ushered her over to the table, and proffered a chair, 'I would like you to assist young Eduardo here with the newsletters.' The bespectacled boy gave her a solemn nod. 'Meanwhile, I need Fortunata to rescue poor Rosa from the typewriter. If you work hard, Serafina, your rewards will be chocolate, and a free Italy.'

This amused the young man by the window a great deal, and he snorted over his cigarette. Fortunata took over at the typewriter, where she proceeded to hammer efficiently at the keys. Serafina had ceased to be surprised at Fortunata's seemingly endless abilities, so the revelation that she could type as well as cook, sew, argue, pray and look effortlessly beautiful came as no great shock to her youthful admirer.

'Well, are you going to gawp, or are you going to help?' Eduardo frowned at her self-importantly through the lenses of his spectacles. Serafina settled at the table.

'What do I have to do?'

'It's simple.' And it was. Eduardo showed her how to gather together the two sheets of paper, one from one pile, one from another, how to fold them once, then again, so that they fitted the envelopes exactly. When the envelopes were filled, the letters were piled in a cardboard box ready for sealing later.

'Why do they send so many leaflets? Don't they have enough customers?' Serafina inquired of her companion.

He gave her a pitying look. 'They're not about the shop, stupid. They're about the blackshirts.'

'Oh.' Serafina did not like to ask what this was, for fear of revealing yet more ignorance. She applied herself to the task contentedly, glad that Eduardo did not appear to want to talk.

39

This gave her the opportunity to observe the many comings and goings, the business and bustle of the room.

It was not clear to Serafina what the many visitors who came and went were doing. Some seemed to be bringing boxes of produce for the shop, stacking them in piles by the door, men with pencils behind their ears and clip boards with order forms for Signor Recchioni to sign. The angry woman with the angular haircut seemed to be involved in these transactions, shouting, 'No, no! The jam on top of the flour, please!' or, 'I said three gross, not two!' Then she would go, fuming, over to the window where the men were, and light a cigarette, coughing and swearing. This rather shocked Serafina, who had never seen a woman smoke before. It looked odd, ridiculous, like a man with a dress on.

Other people arrived waving newspaper cuttings or carrying books. These would join the group by the window, where heated political debate was punctuated by intense moments of silence, when heads would be lowered over some piece of writing, and adjustments would be made to the prose. Then an argument would slowly rise up again, gathering momentum, until someone would break the tension with a joke, and their laughter and groans would carry over to the table where Eduardo and Serafina continued to fold newsletters.

Fortunata seemed in her element. Hammering away at the typewriter she looked radiant. Young men crossed the room to flirt with her, pretending to be interested in the text she was typing. Grinning, they leaned over the table, too close, until Fortunata pushed them away laughing. Serafina felt proud. Fortunata was so beautiful in her cream lace blouse with the tiny pearl buttons, the matching pearl drops in her ears, the black curls framing her face, it was no wonder that all the young men wanted to be close to her, and no wonder that she pushed them away. None of them were good enough for her. Only a knight, or a prince on a white horse would be worthy of Fortunata's attention. It was obvious that Fortunata didn't care for young men – when they wandered away her eyes returned to her work and she became immediately engrossed again. Not for the first time, Serafina pondered on the idea of her father as Fortunata's suitor. He wasn't a proper prince, of course, but he was a hero of 'the struggle' (whatever that was), and surely in Fortunata's eyes, that was better . . .

The noisy scene of combined political and commercial activity continued uninterrupted until almost lunch-time, when suddenly Signor Recchioni ushered in a new visitor and proceeded to introduce him to the men gathered by the window. Serafina watched them as she folded the papers automatically now, almost not heeding what she did. The reason the atmosphere had changed, Serafina decided, was because the men were no longer talking in Italian. The tall stranger who had come in clutching his cap was not Italian. Serafina wondered for a moment where he came from. She heard his soft lilting accent as words drifted across the room, '. . . Michael Collins . . . County Cork . . . Sinn Fein . . .' and realised only after several minutes that he was speaking in English, but with such a strange accent that she barely understood. The men all looked serious and unsmiling, and Serafina felt angry with the stranger for interrupting the comfortable morning.

He towered above the Italians, a strong man with broad shoulders. His hair was a strange bright ginger colour, and as he turned towards the sunlight, Serafina saw that his face was covered with tiny marks of the same hue, peppered all over his skin. She shuddered. Perhaps a witch had put a spell on him, or a curse. That was why he looked so different. Although Serafina noticed that when he smiled, suddenly his face lit up so that you forgot the strange marks and the bright hair. He was obviously important, because the men were listening intently to what he had to say, the room silent apart from the rustle of Eduardo's folding, and the man's voice.

That was it. Serafina looked across at Fortunata, suddenly realising why the atmosphere in the room had changed so. Fortunata was no longer typing. She was sitting, immobile, her fingers frozen on the keys, staring at the stranger.

Then Signor Recchioni remembered Fortunata and, taking the stranger's arm, drew him across the room to make the introductions.

'Forgive me, Fortunata. This is a good friend and supporter of our cause, Joe O'Connell. Joe, this very beautiful and intelligent young woman is Fortunata Vialli.'

'Fortunata Vialli.' The man was standing by Fortunata's desk looking down at her, still holding his cap.

'Joe O'Connell.' She was looking up at him, coolly. But

Serafina could see Fortunata's long white fingers nervously toying with a pearl button at her throat. There was a long pause. Serafina felt anxious. What on earth was the matter with Fortunata? Why did she not just grin and make a joke, as she had with the other men? It was obvious from the look in his eyes that this Joe O'Connell thought Fortunata was beautiful too. Only he didn't flirt, or grin, or lean over the desk. He just stood there, cap in hand, not moving.

The spell was broken by Eduardo. 'Stop slacking, Serafina! We have at least fifty more of these to do—' By the time Serafina dared to look up again, Fortunata had moved over to the window with the tall Irishman, and they were talking with the others in a group.

'Politics!' Eduardo said, energetically stuffing another newsletter into an envelope. 'Politics and more politics. Don't they know it's time to eat?'

They continued their task in silence, Serafina feeling increasingly resentful. The uneasiness she had felt when the Irishman had loomed over Fortunata had not diminished. They stood together now, Fortunata seeming tiny in comparison to the freckle-faced man who gazed at her so seriously. What puzzled Serafina was the change in Fortunata – usually so carefree, so dismissive of admirers, yet in the presence of this man she seemed passive. They talked quietly together, part of the group by the window and yet somehow separate. Serafina frowned to herself. And what had happened to the chocolate she had been promised? Signor Recchioni seemed to have disappeared, and Fortunata had evidently forgotten her. Grumpily she threw another envelope into the cardboard box under the table. What did she care about a free Ireland? And this was a Sunday, and she was working – didn't the Bible forbid it?

'*Finito!*' Eduardo hurled the last envelope into the box with a flourish. 'Now they have to feed us!' He got up from the table and, to Serafina's surprise, went over to the cross woman with the severe black hair. 'Mamma! Serafina and I have finished – can we eat, please?'

The woman's furrowed brow uncreased and she gave Eduardo the shadow of an exhausted smile. 'Of course you can eat.' The smile grew to include Serafina. 'You shall both have lunch with me in the kitchen. And then chocolate.'

'That's very kind of you, *signora*,' Serafina was firm, 'but Fortunata said we would go to La Perla—'

'No, Serafina – it's all right—' Fortunata had joined them, looking a little flushed, 'I'm to go to lunch with the editorial committee. We must discuss some dull business, I'm afraid. You would be very bored.' She played distractedly with a fountain pen she was holding, getting ink on her fingers. 'You stay with Rosa and Eduardo and have lunch and cioccolata – you've earned it.'

'But I—'

'No, it's perfectly all right,' Rosa interrupted, misunderstanding, 'there's plenty for three. And Eduardo will welcome the chance to talk to someone of his own age.'

Eduardo responded with a non-committal grunt, the noise often made by small boys who are expected to be enthusiastic at the prospect of entertaining small girls. Serafina gazed desperately up at Fortunata, but it was useless. The Irishman had come up silently behind her and Fortunata had dropped the fountain pen. Both Serafina and the stranger stooped under the table to retrieve it, their heads almost clashing. Serafina found herself gazing into bright blue eyes. They twinkled at her, their owner grinning. 'Ah! A rival! Allow me, madam!' And picking up the pen he stood up and returned it to Fortunata's inky fingers.

'Don't be losing this, Miss Vialli. They say it's mightier than the sword.'

'And do you agree with what they say, Mr O'Connell?'

They were already moving towards the door, following the group of men heading downstairs. As they passed through to the landing, Fortunata's voice could be heard saying something light and witty, and this was followed by a full-throated laugh, a big, carefree gust of laughter that echoed in the stairwell.

'Serafina! Where are you?' Eduardo peered under the table. There was Serafina, cross-legged and immobile on the floor. For she had recognised that laugh, and a terrible chill hand had clutched at her heart. That laugh belonged to the man who had fought Papa, that awful night so long ago when they had first arrived in London. That laugh had transported her back to a dusty doorway, where she cowered under the bag of belongings Papa had carried all the way from Nemi.

Through her exhaustion, clutching the little Madonna, she had seen Papa fight two strange men, she had seen the dust rising up off the pavement, she had seen one man fall . . . And the other one – this one – had thrown back his head and laughed, that same joyous, full-bellied laugh. Papa's enemy! Like the men who had tortured Papa in Italy, the men who had killed Mamma – this man was to be hated and feared. He would change things, he would make things ugly, if he only could!

'Serafina, come on – let's eat!' She crawled out from under the table, her face set into an odd expression. Rosa raised an eyebrow. What a strange little girl. But then, poor soul, she had had some terrible experiences already.

'Are you hungry, Serafina?'

Serafina, her mind on other matters, nodded grimly, and followed them downstairs.

Serafina was unusually quiet on the tram ride home, but Fortunata appeared not to notice, gazing distractedly out of the window, fingering her pearl buttons, smiling a little smile to herself. But Serafina comforted herself with the thought that eventually, when they got home, Fortunata would notice her silence, her glum face. Then Serafina would say to her: 'Don't see that man again. I don't like that Irish man.' And Fortunata would hug her, and smile and say, 'Of course I won't, my little *topolina*, if you don't want me to.'

But as they entered the house, Serafina's heart sank. Voices could be heard in the front room. Nonna Lucia's visitors were still here. Fortunata pulled a little face at Serafina, but went dutifully inside, removing her hat.

'*Buon giorno*, Signor Vittorini, *buon giorno,* Signora Viazzani,' Serafina heard her say.

She stamped down the hall towards the kitchen, a cross scowl on her face. Nonno Bruno was dozing in his shirtsleeves by the stove, making that curious rumbling sound in his chest. He had told Serafina that it was the plaster dust dancing in his lungs. She shuddered. She hated that noise, she hated the way that awful gurgling pervaded everything. She couldn't sit in the kitchen, and she did not want to sit in the front room with Nonna Lucia and those miserable old ladies, all remembering dead people and crossing themselves and sighing. It had been a wonderful day and now it was miserable – and it was all Fortunata's fault.

She went and sat on the stairs, still in her coat, cross and frowning. Voices were being raised in the front room. Once again Fortunata was arguing about Valentina Moruzzi.

'She shouldn't have died like that! It was an outrage!' Serafina heard her say.

The querulous voice of Signora Viazzani interrupted. 'It was God's will, Fortunata. The girl had sinned.'

Serafina heard something crash on the mahogany table. 'God's will?' Fortunata said, incredulous. Then, after a brief silence, she spoke quietly. 'With respect, *signora*. Forget for a moment that Valentina wasn't married. We all know why girls like Valentina die. It has nothing to do with bad practices. It was because no contraception—'

'Fortunata!' Nonna Lucia sounded close to tears. 'Fortunata, I forbid you to talk like this! You shame me in front of my friends!'

'The Lord have mercy on you,' Mrs Vittorini from next door murmured, but Fortunata was still angry.

'I know what the Church says about contraception, Signora Viazzani, but you and I also know what women do in order not to have babies. All I'm saying is that if people read Marie Stopes' book, girls like Valentina might not have to die.'

'That's enough, Fortunata!' Nonna Lucia's voice had faded to a shocked, embarrassed whisper.

There was a rustle of skirts. Signora Viazzani had stood up. 'I must go, Lucia.'

'No – please – some more coffee—'

'This is not the kind of talk I expect to hear from an unmarried girl.'

'*Signora*, please—'

But Signora Viazzani was implacable. 'I will pray for you, Fortunata,' she said. She was heading for the door. Serafina drew back, hiding behind the banister rail, motionless. The guests were leaving, heads high, faces stiff and offended. They kissed Lucia on both cheeks coldly, and left her on the threshold, upset. Fortunata stood in the hall, unrepentant.

'Mamma, you really must let me lend you my NUSEC pamphlet on these matters. There's a wonderful piece by Eleanor Rathbone, you could pass it on to your friends—'

'Don't speak to me!' Nonna Lucia had slammed the front door shut and was brushing angrily past her daughter in the hall, her eyes brimming with tears of humiliation.

'How could you! How could you! On a Sunday! May God forgive you!'

'Mamma!' Fortunata pursued her into the kitchen. The door closed. The raised voices continued, Nonno Bruno's deep tones joining in.

Serafina sat glumly on the stairs, hugging her knees. No one had noticed her. No one cared about her. This was a horrible, ugly day. If only Papa would come back! She closed her eyes, trying to conjure up his face, but all she saw was that grinning man, the freckled smiling face, and that strange voice saying, 'Ah! A rival!' A tear dampened her cheek. She felt empty, fearful, alone. For a moment, in the darkness of the hall, with the murmur of angry voices humming in the air, she felt as if she had lost Fortunata forever . . .

As autumn followed summer, Serafina's worries about the Irishman began to fade. Fortunata, restored once more in Serafina's eyes, never mentioned Joe O'Connell again. On several further Sundays Serafina had gone again to Soho, to King Bomba, and had sat in the upstairs room with Rosa, Eduardo and the other people who came and went so busily. The red-haired Irishman had not appeared again. Sometimes Serafina would catch his name in the conversations by the window, and she would stiffen, and listen intently. She understood only that the men admired Joe O'Connell, that he was as good as a *compaisano* to the anti-fascist movement, and that what he did was somehow fraught with danger. It was to do with Ireland, the country from which he had come, where Serafina understood there were terrible battles and men shot each other. She thought it sounded exciting. According to the men at King Bomba, Joe O'Connell was always 'crossing the water' back to his native land. Serafina hoped that he would go back to Ireland and stay there. Perhaps he would even get shot, and then he would never come back. The memory of Fortunata, frozen at her typewriter, staring up at Joe O'Connell, would appear unbidden every now and then, casting a shadow over Serafina's generally carefree daily existence.

She attended the Italian School, and proved an eager pupil. It was difficult for her to comprehend the lack of enthusiasm for learning she saw in other children. Serafina remembered the books in Father Antonio's rooms in Nemi, and how she had longed to be able to read them, instead of just looking at the pictures. She remembered how the children of Nemi were reared to work on the land, how the reading of books was regarded with great suspicion, how any kind of learning – other than the pruning of strawberries or the ploughing of a straight furrow – was seen as somehow subversive, dangerous.

Here in London Serafina could see for herself the difference that education made. Fortunata, a star pupil from the Italian School, had risen from the lowly role of shop assistant to assistant book-keeper in the West End gown shop, simply because she had a quick mind and a good grasp of figures. Serafina, while not shining in any particular subject, was noted by her teacher, Miss Perkins, because she worked so determinedly – grimly, almost – at all her lessons. While her classmates giggled and fidgeted, Serafina would struggle with spelling, painstakingly scratching the letters on her slate, or else, frowning over the abacus, she would try to make sense of complex questions involving the number of apples left in a tub if boy A took three, boy B took seven and then put four back, and boy C ate two. Miss Perkins, when she met old Lucia Vialli in the street, would warmly sing the praises of the 'poor motherless child'.

'—But I must say, Mrs Vialli, that Serafina is a very solitary little girl. She doesn't appear to have made many friends at school. Does she play with other children in the neighbourhood?'

Lucia would shake her head, smiling. 'No, Miss Perkins, little Serafina only wants to be with my Fortunata.' Then she would shrug, very Italian. 'She needs time, Miss Perkins. Poor little *ragazza* – she needs time.' Then they would nod, smile, and go their separate ways, Miss Perkins still uneasy about her solitary pupil, Lucia basking in the borrowed glory of Serafina's progress to the top of Class Five.

To add to Lucia's pleasure, Giuseppe Florio was home for two weeks, having finished his tarmac laying in Kent, and awaiting a new assignment, scheduled for December in Liverpool. During these all too brief periods of rest, Giuseppe had taken to working with Bruno Vialli in the studio in Baker's Row, where the statuettes were made. Giuseppe, not a craftsman, simply helped the older man by doing the heavy work, carrying the sacks of plaster, turning the larger moulds when they were filled, to prevent bubbles forming, stirring the great vats of plaster, pulling the bigger statues from the oven and dragging them to the cooling corner. Bruno and Lucia tried to pay him for this work, but he refused.

'You are caring for Serafina,' he would say, simply. 'That's more payment than I deserve.'

The absorption of Giuseppe Florio and his daughter into the Vialli household was a happy affair. Everyone in the little Italian community noticed it. Bruno Vialli, proud and gruff, had at last found in Giuseppe the son he had always longed for. Lucia had a small child to fuss over and worry about. And Fortunata? She clearly had a special place in her heart for the disturbed little girl who had catapulted into her life so suddenly. Serafina went everywhere with her, like a shadow, until gradually people could not remember a time when they had seen Fortunata alone, and not hand-in-hand with the solemn-faced and silent child.

So it was then that the argument which erupted in the Vialli house that November was all the more surprising, since the Grape Street house, cramped though it was, had seemed so harmonious, the only arguments being those Fortunata instigated with her confused parents over politics. Giuseppe always remained enigmatically silent when these eruptions occurred, merely shrugging when Fortunata or Bruno tried to involve him, saying, 'This is family business. I am not family.' However today was an exception.

It had begun over breakfast. Lucia, who never seemed to sit down at meals, had been fussing over a boiling vat of water hissing on the stove, ready for killing bugs in the pantry later. The others sat round a large kitchen table which dominated the tiny dark room and constituted its only furniture apart from an old dresser which housed plates. At this table everything happened: meals, baking, the cleaning of boots, the darning and mending, carpentry, the repair of Bruno's bicycle, even the occasional touching up of a chipped statuette, although Lucia constantly upbraided her husband for bringing this work home and, worse, into her domain. For the kitchen was the centre of Lucia's world, and of the house. The front room was for visitors and important occasions; but the kitchen was the heart of the house, where both the mundane everyday activities and the family dramas occurred – like today.

It had begun peacefully enough. Lucia was busy lugging the steaming cauldron out to the scullery. Serafina was waiting for Nonno Bruno to cut her a slice of fresh bread from the Ruffoni bakery, fetched only this morning, and still warm. Fortunata was daydreaming over her breakfast, smiling to herself, unaware of Giuseppe's dark eyes watching her from across the table.

She was remembering what had happened yesterday, at work. It had all happened so fast, it seemed incredible now. Perhaps it hadn't happened at all. But the paper in her pocket told her it had ... Not that it mattered at all in the great scheme of things, she told herself sternly, but her cheek was flushed and a smile played on her lips as she remembered.

She had been upstairs, working in the miserable attic Mrs Broadbent delighted in calling 'the office', hunched over a large leather-bound ledger, posting invoices in her neat hand-writing, when Sally, the silly young English girl who worked in the shop, had peered round the door.

''Nata,' she said, 'guess what? There's a man in the shop and he's asking for you! He won't go away, either! Mrs Broadbent says she's going to call the police!'

Fortunata looked up, fearful. If she incurred the wrath of Mrs Broadbent she might lose her job.

'Who is it?' she asked.

The girl shrugged, scornful. 'Big bloke. Red hair. A Mick. What you doing, hanging about Irishmen, 'Nata? They're the scum of the earth, my mum says. They never wash, she says.'

Fortunata stood up and slammed the ledger shut. 'Thank you, Sally,' she said, 'I expect your mother has an opinion on Italians as well, does she?'

She headed for the door, angry, brushing past Sally, who had the grace to look slightly ashamed, because of course Fortunata was right. Sally's mother had pronounced all immi-grants filthy and flea-ridden. But then, Sally thought, Fortu-nata isn't like the others, she's made something of herself . . .

The subject of her thoughts had gone downstairs and now hovered, uncertain, in the back room of the shop, hidden by a velvet curtain. Peeping through, her heart turned over; for it was, indeed, Joe O'Connell, standing incongruously next to a cold-faced mannequin in a satin evening gown, holding his hat, polite and silent, dominating the pastel colours and discreet decorations of the little emporium, completely out of place.

'You will have to leave,' Mrs Broadbent was declaring firmly from behind the counter, the only sign of her agitation being the plump hand that played nervously with her pearls. 'We do not allow young men to visit our employees. I will have to talk to Miss Vialli. She knows the rules. I cannot understand why she gave you permission.'

'Oh, but she didn't!' Joe's rich accent contrasted vividly with the strangled vowels of Fortunata's employer. 'Please don't tell her off on account of me!' He looked desperate for a moment. Fortunata remained frozen, staring at him through a gap in the curtain.

'Can I give her a note, at least?' he persisted, his voice urgent. He took a step towards Mrs Broadbent, who involuntarily stepped back, grasping at the display cabinet behind her for support. Fortunata smiled to herself. She thinks he's going to snatch her precious pearls, she thought; or worse. Joe pulled a piece of paper from his pocket, was about to hand it over, and then thought better of it.

'Have you a pen?' he asked. Then, seeing one on the counter by the till, he picked it up and scribbled something on the paper. 'There!' he said, triumphant, grinning. 'Now if you could just give that to Miss Vialli, I'd be more than grateful.'

Mrs Broadbent took the note, holding it delicately between two podgy manicured fingers, as if it were the carrier of a disease. 'You will give it to her?' Joe persisted.

'Very well,' Mrs Broadbent said, her voice tense. 'If you'll go this instant, I'll make sure she gets it.' And he had gone, crashing out of the shop, clumsy with relief, making the delicate bell above the door tinkle furiously as he left.

Fortunata breathed again. She was about to go and apologise to her employer when she saw Mrs Broadbent read the note, make a tutting noise, and then tear it up. To Fortunata's amazement, she then threw the pieces of paper into the wastebasket under the counter.

'Fortunata! Stop frowning! The wind will change and your face will stay like that!' Her mother's voice interrupted her thoughts. Serafina giggled from across the table.

Fortunata smiled and sipped her tea. 'Sorry, Mamma. I was miles away.'

She had been unable to do anything, because a customer had come into the shop, and Mrs Broadbent had pulled the curtain aside, calling imperiously for Sally. Fortunata had crept back upstairs, biting back tears of anger and frustration. How dare she! The note had been for her! But of course to Mrs Broadbent she was less than human, merely the foreign girl with the good brain who did the books. The foreign girl who had given nine years of her life to this claustrophobic little corner of Bond Street, who had always been polite, hard-working, obedient, and this was how she had been repaid!

Later, she had crept downstairs and retrieved the torn scraps of paper from the wastebin, and alone at her desk, she had pieced them together with a pounding heart. It was a leaflet published by the anarchist group, denouncing the British fascist movement. In one corner there was a scribbled message: 'Going to Ireland. Wanted to say goodbye. All the best, Joe O'Connell.'

Fortunata's hands crept down to the pocket of her skirt and found the note, glued back together and folded away. So she would never see him again . . .

Giuseppe looked up from his coffee and addressed Bruno across the table.

'I will be late to the studio this morning, Bruno. I have to go to the West End.'

Fortunata, buttering bread, said, 'I'll come with you.'

Giuseppe shook his head. 'No, Fortunata. You must not come.'

Serafina looked up, interested. 'Why must Fortunata not go to the West End, Papa?'

Giuseppe lowered his eyes again. 'She just shouldn't, that's all.'

'Why not?' Serafina persisted. There was an uncomfortable silence. Then Fortunata stood up suddenly, sending her chair crashing to the floor, her cheeks pink.

'Damn you, Giuseppe!'

'Fortunata!' Lucia, returning from the scullery, was horrified. Her daughter, swearing at the breakfast table, like a common slut! 'Fortunata, how could you speak like that!'

51

Serafina sat gaping, speechless. Fortunata was gripping the edge of the table, glaring at Giuseppe, her eyes blazing.

'When will you stop just seeing a woman when you look at me? I will go, I've got just as much right to go as you! You can't stop me!'

Giuseppe looked at her, mildly. 'You will not go, Fortunata. You know it would not be wise.'

Serafina did not understand any of this. 'Why wouldn't it be wise, Papa?'

Fortunata retrieved her chair and sat down again, bitter. 'Because I'm female, Serafina. You'll learn as you get older. Women are not allowed to do things – interesting things. Women are meant to stay at home and wash the dishes. Especially Italian women!' She spat the words at Giuseppe. His face was impassive. He stirred his coffee, an action that seemed to enrage Fortunata still further. 'Tell her, Giuseppe,' she stormed, close to tears, 'tell her what it will be like for her if she ever wants to – to *do* anything! Go on – tell her!' Giuseppe shrugged and said nothing.

Serafina had seen Fortunata in a rage before – angry with the Italian government, angry with the British Prime Minister, angry over mysterious things like 'contraception', 'women's rights', but she had never seen Fortunata angry with Papa. The situation made her afraid. Why was Fortunata so furious? Why did Papa say nothing? Why did Bruno and Lucia remain silent, exchanging knowing glances and half smiling over their breakfast?

'What is it, Papa?' she asked, fearful. 'Why can't Fortunata go to the West End today?'

Giuseppe replaced his coffee cup carefully and then looked across at his daughter. His eyes travelled to where Fortunata sat, still pink and furious, and then returned to Serafina.

'Today,' he said, 'there will be a procession in London. It is a procession to remember the people in the Great War.'

Serafina nodded. She knew about the Great War from Bruno.

'Many men died in the war,' Giuseppe continued, looking again at Fortunata, 'men we should all remember. They fought for this country. For freedom.'

'Tony Boselli's papa died in the Great War,' Serafina remembered, 'and the Nerone sisters lost their big brother.'

'Fabio Nerone . . .' murmured Lucia, nodding, 'on the Somme . . .'

'There are other men, Serafina, bad men—' Giuseppe, strangely, seemed to be talking to Fortunata rather than to his daughter. His voice sounded urgent, anxious. 'These men are called fascists.'

'You mean the blackshirts?' Serafina had seen the boys in their playground staging mock marches, saying they were the blackshirts.

'*Si*, the blackshirts. They want to join in the procession. I am going with some of the other men to try and stop them.'

'Why?' Serafina still did not understand. This was enough for Fortunata, who leapt to her feet again.

'Oh, I'm not staying here to listen to this! I'm going to get my hat!'

She made for the door, but Bruno's hand suddenly shot out as she passed and gripped her wrist, hard. To Serafina's astonishment, dear old Bruno, who rarely spoke and never raised his voice in anger, was purple with rage.

'Fortunata, you will *not* go! I forbid it, as head of this house! You will go to your room and pray for forgiveness for using profanities under my roof! Go at once!'

For a moment Fortunata stood frozen, staring wide-eyed at her father. Then with a sob she ran from the room. They heard her rushing upstairs, and then the door of her bedroom slammed.

Serafina looked expectantly at her papa. He would decide what to do now. Sure enough, he rose to his feet.

'Please, Bruno,' he said, 'let me go and speak to her. Please?' Bruno, still trembling, nodded, and Giuseppe left the room.

Serafina finished her breakfast in silence, her ears straining for some sound from upstairs, some indication of what was happening. Lucia, uncharacteristically silent, began to clear the table and indicated with a nod in the direction of Serafina that she, too, should help. As Serafina began to carry the jam pot to the larder, she heard Bruno murmur, '*Dio mio!* That girl will be the death of me . . .'

Lucia tutted at the sink: 'Nonsense! She's headstrong, we've always been proud of that. And she knows evil when she sees it. Is that so wrong?'

'They are not her concerns! How many times must I say it—'

'There are more ways than you know of to attract a man, Bruno,' Lucia said, smiling inexplicably. Serafina stared at her. What on earth did that mean?

'If I thought that was her only concern I wouldn't mind one bit.' Bruno stared at the stove, gloomy. 'If it was any other girl—'

'She's just like any other girl, Bruno!'

'I wouldn't be so sure,' he said, darkly. 'All the other girls her age were married long ago. There's something wrong with her, I've told you.'

He and Lucia began one of their grumbling arguments. They had forgotten Serafina, who waited until she was certain they were too engrossed to notice her absence, and then quietly opened the kitchen door and stepped into the hall. Faintly she could hear Fortunata's voice upstairs, saying something softly, urgently.

Serafina tiptoed up the stairs and paused at the top, listening. Fortunata and her papa were on the landing by the door to Fortunata's room. Gingerly Serafina peered round the corner to see what was happening. She need not have worried about being seen, for the couple were engrossed in their argument, and had eyes only for each other. Fortunata was pressed against the wall, as if trying to escape beyond it. Giuseppe stood before her, his entire body stiff with anger.

'If you weren't here,' Fortunata hissed at him, 'if you weren't here then I would have gone! And Mamma and Papa would have said nothing, they would have let me go.'

'Only because they don't understand the danger, Fortunata. Listen to me. Those men – they're animals. There will be bloodshed, I promise you.'

'Yes! I know!' Serafina watched Fortunata impulsively reach out to touch Giuseppe's arm. 'Giuseppe, I want to be there! I've worked hard for the Movement—'

'Damn the Movement!' His voice cracked. Distractedly he gazed at the ceiling and then back into Fortunata's eyes. 'I'm not thinking about the Movement, Fortunata,' he whispered. There was a silence. Then, as Serafina strained to catch what he said, he spoke up quietly but clearly. 'I'm thinking about you.'

He took a step towards Fortunata, and then bent his head and kissed her, his hands pressed against the wall so that she could not escape. Serafina froze. This was not a situation to which she knew how to respond – it excited her and terrified her all at once. Papa and Fortunata kissing! Kissing! Fortunata had just stood there at first, seemingly taken by surprise, but then Serafina saw her slowly reach up and place her hands on Papa's shoulders. The kiss continued. Papa groaned. Fortunata's hand had crept to his hair and was entwined in the black curls. Still they kissed. Would they never come up for air? Papa had pressed even closer to Fortunata, if that were possible, and now they seemed to Serafina like one creature, so entwined were they, so completely and passionately locked together, lost to everything, it seemed, except each other.

Then Fortunata pushed Giuseppe away and, still holding his shoulders, looked into his face with bright eyes and said, '*Now* will you let me come with you to the cenotaph?'

With a cry of rage, Giuseppe released her and spun on his heel, cursing. He strode past Serafina without seeing her and crashed downstairs. A few seconds later, the front door slammed resoundingly. Serafina cried 'Papa!' but it was too late. Behind her she heard a sharp sigh. Fortunata had sunk to the ground and was sitting there, one hand to her pink mouth, her eyes closed. Serafina rushed forward and knelt before her. 'Fortunata! Fortunata! Please don't cry, Fortunata! Papa didn't mean it—'

Fortunata put a distracted hand up to stroke the child's hair, seeing her and yet somehow not seeing her. She was not crying at all. 'Don't be upset, Serafina,' she said, a smile playing on her lips, 'I hope your Papa did mean it. I hope he did.'

Serafina didn't understand. 'Where are you going?' she asked as Fortunata slowly got to her feet. Fortunata looked down at her thoughtfully. Then she made a decision. 'I'm going out,' she said.

Serafina followed her into the bedroom. 'Where are you going?' she repeated. Fortunata was pinning on her hat, a small black cloche with a velvet trim. Their eyes met in the mirror.

'I'm going to the procession,' said Fortunata, smiling mysteriously at the anxious face of the little girl reflected next to her own, 'and I'm going to find your papa and tell him never to touch me again!'

Bruno and Lucia could not understand why, five minutes later, they found Serafina sitting on the stairs sobbing loudly. They questioned her, but her answers made no sense.

'Fortunata has gone out to find my papa! Now everything will change!'

'What do you mean, 'Fina?' Lucia put her arms round the trembling shoulders, while Bruno fumed at his daughter's disobedience.

'I told you!' he raged. 'She's a disobedient headstrong thankless child. It's time someone had her under control—'

Serafina studied Bruno through the gaps in her fingers as she sobbed loudly against Lucia's breast. He really *was* angry this time. 'Papa has her under control,' she said in a small voice.

'Eh?' Bruno was peering at her. 'What did you say?'

Serafina took her hands away from her tear-streaked face, cautious. She had the full attention of both of them. Her heart began to pound.

'I heard him say – to Fortunata – just now – that he had control of her sometimes . . .' She felt powerful now, watching the two old faces gaping above her, waiting for her next words. 'When they are together.'

Lucia's face creased into a smile. She turned to Bruno. 'You see!' she said, triumphant. 'They are already courting. I told you they were.'

Bruno frowned down at Serafina. 'Together, yes! – But – courting?' He shook his head, depressed. 'He'll never get her to the altar. No man will. Least of all Giuseppe. And who would want a disobedient wife?'

Serafina felt her hopes receding. She took a deep breath and started again. 'No, Nonno, you don't understand. When Papa said about being together, he meant – he meant when he comes into our room sometimes – when I'm supposed to be asleep.'

This had the desired effect. Serafina looked up at the shocked faces of Fortunata's parents; watched the narrowing of Lucia's eyes, the grim set of Bruno's mouth, and remembered, at last, to give a little sad sob.

'Did I say something wrong?' she asked.

Fortunata and Giuseppe did not return until the evening. Serafina, seemingly inconsolable, was sitting at the feet of

Bruno, in the kitchen, refusing to go to bed. Bruno smoked his after-dinner pipe, occasionally stroking Serafina's hair in a distracted kind of way, as if she were a small pet to be placated. Lucia, in unusually good spirits, hummed as she darned socks at the table. All three of them started as they heard a key in the lock of the front door.

Fortunata came in first, flustered and breathless. She went straight to Bruno and leaned over to place a penitent kiss on his brow. '*Buona sera*, Papa. Forgive me for disobeying you. I'll say ten *novenas* on Sunday, I'll do anything you say, but please don't be angry with me tonight.'

'You are forgiven,' he said gruffly.

Giuseppe stood in the doorway, his expression, as always, unfathomable. '*Buona sera,*' he said.

Fortunata, surprised by her father's lack of anger, went across to hug her mother, her face uncertain. The room crackled with an air of expectancy. Serafina smiled at Fortunata from her place by the stove, but Fortunata didn't notice her. Something was happening, as Serafina had predicted, something that excluded her, and would change things forever. She was sure it was going to be something good.

'Well?' Lucia's needle paused. 'Well?'

Giuseppe said, 'They were there, the blackshirts. We managed to push six of them into a side street. They broke Guido Ruffoni's arm. And Pino has a gash on his face—'

'The boys from the bakery?' Lucia was shocked.

'—But we beat them!' Fortunata said excitedly. 'We routed them!'

Bruno was leaning forward in his chair, his pipe forgotten.

'We beat them. They won't forget Remembrance Day in a hurry.' Giuseppe still stood by the door, sensing something not quite comfortable about the atmosphere.

There was a tiny silence and then Lucia snorted angrily, and picked up her darning again. Bruno seemed to be studying his hands carefully. 'Is that all you have to tell us?'

'All?' Fortunata looked at them, surprised.

Bruno sprang to his feet so suddenly that Fortunata started back. 'All! All! You heard me!' he bellowed, his face suddenly very red.

'Papa! What is it? What's the matter?' Fortunata tried to restrain him as he strode across the room, but he shook her off, grabbing Giuseppe by the throat and bawling, 'You filthy bastard! You come into my house, you take advantage of my daughter—'

'Bruno – I never—' Giuseppe stuttered, trying to free himself from the old man's enraged grasp. Fortunata, Lucia and Serafina rushed across to intervene, Fortunata reaching her father's side first.

'Papa, have you gone mad? What are you saying? What's the matter?' Fortunata's eyes had filled with angry tears. 'Why are you doing this? I said I was sorry about going to the cenotaph—'

Giuseppe had managed to extricate himself from Bruno's grip. Serafina had reached his side and was shouting at Bruno, incoherent, confused, excited. '*Basta*, Serafina,' Giuseppe said quietly. His eyes met Bruno's.

'What is it, Bruno? What are you saying?' His calmness began to affect his adversary. Bruno hesitated. He looked at the white, shocked face of his daughter and then back at the steady gaze of Giuseppe.

He dropped his eyes. 'I want you to get married,' he said. 'At once. I will have no discussion, no argument.'

Fortunata's jaw dropped. 'Papa!'

Bruno's mouth was set in a grim, determined line. 'I will not discuss it, Fortunata. I have told you my decision. You will do as you are told. Either that or you will leave this house and never come back.'

She was aghast. 'But I – we – we've done nothing, Papa! Nothing to make you ashamed! One kiss—'

Lucia laughed nervously. 'What does it matter, *cara mia*, you know it's what Papa and I have always wanted – and look at Giuseppe! He obviously loves you ... We'll have an autumn wedding, at St Peter's, I'll talk to Father Joseph—'

Fortunata turned on her mother, furious. 'But what if I don't want this – what if I—'

'Then you can leave at once.' Bruno was implacable.

Fortunata's body slumped. 'Leave? How can I? You know I have nowhere to go,' she said dully. There was silence. Then her eyes turned to Giuseppe, a desperate, eloquent look of mute anguish.

'Well, Giuseppe?' she said, 'well? What do you say to this very civilised form of blackmail?'

58

'You know the answer,' he said simply. 'Nothing would make me happier, Fortunata.'

'Yes,' she said, bitter, 'yes, I suppose you're right. A wife for you . . .' she looked across the room suddenly, '. . . and a mother for Serafina.'

Serafina stirred, a little terrified. Fortunata was looming over her. She knelt down and took Serafina's hand. 'I shall be Fortunata Florio!' she said, looking into the child's eyes, her own somehow dead, resigned. 'Fortunata Florio – what do you think of that, little mouse?'

Serafina pressed the cold hand that held hers, tremulous. 'I should be the happiest girl in Little Italy,' she said, shyly.

Lucia was peering at Serafina over Fortunata's shoulder, her old face creased with pleasure. 'You will have a new mamma! Not that you can replace your real mamma, *mia cara*, but you will have Fortunata to look after you.'

Something was pounding in Serafina's head, a wonderful feeling of strength, of power. She could conquer the world. Everyone in the room was staring at her. Papa was smiling, Lucia had tears in her eyes, and Bruno looked grimly satisfied. Only Fortunata, shivering in spite of the heat of the stove, looked unhappy – and that would change, Serafina was sure of it.

She smiled at Fortunata. 'Mamma,' she said, 'My new mamma . . .'

The wedding took place quickly, as if all those involved felt that a delay might mean it would not happen at all. Lucia and Bruno were in a delirium of delight: their only child, married at last! Serafina was transformed, sure that Papa's new bride was the answer to her prayers – and she had made it possible! Only Fortunata seemed subdued by the frantic preparations, the excitement, the fevered sewing and cooking taking place all around her.

'Nerves!' Mrs Vittorini pronounced, her mouth full of pins as she adjusted the hem of Fortunata's breathtaking wedding dress bought at a small discount from Mrs Broadbent. 'I was sick the morning of my wedding!'

'—And didn't your Annunziata faint at the altar?' Lucia's voice held a faint hint of malice.

Mrs Vittorini looked offended. 'That wasn't because she

was nervous,' she said, annoyed. 'She hadn't eaten, if you remember, because she was waiting to take communion – and my Annunziata's used to a good breakfast . . .'

'*Que bella!*' breathed Signora Viazzani, standing back to admire the bride, who was standing on the kitchen table, enduring Mrs Vittorini's ministrations with a small, strained smile. 'Now where's the veil . . .?'

And so Fortunata was swept along, out of the house on her papa's arm, a vision in white, past the cheering neighbours, towards St Peter's. It will be all right, she told herself, smiling automatically at the fond faces of the people she knew all around her. It will be all right. Giuseppe will be good to me and I will respect him. The Ruffoni boys were calling and waving, Guido's arm still in a sling from his fight with the blackshirts. He'll care for me and allow me to be the things I want to be . . . Antonio Viazanni raised a laconic hand from the doorway of the betting shop. Giuseppe's a good man, a good man . . .

They had arrived at the church. As she entered and the organ pealed out, she saw the faces turn towards her: Mamma, in her best hat, crying; Serafina, her face positively shining with pride; Rosa and Eduardo from King Bomba; Elena from the restaurant in Soho; her friends from *Il Comento* and the Women's Matteotti Committee mingling in the pews with her old friends from the Hill, the Moruzzis, the Vittorini girls from next door, the old men from Papa's social club, all smiling, all happy for her.

Yes, it would be the best decision after all. As a married woman she would have more freedom. And Giuseppe loved her. He was a good man.

And so it was, as Mussolini took power in his native land, that Giuseppe Florio stood at the altar in St Peter's and watched his new bride step slowly down the centre aisle, her eyes downcast, the perfect figure of a submissive wife.

CHAPTER THREE

1924

THE MADONNA GAZED down from her plinth, serene. The child she was holding, arms outstretched, had the same calm eyes: blue, fathomless, unquestioning.

Fortunata looked up at the Madonna del Carmine, regretful. 'She's beautiful, Papa. Magnificent.'

Her father came and stood beside her in the dusty yard of his workshop, wiping his paint-covered hands on a rag.

'She's always been beautiful, Fortunata,' he said, his voice gruff with reproach.

'And if you came to Mass more often, you'd see how beautiful she's always been.' Giuseppe had appeared, still holding a paint-brush. He had been hidden behind the statue, adding a pale apricot colour to the plaster roses at the Madonna's feet. Fortunata gave her husband a dutiful peck on the cheek.

'Don't start, Giuseppe. You know I haven't got time for Mass at the moment. Too much to do.'

'Always too much . . .' muttered her father, disappearing inside the studio. He sensed the tension between these two, and did not want Procession Day spoilt by a family quarrel.

But as usual they did not fight. They were merely polite, as disappointed lovers often are.

'Where are my girls?' Giuseppe asked, cool.

Fortunata fingered a delicate plaster rose. 'Where do you think? Do you think when I come out alone I've locked them in a cupboard?'

Giuseppe said nothing, hurt. There was little point.

'Or perhaps,' Fortunata persisted, 'you think I've drowned them? I'm sure Signora Viazzani thinks I'm going to one day. But then,' she continued, bitter, 'she thinks I'm the devil incarnate anyway. Birth control – the work of evil forces!'

'She's a Catholic,' Guiseppe said, deceptively mild, 'and so are you.'

Fortunata made a small angry sound and turned for the door. 'And so are you, Giuseppe Florio, and don't I know it! You've abandoned all your politics in the name of God, and I don't believe God would thank you for it!'

'God and politics don't mix.'

'No? Then perhaps you and I have different Gods.'

'That's blasphemy, Fortunata!' She stared at him for a moment, unnerved. Those words . . . Joe O'Connell had used those same words to her all those years ago – and now he had come back, courting her, determined, indifferent to her married status, uninterested in conformity, implacable in his pursuit. She pushed him away, of course. She was a married woman. She made sure she was never left alone with him after meetings. She returned his notes unopened. She remembered her wedding vows.

She stared at Giuseppe, who was looking up into the face of the Madonna, his eyes soft. This was the embodiment of perfect motherhood, this was everything she had proved not to be. He was a stranger to her still, this silent man she had married. They had nothing to say to each other.

'I'm going,' she said abruptly, and stepped out of the yard into the street, slamming the yard door with her customary mixture of vigour and frustration. It was Procession Day. Today of all days, she must not quarrel . . .

The dress was still beautiful. Lucia was ironing it in the kitchen, carefully smoothing out each frill on the bodice. Serafina sat at the table, watching her. She had longed to wear the dress again, ever since her communion in May. In it she felt like a bride, resplendent in white muslin with a rustling brocade petticoat, the hem bordered with lace. Fortunata had somehow acquired the material through the gown shop where she worked, and Lucia had sat for hours at the treadle sewing machine, concocting a dress to make Serafina look like a queen. How hard they tried to make Serafina smile again! But even though she loved the dress, even though she felt a thrill at the prospect of being in the procession today wearing it, her face and demeanour revealed nothing. Her chin cupped in her hands, Serafina leaned on the table and watched the beautiful cobweb-like dress lose its creases under the capable hands of Lucia, but she did not smile.

Every now and then, Lucia would stand the iron back on the stove and peer into the cradle in the corner. It contained baby Antonia, three months old and sleeping peacefully, one small fist clenched on the pillow, rosebud mouth sucking softly in and out, as if she were dreaming of her mother's milk. Serafina looked at her little half-sister, and her face became even stonier. The birth of Claudia the year previously had been hard enough for Serafina to bear, but this second rival seemed to signal the end of Serafina's childhood. She had sisters now, babies who belonged to Papa and to Fortunata, separating her still further from them both.

''Fina! Stop staring into space!' Lucia's cross voice interrupted her thoughts. 'Go and see what Claudia is up to.' Obediently Serafina stepped out into the back yard. Claudia was sitting up in her pram, gurgling delightedly at a butterfly dancing round a pot of geraniums on the windowsill. The sight of Serafina pleased her even more, and she held out a chubby brown hand, calling ''Fina! 'Fina!' Absently, Serafina jiggled the pram, so that the baby laughed, rocking backwards and forwards and calling 'More! More!'

They were such happy babies, always either contentedly sleeping or amusing themselves, seemingly impervious to the tensions in the Vialli household. Sometimes Serafina would hear Lucia murmuring thanks to the Blessed Virgin that the babies were so good. 'Heaven help us,' she would say, 'if they required any attention, poor little souls. No one has time for them . . .'

Serafina found this remark stupefying in its inaccuracy. The babies were surely the centre of attention! They were always somewhere within the reach of their grandmother, who somehow managed to incorporate boiling nappies, feeding and cuddling into an already overworked day. Nonno Bruno adored his grandchildren, rushing in from his studio at all hours of the day to pluck one or other of the baby girls from the rug or the cradle or the pram, to toss them in the air or hug them roughly, covering them in plaster dust and enraging Lucia, who would snatch the giggling baby away and shout, 'Basta, imbecile!' Papa, hardly ever at home, compensated for his long absences by spoiling his two new daughters, returning with too many presents, pockets full of sweets, a handful of balloons, pieces of satin ribbon, a stuffed toy. He would gaze at them entranced, hypnotised with love for the fruit of his union with Fortunata, his 'English babies', as he never ceased to call them. True, he brought Serafina presents too. He also showed her more affection since the arrival of Claudia and then Antonia. But to Serafina nothing would ever be the same, and she would push Giuseppe away, sounding for all the world like a miniature Fortunata, and snap, 'Don't fuss so, Papa! Leave me alone!'

As for Fortunata, she was the real source of Serafina's unhappiness. The marriage to Papa had not been a happy one. Fortunata bore it politely, without enthusiasm, but had never grown to love Giuseppe as Serafina had hoped. Fortunata was like a sleepwalker when she was at home, going through the motions of being a wife and a mother, but clearly not enthusiastic about either role. The babies made her guilty. Her pregnancies had been miserable, she had been constantly sick, and both births had been difficult. It was a miracle that both babies were now so healthy, for their survival had been in doubt from the start. They were beautiful babies, their even features, creamy skins and wide eyes promising the kind of beauty their mother possessed. Claudia already had a shock of glossy black curls and Antonia had 'the longest eyelashes in London', according to Bruno. But it gave Serafina a sneaking sense of satisfaction that Fortunata seemed impervious to the charms of her own children who were so admired by everyone else. Motherhood had not been 'the making of her', as Lucia had hoped and predicted. Fortunata had loathed breast feeding, and had insisted that the babies be weaned at the earliest opportunity. 'I must get back to work,' she had argued. 'We need the money. I can't stay at home and look after them – I'm sorry but I just can't!'

Serafina knew that Fortunata was not sorry at all. Even when her work at the gown shop was over, at the end of the day Fortunata did not rush home to her children. She seemed more immersed than ever in political work, and often did not get back to the house in Grape Street until the babies were asleep. She would regale Bruno with news of the various meetings and committees she attended, mentioning oddsounding names – NUSEC, the WFL – recounting excitedly how this committee member had resigned, or that speaker had been booed off the platform after a passionate debate over the New Feminism or the birth control question. Only after these stories had been told, and Bruno's questions answered, would she look up from her tea and ask her mother, '. . . and how were my girls today?'

Her girls! Serafina scowled at Claudia, rocking in her pram. Claudia dimpled and gurgled. 'More!' she said. 'More!'

For Serafina, the only puzzle in all this was why Fortunata still seemed to love *her*. But then, she would tell herself guiltily, her stepmother had no idea that it was Serafina who had engineered the hasty wedding, who had forced her into a loveless marriage, who felt responsible for the presence of the babies Fortunata didn't want . . . Somewhere in Serafina's heart, the struggle continued. She wanted to hate Fortunata, because she had made Papa unhappy, but she could not. Something about Fortunata's beauty and intelligence made her impossible to hate.

A door slammed somewhere in the house and Fortunata could be heard calling to her mother, 'I'm back! Where's Serafina?'

A few moments later she appeared on the back kitchen doorstep. 'There you are, mouse!' She dropped a light kiss onto Serafina's brow, and then leaned for a second over the pram, smiling at baby Claudia. 'I see they're forcing you to play mamma, as usual.'

Serafina shrugged. 'I don't mind.'

Fortunata turned and straightened the red ribbon in Serafina's hair. 'Well, you *should* mind. It's far too nice a day to be stuck in the house with the babies, like some housewife.' She smiled, her eyes creased against the sun, 'Why don't you go and see what's happening in Back Hill? There are crowds of people already.'

Serafina was silent. She didn't want to go and see the preparations for the procession. It would spoil it, somehow. The Festival of Our Lady of Mount Carmel was a special day, a magic moment. Serafina had no desire to join her classmates, who even now would be climbing all over the floats and trying to sneak a look at the costumes hanging in the back room of St Peter's. To them the procession was merely an excuse for fun, a Sunday when parents paid you less attention than usual once Mass was over; a day when, once the procession had passed, solemnity would give way to wine drinking and dancing, and possibly a fight or two.

For Serafina, still under the spell of the Madonna and even more weighed down by a sense of the spiritual since her Holy Communion, this day held a particular, magical significance. On this day, marching in the procession with the First Communicants, Serafina felt she would free herself finally from her unhappiness. Somehow in the noise and bustle of this important day for the Italian Quarter, Our Lady would bring peace to Serafina's miserable soul, so tormented for so long.

'I'll stay here until the procession begins,' she told Fortunata, decisive but with her eyes downcast.

Fortunata gave her a long look. 'Are you all right?'

'*Si, va bene.*' Serafina pulled away from the affectionate hand that reached out to touch her. 'Can I go in now?'

Fortunata sighed. 'Yes, go on. I'll come and help you with your dress in a moment.'

Serafina paused in the doorway. 'Will you be coming with me to the church?'

'Of course I will.'

'. . . and Claudia? . . . and Antonia?'

'I don't know. Perhaps Mamma will bring them.'

'. . . and Papa?'

A shadow crossed Fortunata's face, as it often did, at the mention of Giuseppe. 'Your papa is helping Nonno Bruno put the finishing touches to Our Lady, at the studio. He'll be here soon.'

'Can I go to the studio to see Our Lady?'

Bruno had been assigned the annual refurbishment of the enormous statue which stood in St Peter's but which, on the third Sunday in July every year, was carried proudly through the streets of the Hill, a symbol of the faith the Italians held so dear. Serafina was proud of the fact that it was Bruno's steady hand which annually brushed a fresh coat of carmine onto the lips of Our Lady, which so delicately traced the gold flowers on her white robe and tinted her cheeks with a flush of pink.

Fortunata was shaking her head. 'Bruno hates to be disturbed when he's working on the statue, Serafina – you know that. Remember last year?'

Serafina bit her lip. Last year, in a fit of jealousy over the recently arrived baby Claudia, she had shouted at Fortunata who, pale and pregnant, had burst into tears. Horrified at herself, Serafina had run to Bruno's studio, sobbing unseeingly past the crowds in Hatton Garden and, bursting through the small wooden door cut into the tall locked doors of the studio, she had almost toppled the statue, balanced on a bench near the entrance. Only Bruno's quick reflexes had saved the statue from being smashed to pieces on the stone floor. Serafina shuddered at the memory of Bruno's fury, and Fortunata laughed and came over to hug her again.

'Don't worry, mouse. That was last year. This year you'll have a wonderful day, you'll see.'

Serafina extricated herself from Fortunata's embrace. 'I'll go and see if Nonna Lucia has finished my dress,' she said gruffly, and disappeared inside, torn as usual between a loathing of Fortunata and a powerful desire to love and be loved in return, without guilt, as it used to be.

The finished dress was now hanging resplendent on the picture rail in the kitchen. Serafina went upstairs, under instructions from Lucia to fetch her white cotton stockings, which had been washed and hung to dry over Fortunata's dressing-table mirror. Reluctantly Serafina entered the bedroom. The haven she had once shared with Fortunata was hers no longer. Now the narrow bed she had shared with Fortunata had been replaced by a double bed for Giuseppe and his bride. A crib stood by the window, and Fortunata's clothes, which had always been strewn around the room in perfume-scented and sensuous piles of velvet, lace and muslin, were now locked away in the new oak wardrobe, a wedding present from Bruno and Lucia. The room looked dead to Serafina, shorn of Fortunata's vibrant and careless pre-marital personality. Sighing, she went to collect the stockings hanging over the mirror. She sat down and gazed forlornly at her reflection. Staring back at her was the proud, pale face of a lonely child – not a beauty, but with plenty of character in the broad forehead and the determined chin. Serafina had the same unfathomable eyes as her father, but there the likeness ended, for she had inherited the fine straight hair of her mother as well as her strong bones, snub nose and small rosebud mouth. She scraped her long hair back and frowned. If only she had full glossy curls like Fortunata, who could shove her hair up with one hairpin and look as if she had been coiffed by a lady's maid! If only her mouth was full and generous, if only a quick pinch of her cheeks would give her the glow of Fortunata!

A shadow crossed by the window, and the object of her thoughts appeared next to her in the looking glass, as if to emphasise the unhappy comparison she had been making.

'What a thoughtful mouse!' said Fortunata. 'Why so glum?'

Serafina pulled at a strand of her hair, miserable. 'Look at this! What can I do with my hair? Nonna will only scrape it back into plaits, and I look awful with plaits!'

Fortunata picked up a hairbrush and began to brush Serafina's hair, thoughtful. 'Leave it to me, *topolina*, we can't have an angel flower unhappy about her hair!'

This was how Fortunata always made her unhappy stepdaughter feel beautiful; for she had been the only person in England who had ever noticed that Serafina's name, coupled with her family name of Florio, made such a poetic combination. Angel flower. No one else ever saw her as anything so lovely.

Deftly Fortunata began to thread some white satin ribbon through Serafina's dark tresses. Humming through a mouthful of hairpins, she began the transformation. Serafina watched, transfixed. How could Fortunata do these things? Everything was so easy for her!

'Tell me,' Fortunata was saying, as she pinned up another satin-braided lock of hair, 'what do you dream, Serafina?'

Serafina looked at her stepmother's reflection in the mirror, bending over her, frowning and concerned.

'What do you mean?'

'That's it – turn your head to the left – good.' Another pin was positioned. Fortunata paused to examine her handiwork. 'I mean – we all dream about what we'll be when we grow up. I wondered what your dream was.' Their eyes met.

'What was your dream, Fortunata?' Serafina asked shyly. She had forgotten the warmth of these shared, private moments, abandoned since the arrival of the babies.

Fortunata was staring unseeingly into the mirror, her face an odd mixture of emotions. 'I dreamed . . . I dreamed of one day being a great public speaker, like Mrs Pankhurst.' She bit her lip. 'I wanted to stand on a high platform and say things to make people change the way they think! I wanted to be a name in the history books—' Suddenly she subsided, and the gleam disappeared from her eyes. She began, slowly, to brush another lock of hair.

Serafina gazed anxiously at the face in the mirror so close to her own. Surely Fortunata wasn't going to cry? 'You can still do those things, Fortunata!'

Fortunata's brushing became more brisk. 'No, *topolina*, I'll never have my dream. Now I'm married and I have the children—'

'You have to be a good Italian wife,' Serafina concluded, repeating the phrase she had so often heard Nonna use.

Fortunata laughed, bitter. 'I'll never be a good Italian wife! I will only ever be an adequate one. And I'll probably go to my grave with all the local biddies still gossiping about me; still saying I'm not a good mother or a good wife; still saying—' She stopped and looked at Serafina with a strange expression. 'What are they saying? You must know, 'Fina.'

Serafina concentrated rather hard on the box of hairpins she was holding. 'They don't say anything—'

'Oh, rubbish!' Fortunata tugged at a strand of hair a little too harshly. 'Come on, Serafina – this is me! We're friends, aren't we? – or rather we were. Tell me the truth. I've never been afraid of the truth.'

'They don't say anything,' Serafina repeated miserably. Fortunata made a noise like a long, sharp intake of breath, and silently continued her styling. Serafina's lips trembled. How could she tell Fortunata what the Boselli boys had shouted after her in the alleyway, how they had said Fortunata was a tart? And Mrs Vittorini had made a remark only yesterday, when she had seen Serafina carrying Claudia down the street. What was it she had said? Something about letting a girl do a woman's job, while the woman ran off and interfered in men's business . . . Serafina couldn't tell Fortunata these things – she did not dare. For Fortunata would get furious and she would shake Serafina by the shoulders until she told her the names of these accusers, and then Fortunata would storm round to their houses, and there would be an almighty row, and Bruno would start shouting, and the day – the wonderful day of the Procession of Our Lady of Mount Carmel – would be ruined.

On any other day she might have taken some small pleasure in reporting to Fortunata the gossip, and watching the sparks fly. She had done it often enough in the past. But not today. Not today.

'Don't look so tortured, you silly girl!' Fortunata planted a kiss firmly on the back of Serafina's newly exposed neck. 'It doesn't matter. I can guess what they say.' Her mood had swung back again, as it so often did these days, and she was calm. 'You were supposed to be telling me about your dream, you sly little monkey, and you got me off the subject very successfully. But you don't escape that easily! Come on, Serafina. Do you have an ambition?'

Serafina was silent.

'I promise I won't laugh, I promise! I told you my stupid dream, didn't I? Now – what's yours?'

Serafina fingered the white cotton stockings coiled on the dressing-table in front of her. 'You won't approve, Fortunata. It's not a – a –' she sought the right word, '– it's not a noble dream, like yours.'

Fortunata laughed, a little cold laugh. 'I gave up trying to turn you into a socialist long ago, 'Fina! Anyway, you must be your own person, not what other people want you to be. Well?'

Again her eyes met Serafina's in the mirror. Suddenly brave, Serafina blurted out, 'I want to make statues, like Nonno! Only I want to make beautiful Madonnas, like my Madonna—'

'The one from Nemi?'

Serafina nodded, tremulous. Fortunata hadn't laughed at her! Encouraged, she went on, 'I've watched Nonno for hours and helped him with the mould making and I've done a bit of painting on the rejects. I'm good at it, Fortunata! I want to make beautiful statues, and then I'll be rich—' She broke off, knowing that her desire for riches would bring a frown to Fortunata's face. Sure enough, it was there.

'making beautiful statues is one thing,' she said crisply, 'making money is quite another. Stick to the first bit of the dream, but if you've got any sense you'll forget about the second part. It's much harder to achieve and it won't make you happy. There!' She put down the brush. 'What do you think?'

Serafina, her ambitions forgotten, gazed at her reflection with delight. The long stringy hair had been transformed into a thick pile of beribboned braids, wound round her head and topped with a spray of lilies-of-the-valley – not real, but bobbing delicately and prettily just the same.

Fortunata grinned at Serafina's obvious delight. '. . . And so, Cinderella,' she said, 'you shall go to the ball!' she looked into the mirror too, still beautiful, still vibrant, '– and so shall I!'

Eyre Street Hill had been transformed. Multi-coloured bunting had been threaded from lamp post to lamp post and flapped overhead; the Italian flag and the Union Jack fluttered garishly together above the door of the delicatessen, and everywhere crowds of people were all talking Italian at once, voluble, hands gesticulating, excited. They had come from all over London. Serafina was always surprised on this July feast day at the enormous number of Italians who materialised for the procession, filling the narrow streets of the Hill to bursting point. If she shut her eyes, she could imagine it was market day in Nemi . . . She shook the thought away. It would not do to be thinking about Mamma now, not when she had Fortunata all to herself for a few moments.

For miraculously Fortunata was here, firmly holding her hand and chatting to Signora Vittorini on the corner of Summer Street, for all the world as if it were three years ago, before life had been spoilt by marrying Papa and having babies. She looked beautiful, too, in her best cream lace Sunday dress and close-fitting velvet cloche hat. Fortunata, with access to the exclusive dressmakers of the West End, always outshone the other women on Procession Day, and this year was no exception. Her figure was as trim as ever, in spite of the babies she had borne, and men still watched her from the corners of their eyes, glumly comparing her to their plump and passive wives, and wondering for the hundredth time what she saw in Giuseppe Florio.

Serafina looked up at Fortunata. She was smiling at Mrs Vittorini, a small glow of triumph in her eyes. 'You mean *Wise Parenthood*?' she was saying, 'the Marie Stopes book?' Mrs Vittorini looked around, furtive, not wanting anyone to hear.

71

'It's my eldest, Annunziata,' she whispered, 'she's already expecting her fourth and she's only twenty-one!'

'Poor soul,' said Fortunata, genuinely sympathetic.

'Why does she need a book,' Serafina asked, innocent, 'if she's having a baby?'

Mrs Vittorini looked agonised. Fortunata grinned down at her step-daughter, 'That's exactly why she needs this particular book, *cara*,' she said. Then turning back to her neighbour, she said, politely, 'Don't worry. I'll talk to Annunziata, if you like.'

The older woman blanched. Fortunata was enjoying her discomfort. 'I'm married now, remember?' she said. 'This kind of talk is permitted now, isn't it? And anyway . . .' she leaned forward, mischievous, whispering, 'why do you think it is I have only two babies myself . . .?'

Mrs Vittorini drew back, pained, and made a discreet sign of the cross. Her hand dropped to her side as she became aware of the sharp, interested gaze of the funny little Florio child, who, as usual, seemed to have been listening in to an adult conversation instead of occupying herself as other children did.

'How pretty Serafina looks!' she simpered, changing the subject. 'Quite a transformation – you must have been working on her all morning, Fortunata.' Serafina's hand was squeezed gently.

'Not at all,' Fortunata answered politely, 'Serafina is a natural beauty in my opinion, and needs no work. Talking of which, where is little Anna? Still having the rags put in for her ringlets?' With a mischievous grin, Fortunata tugged Serafina into the crowd, waving a careless goodbye to her neighbour. '*Ciao*, Signora Vittorini – see you at the procession!'

Giggling, she and Serafina threaded their way through the busy throng on Summer Street and into Back Hill. Here the level of chaos was even greater, as horses and carts jostled for position in the procession, and people in costumes ran in and out of the side door of the church, shouting instructions, searching for lost children, clutching false beards and biblical robes in a welter of colour and confusion.

Fortunata bought them both an ice-cream wafer from a nearby stall, and they settled on a low wall outside a small printing works facing the side door of St Peter's, in the

72

sunshine and with a perfect view of the starting point of the procession.

Fortunata looked at the silver fob watch she kept in her purse. 'We can relax for at least half an hour,' she told Serafina, 'then I'll deliver you to Sister Catherine.'

'Are you going to wait for me?' Serafina asked, surprised. 'Shouldn't you go and get the babies?'

Fortunata shrugged. 'Mamma said she'll bring them along later.'

'And what about Papa? Shouldn't you go and find Papa?'

Fortunata laughed her delicious musical laugh. 'Papa's with Nonno, fussing over the statue! I'm free, Serafina – I've been given the afternoon off to be with you! I'm free!' Serafina pondered this, a pleased smile playing around her mouth. Fortunata was free, and she chose to be with Serafina! Perhaps life wasn't so bad after all. She and Fortunata could still be friends. Today Fortunata was like her old self, concentrating on Serafina, taking her away from the stuffy little house on Grape Street, making her feel wanted and loved. When Fortunata was like this, the world seemed full of possibilities.

Together they licked at their ice-creams and watched the world go by, occasionally calling to someone they knew in the crowd or waving to a familiar face peering from a window in the church. Serafina asked about Mrs Vittorini, puzzled. 'Why did she make the sign of the cross? Does she think you're really wicked?'

Fortunata sighed and patted Serafina's hand. 'She doesn't know what to think, *topolina*,' she said. 'Forget it. She's just a foolish old hypocrite. Watch the procession!'

Everywhere was colour. A group of men dressed as shepherds went by, actually pulling two live sheep along behind them. Fortunata nudged Serafina. 'It's old Santini and his two brothers from Finchley – see the one with the striped headdress? He's got a café off the Tottenham Court Road.' Several girls in Italian regional costumes ran up the hill towards the Clerkenwell Road, screaming with delight, chased by a Roman centurion.

'It's Vittorio Boselli,' Serafina told Fortunata in a stage whisper, 'he's in class seven, and he likes Gloria – the girl at the front with the red ribbons.'

A man in white robes with a false grey beard was ordering

a group of angels onto a cart decorated with blue and silver streamers.

'Who's he?' asked Serafina.

'God!' Fortunata replied, and they both collapsed into fits of giggles.

Gradually a semblance of order appeared, and the horses and carts began to form a line stretching up the hill and around the corner out of sight. Groups of nuns began to collect and flutter about behind the carts in nervous little flocks, prayer books ready. The children on the nativity float appeared and were directed by 'God' to their cart. A tragic-faced young woman in blue and white was helped onto a cart with the aid of an upturned crate and two strong-armed kings in dyed purple bedsheets.

'Olivia Brosso,' Fortunata told Serafina, 'the last person in the world they should have picked for the Virgin Mary!'

'Why?'

Fortunata grinned and flicked at Serafina's braids. 'Guess!'

Serafina was still pondering this enigma when she heard a cry of 'Fortunata! Serafina!' It was Rosa and Eduardo, from King Bomba. Rosa, managing to look cross and pleased all at once, was hugging Fortunata to her bosom, while Eduardo – taller now, and shyer, hung back, twisting his cap in his hands, uncomfortable in his Sunday suit.

'Say hello, you two!' commanded Rosa.

Eduardo came and sat next to Serafina on the wall.

'How are you?' he asked.

'Fine. You?' She watched him remove his glasses and polish them carefully with his cap.

'I'm all right. You haven't been to the shop for ages.' He had a nice face, Serafina decided, stealing a look at his short-sighted profile before he replaced the spectacles.

'I've been too busy,' she said importantly. They subsided into silence and watched the passers-by. Serafina wished she hadn't answered the way she had. It wasn't the truth. Her absence from King Bomba was actually a kind of punishment. When Fortunata would rise from the breakfast table on a Sunday morning and cause consternation in her family by announcing her intention to 'work on the paper' for the day, Serafina took a grim delight in turning down the offer to accompany her, much as she would have liked to go. It felt like a final slap in the face, the cruellest reprimand of all. Nonna would be angry with Fortunata for neglecting her babies, and would slam the plates about. Nonno would be angry with Fortunata for neglecting her duties as a wife, and would shout at her about missing Mass. Papa would say nothing – he would just *look* angry. And Serafina – she didn't know exactly why she was angry with Fortunata, but she knew it hurt her to go to Old Compton Street alone, without her small companion. Now, faced by the gentle Eduardo, Serafina felt mean and petty.

'Have you been working hard for *Il Comento*?' she asked.

Eduardo nodded, his gaze following two white-robed priests who were strolling past, deep in conversation. 'Yes. Since Mussolini came to power we've had twice as much work.'

'Why?'

Eduardo could not help shooting her a look of quiet condescension. 'We have to tell people,' he said simply, 'about what he stands for. People don't realise – he's taken over Italy and he'll destroy it.'

Fortunata interrupted them gaily, 'That's right, Eduardo, she needs a political education! Nine years old and not worried about Mussolini – the joys of childhood! I don't think she even noticed that Lenin died!' She lowered herself from the wall. 'Come on, we must deliver you into the hands of the sisters – the procession will be starting soon. *Ciao*, Rosa!'

As she turned to go, Rosa pulled Fortunata back. The crowds had suddenly increased, and Serafina was thrust against Fortunata's lace skirts. Above her head, Serafina heard Rosa saying urgently, 'I shouldn't tell you this, Fortunata, but he's here.'

Serafina felt Fortunata's entire body go rigid. 'Here?' She looked down suddenly, nervously, at Serafina.

Rosa was still holding Fortunata's arm. 'He's here, on the Hill somewhere.'

'Oh God!' Fortunata stood there, oblivious to the crowds and to Serafina, pressed against her skirts. She bit her lip and gazed at Rosa.

'I must go, Rosa.'

'What shall I tell him?'

'Nothing! Don't tell him anything!' Brusquely she pulled

75

Serafina away through the crowds towards the side door of St Peter's.

'I didn't say goodbye to Eduardo!' Serafina shouted indignantly above the noise.

'Sorry, *topolina*.' Fortunata seemed agitated, pushing her way through the crush of bodies. 'We mustn't be late.' Suddenly they were inside, where it was cool and dark. Father Guido greeted them both and directed them to a room at the end of the corridor, where a plump, flustered nun with sweat on her upper lip was trying to keep order among twenty little girls, over-excited in their communion dresses.

'Sister Catherine – here is Serafina,' said Fortunata, her voice sounding dazed and distant.

'Serafina! Good. You will be walking in the third row, between Bridie and Angela. Got that? Third row. Good!' Her voice became suddenly stern, as she was distracted by a scuffle in the corner. 'Mary Feeney! Let Anita have a turn in front of that mirror, her veil is all askew!' She turned back to Serafina, 'You look lovely, Serafina, really lovely, it does my heart good to see you. I remember Fortunata in the procession, you know—'

Fortunata smiled a sad smile at the old nun, 'It seems a million years ago, Sister.'

The two women exchanged a silent look which spoke volumes. Sister Catherine placed a cool hand on Fortunata's flushed cheek. 'The women – they still complain about you.'

'I know, Sister.'

The old woman studied the face before her, thoughtful. 'They say you've been offering advice contrary to the teachings of the Church.'

Fortunata's eyes met hers for a moment, defiant. 'Do they?'

The old nun patted the soft cheek and smiled, too full of affection for this proud product of Little Italy to have the argument now, today of all days. She would do penance later. There would be other times . . .

'Come and talk to me, Fortunata. Some other day.'

'I will, Sister Catherine.'

'God bless you, Fortunata.'

Fortunata's eyes were downcast. 'Thank you, Sister Catherine.' She looked at Serafina, but distractedly, as though she saw something – or someone – else standing there in the shadow of the doorway. 'I must go.' Her eyes focused at last and she saw Serafina gazing up at her. Her face softened. 'You look so beautiful, Serafina. I'm proud of you. Hold your head up in the procession and remember you're representing the Viallis and the Florios – that's quite a responsibility!'

'Will you be there, watching?'

'Yes, I'll be there.'

'Where?'

Fortunata was already heading for the door. 'I'll be in Warner Street, outside the shoemender's – do you know where I mean?'

Serafina nodded. 'But will Papa know where to find you—?' It was too late. Fortunata had gone.

'Come upstairs, children!' Sister Catherine was calling, 'Father Guido says we can watch most of the procession before we join in . . .'

Serafina clattered excitedly upstairs with the other children, Fortunata forgotten. They reached the window just as the Cross of Peace, an enormous wooden cross covered in pink flowers, wobbled away down the hill atop a horse-drawn milk float festooned with white sheets. One by one the stories Serafina knew so well from the Bible sprang to life in the procession below, as she watched, entranced. After the Cross of Peace came Salvatore and Rosa Medici, from the print works, dressed as San Francesco and Santa Caterina. Behind them a group of Franciscan monks walked silently, their lips moving in prayer. The crowd, forgetting piety for a moment, called and waved as a group of teenagers followed in the colourful costumes of the different regions of their homeland. Rumbling down the cobblestones came a cart depicting Our Lady of Lourdes, with Serafina's neighbour, the generally bad-tempered Rosa Vittorini, occupying the grotto, her face soulful and eyes raised heavenward.

'Look, Anna,' Sister Catherine called, 'it's your sister! How wonderfully saintly she looks.'

'*Guarda*, Sister!' another child called. 'Look at the men in their satin capes!' Another involuntary cry went up from the crowd as a band began to play, and behind the band came Mr Terroni's delivery cart, swathed in muslin, with the girls from the delicatessen magically transformed into angels, tinsel wings a-quiver. The little girls gazing from the upstairs window sighed enviously.

'I wish I was an angel,' said Anna Vittorini, sucking sulkily at one of her ringlets. But I am one, Serafina thought proudly. Angel flower . . .

'Plenty of time for that in years to come,' said Sister Catherine firmly. 'Now we must go down and get into our places. Remember your positions, please! Roberto – what is the matter with your shirt front? Have you all got your prayer books?'

Down in the street they took their places behind four men in suits carrying a statue of Santa Lucia. Behind them another marching band began to play. Slowly they moved away down Back Hill, hands clasped over their prayer books as instructed, hearts thudding in time to the big bass drum. Disobeying Sister Catherine's orders to keep eyes fixed on the road, Serafina sneakily scanned the crowds for familiar faces. Yes, there was the bird-like face of Miss Perkins, her teacher, transformed with pride as her white-clad pupils marched past. Serafina ran out of her place to guide the wandering Bridie O'Farrell back beside her (Bridie was only six, and it was her first procession, so she would be forgiven for straying slightly from the fold).

''Fina!' It was Eduardo and his mother, smiling and waving from the wall outside the printing works, Eduardo grinning from ear to ear and waving a small Italian flag. She allowed them a quick smile before resuming her solemn 'procession expression' as Sister Catherine called it.

Now they were turning the corner at the foot of the hill and entering Warner Street. Serafina clutched her prayer book tightly and adjusted her step to keep perfect, measured time with Bridie and Angela. The crowd murmured, people crossing themselves as the band boomed behind the First Communicants making their way towards Rosebery Avenue, where the cries of pleasure ahead indicated an even bigger crowd had gathered. Now they were drawing level with the shoemender's. Serafina dared to raise her eyes and look for Fortunata as they passed by. The girls in the row behind murmured a prayer in unison, '*Santa Maria, Madre di Dio, prega per noi peccatori* . . .' Fortunata was not there. Serafina looked again, disobeying Sister Catherine and craning her neck round. No, a young couple with a baby stood in the shoemender's doorway, and a gang of youths lounged against the narrow, dusty window. Fortunata had not kept her promise.

'Serafina! *Qui*, 'Fina – over here!' It was Nonna, standing on the corner as the procession turned, holding baby Claudia, and there was Papa with Antonia in the perambulator, and next to him was dear old Nonno, waving a paint-smeared hand, proud as Punch, a tear in his eye at the sight of Serafina, so solemn in her white dress. She passed them, unsmiling. Around her the noise was deafening, as the crowds called to people in the procession, the music blared, and the murmur of prayers rose and fell in the hot afternoon. Blindly she followed the statue of Santa Lucia, keeping the blue-robed plaster figure always the same distance ahead, as Sister Catherine had instructed. Fortunata! Where was Fortunata?

The cold hand around her heart had returned. For a brief morning it had left Serafina and she had felt somehow normal, sunny, excited – like other children. Now she was different again, alone, silent, stony. Now it was as if the gay morning had never happened. The wonderful hair ribbons, the ice-cream in the sunshine, meeting Eduardo – it was all spoilt. Fortunata, who always promised so much, had let her down again.

Behind her, the crowd let out a great 'ooooh!' of surprise and then a cheer rose up. Serafina knew it meant that the statue of Our Lady of Mount Carmel had arrived below the ball of flowers suspended above the crowd in Eyre Street Hill, and the doves and confetti had fluttered out. This was the highlight of the procession, and it was torture for the First Communicants, ordered to keep their eyes ahead and not turn around to see the spectacle. Little Bridie gave a frustrated moan, earning a frown from Sister Catherine, but Serafina's step did not falter and her eyes did not waver as they approached the steps of St Peter's, where they would pass into the cool darkness. There the statue so lovingly tended by Nonno would be placed at the foot of the High Altar, and all would bow their heads for the Benediction of the Blessed Sacrament, before a myriad of glimmering candles.

For Serafina it all meant nothing now. The magic had died, and all that remained was to get through the day, until the oblivion of sleep. She hated Fortunata. Fortunata had promised to be there, and Fortunata had lied.

By ten o'clock the solemnity of the procession was forgotten, and the streets of Little Italy echoed to the sound of dance music, the chink of glasses and the raucous cries of young men who had drunk too much wine. Old women tutted tolerantly on their doorsteps, wearing their best shawls. Children, still in their communion outfits or procession costumes, ran through the streets over-tired and excited, anxious to avoid being sent to bed while the *sagra* was in progress. Serafina was wandering disconsolately through the swaying, dancing mass in Hatton Garden when Giuseppe found her.

'At last!' he panted. 'Where have you been? Have you had any supper? Where's Fortunata?' He clutched her thin shoulder, his face creased into a frown, lit by a kerosene lamp hanging from a nearby polenta stall.

'I'm not hungry,' Serafina mumbled, not raising her head.

'Nonno's been looking for you. He was worried. I've sent him home with Nonna and the babies to wait. I said you would be with Fortunata.' Giuseppe looked around hopefully, craning his neck to peer at faces in the crowd, as if the act of looking would produce his errant wife. Instead the crowd opened up and three men, dressed very smartly and all much the worse for drink, staggered towards them. Giuseppe's hand tightened on Serafina's shoulder. She looked up and recognised the tall man in the grey hat squaring up to her father. It was Antonio Viazzani, whom Nonna always referred to as 'that gangster'. Behind him was his brother Federico, his mouth drooping drunkenly as he supported his unknown companion.

'Lost your wife, Florio?' Antonio sneered, lurching dangerously.

'Mind your own business,' Giuseppe snapped, pulling his daughter towards him and turning away.

'He's lost Fortunata again!' Federico's voice was slurred. He leered at Serafina, 'Here's the only pure one left in the family—'

'And I don't expect she'll last long!' The two brothers laughed unpleasantly.

'Come on, Serafina,' Giuseppe stepped back, his face revealing nothing. Only the hand on her shoulder, hurting now, indicated his silent rage. But he would not fight, Serafina realised. Papa would not defend her honour, nor that of Fortunata. She felt hot with shame at his public cowardice.

Antonio had followed them, and was prodding at Giuseppe, drunkenly persistent. 'Where's your wife, eh? Lost your wife?'

Giuseppe remained silent, his jaw set. Antonio leaned down to grin at Serafina, his breath heavy with alcohol.

'She's fighting the fascists still, is she? She's a communist, your stepmother, you know that? She's a red.'

'Come on, 'Fina.' Giuseppe's hand on her shoulder became more insistent.

'She's an anarchist!' It was Federico, hanging back behind his brother, but eager to have his say. 'A troublemaker! She's not a proper Italian, your wife! She should behave herself! We're guests in this country!'

Antonio yelled his agreement, egged on by some of the crowd. 'That's right! Fortunata Florio's a troublemaker!'

'Papa,' Serafina hissed, 'don't let him—'

'Quiet, 'Fina! Take no notice. He's drunk.'

Antonio prodded at Giuseppe. 'Are you calling me drunk?' Giuseppe moved away again. The crowd around them had fallen silent. Her cheeks burning, Serafina could hear the murmurs.

'. . . It's the Viazzani brothers, looking for trouble.'

'They say Fortunata jilted him . . .'

'Be careful, he carries a knife . . .'

Giuseppe pushed his daughter ahead of him. 'Keep walking, 'Fina,' he said quietly. She thought she would probably die of shame as they retreated into the crowd. Then once more Antonio appeared before them.

'I asked you a question, Florio. Where's your wife?'

Giuseppe stopped, but did not raise his eyes. 'She's at home, I expect.'

Antonio guffawed and lurched forward. 'You expect! You expect wrong, Florio. Your wife is out whoring, as usual! Fortunata's gone off with another man, *whoring*,' he stressed the word, enunciating it drunkenly, 'giving us Italians a bad name—' He never finished his sentence, for Giuseppe had pushed him suddenly in the chest, and he fell heavily to the pavement. Before he could struggle to his feet, Giuseppe was upon him and the two rolled, panting, in the dust, fists flying, while the crowd jostled and cheered.

Sobbing, Serafina fled, struggling through the sea of legs

until she reached the edge of the crowd. With cries of 'Hit him, Giuseppe!' and 'Watch your back, Viazzani!' still echoing in her head, Serafina ran through the noisy streets towards home. The nightmare had returned. Papa fighting for Fortunata, poor Papa forced to defend her honour, and she didn't care – she didn't care what he did for her, it made no difference. As she ran, ignoring the calls of recognition from neighbours and ducking out of sight when she saw Miss Perkins looming up from a side street, Serafina knew that although instinct took her to Grape Street, she didn't want to see Nonno and Nonna. She did not want to have to tell them about the fight, or about what those men had called Fortunata.

She slowed down as she turned the corner, gasping for breath. She would not go home after all. She would go to Nonno's studio and sit in the dark for a while, until the hurt went away. She would sneak into the back yard of the house and get the spare studio key that always hung from a hook in the outside privy.

Within minutes Serafina had groped her way along the passage at the back of the houses, into the yard and then into the shed. Her hand felt along the rough bricks for the key, but met only an empty hook. Strange, she thought. The key was always there. Papa or Nonno must have taken it and in the excitement of Procession Day had forgotten to put it back. She tiptoed back into the yard. Through the kitchen window she could see Nonna rocking the baby in her arms by the stove, crooning to it. Serafina's mouth set in a cold grim line. No one would miss her. She would go to the studio anyway, and climb in through the skylight window. She would sit in the dark amidst the silence and the smell of drying plaster and she would feel better, because nothing in the studio ever changed, it was always the same, always comfortingly the same.

She retraced her steps along the passage and out again into Grape Street. Then she turned away from the lights and noise coming from the *sagra* and set off towards Vine Hill and the courtyard where she had spent so many happy hours with Nonno, learning how to make statues. She turned the corner, arriving at the gloomy unlit yard, where the huge double doors of the studio were closed.

Serafina, who knew every inch of the yard, wasted no time. She climbed up onto the water butt in the corner, mindful of her white dress, and pulled herself quickly up the drainpipe onto the low roof of the front of the building. Panting, she paused, peering over the edge into the cobbled yard below. She could hear faint music coming from the direction of Hatton Garden, and somewhere overhead a firework crackled into life, exploding into a fountain of silver sparks in the night sky. She could see the skylight window behind her; once inside it was a simple matter of lowering herself on to Nonno's painting bench, which was directly beneath (Nonno said you needed light from all angles in order to paint accurately).

To Serafina's puzzlement, there was a tiny gleam of flickering light showing through the grimy glass of the skylight. A candle was burning somewhere in the studio. She hesitated. Perhaps Nonno had come back here – that would explain the missing key. But then again, perhaps it was burglars, come to steal Nonno's tools. Her heart skipped a beat. They might kill her if they found her up here! Then her courage took hold. She must at least have a look. If it was burglars, she must see them, so that she could describe them to Nonno. She crept towards the skylight, terrified and elated at the same time. Imagine if there really were burglars in the studio, and she was responsible for their capture! How pleased Nonno would be!

Careful not to make a noise on the slates, Serafina edged forward, inch by inch, until she was level with the dusty glass. The light still flickered within. She craned her neck and peered down. Through the grime she could make out movement, something light-coloured below, someone was there – or perhaps two people?

Hardly daring to breathe, she delicately rubbed the dirt away from a corner of the pane and peered in. For a second, as her eyes focused on the studio below, she did not understand what she saw. Then, as the gloom became familiar, she saw them, moving urgently, rapt, intent only on the moment, unaware of Serafina staring down at them. Fortunata was pressed against the painting bench, her head thrown back. Her mouth was moving, murmuring something. Her blouse was in disarray, the lace clinging to one shoulder but not the

other, one white breast shockingly exposed in the candlelight
... and leaning into her, his face invisible, groaning and
pressing his thighs against her, his head buried in Fortunata's
neck – yes, it was the unmistakable bright head of Joe
O'Connell.

Serafina turned to stone. Fortunata and Joe O'Connell!
Together they moved, his thrusting becoming more urgent.
For a second Serafina thought of crashing through the skylight
to rescue Fortunata, but just as the thought entered her confused brain, she saw Fortunata writhe, laugh, and pull the
Irishman's head to her breast. Fortunata was laughing! Serafina
watched, aghast. Joe O'Connell was sucking at that huge
blue-veined breast, just as baby Antonia had done – only
Fortunata's face was glazed, smiling, her hands moving
through that red hair.

Suddenly he pulled his head away and pushed again at
Fortunata more violently, his hands disappearing under her
bunched-up skirts, the cream lace spread on the bench. Fortunata was moving too, in the same strange way, her eyes
closed, but her mouth open, moaning now, her hands on his
shoulders as they thrust together. Faster they moved, in a
strange spasmodic rhythm, Fortunata giving a series of small
cries, one hand clutching at the red hair – and then, suddenly,
she opened her eyes. She was staring straight at Serafina,
frozen above her. But before Serafina could move, the Irishman gave a great violent shove at Fortunata, and let out a
groan. Fortunata's eyes widened for a second, she gasped, and
seemed to crumple.

Serafina scrambled across the roof tiles, no longer caring if
she could be heard. She hurled herself onto the pipe, onto the
water butt and back onto the cobblestones. She ran like light-
ning back into Grape Street, her mind racing, her head full of
horror and bewilderment. The world was an ugly, ugly place,
full of betrayal and deceit. People were like animals, like dogs
– fighting and doing that unnameable thing she had seen
mongrels doing in the street, when people gathered and
laughed and threw buckets of water over them. Papa was
rolling about in the road like a savage dog, Fortunata was
doing that unspeakable thing with Joe O'Connell, that hated
Irishman. Serafina would never trust anyone – no, not anyone
– again.

CHAPTER FOUR

1932

THE CURTAINS OF of the house in Grape Street remained closed, even though the friends and relatives of the deceased Bruno Vialli had long since departed. In the front room Fortunata was clearing the remains of the tea things on to a tray. She was in a kind of trance, trying to accept that Papa really was dead. She had been busy all day trying to organise the funeral, since Giuseppe was worse than useless at that kind of thing, and Mamma was paralysed by grief. She knew it was the kind of funeral Papa would have wanted. It told the world that here was a man who had come from another land and had bettered himself. He may have arrived here as an illiterate peasant, but he left with a little more. The crowds at the cemetery had proved that, as had the tributes they left by the newly turned grave.

There had been a floral tribute from the Mazzini-Garibaldi people, and another from the Club Co-operativo in Greek Street, as well as flowers from neighbours and friends from all over the Hill. How everyone had loved Bruno! Lucia had been so proud when the funeral cortège had stretched from St Peter's right down the Clerkenwell Road. It had been a grand funeral, in true Italian tradition, with great grief and magnificent singing, leaving the mourners drained but satisfied. Bruno had been buried in style, in spite of the family's poverty, thanks to Lucia's determination over the years to make regular payments to the funeral club.

As usual, Fortunata thought, it was the woman behind the man, making the sacrifices, thinking ahead, holding things together. She looked across for a moment at her mother, her heart full of love. Dear Mamma. She was the embodiment of everything a good Italian woman should be. How disappointed she must be with her daughter!

Lucia was staring blankly into the fire (lit only rarely in this room) and said nothing. Serafina peeked through a gap in the curtains at Papa, who was standing at the front gate in the rain talking sadly to Signor Vittorini from next door. How sombre they looked in their black Sunday suits and armbands! Serafina sighed. Dear Nonno. It was hard to believe she would never see him again.

''Fina! Come away from the window!' Fortunata frowned at her, piling up teacups. 'You can help me with these.'

'But I wanted to go to the studio—'

Fortunata crashed some plates expressively, raising her eyes to the ceiling. '*Dio mio!* The day Papa is buried and she wants to go out.'

'You went out when Nonno was ill. You went to feed those hunger marchers when Nonno was lying upstairs calling for you—'

'I went because I had to, Serafina. Papa understood.'

'And Nonno would have understood my wanting to go to the studio.'

'Well, I don't. You can stay here and help me with all these dishes.'

'I don't have to do what you say! I'm seventeen! I can do what I like!'

''Fina, please!' It was Lucia, made feeble by the sudden death of her husband, intervening from her armchair in a quavering voice. 'Please help Fortunata – for me . . .'

Serafina snatched up the teapot from its stand, burning her fingers in the process, and stormed out to the kitchen, followed by Fortunata carrying the tray.

'How dare you!' Fortunata hissed, slamming the tray down. 'Papa's hardly cold in his grave and you're behaving like a spoilt brat. The studio, indeed! On the day of Papa's funeral!'

Serafina poured boiling water from a kettle on the stove into the sink, and said nothing. She had learned over the years that the best policy was to keep a low profile and then do what she wanted when no one was paying attention; unfortunately every now and then her Italian, argumentative nature got the better of her and she forgot her usual self-contained comportment. She bit her lip, as she washed the plates and placed them, dripping, on the draining-board. Losing her temper like that was stupid – it only focused Fortunata's eyes on to her, and that was the last thing she wanted.

'Speak to me when I'm talking to you!' Fortunata was standing, hands on hips, eyes blazing. *Que bella*, Serafina thought dispassionately; she is still beautiful, in spite of the tiny wrinkles at the corners of her eyes. How I hate her!

The door opened, and Giuseppe came in, shaking the rain from his hat.

'Ah, good – I'm glad to see you helping, 'Fina. Is Mamma all right?' he asked Fortunata.

She nodded. 'Yes, she's all right. Dozing by the fire. I've told the girls not to disturb her. They've gone next door to Mrs Vittorini for a while. Poor lambs, they were so good at the funeral and afterwards – I thought they deserved an hour's play before bedtime.' Inexplicably, her eyes filled with tears. Giuseppe went over and placed an arm silently round her shoulders.

Serafina paid exaggerated attention to the teacup she was scrubbing. 'Did you see Anna Vittorini in the church, Fortunata?' she asked, casual. She could never bring herself to call Fortunata 'Mamma'.

Fortunata shook her head tearfully. 'No, I was too upset. I hardly saw who was there. Why?'

Serafina placed the cup carefully on the draining-board, relishing the moment. 'Oh, I just asked because she came in her *ballila* uniform.'

'*What?*'

Fortunata's outrage did not surprise Serafina in the least. She washed another cup, smiling quietly to herself. 'Didn't you know she'd joined?'

'How dare she!' Fortunata was furious, trembling with emotion. 'How dare she defile Papa's funeral in the uniform of that scum! I can't believe the Vittorinis would insult us in that way, they know how I feel—'

Giuseppe reached for his pipe, calm as usual. 'Yes, of course, Fortunata. They know how *you* feel. But it wasn't your day, was it? It was your father's funeral.'

Fortunata snorted. 'Oh, you!' She moved a step away from him as if wanting to shake off the moment of sympathy he had offered a moment before. 'I can always rely on you to be feeble and see all sides of the argument.'

'There is no argument.' Giuseppe began slowly to fill his pipe from his tobacco tin. 'You have your views, other people have theirs, and most people think the *fascio* is a good thing.'

'What happened to you, Giuseppe?' A tear was trickling down Fortunata's cheek. She dashed it away. 'This is the man who had to leave Italy because of his political beliefs! This is the man whose wife died because of those thugs—'

Giuseppe had lit his pipe and was drawing on it, slowly. Only a slight tremor of his hand revealed emotion. He shook his head. 'Not the same thugs, exactly. Anyway, I can hardly see that a young girl in a silly fascist uniform is going to change the world.'

'It's rather a nice uniform,' said Serafina from the sink, 'and I like the tune of the "Giovinezza" – it's pretty.' She began humming to herself. Suddenly she was pulled around, and received a stinging blow across the face. Fortunata stood before her, arm still raised. 'You little bitch! How dare you say that! How dare you sing that wicked song! You're evil, you know that?'

'Fortunata!' Giuseppe had leapt up and stood between them. 'Don't say things like that to 'Fina! We're all upset about Nonno – we must stay together as a family.'

Serafina, her face throbbing, laughed out loud, staring defiantly at her stepmother. 'A family! That's a joke!'

'Enough!' Giuseppe meant business. 'Go upstairs, Serafina. Don't come down until you're ready to apologise to your mother.'

'She is not my mother,' said Serafina. 'And I don't see why she should take it out on me just because her precious comrades didn't succeed in killing Mussolini like they planned.'

'Serafina!' her father whispered, his face white with fear. 'Don't ever – ever – say a thing like that! You want us all arrested? Now go, before I do something I might regret!'

She left the room in what she hoped was a dignified manner, and went upstairs to the room she shared with her two small sisters. She flung herself on the bed and lay gazing at a stain on the ceiling, her heart still pounding. The slap had been worth it. She could hear Fortunata and her father arguing, their voices gradually gathering momentum, until Lucia called into the passage, *'Que succede . . .?'* and Giuseppe answered, *'Niente*, Lucia!' Then the voices subsided to a low, angry murmur. Serafina allowed herself a small smile. Fortunata behaved like a pig to Papa. She deserved a good beating. It was a pity that he would never raise a hand to her, but a good argument was better than nothing.

After a few moments Serafina went over to the window, which looked out over the rain-sodden street. She picked up her little statue from its place on the windowsill, and caressed the plaster folds of the Madonna's skirts. She was fading, and tiny flakes of gold paint from the hem of her cloak had fallen off. She sighed, and kissed the head of the statuette. Life had to continue, even though Nonno had gone.

She heard a knock on the front door. Giuseppe was calling her. 'Serafina! Come downstairs – someone to see you.' She went quickly into the main bedroom to get a glimpse in Fortunata's mirror of her reflection dimly revealed by the street light shining through the window. A pale, round-faced girl stared back at her, unfashionably long, straight hair framing an unsmiling face. Her appearance meant nothing to her; she was not vain, and accepted that she was not a great beauty like her stepmother. But she understood that her body, developing rapidly as she progressed through her teenage years, now had the kind of voluptuous curves that made men look twice. She was not beautiful, but if she combed her hair and smiled, she had learned that people – and men in particular – took note only of the rounded curve of her hips, her well-developed breasts and her fine ankles, and imagined that they saw a pretty girl . . . And pretty girls, Serafina thought bitterly, often got what they wanted simply because they were pretty girls. This she had learned from her stepmother.

Satisfied with her appearance, in spite of the plain black dress she had to wear, Serafina went downstairs. In the front room she found Rosa from King Bomba offering condolences to Lucia and Fortunata. Eduardo stood by the window, and Serafina noted with satisfaction the way his eyes lit up when he saw her.

'Hello, Serafina!' he said eagerly, stepping forward into the light. He held out his hand, and she took it politely. Even with his spectacles he had grown into a handsome young man, although prone to over-seriousness.

'I'm so sorry – about your grandfather,' he said, suddenly shy, still gripping her hand.

She withdrew it, smiling. 'It was kind of you to come, Eduardo.'

Serafina was aware that her father had retreated once again into the kitchen. The presence of Rosa always made him uncomfortable. He would argue that he did not want 'known agitators' in his house, that it might anger the British authorities and he would lose his right to stay in the country. 'We should keep a low profile,' he would say. 'We are guests of Britain.' Since the scandal of the June attempt on Mussolini's life and hints of involvement by some of the men who gathered above King Bomba, Giuseppe was doubly agitated by the visitors. Fortunata would simply accuse him of cowardice and invite Rosa to come again.

'Shall we go and sit with Papa in the kitchen?' Serafina asked her stepmother deviously. Papa distrusted Eduardo.

'No, no!' It was Lucia who intervened again from her armchair, anxious to avoid confrontations. 'Why don't you take the boy to see Bruno's studio, 'Fina? He might like to see the statues.'

'I'd love to!' Eduardo's enthusiasm effectively prevented Fortunata from objecting. Serafina could not help a small glow of pleasure at her stepmother's hesitation. Fortunata stepped forward as if to say something, then bit her lip. She looked steadily at Serafina.

'Yes, Serafina. Take Eduardo to the studio. Be home by nine o'clock. Don't forget to take the key.'

Serafina raised an eyebrow. 'Ah, yes. The key. Is it hanging where it should be, Fortunata?'

There was a silence, the air heavy in the gloomy firelight.

'What does she mean?' Lucia looked up. 'Have you moved Bruno's key, Fortunata?'

'Of course I haven't.' Fortunata had turned away and was fiddling with the chenille fringes of the tablecloth, to disguise her trembling hands. What did Serafina know? 'Go on, Serafina. We'll see you both at nine o'clock.'

'What was all that about?' Eduardo wanted to know, as he and Serafina stepped out into the rainy evening. Serafina had run through to the back of the house, retrieved the studio key from its hook in the privy, kissed Papa on the forehead, and thrust on her coat and hat, all in the space of a very short time. Her eagerness to get out of the stuffy house had not been lost on any of its occupants.

'Hurry up with that umbrella, Eduardo — I'm getting drenched.' Together they headed down the street under the darkening sky.

'What was that awful atmosphere about, back there? Have you been fighting with Fortunata again?'

Serafina shrugged, suddenly carefree. The evening air felt cool on her cheeks and the rain drummed on their shared umbrella. It was good to be alive.

'Just a family squabble. Surely you and Rosa fight sometimes?'

Eduardo considered this question solemnly as they turned into Vine Street. 'No, we don't really fight. The occasional political disagreement—'

Serafina pulled a face in the darkness. 'Politics! What a waste of time.'

Eduardo looked sideways at her. 'You don't really mean that.'

She shrugged. 'I've listened to Fortunata going on about Mussolini for years now. He doesn't seem to have destroyed Italy, as she predicted.'

Eduardo stopped on the wet pavement, still clutching the umbrella. '*Il Duce* isn't important,' he said. 'He just sits alone in his office eating fruit and reading newspapers, by all accounts. It's the people he's put in power – Guidi, Ciano—'

'Oh, do be quiet, Eduardo!' Serafina said, irritably. 'We live in London, not in Rome! I don't want to talk about a lot of stupid men hundreds of miles away.'

Eduardo suddenly blurted out, 'I was going to invite you to a meeting in the Finsbury Library on Friday night. But I don't suppose you'd want to go – it's political.'

Serafina turned up the collar of her coat, huddling under the shelter of the umbrella. 'What kind of political?' she asked, enjoying Eduardo's discomfiture.

'Some speakers – you know – Anzani, and maybe someone from the Italian League—'

Serafina groaned. 'Don't tell me! and then at the end you all clasp hands and sing "La Bandera Rossa" and the world is a better place – oh, Eduardo!' She laughed at the sight of his downcast face.

'There will be music afterwards,' he said, in a final bid.

'What kind of music?'

'Only the gramophone and Romano with his accordion and a couple of singers – but Mamma says the older people will leave when the talking stops and we'll be left to dance on our own.'

Serafina pulled him along the pavement again. 'Come on! We've only got 'til nine, remember?'

'Will you come? To the meeting?'

Serafina smiled mischievously and shook her head. 'No, I won't come to the meeting . . . But I'll come along later for the dancing if Papa will let me.'

'You will?' Eduardo's eyes widened in amazement. His joy was apparent. 'I never thought you would say yes!' he said exultantly. 'You're always so opposed to anything connected with politics!'

They had reached the studio. Eduardo held the umbrella over Serafina as she fumbled with the padlock. 'Politics killed my mother,' she said, 'you seem to forget that. There!' Triumphantly she pushed open the small door cut into the great wooden one, and stepped inside. 'Wait a second until I light the lamp. That's better.' Her face appeared suddenly in the gloom, illuminated by the kerosene lamp she was holding. 'Come in – but careful where you stand. You might break something.'

She took Eduardo on a lamplit tour of Nonno's studio: past the huge aspidistra plant which threatened to grow all the way up to the skylight; around the enormous sacks of plaster heaped in one corner and the shelves of gleaming white statuettes waiting to be painted – rows of cats and windmills and Madonnas and cherubs. On the other side of the giant oven with its great black chimney reaching through the roof stood the painted statues ready for packing. A row of brown painted horses, each prancing in perfect frozen unison with its companions, stood forlornly on the floor. Above them dozens of little shepherdesses posed in attitudes of coyness, pink fingers pressed against painted dimples. Eduardo paused here, and carefully picked up one of the shepherdesses.

'Sad, isn't it?' said Serafina, holding the lamp aloft, and gazing with him at the smiling figurine.

'What will happen to the business now?'

Serafina took the shepherdess from him and replaced it on the shelf. 'Nonno left all this to me – the oven, the moulds, his designs. All I have to do is find the money to pay old Albinoni his rent every week.'

Eduardo looked at her, surprised. 'You don't mean you're going to make statues?'

'Why not?' She wandered over to the painting bench, where a small pack of black Scottie dogs waited for someone to apply tartan collars. 'I hate waitressing, and I hate the restaurant. I hate the fact that it was Fortunata who found me a job there. I don't want to be a waitress or a shop girl, like she is. I want to run a business. I'll have to start off by working here at night when I come back from the restaurant, but I'm sure that in a few months I'll be able to stop waitressing and just do this. It's what I want.'

Eduardo looked bewildered. 'But surely—'

'What? What do you want to say? — that everyone knows the business was failing?' She put the lamp down on the table and turned to Eduardo. 'I know that. But I have new ideas. Nonno would never listen to me, but I have plans. I'll make a lot of money, you'll see.'

In the glow of the lamp she looked suddenly passionate, her mouth parted, her eyes dark. Invitingly she smiled at him, tossing her damp hair back over her shoulders.

'Serafina—' Eduardo stepped towards her, inflamed. She pulled him closer and kissed him for a long time on the mouth, expertly. His body, stiffening in surprise at her boldness at first, began to relax. He was sinking, lost. He had dreamed of this moment.

'Eduardo . . .' she murmured. 'Make love to me, Eduardo . . .' She nuzzled his neck, her lips soft and warm on his skin, and then sighed and leaned away from him so that he had to come closer, overcome with a terrible desire for her that he knew would somehow never be assuaged. Her throat looked very white in the lamplight, contrasted against the sombre fabric of her mourning dress. Eduardo lifted his head and looked into Serafina's face. She was staring distractedly at the skylight above their heads, an odd smile flickering across her lips.

The spell was broken. Eduardo pulled away abruptly. 'We mustn't,' he said, in a voice trembling with emotion, 'not here, not now. It wouldn't be right.'

Serafina looked coldly at him. Slowly she began to button

her coat. 'Of course,' she said, in a flat voice, 'it wouldn't be right.'

'We'd better get back.' Eduardo picked up the lamp, avoiding Serafina's eyes. 'It's almost nine.'

Serafina's intention to meet Eduardo after the library meeting caused a ripple of conflict in the Vialli house. Giuseppe declared that it was inappropriate for Bruno's granddaughter to be seen socialising less than a week after the funeral. He was adamant. Serafina would not be permitted to go.

Fortunata was torn: she had arranged to be at the meeting herself, but had not yet told her husband. She could hardly prevent Serafina from going, it would be hypocritical. But she had her own reasons for not wanting her difficult, sulky step-daughter there. Consequently she confused Giuseppe by alternately supporting him and then berating him.

Lucia tearfully announced that poor dear Bruno would have wanted Serafina to enjoy herself, and anyway, she would prefer Serafina to go out, because the alternative was the prospect of her granddaughter slamming round the house in a fury, punishing her innocent sisters. Claudia and Antonia, placid and even-tempered children, simply removed themselves if the argument threatened to explode into a torrent of recriminations, as it frequently did.

On the morning of the Friday in question, the problem was solved by a summons to work for Giuseppe. He had to leave immediately for York, with a tarmac-laying gang. The household breathed a sigh of relief, not only because of the much needed money the work would bring, but also at the prospect of an end to hostilities. As he left, bestowing a warm kiss on Serafina's brow, Giuseppe was philosophical, having been spared the humiliation of defeat or the dubious pleasure of victory.

'I leave it to you to sort out a civilised compromise,' he announced, 'but remember, whatever you decide it must not dishonour the memory of Bruno. Are you listening, Serafina? If you misbehave, someone is bound to tell me when I get back.'

'I won't, Papa.'

Fortunata kissed her husband coldly on the cheek, and then the door closed behind him. There was an expectant hush round the breakfast table. Claudia and Antonia ate their porridge, staring from Fortunata to Serafina and back again, instinctively understanding that it was wise to stay silent. Lucia, exhausted by the conflict, leaned back in her chair and waited for her daughter to speak.

Fortunata carefully buttered some bread. 'I have a proposition, 'Fina.' She reached for the strawberry jam. 'I don't expect you'll like it, but it's the only way I'm going to allow you to go to the meeting.'

Serafina's eyes widened. 'You're going to let me go?'

Fortunata cut the bread into neat slices and handed one each to her two daughters. They ate them silently, watching Serafina.

Fortunata put the knife down on her plate. 'I have promised to be at the meeting myself, as a representative of the Women's Matteotti Committee. I'm reporting on it for their paper. I need you to look after the girls. No, Mamma—' she raised her hand, as Lucia tried to intervene, 'you always have the girls, we make you do too much. This week you need some peace and quiet, some moments alone in the house with your memories. I've decided. Serafina will look after the girls, she will bring them to the library as the meeting ends and the dance begins, and then I will take them home. And you may stay until ten o'clock, Serafina, and no later. Is that clear?'

Serafina realised that this was the closest to victory she would get. Demurely she lowered her eyes. 'Yes, Fortunata. Thank you. I'll behave myself, and Eduardo will walk me home.'

So it was that at eight o'clock that evening, Serafina took her sisters to the Finsbury playground behind the library. They had walked all the way to Upper Street so that Antonia and Claudia could look in the window of the toy shop, and had caught the bus back, alighting in St John Street outside the library. A notice was pinned to the door: ISLINGTON ANGLO-ITALIAN WORKERS' ASSOCIATION MEETING: WHAT PRICE FREEDOM? MAIN SPEAKER: DECIO ANZANI, SECRETARY OF THE LEAGUE OF THE RIGHTS OF MAN, ITALIAN SECTION. QUESTIONS FROM THE FLOOR. LOCAL COUNCILLORS WILL BE PRESENT. MEETING BEGINS AT 7 P.M. REFRESHMENTS AND SOCIAL AT 8.30 P.M. ALL WELCOME.

Serafina sat on a swing, careful not to crease her best dress, a demure pink moss crêpe with a fluted skirt which peeked out from below her coat. Her sisters were spinning round and round on the wooden roundabout, their faces frozen in the rapt, ecstatic expressions that children acquire when they are engaged in something dangerous and pleasurable.

Serafina watched them, dispassionate. They were very pretty girls; it was difficult to dislike these doll-like creatures with their sunny dispositions and their ready smiles. They both adored their older sister, a fact which never ceased to amaze Serafina, who avoided showing them any affection. Sometimes one or the other would climb on to her lap, clasp their chubby arms round her neck and say 'Lovely Serafina! *Bella topolina!*' – a phrase they had learned from Fortunata. Serafina would shrug them off with an uneasy laugh, saying '*Basta, ragazza!* Enough, for pity's sake – you'll choke me!' She could not understand what they saw in her to love, especially when she certainly did not love them. They are either very blind or very stupid, she decided, swinging slowly back and forth, listening to their shouts.

But even she could not deny the fact that they made a charming picture: nine-year-old Claudia with her bright eyes and dimples, and Antonia, a year younger, with those long lashes, perfect skin and a mysterious smile like La Gioconda. They were beautiful like their mother, but they had not inherited her strong, defiant spirit. Like Giuseppe they would retreat into silence if argument loomed, and preferred compromise to confrontation. Consequently they were popular children, loved by everyone, and the pride and joy of their father – something which did not endear them to Serafina.

''Fina!' Claudia was tugging at her skirt. 'The clock just struck – is it time to go and meet Mamma?'

It was. They arrived at the library as the first straggle of people were leaving the meeting. Holding her sisters by the hand, Serafina went into the crowded lobby where people drank tea and argued, milling about in excited confusion, animated by the meeting. Serafina could hear people talking about Fortunata. She had caused some kind of sensation by standing up and speaking from the floor with some vigour about the role of women in 'the struggle'. (Serafina was never quite clear about exactly what the struggle was, only that the mention of it animated her stepmother in a way that nothing else did.)

'A brilliant speaker, that woman!' someone was saying excitedly. 'She completely crushed old Boselli's nonsense!'

'She ought to be in Parliament!' someone else said. 'She ought to represent us!'

The object of this debate was at that moment crushed in the embrace of Joe O'Connell, hidden from view in a tiny cloakroom on the other side of the lobby.

'Joe, Joe!' she gasped, 'You mustn't! We'll be seen!'

'I can't help it!' he laughed, gazing at her for a moment. 'You know I find you irresistible when you're all fired up like that, yelling at some reactionary as if he were a naughty boy caught thieving!'

He kissed her again and she wriggled a little, reluctant to break away but knowing she had to.

'Joe . . .' she whispered, 'my girls will be waiting . . .'

He groaned. 'Of course! *La Famiglia!*'

She touched his cheek, tender. 'There'll be other times . . .' There was a moment between them, desperate, full of love.

'Of course,' he said quietly, and kissed her hand. 'You go first, I'll be right behind . . .'

Antonia pulled at Serafina's hand. 'Look, there's Mamma!' Serafina looked up. There at the top of the steps leading into the main library stood Fortunata, a still slender figure in black, talking intently to a group of men. Slowly, Serafina mounted the stairs. Not until she reached the top step did Fortunata see her, and Serafina registered the shocked expression, the guilt, and then the determination to keep control of the situation.

'There you are,' Fortunata said. 'Good. I would like you gentlemen to meet my daughters. This is Serafina, and this is Antonia and this is Claudia. Girls, please shake hands with my friends. This is Signor Anzani. This is Signor Bellini, who you've already met, Serafina. And this is Councillor O'Connell.'

Serafina placed a cold hand in that large freckled one. She could not bear to look up, but she could feel those bright blue eyes gazing intently at her.

'Have we not met before?' Joe O'Connell asked, his Irish brogue as strong as ever.

Serafina did not – could not – answer. She withdrew her hand and said nothing.

'Serafina is very shy, Councillor,' Fortunata was saying, unable to hide the quaver in her voice. 'You did indeed meet, many years ago, above King Bomba.' The lovers could not resist exchanging a brilliant, panic-stricken glance, loaded with significance, at the memory of that meeting. Serafina looked up and intercepted it, her face expressionless.

'I must be going.' Fortunata pulled Claudia and Antonia to her and began to fuss with their coats, unable to meet anyone's eyes. 'Thank you, Serafina. You may go and look for Eduardo now. He's in there, putting the chairs away.'

'It was nice to meet you,' Serafina said, addressing her own feet. The three men bowed politely, and she walked away. She found Eduardo piling up chairs in the meeting room, where groups of young people were beginning to gather expectantly. His face lit up when he saw her.

'You came!'

'I said I would, didn't I? How was the meeting?' She stood watching him as he worked his way along a row of chairs, folding them shut and piling them in a stack at one end.

'Anzani was brilliant, as usual.' He paused for a moment. 'There was a good row during the questions – someone kept saying that the *ballila* were no different from Baden-Powell's scouts. You can imagine what your mother thought about that!'

'She's not my mother.'

'Serafina!' Eduardo was despairing, 'why must you always be so – so angry with Fortunata? She's an amazing woman, everyone thinks so. They say she may end up on Islington Council.'

'I wouldn't be at all surprised,' Serafina said drily. 'Now, where can I put my coat?'

The room had quickly filled up, and soon the sound of Henry Hall and the BBC Dance Orchestra could be heard – a scratchy rendition of 'The Teddy Bears' Picnic' – and couples began to dance. Several disapproving old Italian faces could be seen glowering through the glass panels of the lobby. The idea of young people dancing together without close observation by a chaperone was still rather shocking to first generation Italians. They were being gradually introduced to this 'modern' British approach by their sons and daughters, but for many the changes were almost impossible to bear. Most of the young people foxtrotting back and forth across the meeting room floor had fought, like Serafina, some kind of a battle just to be permitted an hour's dancing; consequently the air was filled with exultant laughter and an atmosphere of excitement.

Serafina and Eduardo were whirling round to the strains of 'Oh! Mo'nah', when Eduardo looked across the room and panted, 'Someone I want you to meet, 'Fina — come with me!' Still out of breath, Serafina allowed him to lead her by the hand through the throng of dancers to the far corner, where some girls were drinking lemonade and two boys leaned against the wall, deep in earnest conversation.

'*Ciao*, you two! I want you to meet Serafina Vialli — she's Fortunata Vialli's step-daughter.'

Serafina was outraged. 'My name is Florio,' she said stiffly, 'and since Fortunata has married my father, her name is Florio too — unless your politics allows married women to forget that they're married?'

There was a moment's silence. The two young men looked at her with interest. One held out his hand and grinned. 'Hello. My name's Joe Lucente — and this is my younger brother Roberto. We're great admirers of your stepmother.' Serafina acknowledged them both coolly. She was never shy in the presence of boys. She knew that her mature curves guaranteed attention. To her surprise, however, the three friends immediately began a spirited discussion of the meeting, seemingly uninterested in her female charms. She leaned against the wall and listened to their conversation, content for the moment to have a rest from dancing. Eduardo had a tendency to crush her toes.

'At least Anzani recognises the threat coming from the German National Socialists,' Joe Lucente was saying earnestly. 'Half the people at the meeting didn't seem to see the significance.'

His brother shrugged. 'What do you expect? Most of them never even read a newspaper, and they only switch the wireless on when there's a dance band playing!'

Serafina studied them both. Joe was the more thick-set of the two, with broad shoulders and a muscular neck. He was probably about twenty, she decided. Roberto, the younger brother, was almost as tall, but more slender. Serafina found herself staring at him. He was impossibly good looking, with intense deep-set eyes, a soft mouth and a strong chin. His black hair was slightly longer than was usually acceptable. He probably fancies himself as a poet, Serafina thought. She had become mesmerised by his face, by the perfectly straight nose, the line of his cheekbones, the lock of hair which he swept impatiently out of his eyes. He reminded her of some statues she had seen once, in the British Museum. A young Caesar. He would make a handsome statue, she mused. Perhaps that was what she should make first in the studio . . . He had become aware of her gaze and turned towards her, smiling.

'Sorry, Serafina. What do you think?'

'About what?' she asked, feeling foolish. She had not been listening.

Eduardo groaned. 'I wouldn't bother! Serafina's not that keen on politics, are you, 'Fina?'

She tried to look nonchalant. 'It depends. What were you talking about? Sorry, I was watching the dancing.'

Roberto smiled knowingly, and Serafina felt a blush rising to her cheeks.

His eyes met hers. 'We were talking about the NUWM.'

There was a small silence. Finally, Serafina was obliged to ask, 'What is it?'

'See what I mean?' Eduardo laughed affectionately. 'You're hopeless, 'Fina! It's the National Unemployed Workers' Movement – surely you've heard Fortunata talking about them—'

Joe Lucente interrupted, irritated. 'But they're not significant! The Labour Party won't get involved with them, because they're all communists—'

Eduardo pulled Serafina away towards the dancers. 'Let me rescue you from these fanatics, 'Fina. See you later, boys!'

Serafina and Eduardo danced until they were exhausted, enjoying each other's company, comfortable with their friendship, both choosing to forget that their relationship had for a few moments in Bruno's studio become something more. Serafina noticed Roberto and Joe moving amongst the girls, dancing with various partners. She wondered fleetingly why neither of them interrupted Eduardo to request a dance with her. She felt faintly indignant. There was Roberto dancing with that plain little thing from the bakery, laughing at something she said – and he didn't even glance in her direction!

Suddenly there was a commotion at the door. People began shouting above the music, and several boys left their partners and made hurriedly for the exit.

'What is it? What happened?' Serafina asked, fearful.

'*Ballila* outside,' a girl next to her said. 'One of the Boselli boys, and that Paolo Bianchi, and Anna Vittorini's boyfriend – they're fighting!'

Serafina clutched at Eduardo. 'Don't go, Eduardo. I'm afraid!' He looked at her, surprised. Fear was not an emotion he associated with Serafina. He could not know that fighting among men sent a terrible shudder though her soul, transporting her back to that hot, dusty village street, to Papa's humiliation, and to Mamma's sad, surprised, dead face on the cobblestones.

Eduardo put an arm protectively around her shoulders. 'I won't leave you,' he said. 'I promised Fortunata I would see you home, and I will.' He smiled down at her. 'Anyway, I'm a coward. I don't want to fight. It doesn't solve anything.'

The jostling at the door grew more urgent. Several girls were crying. One that Serafina recognised from St Peters was sobbing, '. . . But my brother's in the *ballila*! He might be out there—'

Serafina tutted crossly, recovering her composure. 'How stupid this all is! I wanted to dance!' She saw Roberto and Joe Lucente shouldering their way determinedly through the crowd. They disappeared outside. Soon the room was almost empty. The man playing the records was disconsolately packing up.

'Sorry, folks,' he said. 'It's almost ten o'clock anyway. No point in carrying on now.'

Someone appeared in the doorway, out of breath. 'They've gone!' he announced triumphantly. 'We chased them off!'

Eduardo applauded this news with a sardonic slow handclap. 'Bravo!' he called. The messenger gave him a frosty look and departed.

'Take me home, Eduardo,' Serafina said, suddenly tired. 'Fortunata will be waiting up for us.'

They walked back to Grape Street in silence, lost in their own thoughts, arm-in-arm. When they reached the front gate Eduardo suddenly pulled Serafina towards him. Smiling, she clasped her arms round his neck and looked into his eyes. She felt very safe with Eduardo, even though she knew the effect she could have on him. She enjoyed the feeling of power it gave her. They kissed, gently, lingeringly.

'Thank you for the evening, Eduardo,' she whispered. 'Will you come in for a while? I know Fortunata would like to talk to you about the meeting.' She could feel his heart pounding against her. She knew he was plucking up courage to ask her out again.

His face wore an anxious expression. 'Will you come with me to the Odeon next week?'

Serafina was teasingly regretful. 'Papa might be back. He probably wouldn't allow it.'

'We could go with the Lucente brothers. Your father knows their father. They play snooker together at the Club Co-operativo.'

'What film is it?'

He groaned. 'You're a tease, Serafina! I haven't a clue – I think Douglas Fairbanks is in it.'

She headed towards the front door, grinning at him over her shoulder. 'I'll *definitely* come if it's Douglas Fairbanks!'

To her surprise Lucia appeared in the hallway to greet them. 'Hello, Nonna! Where's Fortunata? Why, what's the matter?'

Her grandmother began to sob loudly, dabbing at her face with a crumpled tea towel. Alarmed, Serafina and Eduardo ushered the old woman into the kitchen and made her sit down.

'I'll put the kettle on,' Eduardo said, taking off his overcoat and discreetly making himself busy at the sink. Lucia's sobs had reached a crescendo. Serafina could not understand the strangled Latin and Italian issuing forth, a mixture of prayers and exhortations. Then she heard the front door slam, and Fortunata appeared in the doorway, taking off the black shawl which had covered her head and shaking out her curls.

'Oh, *basta*, Mamma,' she said crossly, 'he's not worth your tears.'

'Who? What happened?' Serafina asked, one arm still round her grandmother's heaving shoulders.

Fortunata sighed and shrugged off her coat. 'You remember the Viazzani brothers? They live above old Oriani, the clock-mender.'

Serafina remembered them only too well. The memory of that dreadful Procession Day when they had fought her father had never gone away. Papa had had a cut lip and a bruised cheek for weeks afterwards, and although no one had said a word, Serafina had been dreadfully ashamed. She knew that everyone had talked about them; about the fight; about Fortunata; about funny little Serafina running away like that ... She still felt a surge of shame at the thought of that fight between Papa and the Viazzani brothers. They had called Fortunata a whore, publicly. The irony of the situation had not escaped Serafina, young as she had been at the time; and with the years her anger had increased. The Viazzanis had called Fortunata a whore, and while Papa had fought for her she had been with that Irishman ... and was still with that Irishman. Eduardo was pouring tea, remaining quietly in the background. How perfectly he behaves, Serafina thought irrelevantly.

'What about the Viazzanis?' she asked aloud. Nonna's sobs increased.

Fortunata sat down at the kitchen table. 'Antonio Viazzani's dead,' she said wearily '– murdered.'

Good, Serafina thought. There is some justice after all. 'How?'

Fortunata smiled gratefully at Eduardo who was handing her a cup of tea. 'Thanks, Eduardo. You're a saint.' She took a sip, and then closed her eyes as the warmth of the tea seeped through her body. 'He was knifed at Kempton racecourse.'

'The Darby Sabini gang!' Lucia exclaimed, crossing herself and murmuring a prayer.

Fortunata shook her head. 'Don't be silly, Mamma. Sabini died ten years ago.'

'But didn't Papa say his son Harry took over the gang?' Serafina asked, interested. She had always been fascinated by her father's stories of the racecourse gambling rackets, the terrible vendettas, the protection mobs. She had listened with awed fascination to his colourful accounts of the razor gangs who stalked the streets of Soho, fighting for control of the mysterious underworld.

'They meet in the Yorkshire Grey on Theobalds Road,' said Lucia, fearful, twisting the damp tea towel in her hands. 'The Viazzani brothers used to go there all the time.'

'You're getting confused, Mamma,' said Fortunata. 'That was years ago. Harry Boy Sabini is still out and about, but Signora Viazzani says it was nothing to do with gambling. Not that I believe her,' she shrugged, 'but she's in a terrible state – I left her with Father Guido – she needs to imagine that Antonio was a good boy, murdered by accident.'

'How has she taken the news?' Serafina wanted to know. She remembered seeing the old lady in church; she had seemed harmless enough, unlike her sons.

'Badly. What do you expect? And Federico's gone off on the rampage looking for revenge. He'll be in prison by the morning if the neighbours don't get to him first – they're all out looking for him now—'

There was a terrible hammering on the front door. The four of them froze, exchanging frightened glances. Then Eduardo put down his cup.

'I'll go,' he said.

Fortunata put out an anxious hand. 'You don't think – Federico's always hated Giuseppe. You don't think he would come here—'

'Don't answer it, Eduardo!' The banging grew more insistent. Inside Serafina's head it was the pounding of marching feet, on the cobblestones of Nemi. 'It's Federico – he's come to kill us!'

They could hear someone shouting outside. Eduardo made for the hallway. The three women were paralysed, their ears straining to hear what was happening at the front door. They heard Eduardo open it. They heard the low murmur of voices, talking urgently. Still they waited. The voices stopped, and there was a silence. Then they heard Eduardo say, '*Grazie*,' and the front door clicked shut. After a long pause he appeared in the doorway. Serafina was still bending over Lucia, Fortunata still sitting at the kitchen table, exactly as he had left them.

'I'm sorry, Fortunata,' he said gravely. 'It's bad news. That was Rosa Vittorini from next door. Her father has just come back from the Garibaldi-Mazzini Club. Someone telephoned there from York.'

Fortunata stiffened. 'Giuseppe—'

He nodded. 'I'm afraid so. There was an accident on the site, as they were settling in. A truck backed into their hut. Signor Giuliano the foreman was killed and three men were injured.'

'Giuseppe was one of them?'

'Yes. He's been taken to hospital.' Eduardo hesitated.

'You know more,' Fortunata said, slowly standing up. 'Tell me!'

He bit his lip and looked at the floor. 'His back is broken. He may not walk again. Rosa said the doctors are certain he won't work on the roads again—' Before he had finished, Fortunata had crossed the room and knelt at her mother's feet. Lucia leaned forward and held her daughter, rocking her slightly. Shocked and silent, the two women clutched each other, Lucia exhausted by her earlier tears for Antonio, and Fortunata numb with guilt. Serafina gazed down at them, unmoving, from behind her grandmother's chair. Fortunata looked up at her and put out a hand – whether for comfort or to include Serafina in her grief it was not clear. Serafina stared back, blankly.

Papa would not work again. How could they live? Times were impossibly hard already, with Nonno dead, and Fortunata's wages usually having to support them all. Her lips trembled. Papa! What on earth had he done to deserve this terrible blow?

'Good people are always punished,' she said slowly to Fortunata, 'the wicked ones prosper, and the good ones are punished. Surely that isn't right?'

'It's not true, Serafina,' Eduardo said softly. 'Antonio Viazzani wasn't a good man – and he's dead, remember? Your papa has been saved—'

'Saved?' she stormed. 'Saved? What sin did he ever commit? Yet his life has been all suffering.'

Fortunata got clumsily to her feet, her eyes brimming. 'Stop it, 'Fina. It won't do any good. We must think clearly, we must be practical. I must go to York. I'll leave in the morning. You must take care of the girls while I'm gone.'

Serafina shook her head. 'No, I won't.'

'Serafina!' Eduardo was horrified. Lucia simply stared at her, too stunned by the news to absorb her granddaughter's words.

'Don't be difficult, 'Fina,' Fortunata said wearily. 'Not now, of all times.'

'I'm not being difficult!' Serafina's face was transformed. She was still crying, but a new light had appeared in her eyes. 'Nonna will have to have the girls. I'll start tomorrow – I'll not go back to the restaurant.'

'I'll call in and tell them what's happened,' Eduardo said, helpfully. 'I'm sure they won't expect you back for a few days.'

'No, no – you don't understand!' she said, impatient. 'I've told you – I'm going to make statues, like Nonno did. Only mine will be better – *scusi*, Nonna, but Bruno's ideas were too modest – I'll produce them more efficiently. That way, if I can keep the studio going, the business can support us all, instead of Papa.'

'Serafina, don't—'

'No, listen!' She scrubbed a tear from her cheek. 'I'll go round the West End hotels, I'll get orders for bigger statues, Greek gods and Roman emperors and things, and busts of composers for the big houses.'

'Not now, Serafina. This isn't the time . . .'

'Yes, now!' she began to raise her voice. Her face was very white, and she trembled from head to foot. 'Now! And Papa can come and work for me when he's better. When you bring him home he can paint the smaller statuettes. You don't have to be able to walk to paint statues—'

She was unable to continue, choking on her words. Eduardo was there when she crumpled, sobbing, into his arms, still saying to no one in particular, 'I'll go to the studio tomorrow! I'll start tomorrow!'

Fortunata stared at her, any words of comfort frozen on her lips. The girl was mad. Here they were, on the brink of destitution, and Serafina was talking about making statues! Her heart constricted. Life was hard, very hard. Now it would be worse. Giuseppe would need full-time care. Lucia was already too old to cope. The girls were growing up. Serafina obviously had no intention of supporting the family. As usual, Fortunata realised, it was going to be her responsibility to see that the family survived . . . It would mean even less time for the things she loved – the meetings, the campaigning, the late nights drinking wine and planning action with Sylvia

Pankhurst or the tea-filled strategy meetings with Dora Russell. There would be no time for all that now. And worse, there would be no time for the one man who gave her a belief in things, the man who made it possible for her to go on. There would be no more time for Joe O'Connell.

'Fortunata! Please, Fortunata, you mustn't cry so—' At the sound of Eduardo's voice, Fortunata looked up in surprise. Without realising it, she had sunk to the floor in despair, her face wet with tears. Eduardo was helping her to her feet, concerned. Serafina watched, unsmiling, from across the room.

'No, it's all right, I'll be all right.' Fortunata smiled at him with a courage she did not feel. 'It's all right, Eduardo. I know what I must do. And I'll do it.' She looked at Serafina, suddenly fierce, 'I will!'

CHAPTER FIVE

1940

'**B**LOODY EYTIES!'
'Why don't you go back to where you came from?'

Fortunata lowered her head and stifled the desire to say 'But I was born here!' She must not start an argument, today of all days. She imagined for a moment the faces of her daughters being told their mother had been arrested. No. She must remain silent.

The woman in the greengrocer's eyed her, sourly. 'Beats me why some people get given coupons,' one said loudly. 'We should be feeding our own, not a bunch of foreigners.'

Fortunata gave the girl behind the till her coupon book and hurriedly put the swedes in her basket. If only the Italian greengrocer on Saffron Hill had stocked swedes, if only Guido's vegetable stall hadn't closed down because of the shortages. She did not usually stray far from the Hill in these times, and the unfriendly faces around her now were a sharp reminder of why the Italians stayed in their own corner of London as much as possible.

The girl behind the counter handed the coupon book back, and shot Fortunata a sympathetic glance. Best not to say anything though, she decided, they'd start losing customers if people thought the shop was pro-Italian . . .

Fortunata stepped outside into the sunshine, ignoring the glowering faces, and hurried back towards Rosebery Avenue and the safety of her world. Only the *bomboniere* to collect from the shop next to the church, and then she could go home. A small smile of relief appeared, as she rounded a corner and saw before her the welcoming marble columns of the entrance to St Peter's, and the familiar faces of Italians climbing from the pavement up the steep stone steps to confession . . .

'Father forgive me, for I have sinned. It is three weeks since my last confession.'

'Have you been regularly to Mass?'

'Yes, Father.'

'But you have not come to confession? Have you committed any mortal sin?'

'Yes, Father. I have been impure.'

A slight pause. The confession box was almost completely airless. Serafina gripped the rail below the grille dividing her from Father Joseph, and closed her eyes.

'What were the circumstances that led you to commit this sin, my child?'

He had been waiting for her, outside the studio. He must have waited until he saw that everyone else had gone home. How did he know that she always stayed late on Wednesdays, putting the books in order?

He had suddenly appeared in the doorway, and she had started, dropping her pen and making an ink blot in her account book.

'Hello!' she had said, trying to make her voice light. 'What are you doing here?'

He had not even spoken. He had simply walked around the desk, pulled her roughly to her feet, and kissed her.

She had tried to pull away, but he would not let her go. She had tried to struggle, but how could she struggle when her body ached for him, when having him this close was the secret dream she had been harbouring?

'We mustn't do this,' she whispered. 'It's wrong.'

He still had not spoken. He took her by the arm and led her, unprotesting, to the far corner of the studio, by the plaster sacks, where it was dark. He took off his coat and threw it down. For a moment she could see his eyes gleaming, as he looked at her. She felt exultant. The moment had come. She had always somehow known it would.

'Father – I – I don't know what came over me. I knew it was sin. I couldn't stop myself.'

'Was this adultery, my child?'

'No, Father. No. But—' Serafina paused. 'It wasn't adultery, but he is promised to another.'

She heard the priest sigh. 'Then this is a grievous fault.'

There was no need for words. They had both fought a

109

battle within themselves, and they had both lost. This act was a necessity, borne of a mutual obsession – not proper, not right, not wanted or desired, but it had to be.

He had pushed her to the ground, and knelt over her, a shadow between her and the light. He pushed her skirt up, he fumbled at his clothes, and then he was inside her. It was a terrible relief, it made them both cry out, and then he simply rammed himself against her, repeatedly, silently, as if his life depended on it. It was a joyless union, this urgent coupling in the dark corner, like two beasts driven by centuries of innate, inherited lust. She received him with the same sense of urgency, the same release, although he was hurting her. Together they grunted and pushed, until he shuddered and was still. He lay on her, panting, and Serafina smiled to herself in the darkness. He was still inside her, warm and wet, and she wanted him never to move.

'It will not happen again, Father. It was a temporary madness, brought on by the war and all the upset—'

'We should not use the unusual circumstances of the times to excuse our behaviour.'

'No, Father. Of course not.'

'This is a serious business. Have you thought of the repercussions?'

'I have, Father. It will not happen again.'

Slowly, he withdrew from her. Then he sat up. She could hear him adjusting his clothing. She lay there, her skirt still up round her waist, her pants round her ankles, a cold stickiness on her thighs. She liked the feeling, the wicked, wanton feeling of having just performed the unspeakable . . . and in the studio!

'Fortunata would never forgive us,' she whispered.

She heard the rasp of a match, and for a second she saw his face as he lit a cigarette. His hands were trembling.

'Fortunata will never know,' he said. 'No one will ever know. I hate you, Serafina. Why did you do those things to me? Why did you make me want you? Why did you want to make my life ugly?'

'I didn't!' She sat up on her elbows and looked at his profile, just visible in the glow of his cigarette. 'I didn't mean this to happen—'

He had stood up. 'Ask yourself,' he said, pulling his coat

110

from under her, 'ask yourself if that's true.' He stood, unmoving, above her. 'This shouldn't have happened. Forget it did. It won't happen again.' He was gone. Serafina smiled to herself. He would be back.

'Fifteen Mysteries of the Rosary, my child.'

'Thank you, Father.' She could hear him murmuring a prayer. She clasped her hands together and tried to concentrate on penitence, on her own act of contrition. The murmuring stopped.

'Go, and try not to sin again.'

'Thank you, Father.'

'God be with you.'

'God be with you, Father.'

She stepped out into the airless church, and resumed her seat on a pew near the statue of Our Lady of Mount Carmel. The wooden benches were unusually crowded for a Saturday in June. Serafina smiled wryly to herself. Whatever Father Joseph said, the outbreak of war had brought changes, one of which was the number of lapsed Catholics brought back to the fold.

She knelt, holding her rosary, and began to murmur the prayers. 'Hail Mary, full of grace, the Lord is with thee. Blessed art thou among women and blessed is the fruit of thy womb, Jesus . . .'

Ahead of her she could see Signora Viazzani, hunched over in prayer, fanning herself with a copy of the *Daily Express*. Even in this blistering heat she had a black woollen shawl over her head.

'Holy Mary, Mother of God, pray for us sinners now, and at the hour of our death . . .'

Serafina knew that the old woman would be praying for the safe return of Federico from France, on one of the little boats ferrying troops back from Dunkirk. London seemed to be full of people waiting for news.

Serafina tried to concentrate on the rosary. It was pointless reciting the prayers if her mind was somewhere else. She started again, willing herself to think about the Joyful Mysteries, as she fingered the beads. She know almost the whole of the book of Luke by heart . . . 'And the angel came in unto her and said, Hail, thou that art highly favoured, the Lord is with thee: blessed art thou among women . . .' The beads

111

slipped through her fingers, damp with sweat. 'Then Mary said unto the angel, How shall this be, seeing I know not a man? And the angel answered and said unto her, The Holy Ghost shall come upon thee, and the power of the Highest shall overshadow thee . . .' She shuddered. Best not to think of the Annunciation. 'Hail, Mary, full of grace . . .'

Eduardo had still not come home. Was he dead, crumpled in a trench somewhere in Europe? Or was he even now knocking on the door in Grape Street, smart in his army uniform, come back to claim her? He had asked her to marry him, but she had stubbornly refused. She could not understand why he had enlisted, he who had always been a pacifist.

'I can't explain,' he had said quietly, 'it's just something I have to do. I feel so useless here. If we don't put a stop to what's happening—'

'I need you here!' she had stormed. 'I need help in the studio, I can't keep up with the orders now my painter's joined up. He couldn't get a deferment, and now I'm a man short.'

'Which is more use – painting statues or fighting for one's country?'

'It's not our country!' she stormed. 'You forget that.'

'It may not be yours, Serafina, but it is mine. My father was English, remember?' He had grinned at her disarmingly. 'My Italian half would like to stay here with you, but I'm afraid my English half thinks differently.'

Her eyes had filled with tears. 'I certainly won't marry you now. I don't want to be a widow at twenty-six.'

'But you will wait for me?'

She had shrugged. 'I suppose I will. But I'm not promising anything.'

She knew she had been cruel, but she could not understand his desire to be part of the war, to fight for this unfriendly country. The papers were full of stories about the Fifth Column, rumours circulated, and every foreigner in London was now viewed with deep suspicion. Mussolini's talks with Hitler had made life difficult for the Italians on the Hill, whether or not they were fascist sympathisers. Some had been dismissed from their jobs, simply on the grounds of their nationality. Children followed them in the streets singing ugly ditties about wops. English women jostled the Italian housewives in shops, and had taken to boycotting the delicatessens in Soho. Fights broke out in pubs between uniformed soldiers and anyone with a foreign accent. These were difficult times.

Serafina sighed. Why on earth had Eduardo wanted to risk his life, risk everything, to fight for these miserable people, this petty-minded little island?

Signora Viazzani was getting up to leave. Serafina decided that this was not, after all, a good time to do penance in St Peter's. She had come to confess, but she still felt tormented. The world had gone mad on a large scale, but what did that matter, when inside her own head a million unanswered questions were buzzing like fretful bees? She paused in the central aisle and crossed herself before heading towards the doors leading on to Clerkenwell Road.

At the top of the steps she paused in the shade of the entrance. The street below was bathed in dazzling sunlight. Spring had come early this year, and it was very hot, adding yet another unreal, unnatural quality to these strange times.

'Serafina!' Her heart quickened at the sight of Roberto Lucente, waving at her on the pavement. She descended the steps, smiling and composed. 'Hello, Roberto. Shouldn't you be getting ready for this afternoon?'

'Yes, I know – I'm about to go home.' That said, he fell into step beside her, heading in the opposite direction from where he lived, down towards Vine Hill. 'Where's your gas mask?' he asked.

'Oh, I can't be bothered to carry that ugly thing about.'

He smiled his heart-stopping smile at her. 'Bad girl!'

Annunziata Vittorini was calling and waving from the other side of the street, accompanied by her brood of sulky daughters.

'Ready for this afternoon, Roberto?' she called.

Serafina smiled politely and raised a hand in reply. 'Answer her, Roberto!'

But Roberto had walked on, obstinate. 'Why should I? Her husband's a fascist. If we were in Italy he'd shoot me. Come on. I'll walk with you as far as the studio.'

'We might meet Claudia. It's bad luck to see your bride on your wedding day.' She kept her voice light and managed to return his smile, revealing no sign of her inner anger. He was going to marry Claudia. Beautiful, stupid Claudia!

113

'She'll be at home, won't she?' he asked.

'I suppose so. Fortunata is still doing something with the wedding dresses, I think.'

His face softened. 'Fortunata has been wonderful.'

Reluctantly, Serafina had to agree. 'Where on earth she managed to get material for two identical wedding dresses is beyond me. She must have been fiddling the coupons.'

Roberto laughed. 'Your mother is about the only person I know who could cope with a double wedding in wartime!'

'She's not my mother.'

Roberto chose to ignore the coldness in Serafina's tone. 'Oh well, as good as, surely? Anyway, we'd better not talk about the wedding – it's bad luck, isn't it?'

'Probably.' Serafina suppressed the desire to make a dry, cynical remark. Roberto loathed sarcasm, he would not appreciate jokes about his wedding, and Serafina would not upset him for the world, even though his love for her sister disappointed her dreadfully. She had thought Roberto capable of better: a noble, romantic love, or an undying passion – not the dull, steady relationship he had had with Claudia for several years, ever since Serafina had introduced the Lucente brothers into her family home. To make matters worse, Fortunata approved. In fact she had positively basked in the lovers' glow, when their engagement had been announced. Only Serafina had been shocked and silent; it seemed that everyone else had watched Claudia and Roberto fall in love, and only Serafina had not noticed.

'If you spent less time covered in plaster dust making money, you might notice what other human beings get up to,' Fortunata had said, frostily, 'and you might notice a certain young man breaking his heart over you—'

'Eduardo knows how I feel!' Serafina had snapped.

'Yes, but do *you* know how you feel?' Fortunata had gazed at the stubborn, set face of her step-daughter and shaken her head, despairing. 'When will you let go, Serafina, and let someone love you?'

Serafina and Roberto were forced to step into a doorway, out of the sunlight, as a long procession of glum-faced workmen, laden with tools, passed by.

'They're not still digging trenches in the parks, surely?'

He shook his head. 'No. They're building another bomb

114

shelter in Laystall Street. That's where this lot'll be going.' Roberto turned towards her, his face serious. 'Guess where I went this morning.'

She smiled wryly. 'I bet it wasn't to confession!'

'No, you're right. I went to try and sign up with the Local Defence Volunteers.'

'Roberto! On your wedding day!'

They continued their journey. 'It doesn't matter. They wouldn't take me. In fact the man in charge was pretty rude.'

'Because you're Italian?'

He nodded. 'Said they couldn't risk it, not now. You know they've arrested almost anyone with a German accent – well, I think it's our turn next. He wanted to know if I'd registered with the police.'

Serafina was bitter. 'Don't they realise we have no choice?'

'Apparently not. He seemed to think a lot of Italians had refused to register. I explained to him, as politely as possible, that we were obliged to register. Then he said, "if the army won't take you, we certainly don't want your sort in the LDV" – or words to that effect.'

'*Stronzo!*' Serafina swore, emphatically. 'I hate the British! They deserve what they get!'

'Sssh! You'll get us lynched, 'Fina!' They had arrived at the yard. 'I must get back.' Roberto stood uncertainly before her, and then brushed a lock of hair out of his eyes, a gesture which never failed to melt her heart. 'I – I'll see you in church, 'Fina.'

Yes, she thought. But I won't be the one waiting for you at the altar.

Tentatively he reached out and lightly touched her arm. 'I just wanted to make sure – we will be friends still, won't we, 'Fina?'

She wanted to die. She wanted to pull him to her, to hold him and tell him – but what was the use? She fixed her eyes on the cobblestones. 'We'll always be friends, Roberto,' she said, 'whatever happens.'

'Good – I just thought – I probably won't get a chance to be alone with you again—'

'You'd better go!' And he was gone, and she stood there alone, the colour drained from her cheeks.

Damn him! Why did he have to appear outside the church

115

this morning, of all mornings, looking like an angel and increasing her guilt and sense of sin, with his innocent smile and his desire for friendship? She stepped into the studio, angry with herself for being so affected by Roberto's presence, as usual.

'*Buon giorno*, Signorina Florio – *va bene?*'

It was Pino, the foreman, who had emerged from the tiny office where Serafina ruled her little statue kingdom every day. She murmured a greeting, went inside, shutting the door firmly and sat at her desk. Pino, accustomed to the moods of his employer, disappeared discreetly. Serafina leafed through a pile of letters in front of her. Pino had obviously been reading through them. She would have to tell him off about snooping through paperwork again. Sighing, she began to read. An order for a bust of Shakespeare from a private customer. Two of the laughing cherubs for a department store. A complaint about a consignment for the 'Farewell' statues, chipped on delivery. There was a problem there. The 'Farewell' depicted a young mother and her two children waving goodbye, presumably to a departing husband and father going away to fight. It was selling very well, but the mother's right hand, frozen above her head and holding a handkerchief, often broke off in transit. They would have to insert wire into the offending arm before the plaster set, to strengthen it. She frowned. More time wasted in production, when she should be finding ways to cut corners, particularly as she was losing staff . . .

She ran a hand through her hair, now fashionably permed into the curls she had always envied in Fortunata. The office was unbearably hot. Outside she could hear the men shouting at each other as they worked. She knew what they would be thinking. It was her sisters' wedding day – both sisters! – and yet here she was, in her studio, as if it were an ordinary day. She leafed through the remainder of the letters, hardly absorbing their contents. They were right, of course. She should not be here. It would appear as if she were sulking – or hiding. After all, she was the oldest in the family, and still not married. And Antonia was only seventeen, yet today she would be married and in Italian eyes would rise in status above Serafina. She and Claudia would join that exclusive coterie of young married women who had babies, cooked, sewed, and talked endlessly about their husbands. Serafina knew that this was not what the future held for her. She remembered her grandmother in Nemi. Nonna had known that Serafina was not destined for a life of traditional domesticity. She had often said that Serafina would become a nun. Tears stung her eyes. She would never enter Holy Orders. She would never get closer to God. She had sinned, she had sinned in the most wicked way. Why on earth had she done it?

'Tears, Serafina? This isn't like you.' It was Papa, leaning in the doorway, holding his two walking sticks, his face grey with fatigue.

'Papa! What are you doing here? I said not to work today—'

'I know. I'm not here to work. I've come from the house to fetch you. Fortunata said you would come here after confession. She knows you better than you know yourself. Come on, we must get back.'

Serafina stood up, full of concern. 'I'm so sorry, Papa. How thoughtless of me. You shouldn't have come all the way to the studio to fetch me.'

He leaned heavily on his sticks as he made the painful manoeuvre towards the studio door. Serafina rushed to help him, but as usual he shook her off. 'I don't mind. It was good to get out of the house. It's full of women running about in their petticoats, crying.' He looked rueful. 'It's hard to believe there's a war on.'

They stepped out into the sunlit street, and Giuseppe, resting on his sticks, gazed up at the sun for a moment. 'It's hard to believe . . .' he sighed. Serafina knew that he, too, was thinking of Nemi, of Maria, of that sun-baked place they had left behind. Now, after the wedding of Claudia and Antonia, there would only be the two of them again. Fortunata, after all, had long been lost to both of them.

'Come on, Papa,' Serafina took his elbow, 'let's go and get this over with!'

Antonia was shouting up the stairs. 'Mamma, I can't find my face powder! Did you take it?'

Fortunata looked over the banister and smiled at her daughter, pink-faced in her silk petticoat at the foot of the stairs. 'No, *cara*, of course not. Try Claudia.'

Antonia, about to turn away, hesitated at the sight of her mother. 'Mamma? Are you all right?'

Fortunata was still smiling, although Antonia could see a tremor around her mouth. 'Of course I am.'

'You've been crying.'

Claudia emerged from the tiny bedroom she shared with her sister. 'Powder's up here,' she said. She examined her mother's face. 'You're right,' she told Antonia, 'she has been crying . . .' She moved to put an arm around Fortunata's shoulders, but she was shrugged off briskly.

'Don't be silly, I'm fine,' Fortunata was already heading back to her bedroom. 'It was just a moment – the wedding – you know. A mother's allowed to cry a little, isn't she?' . . . and she was gone, firmly closing the door behind her. The two brides-to-be exchanged an understanding look before returning to their pre-nuptial preparations.

Behind the closed door, in the safe and private haven of her room, Fortunata walked slowly over to the dressing-table and sat down again. She picked up the newspaper she had been studying so avidly before Antonia had called to her. There, on page four, was the picture.

A tear trickled down her cheek and she dashed it away angrily, staring at the headline: COUNCILLOR JOINS LABOUR PROTEST OVER NEW PURCHASE TAX. It was Joe, of course, dear Joe, militant as ever, making statements about last month's budget being 'a slap in the face for the working classes'. He never gave up. She gazed at the picture with an intensity her family never saw, her finger sadly tracing the contours of his face, as it gazed out from the page. He looked proud, a little grim, his eyes not showing the sparkle she remembered so well. No black and white portrait could capture his vitality, she decided. She wondered when the photograph had been taken. Had it been since they had parted? And then she wondered, half hopefully, if perhaps, like her, Joe had lost that spark, that energy for living because, like her, he could not face life alone . . .

It had been eight years since that night when she had told Joe O'Connell that their affair was over. After that fateful night when Giuseppe had been injured, the night when she and her love had stolen a kiss at the library, Joe had been called away, to the Irish Free State, speaking at rallies for

Eamon de Valera, returning triumphant and excited after the success of the Fianna Fail in the elections. She had been waiting for him in his rooms in Holborn and had stood, frozen, while he hugged her excitedly and talked about the freeing of IRA prisoners.

'It's started a real red scare over there, darlin', I can tell you.' He paced the room, as always too big for it, his eyes shining. 'All the reactionaries are showing their true colours now, they're in a blue funk because de Valera's going to let republicanism have a voice at last!' He hugged Fortunata again, almost ferocious with delight. 'A proper voice! Do you hear me?'

Finally her silence had penetrated his buoyancy. He pulled back and looked at her. Her eyes were full of pain. He pushed a stray curl from her cheek, tender.

'What is it, Fortunata?'

She loved the way he said her name. He made it sound like poetry. She had lowered her eyes, afraid that if she did not she would be weak, she would remain silent, she would stay here with him.

'I can't see you again, Joe,' she said, her voice dull. 'It's over between us.'

Then had come the questions, the disbelief, the anger, the hurt – everything she had feared and expected. She had known it would be hard, but dear God, not this hard . . . And when Joe had finally stopped arguing and had sat, head bowed in defeat, she had almost capitulated. Then, when he had pulled her into his arms and kissed her roughly, angrily, she had almost wept with him, so great was the temptation to simply fall back on the bed and give in again . . .

'No,' she had murmured, pulling away from his kiss, 'no . . .'

They had parted in anger, both too wounded to make their farewell an easy, tender thing.

'I'll never understand,' Joe had said finally, his voice hard. 'I could help you! I could give you money—'

'I don't want your money, Joe. How could I explain it to Giuseppe? No. The family must find a way to take care of itself.'

'The family!' he spat the word. 'That cursed Italian straitjacket!'

She had stood at the door, numb. 'I can't help who I am, Joe,' she had said, her voice barely a whisper. 'Fortunata Florio – that's who I am ...' and she had gone, running down the narrow stairs, half-hoping Joe would follow her but knowing he would not. And so, in that banal little bed-sitting room above the tobacconist's, it had ended.

She realised, to her surprise, that her heart was pounding, and in the pit of her stomach was that same fluttering she had experienced whenever she had been heading off to see Joe. It was the anticipation of their love being consummated, how-ever furtively, in Joe's scruffy little flat in Holborn ... She flung the newspaper across the room. It was no use. She might well feel weak-kneed still at the thought of her old lover, but it was a crazy, pointless obsession she carried with her. For she would never again be held in that strong grip, never again lie in that old iron bed in the light of the gas fire and secretly worship that strong Irish body ... That was all in the past. All she had to look forward to now was a lifetime of penitence with a man she did not love, and the guilt of having committed a mortal sin. But worse was the guilt of knowing that all she longed for, in spite of her soul, was to commit that sin again ...

The reception was being held in the Italian School's assembly hall, festooned for the occasion with bright paper streamers. All the chairs had been pushed back to create a space for dancing, and in one corner Romano's quartet were tuning up in readiness. In spite of rationing and ever-increasing short-ages, the Italian women of the Hill had shown their usual ingenuity in producing a wedding feast, which awaited con-sumption on three enormous trestle tables erected under the windows looking over Clerkenwell Road. Serafina had slipped down the street to the school to ensure that everything was in order while the wedding party posed for photographs on the steps of the church; and now, suitably composed, and with a fresh layer of lipstick applied, Serafina was ready to greet the Italian community. The doors were suddenly flung open and into the room they came, all talking at once in a noisy mixture of Italian and English, all dressed up in their best clothes, excited to be part of Little Italy's wedding of the year. Serafina felt a strange rush of emotion as she smiled and nodded, directing them to the food, finding chairs for Nonna Lucia and the other old ladies, directing the men to organise the drinks. These were her people, these Cockney Italians. These were the people that mattered, never mind the stupid war. Here in Clerkenwell they would maintain their corner of Italy, whatever happened 'out there'.

Romano had struck up the Wedding March on his accordion, and a murmur went through the crowd, then a shout and a ripple of applause, as the two bridal couples arrived, the four of them linking arms, smiling and self-conscious.

Serafina watched the couples as they circled the room in a waltz, cheered on by the guests. Antonia and Paolo Bianchi were whirling round in a flurry of white tulle, Antonia's veil floating in a glorious pale cloud around them. The wedding dress, demure and simple, had been cunningly styled by Fortunata to disguise her youngest daughter's misdemeanour. No one would be able to tell that Antonia was almost five months pregnant, Serafina thought. She and Paolo were gazing into each other's eyes. They looked very much in love. Serafina tried not to think sourly of the hours of argument in the Grape Street front room, when Antonia had confessed her sin. Fortunata had been angrier than Serafina could ever remember, and it had been Serafina who had leapt to intervene when Fortunata had raised her hand to strike her youngest daughter, shouting, '*Stronza!* Whore! Couldn't you wait?' Fortunata did not like Paolo. She had never liked him. When he called at the house for Antonia, Fortunata would shrug and say to Serafina, 'It's only a phase she's going through. It won't last. She'll find someone better.' For Paolo was a supporter of Mussolini.

He was not an active fascist – he was too lazy for that – but he genuinely could not understand Fortunata's hatred of Italy's leader, nor would he listen to Giuseppe's horror stories of the *squadristi* who had terrorised the villagers in Italy.

'It's not the same,' Paolo would argue, 'you can't hold *Il Duce* responsible for something that happened in your village twenty years ago. His supporters got out of hand sometimes in the past, I grant you, but not any more. And his policies work. Think what the *fascio* in London have done! My family would never have had holidays if it hadn't been for the Casa del Littorio ... Mussolini – well, he's put Italy back on her feet again, he's made her a power that the world has to take seriously, can't you see that?' They could not. After the initial arguments, Fortunata and Giuseppe simply steered the conversation away from current affairs, hoping that Antonia would tire of this arrogant young Italian whose ill-informed politics made them shudder.

Fortunata studied him as he danced, his head bent towards his new bride, a smile on his lips. Those cruel lips. Paolo was tall and well built, with an odd charisma that derived from his air of supreme confidence rather than from good looks. For he was not heart-stoppingly handsome as Roberto was (she was able to compare these two bridegrooms circling the floor closely now). Paolo's brow was broad, his hair thick and black. His rather close-set brown eyes seemed to have a bright intensity, at odds with his cynical view of the world, which had left one eyebrow constantly raised in a quizzical manner; but it was his mouth that had always fascinated Fortunata. The upper lip was thin, with a touch of cruelty, while the lower lip was full and fleshy, hinting at a powerful sensuality. The mouth was usually curved into a sardonic smile, revealing nothing of its owner's thoughts. When he caught her staring at him, transfixed by his hypnotic mouth, he would draw those lips back in a cruel and knowing smile and say nothing.

Serafina, too, did not like him, but she took a sadistic pleasure in watching him insinuate himself into the house and into the Florio family. Seducing silly, pretty little Antonia was exactly the kind of thing one could expect from someone like Paolo. In English circles, Serafina mused, he would have been called a cad. Fortunata had some even more expressive Italian words for her daughter's seducer, but today she seemed benign, standing next to Giuseppe (for whom a chair had been found on the edge of the dance floor) and smiling beatifically at the sight of her two daughters in their matching wedding gowns.

Serafina's gaze followed Fortunata's, to where Roberto whirled his new bride around the floor, both of them laughing, heads thrown back. Claudia blew a kiss at her younger sister, dancing past, and it was returned, laughingly. Serafina watched the two men. Roberto had averted his head, so that he did not have to acknowledge his new brother-in-law, as

122

the two swept their wives round in a polka. Only Serafina noticed how Paolo's eyes narrowed, how Roberto's back stiffened, how much the men hated each other. Roberto had given Paolo a black eye during that fight outside the library eight years ago, when the young communist had gone to fight the boys who had joined the *ballila*, of whom Paolo was one. They were poles apart, neither understanding the other, although to their credit both had made a half-hearted attempt at friendship because of their mutual link to the Florio family; but both had failed. Each despised the other. Serafina stared at them thoughtfully, a mechanical smile on her face, befitting the devoted sister of the brides, and knew that the future for the Florio family would be made or broken by these two men who disliked each other so much. They would continue the family, after all. She would not. And now that Antonia and Claudia were married, they had lost the name of Florio. The Florios were finished. Their name would be lost for ever when Serafina died.

The music changed, there was a burst of applause, and then other guests began to join in the dancing. People turned away and headed for the buffet. Serafina sighed. Now she would have to play the dutiful older daughter and go and look after the old women, fetching them plates of food and glasses of wine, listening to their complaints about the war, their memories of Italy in happier times, the tales of their many ailments, and agreeing to dance with their sons. How long the day seemed!

Romano's quartet were playing 'South of the Border' and Serafina was clasped in a bear hug by a large, sweating workmate of Roberto's, when someone tapped her on the shoulder and a familiar voice said, 'Is this an Excuse Me? Can I have this dance?'

'Eduardo!' A great rush of pleasure brought a pink glow to her cheeks. Her dance partner stepped back politely, and she rushed into Eduardo's embrace, never so pleased to see someone in her life. He hugged her very tight, almost crushing the breath out of her.

'Serafina . . .' there was a catch in his voice, 'you don't know how good it is to see you . . .'

She pulled back and held him at arm's length, 'Why, you look just the same! I was expecting – I don't know what I was expecting—' Eduardo had come back! Serafina wanted to cry and laugh all at once. He had survived!

'I came back this afternoon. I've been travelling for three days non-stop. When Mamma told me about the wedding, I thought I'd sleep for a few hours and then come to the reception.'

She hugged him again, transformed with happiness. 'You've been home for hours, and I didn't know.'

He took her hand and walked with her through the crowd of wedding guests. People smiled at them knowingly, slapping Eduardo on the back, and calling 'Benvenuto, Eduardo!' He led her into the corridor outside, where the blackout curtains were already drawn, and the light was fading fast. He drew her into his arms and studied her face. The noise of music and laughter filtered through the door.

'I've missed you so much,' he said, and then with a sound strangely like a sob, his lips descended on hers. It was a kiss unlike any they had ever shared, full of pent-up passion and anger, exploding inside Serafina like a starburst. His grip tightened on her shoulders, and she felt her body go weak, unresisting. Somewhere in the pit of her stomach everything stirred and fluttered. Her body was responding to Eduardo as never before; she was overcome with a powerful sexual desire – for Eduardo, who had been her friend, her confidant, her swain, but until now not her lover. Something had happened to Eduardo, something had changed within him. It was as if a soft boy had gone to France and a brutalised man had returned. The kiss became unbearable in its urgency. Eduardo's hand pressed against her stockinged thigh, under her dress. She was drowning, lost, her face wet from his frantic kiss, her heart pounding. Then she pulled away, suddenly back in control.

She laughed softly. 'Eduardo!' She could hear his breathing in the dark, see the outline of his face. 'Not here! We mustn't – not now. We'll be missed. Fortunata watched us leave. We must go back in.'

He reached out a hand and touched her gently, on her breast. She shuddered, still weakened by the power of his embrace.

'I'm sorry,' he said. Then, 'No, I'm not. I'm not sorry at all.' He lifted her hand and held it to his lips for a moment.

Then he looked at her. 'We'll go back to the reception. You're right, of course. I'm on leave – we have ten days.'

'Ten days.'

'All the time in the world . . . come on!' Together, hand-in-hand and smiling, they went back to the wedding party, Serafina slightly giddy from the intensity of the encounter, remembering another day, another embrace . . .

They had been in the house alone together, she in the kitchen, he upstairs, repairing a window frame in Lucia's bedroom. The air was heavy with their awareness of each other. She had been standing at the sink, trance-like, slowly washing some stockings, stirring them around in the soapy water, thinking about him. She could hear the sound of his hammer, firm and regular, thudding upstairs. The noise resonated within her like a heartbeat. She lifted the stockings out of the water and noticed her hands were trembling . . .

As the evening drew on, the wedding party seemed to become bathed in a warm pink glow, aided, perhaps, by the alcohol, the heat, and the suffocating airless atmosphere. The blackouts were in place, and round the walls the little lights shone under their pink shades, casting a soft rose light on the faces of those who sat beneath them. A group of men, some, like Eduardo, in uniform, were arguing affably in a crowd by the bar, their faces red and sweating, the sound of laughter rising from their corner every now and then. Young couples danced together, their faces solemn, intent on intricate foot-work learned at the local dance halls. Father Joseph danced stiffly with daughters, while old women fanned themselves and asked each other when it would rain and bring them some relief. One of the priests was crouched down next to Giuseppe's chair, talking quietly, one hand playing idly with his crucifix. Fortunata, glorious in the palest of pink chiffon frocks, was hugging Claudia and then Roberto, and then Claudia again, perhaps overcome by too much wine, or just overwhelmed with joy at the sight of her daughter married to the beautiful Roberto Lucente. Serafina, standing by the buffet with Eduardo's arm around her shoulders, felt the pink glow pervade her, too. Everyone was happy. It was a wonderful day . . . So why was the guilt still there, like a goblin on her back, whispering in her ear that she was a sinner . . .?

She had climbed the stairs, pretending to herself that she

was merely going to see whether he had finished the job, whether he would like some coffee. He looked up, unsmiling. Of course it was useless to pretend. There were no games to play, no games, at least, that he need know about. Only her own torment, to be expiated before the Blessed Virgin, who sees all and knows. She thrust the thought aside. Mary, Mother of God . . . Later, later . . .

Paolo and Antonia were whispering to each other, heads close, standing next to the wedding cake. (How on earth had Fortunata managed to make a cake?) He lifted his hand and placed it on her stomach, proprietorial. Antonia placed her own hand over his, the wedding band gleaming on her finger, and they smiled a secret smile together, through the gauze of her wedding veil.

They had been naked together on the bed. He was stretched out next to her, and his eyes ran the length of Serafina's body, appraising, unfathomable.

'Don't!' he said, as she made to cover herself with a sheet. 'I want to look at you.'

She reached out and touched his face, gently.

'You never speak,' he said, 'why is that?'

She shook her head and smiled. Overhead, a bee buzzed around the ceiling, the only sound in the otherwise empty house. She just wanted the moment to last forever.

'Aren't you afraid?' he persisted. 'Afraid we'll get caught?' He kissed her shoulder. 'Someone could come home – at any minute.'

'I don't care,' she whispered, 'I don't want to think about it.'

His lips moved up her neck and she shuddered with pleasure. As they moved together on the narrow bed, the bee banged against the window pane, made its way blindly upwards, and was suddenly free . . .

Lucia Vialli made her way slowly through the throng to a quiet chair in the corner. It was getting late, and soon the wedding guests would disperse. A week previously the Home Office had announced a curfew for all foreigners: the Italians had to be home by midnight, or they would be arrested.

Lucia settled herself down to watch the festivities, saddened by the absence of children in the room. Never a particularly sentimental woman as far as children were concerned (and

126

Fortunata had not been the kind of daughter to be sentimental about), she found herself missing the sound of children. Perhaps it was because today her granddaughters were finally growing up, were finally leaving. No more children.

Mrs Viazzani was drawing up a nearby chair and settling herself into it, resplendent in a hat with peacock feathers.

'Why so sad, Lucia? This is a wonderful day!' The two old women sat gazing across the floor, taking in the laughter, the music.

'I was thinking about the children,' Lucia said. 'What's an Italian wedding without children?'

Children in London had been sent to the country, evacuated for the duration of the war. Mrs Viazzani sighed, flapping a small lace handkerchief, thinking for a moment of her missing son. 'I know, I know . . .' She shook the thought away, afraid she might cry. 'But the Valori boys and little Rosa Santini have come back, you know.'

'Have they?' Lucia looked at her friend, interested. Mrs Viazzani nodded, mopping her brow a little with the scrap of lace. 'Signora Santini said to me, "If we're going to be gassed by the Nazis then we'll all go together!"'

The two women smiled, pleased at this very Italian show of family solidarity. Perhaps, Lucia thought, the return of the three children would be the beginning of a steady trickle of returning offspring. Italians adored their children, and these separations were proving hard to endure.

'What's the point of it all?' she asked, throwing her hands out in a very Italian gesture. 'The children are so unhappy! Stuck away in the middle of nowhere – have you heard the names of some of these places where they're staying? Melchett! Islip! Woodham Ferrers!' She spat them out, as if they were corners of hell itself. 'What do people there know about us, about how we live?'

Mrs Viazzani nodded agreement. 'Mrs Santini told me that little Rosa was told she mustn't speak Italian in the village where she was staying, for fear of being stoned by other children.' Lucia listened, round-eyed, as Mrs Viazzani continued, warming to her story. '—Well, apparently the same thing had happened to a little boy with a German surname a few months before!'

'Yes, but – German!' Lucia spluttered. 'That's different! We're not German!'

So what was the point of it? A few bombs had fallen on the outskirts of London, but people here seemed in no more danger than anywhere else in the country. Sending the children away to cope with the additional miseries of homesickness and mistrust seemed only to have made matters worse . . .

Lucia's thoughts were interrupted by the arrival of two newcomers, men in dark suits, neither of whom she recognised. She beckoned Giuseppe to her side, and he hobbled over obediently.

'You want a drink, Mamma? Signora Vittorini?'

'Who are those men?' she asked. Giuseppe peered shortsightedly across the room. 'Those two, by the door, talking to Father Joseph!'

Before Giuseppe could reply, the two men suddenly strode purposefully through the dancers towards them. Fortunata, who had been dancing with Joe Lucente, saw them and followed, frowning, to where Lucia sat.

'What do you want?' Fortunata demanded. 'Who are you? This is a private party.'

The two men ignored her. One of them addressed Giuseppe, consulting a notebook he had pulled from his inside pocket. 'Giuseppe Florio?'

'Yes, I am Giuseppe Florio. Who wishes to know?'

The man waved a card at him. 'Police, sir. Do you reside at Seven, Grape Street, EC1?'

'Well, yes, I—'

Fortunata stepped forward. 'Can I help you? My husband's English isn't that good—'

The man consulted his notebook, and then studied her, his face expressionless. 'Mrs Florio, residing at the same address – am I right?' Fortunata's jaw dropped.

People were beginning to notice that something unusual was occurring. Serafina and Eduardo joined the group, their faces anxious.

'What's this all about?' Eduardo wanted to know.

The second man eyed Eduardo's uniform thoughtfully. 'May I ask your name, sir?'

'Williams.'

'Ah. English.'

'Eduardo Williams. My father was English. My mother's Italian.'

The policeman stared at the notebook, and then looked up at Eduardo again.

'If I could have a word in private, sir,' he said, 'we'll do this as painlessly as possible.'

'Do what?' Serafina could feel the terror return, the fear that had stalked her all the way from Nemi. 'What do you want?'

The policeman looked appealingly at Eduardo, but before he could speak, Giuseppe cut in. 'Gentlemen,' he said politely, in his quiet, calm voice, 'if a crime has been committed you must tell us. We are a close community, we will all know eventually. We have no secrets. What do you want?'

The man shifted uncomfortably, his eyes avoiding the anxious faces surrounding him. Incongruously in the background Romano's quartet struck up 'Honeysuckle Rose' and a cheer went up from the dance floor.

'The fact is,' the man said, 'there's rather a long list.' He flicked the page of his notepad and began to read. 'Giuseppe Florio, Roberto Lucente, Joseph Lucente, Piero Fiorini, William Zavattoni, Anthony Salerni, Paolo Bianchi—'

Antonia, who had been listening, standing on the edge of the group, gave a little scream and turned to her new husband.

'Paolo! *Que ha fatto?*' she asked.

'*Niente!*' Paolo's face was frozen with shock. 'I've done nothing! I've committed no crime!'

The two policemen were beginning to shoot nervous sidelong glances in the direction of the exit. More people were beginning to wander towards the small commotion in the corner, their curiosity roused.

'I should say to you all that we have uniformed officers outside, ready to escort you to the police station,' one of them said, as if to reassure himself that help was at hand.

'What are these men supposed to have done?' Fortunata was clutching Giuseppe's arm, as if the act of holding on to him would prevent his removal.

The man she had addressed looked at her. 'Fortunata Florio, isn't it?'

Her face again expressed her amazement at this stranger who knew her name. 'How did you know?'

He eyed her thoughtfully. 'It's our job to keep an eye on known subversives.'

'Subversives!' Fortunata exploded. 'Since when has social-ism been a crime?'

The man ignored her and turned back to Giuseppe. 'Haven't you listened to the wireless today, any of you?' he asked. 'Surely you know what's happened?'

They looked at him blankly.

'The wedding . . .' Giuseppe waved an expressive hand, '. . . we have been busy with the wedding.'

'Why?' Fortunata asked, remembering the newspaper she had been disloyally engrossed in earlier. She had no mem-ory of anything in it, other than Joe's picture. 'What has happened?'

Romano finished the chorus of 'Honeysuckle Rose' and embarked on the next verse. Roberto and Claudia still encir-cled the floor, engrossed in each other, oblivious to the world.

'Don't you know?' The man seemed genuinely taken aback. 'You must know! Mussolini has entered the war – we're at war with Italy!'

There was a stunned silence. 'We have our instructions,' the policeman continued, ruefully, 'I'm afraid the wedding party's over, ladies and gentlemen. All those on my list are under arrest. You will be escorted home to collect some clothes, and you must be ready to travel.' Romano had stopped playing. Fortunata stared across at Roberto and Clau-dia, so young, so vulnerable, still panting slightly from the exertion of dancing. Roberto's eyes met hers, full of concern. She had a special affinity with this gentle, romantic boy who shared so many of her views, who seemed to understand her. Surely she was not going to lose him, her one ally, as she had lost Joe?

Everyone seemed frozen, shocked into immobility. 'Say goodbye to your families, and we'll get started,' the man said, referring once again to his notebook. He cleared his throat and began to read again. 'Giuseppe Florio, Roberto Lucente, Joseph Lucente, Piero Fiorini . . .'

His voice was drowned in a babble of voices, some hysteri-cal, some shouting, a mixture of Italian and English.

'I don't believe it! *Ma come . . .?*'

'I knew this would happen! *Sai cosa ti dico?*'

'But surely, Churchill can't put us all away!'

'*Madonna!* We'll all be deported!'

'They'll send us back to Italy!'

'All I can say is, it's about bloody time!'

Fortunata heard this last remark and turned, angry. It was Paolo. He grinned at his new mother-in-law. 'Only a joke,' he said, 'only a joke . . .'

Still the man was reading the list. Gradually as the names registered and the first shock wave dissipated, the wedding guests began to leave, some with voices raised, angry, others sobbing, fearfully.

Eduardo was arguing with the policeman, Serafina pulling at him. 'It's no use,' she was saying. 'What's the point?'

Roberto hugged Claudia. Paolo whispered something to Antonia. Giuseppe's hand was clamped on Fortunata's wrist, tightening, panic-stricken. The wedding was over.

CHAPTER SIX

1940

THE SUN SHONE relentlessly as June turned to July. A terrible quiet had descended on the streets of Little Italy, a dumb despair. People seemed paralysed by the shock of events. Many men had been taken away during those terrible first few days after the announcement that Mussolini had joined the war. There was no news, only eternal rumour, washing over the community in enormous waves, only to be quashed by a further, more outlandish set of suppositions.

'They've all been shipped out to sea,' Mrs Vittorini wailed to Lucia in the kitchen, bereft without her husband of forty-five years. 'Shipped out and dumped in the Channel!'

Lucia clutched at the crucifix on her breast, horrified. 'They'll be bombed by the Nazis!'

Serafina, perched on the table darning some stockings, said as she threaded her needle, 'Mrs Ruffoni said she'd heard someone down the Red Lion saying they've all been shipped to South Africa.'

'What nonsense!' said Fortunata, casting an anxious eye in the direction of Antonia and Claudia. 'How do they know?'

'The man said his brother was a policeman. He saw some document down at Vine Street Police Station. Something about Category "B" aliens. It mentioned deportation. Africa. Or it might have been Australia.'

Claudia, huddled by the stove with her sister, burst into tears. 'They're all dead,' she sobbed, 'I bet you they're all dead! They'll be in a mass grave somewhere, in the country, a long way out of sight . . .'

Mrs Vittorini's lips trembled in sympathy. 'They came and took old Boselli last night. Imagine! He's eighty-two!'

Claudia was inconsolable. 'They're all dead! I'm sure they're dead!'

Fortunata, with her customary disdain for the general opinion of the common herd, refused to entertain these stories. 'It's all rubbish!' she told her daughters brightly, a week after the arrests and with no news at all. 'They'll be in prison somewhere while their papers are checked. They'll be released soon, when it's realised they're not in the *fascio*.'

'But – Paolo is in the *fascio*!' Antonia sobbed. 'He wanted to join their club on the Charing Cross Road, because they had coffee machines and dancing.' Fortunata looked at her, aghast, as Antonia continued, between outbursts of crying, to explain how Paolo had paid his subscription fee of one guinea, had made 'a kind of oath of allegiance' and had sometimes gone there to meet friends when his shift ended at the Soho restaurant where he worked.

'You mean he was actually a *member*?' Fortunata could not believe it. 'He really belonged to the *fascio*?' She had known where Paolo's allegiances lay, vague and ill-informed as they were. But this!

Antonia raised a blotched, tear-stained face, made ugly by days of uncontrollable weeping. 'I promised not to tell you, Mamma. He said you would not have permitted the wedding. Now they'll shoot him!'

Fortunata sighed, and put a comforting arm around the heaving shoulders of her youngest daughter. 'I don't expect they will,' she said soothingly. 'They'll probably send him back to Italy until the war's over – exchange him for a British prisoner, or something.' Her voice did not reflect her deep anxiety. The men had disappeared. After energetic research, endless secret telephone calls from the back room of the gown shop, repeated visits to the police, Fortunata had found out almost nothing. A kindly Sergeant at the local police station had told her that the men had been taken to a school 'for processing'. Frantic pleas for more details, and her continued noisy pestering of the station's front desk eventually won her a brief meeting with the station superintendent. He told her wearily that most of the men in his custody had been taken to the Oratory School at Brompton. 'After that,' he shrugged, 'I'm sorry, Mrs Florio, I can't tell you. To be honest, I don't know. My job's finished once I've got them to Brompton Oratory. Anyway, I wouldn't tell you even if I *did* know. You must realise that. There's a war on.' Fortunata

133

had swept out regally. She thought that if one more person told her there was a war on, she would scream.

Serafina had been reluctant to take over the running of the house while Fortunata went on wild goose chases in search of information about the missing men. Someone had to bring in an income, she argued: it was more important to keep the factory going, somehow. So it was Fortunata who organised the ration books, queued for scarce provisions, produced edible meals out of the odd combinations of foodstuffs now on offer. She organised the temporary removal of both daughters from the flats they had rented in anticipation of a life with their future husbands, back to the familiar haven of Grape Street. She made them cups of tea, talked briskly to them when they cried, distracted them with knitting patterns for Antonia's forthcoming baby, and made them listen to ITMA on the wireless, giggling with them over the antics of Tommy Handley. Fortunata became suddenly a gracious hostess, obliged to entertain half the neighbourhood as people began to hear of her strenuous search for news. They would appear at the back door, hovering uncertainly, under some pretext, eventually asking Fortunata (of whom many were frightened), 'Is there any news?'

'Come in,' Fortunata would say, surprising them with a sudden smile, 'come in and sit down for a while, and I'll tell you what I know.' For Fortunata felt fiercely for these people. The realisation that she was a part of this community after all, and not an outsider as she had always supposed, had been growing gradually, and the day of the wedding party had somehow crystallised everything. They must show the British they could survive this terrible blow. They would never be defeated as Italians, whatever nonsense was being fought for in their name in Italy.

'Blast Mussolini!' she would say angrily to visitors over the teacups. 'Blast him for causing so much trouble!' Unlike in the past, her new-found fury with *Il Duce* was not grounded in politics, but in the compassion she felt for all these bereft, frightened women who had suddenly lost their menfolk – and the terror she herself was so efficiently suppressing. For she would wake up in the middle of the night sometimes, her body cold with fear at the thought that she might never see Giuseppe, Roberto – even Paolo – again. Yet this fear made her strong, implacable in her determination to trace the men. Even Serafina was reluctantly impressed by her stepmother's grim determination to find her beloved papa. Worried not only about her family but about Eduardo who had been summoned back suddenly to his regiment, Serafina hid her fear by devoting herself even more ferociously to her business. Yes, it was best that Fortunata do the searching . . . Fortunata was the right person to send on these investigative forays into the bureaucracy of police stations, Home Office buildings, army offices. The community agreed. If anyone could find out anything, it would be Fortunata!

However, Fortunata's resourcefulness failed to elicit any information. As June drifted in a haze of muggy weather towards July, Fortunata's optimism began to fade. Her daily trips to Italian organisations and police stations began to flag, as she heard of more and more friends being arrested and marched away. Gradually other families had begun to hear news of their men. Two postcards arrived from Huyton, near Liverpool, officially informing two wives in Eyre Street Hill that their husbands were interned. Old Mrs Fiorini received a telegram from one of her sons from Lancashire, tersely reassuring her: 'Am in Wharf Mills Camp. Don't worry.'

This news deepened everyone's anxiety. The Italians were not all together somewhere, then. Why not? Were there particular camps for particular categories of internees? Would different things happen to them? Were the Jews all together, perhaps, and the fascists somewhere else? The rumours and suppositions increased. In the Vialli house, Antonia and Claudia were permanently distraught, and Nonna Lucia, shrunk and suddenly very old, had taken to sitting in the front parlour with the blackout blind permanently down, staring into the gloom with a rug over her knees, her mouth half-open, as if surprised. Serafina and Fortunata, tentatively united by this new trauma, spent more and more time together, sitting for long periods in the evenings over a strong pot of tea, trying vainly to reassure each other.

'Papa will write when he can,' Serafina would say, attempting a smile. 'I expect his legs make it difficult for him to get to the post . . .'

'Yes, but – why on earth no word from Roberto?' Fortunata would fret. 'I can understand Paolo not bothering to write, but Roberto—'

'Paolo's restaurant has heard nothing, either. You would think he would contact them if he could. He loved his job – he would want to hang on to it for after the war . . .'

Fortunata's cheeks would glisten with tears in the firelight. 'We must be strong,' she would say, her voice trembling. 'We mustn't give up hope . . .' But Serafina could see that the normally resourceful Fortunata was sinking into a terrible despair, slowly becoming paralysed by the lack of news. There seemed to be nothing they could do . . . And still they heard nothing.

Serafina, in the face of Fortunata's growing depression, took to braving the local public houses in search of news. Aware that she shocked people by walking into smoke-filled public bars alone, but determined to pursue any rumour that might lead to the return of her beloved papa and her brothers-in-law, she went out after supper every evening and did not return until late. Her sisters were too preoccupied to ask where she went, her stepmother too low in spirit to care, after a weary day spent tramping the streets in search of news.

The pubs seemed more crowded than ever since the onset of war. It was as if the people of London had made a collective decision to keep laughter in their lives in spite of the privations they experienced. Serafina was constantly surprised by the seeming indifference Londoners had to the drama unfolding around them. She would stand quietly in a corner, trying to look unobtrusive as she sipped her drink, listening in numb amazement to the complaints about the latest cricket scores, or the price of cigarettes. Half her family had disappeared, and no one seemed to care! She would approach anyone who looked like they might have some authority – an off-duty policeman, someone with an LDV armband – and ask nervously if they had any news of the Italians who had been arrested. This required great courage on Serafina's part, for suspicion of anyone connected to Italy had reached fever pitch; but she relied on the fact that she was female, that she did not have an Italian accent, and that there was usually someone in the pub who recognised her as 'the statue lady'. Generally the drinkers were polite and disinterested rather than overtly aggressive towards this timid, determined young woman. She did, however, carry a sharp kitchen knife in her bag, in case her good luck ran out, as indeed one night it did.

She had ventured into a public house in a side road off Fleet Street, and had begun her round of the groups of men drinking there, showing them a photograph of her father. She had never ventured this far away from the Hill before in her search, but the days were passing and worry made her bold. The pub was crowded, hot and loud and she could feel the stares of a group of men following her as she struggled round. Then the murmuring began. 'It's a bleedin' Eytie!' 'Who's that tart?' Cheeks burning, Serafina realised she had made a mistake. She should never have come in here, it was obviously not a place where women either went or were welcome, and they were clearly not over-fond of Italians. She turned, trying to leave, but found her way blocked.

'Please — excuse me, please—' She kept her eyes lowered, hoping to avert trouble, aware of the sweat trickling between her shoulder blades in the muggy heat.

'You Italian?' someone demanded. 'Why don't you bugger off back there?'

'What are you doing in London?' She seemed to be surrounded by tall men, faces creased with suspicion.

'How come you speak such good English?' One of them pressed himself uncomfortably close, his breath foul on her face. 'You never come in this pub before — what do you want?'

Before Serafina could reply, someone stepped between her and her aggressor. She looked up and found herself gazing into the bright blue eyes of Joe O'Connell. Shock made her silent.

'Come on,' he said, 'I'll buy you a drink and they'll leave you alone.' He grinned at the man who had insulted Serafina. 'It's all right, mate,' he said, 'she's with me.'

'Sorry, Mr O'Connell,' the man said, humbly, 'I didn't know . . .'

'I don't want a drink with you,' Serafina said.

'Don't be ridiculous. You can't stay in here on your own. You've just been made aware of that. You look like a Guinness would help.' He turned and yelled, 'Two here, Sean!' to the barman, and then ushered the protesting Serafina to a corner where the crush was not so oppressive.

'Stay there,' he said, and headed towards the bar. Angrily she watched him as he struggled through the crowd. He was the last person she wanted to see! She studied his face as he carried the drinks to their table, returning the greetings of drinkers and unaware of her scrutiny. She could see why her stepmother had found him so attractive. It was something about his height, his air of confidence, his openness. He was clearly a popular man with a big personality. She heard that memorable laugh as someone joked with him, and she shuddered.

'You all right?' He pushed a drink into her hand, concerned. 'Sorry about what happened. They've been drinking since opening time. We had a big row at the union meeting and they're a bit – you know – inflamed. They didn't mean to insult you.'

'Yes, they did,' Serafina said, coldly. 'I'm Italian. I know how they feel. I'm the enemy as far as they're concerned.'

He stared at her, shocked by the hatred in her eyes. 'Well, that's as may be,' he said, sounding suddenly very Irish, 'but they'll forget soon enough, after a few drinks.' He gulped back his own, unnerved by this meeting, this sudden reminder of Fortunata. Someone put another pint on the table in front of him. 'Here y'are, Councillor,' he said, 'thanks for sorting out the shop stewards.'

Serafina, sipping at her drink, raised a cynical eyebrow. 'Still the people's hero, then,' she said.

He looked at her, so flushed and angry, so Italian, and he remained silent. She looked down. Those blue eyes unnerved her. 'Why aren't you in uniform?' she asked.

'Why?' She could feel his grin. 'Were you hoping to present me with a white feather?' He gulped at the last of his pint and started on the second. 'Sorry to disappoint you, Miss Florio. I have a pin in my leg from an accident on a building site.' She could see that she had hit a nerve. He was drinking steadily. 'Still, maybe it was meant to be,' he said, his eyes bleak. 'Maybe my place is here, keeping the home fires burning.' He replaced his glass on the table with a small crash. 'Stupid, isn't it,' he said, 'a country full of foreigners wanting to fight and no one wants us. They think I'm just as much a foreigner as you, you know. O'Connell. Florio . . .' He stared at her. 'We're none of us very English-sounding, are we? We're all outsiders.' There was a small silence.

'Aren't you going to ask me?' she said as she brushed the

138

damp tendrils of her fringe away from her forehead, her head spinning from the noise and the heat.

'Ask you what?'

'About Fortunata.'

She watched his strong fingers grip his pint mug tightly. 'No,' he said. 'No, I'm not.'

Her confidence, badly shaken by this encounter, was returning. 'Well, perhaps you should,' she said. She waited, savouring the intensity of the moment, enjoying the feeling of power she held over this man. But also, she realised, he might be able to help. He was, after all, a local politician. He might have heard something. Now that *would* be an irony!

'Have you no idea,' she said, 'what has happened to us? The people on the Hill?'

He was drinking steadily, his eyes unhappy. 'Some,' he said

She leaned forward. 'Well, let me give you some details,' she said. 'The men have been arrested. All of them, Mr O'Connell. We don't know where they are. They're probably dead.'

He stared at her. She had his full attention now. 'That was weeks ago. We've heard nothing. My father. My brothers-in-law. My friends. My workers. All gone.'

'Brothers-in-law?'

'My sisters got married, Mr O'Connell.' She saw the look of amazement, and smiled grimly. 'It's been a long time since you saw my stepmother, obviously. They've grown up now, my sisters.' She laughed to herself, bitter. 'Very grown up. This war changes people. They're like a couple of old women, sitting by the stove every night, crying into their aprons.'

'Have you asked? Made inquiries? The Foreign Office? The Home Office? Your MP? What about the Parliamentary Committee on Refugees? Eleanor Rathbone's the secretary. I could—'

She was looking at him with a wry expression. 'Aren't you forgetting something, Councillor?'

His face softened into a smile, remembering. 'Of course. Fortunata.'

She was surprised by the sudden vulnerability she saw. Her voice became hard, but she could not disguise her reluctant admiration for her old adversary. 'She's tried everywhere. She's hardly slept. She's pestered every official, she's written

139

letters, she's organised petitions, she's gone to meetings and heckled the speakers – I'm sure I don't have to give you the gory details.'

He smiled again, his face alight. 'No, no. You don't.' She knew that for a moment she no longer existed; the pub and the noise and the smoke no longer existed, for Joe O'Connell could see only Fortunata.

He was silent for a moment. More drinks had been lined up on the table for him. He gulped back a shot of whisky, staring into the distance, remembering. 'I knew about the arrests,' he said. 'Some of the Italians have been to see me. But I had no idea things were this bad.'

'Not exactly got your finger on the pulse, have you?' Serafina said.

Joe, pained, brought his gaze back round to her, through the haze of smoke. He could feel the alcohol doing its work.

'I've been tied up,' he said. She had the same lustrous dark eyes as Fortunata. He supposed all Italians did. So dark. You could lose yourself in those eyes. 'I've been involved in a union campaign – organising support for Nye Bevan.' He did not need to tell her he had buried himself in an orgy of work in order to forget Fortunata.

Serafina snorted. 'Don't you people ever give up? There's a war on, Councillor! This isn't the time for fancy anti-Churchill speeches and slogans about ending the war! That's what Bevan says, isn't it? Is that why these thugs love you so much?' she waved her arms expressively at the drinkers, 'because you all agree there should be no war?' He stared at her, silent and angry. 'Very easy to be anti-war when you aren't wearing a uniform.' She lifted the glass to her lips, smiling. He leaned across the table and grabbed her wrist, forcing the glass back to the table.

'You little bitch,' he said, his face close to hers. 'I'd like to slap you one—'

But Serafina understood that grip on her wrist. This man was sexually frustrated, alone, angry, desperate. And she had suddenly appeared, a provocative reminder of everything he had lost: and this was the man who had destroyed her happiness, who had seduced Fortunata away from her duty, who was the cause of the dead look in Papa's eyes. Joe O'Connell needed to be driven away from the Florios forever . . . and

140

the moment had come. Fortunata may be beautiful, she thought, but she isn't here, and I'm younger. She could feel Joe O'Connell's eyes raking over her body, over the flimsy crêpe-de-chine blouse clinging damply to her dark skin. She smelled the alcohol on his breath. Their heads were very close. Some men at the bar saw them, nudged each other and winked.

She looked down coolly at that strong hand crushing hers. Then she looked back at him, anger and bitterness giving her courage. 'You'd like to slap me, would you, Councillor O'Connell?' Her face was close to his now. He was hypnotised by that angry stare, those black eyes. 'Is that what you'd like to do?' She had turned her hand in his and he felt her fingers, delicate as a butterfly's wings, caress his palm. 'Are you sure?' He could feel her breath on his lips, so close was she. 'Are you sure that's what you would like?'

One evening in early July, the two women were sitting in their usual places either side of the stove, listening to a dance band concert on the wireless, Fortunata knitting some bootees for her forthcoming grandchild, Serafina staring into space. She had taken to daydreaming a great deal, Fortunata thought, listening to 'Moonlight Serenade' and surreptitiously studying her step-daughter's face. The war had certainly not harmed Serafina – on the contrary, she had lost that tense, lonely look and had relaxed, her features now softer and a smile often on her lips.

Fortunata paused at the end of her row, and placed the needles on her lap. 'Are you missing Eduardo?' she asked Serafina, gently.

Serafina's eyes met hers in the half-darkness. 'Of course I am. I wish he would write.'

Fortunata sighed. 'This waiting – we all seem to be waiting.' She resumed her knitting, aware that Serafina was now study-ing her placidly. I wonder what she is really thinking, Fortu-nata thought to herself for the thousandth time. There would always be a distance between Serafina and the rest of the world, even in times like these. Those men in Nemi had a lot to answer for.

'How thoughtless we've been!' Fortunata's voice was over-bright. 'All of us so worried about Giuseppe and the boys.

But you must be just as anxious about Eduardo, called back to his regiment so suddenly – and only a day after he got back from Dunkirk. How on earth do they expect men to fight when they never get a rest?'

Serafina's eyes were focused on a spot somewhere behind Fortunata as she answered, her voice low. 'Eduardo was due ten days' leave'. He wanted us to get married while he was home. I didn't have a chance to tell you, what with all the arrests.' She was staring at the statue of the little faded Madonna, now standing on a small wooden shelf fixed to the wall behind Fortunata. Roberto had made the shelf for her, when he saw how much she loved the statue.

The dance band concert was coming to an end. Fortunata had stopped knitting again. 'Would you have done it? Would you have married him?'

She did not receive an answer, for a familiar voice was intoning, 'This is the Nine O'Clock News from the BBC' – a universal signal for silence in households all over the country. Both women leaned forward, their conversation forgotten. The bland and comforting voice of the announcer began. 'The fifteen-thousand-ton Blue Star liner, *Arandora Star*, on its way to Canada with fifteen hundred German and Italian internees on board, has been torpedoed by a Nazi U-boat off the west coast of Ireland.'

'*Madonna mia . . .*' whispered Fortunata.

'The number of survivors is not yet known,' the voice continued, 'but early reports have suggested that the Nazi internees on board swept everyone aside in their rush for the lifeboats. It is understood that the Italian prisoners on board had little chance to escape, and many have drowned.'

The two women stared at each other. The announcer moved on to another item of news, droning on unheard in the stillness of the kitchen. Fortunata's eyes filled with tears. She stood, her knitting falling forgotten to the floor. 'I'd better go up and tell the girls,' she said, and hurriedly left the room.

Serafina had not moved, her eyes fixed on the Nemi Madonna gazing graciously from the other side of the room. '*Signore, pieta,*' she murmured, crossing herself. 'Don't let it be Papa on the ship! Please, please don't let it be Papa!' She pulled her rosary out of her pocket and kissed it, tasting her own tears, '*Nel nome del Padre e del Figlio e dello Spirito Santo – pieta di noi, Signore!*' As she bent her head and began to pray frantically, the voice on the wireless continued, the cool tones filling the dark corners of the room, interrupted only by the intense sound of Serafina's prayers.

'The liner *Duchess of York* has arrived safely in Canada with her complement of Nazi prisoners of war . . .'

'Our Father, which art in heaven, hallowed be Thy name . . .' Somewhere, through her prayers, the thought came to Serafina – they are shipping them all out – all of them!

The next few days passed slowly, like a nightmare, never to be forgotten by anyone who knew men who were taken away in the June arrests.

The newspapers were full of furious and dramatic headlines: NAZIS PUSH ITALIANS ASIDE IN PANIC DASH! NAZIS PANIC AND RUSH LIFEBOATS! The *Daily Express* went further: GERMANS AND ITALIANS FIGHT FOR LIFEBOATS! Fortunata had thrown the paper in a fury across the room, when she had read the story by a survivor claiming that the Italians had fought just as viciously as the Germans in the scramble for a place in the lifeboats. Perhaps even worse, no one seemed to care. The politicians claimed that the internees on the ship that had sunk so dramatically had all been Nazi sympathisers. The public seemed to enjoy the irony of a Nazi U-boat sinking a ship carrying its own supporters.

In Little Italy, emotions were at boiling point. Fights broke out on street corners, bitterness was everywhere. Unforgivable things were said. Italians were evicted by English landlords. Italian youths would return home from work with bloody noses and black eyes. Old men wept openly on their doorsteps, bemoaning the wickedness of war. The women seemed paralysed, in a frozen state of waiting, eternally hoping for news. The young women like Antonia and Claudia aged almost overnight, shadows appearing beneath their eyes, faces taut with worry. The older ones became uncharacteristically silent, withdrawing into themselves, only their eyes revealing their terrible fears, as they went about their housework and shopping as usual.

The Hill, now that there were only boys and a few old

men left, seemed suddenly to be a strangely female universe, with Fortunata as its authoritative voice. She listened to the terrible fears of the women patiently, and then hustled them off to St Peter's. 'Go and pray with Father Joseph,' she told them. 'All we can do is pray.'

But she could not pray herself. Instead she stared at her reflection, white-faced, in the mirror, and murmured, 'It's all my fault.' She felt as if she was slowly going mad, waiting in this house full of weeping women, waiting for some kind of sign that never came, some indication of what the sinking of the *Arandora Star* would mean to her and to those she loved. Finally, after two days of agonised waiting, she decided that it was time to act, even if her efforts were futile. She could not bear to stay in the house in Grape Street, hunched over the wireless, listening to the fervent mumbled prayers of her mother and the wailing of her daughters. She would go out and start the long round of inquiries again. Surprisingly, Serafina offered to help. So it was that Fortunata and Serafina stepped out into the silent, stunned streets of the Hill in search of news, Serafina to Bloomsbury House (where refugee organisations operated) and Fortunata to the police station.

Without much hope of success, Fortunata mounted the steps of the Rosebery Avenue police station, her eyes dulled with worry and the knowledge that her family was in tatters. As she approached the swing doors, a tall figure was pushing his way out, putting on his hat. They both halted in the doorway, speechless. Fortunata felt that flutter in the pit of her stomach, suppressed for so long.

Finally she spoke. 'Hello, Joe.' The pain of meeting him was almost too much. The sleepless nights, the grinding fear, the guilt – and now Joe, standing here, the same Joe, exactly as she remembered him. She began to tremble.

'Fortunata?' He spoke, with that same sing-song way of saying her name that had always made her melt. She staggered back slightly, and his arm came out and caught her, preventing her from falling.

'Please, Joe—'

'Come and sit down, Fortunata – you're going to faint.' He pulled her down on to the step, clutching her hands, gazing at her, concerned.

'Joe, we mustn't, not here – people will see.'

'To hell with people!' he said, his old vigour returned. 'You're in a hell of a state, Fortunata.' He looked at her closely, unable to suppress his joy at seeing her again. 'You've changed your hairstyle,' he said softly. 'It suits you.' Fortunata's curls were now falling on her shoulders in a fashionable long style. He longed to reach out and touch that glorious halo of extravagant black curls, but instead he said, ever-practical, 'Maybe you should put your head between your knees.'

Fortunata pulled her hands away from his and made to stand up again. 'I'm fine – really, I'm fine. I must go in there–' Joe helped her to her feet.

'If it's news of the *Arandora Star* you're after,' he said, 'there is none. Why do you think I was in there?'

Fortunata could not meet his eyes. 'Oh Joe,' she said, 'you were looking for news.'

Joe put a hand under her chin and forced her to meet his eyes. 'What else would I do?'

Uncharacteristically, Fortunata began to cry. She backed away down the steps, as Joe moved towards her. 'No,' she said. 'No – please don't follow me, Joe—' and she ran, away down the steps and along Rosebery Avenue, her tears becoming sobs. But he was behind her, running too, and he pulled her back.

'I'm not letting you go like this,' he said, firmly, 'I don't care what you say.'

She turned to him, her face anguished, streaked with tears. 'I can't be seen with you, not now—'

He looked down at her, all the love he felt making his face vulnerable, softer than usual. 'Then don't be seen with me,' he said quietly, 'come home with me, Fortunata.'

There was a moment, when he felt the world had held its breath as he waited, his hand on her arm, for her reply.

Then, slowly, he felt the gentle pressure of her hand on his. 'All right, Joe,' she said, tired, 'all right . . .'

They had gone back to his small flat in Holborn, and he had made her some tea. They had sat, drinking it silently, opposite each other in the old leather armchairs that were so familiar to Fortunata. She had recovered from the terrible feeling of faintness she had experienced on seeing Joe, and now she was talking, slowly and carefully, like someone in a trance.

'I'm sure they're all dead,' she was saying, 'Roberto, his brother Joe, Paolo . . . Giuseppe.'

'I'm sorry,' was all Joe could say.

Fortunata shook her head, as if shaking off his condolences. 'It's because of us,' she said, staring at the carpet, her voice very low. 'Don't you see? It's because of us that I have to be punished. I've committed a mortal sin and now I'm damned to hell—'

'You don't believe in all that mumbo-jumbo!' Joe said angrily. 'Don't forget I know you, Fortunata – I know you better than I know myself. Since when have you believed in damnation?' She was silent. 'And anyway –' Joe tried to be reasonable – 'why should you be punished? You and I – it's over. We ended it, didn't we? So why should you be punished now?'

Fortunata's eyes met his. She stared at him for a moment. He tried not to think about how beautiful she looked, nor to feel a small, evil quiver of exultation at the thought that Giuseppe might be dead, and that Fortunata might be free.

'I know what you're thinking,' she said, 'and the terrible thing is – I'm thinking it too. Don't you see? That's why I've been punished, because I've never stopped thinking about you, wanting you – not for one minute.'

She put down her teacup and stood up. Joe sat, unmoving, unsure what to do, what to say.

'Fortunata—' he began, helplessly.

'Please—' she said, 'don't say anything.' Slowly she began to unbutton her dress, her eyes never leaving his. He watched, transfixed, as she slowly revealed the pale slip she wore underneath, and let the dress drop to her feet. She stepped out of it and stood there, trembling. 'I love you, Joe,' she said, 'I just can't help myself,' and she crossed the room and leaned over him, pulling his face to hers to be kissed.

When Serafina returned that afternoon to find Fortunata calmly making suet pudding in the kitchen, she had to report that the Italian Embassy had been closed, and that they had been instructed to go instead to the Brazilian Embassy in the morning.

'We'll go together,' Fortunata said, her head bent over the mixing bowl. Serafina raised her eyebrows but said nothing.

When they arrived they found it besieged by hundreds of their neighbours and fellow Italians. Fighting their way through the crush in the main entrance, Serafina and Fortunata, hand in hand, struggled into a large meeting room which seemed to be the focus for the crowds. Unable to see beyond the backs of the men in front of them, Fortunata peered around for a familiar face. Eventually she sighted a friend from the local Labour Party, and waved and called to him frantically. He shouldered his way towards them, and hugged them both, much to Serafina's surprise (for she hardly knew the man).

'Hundreds are dead,' he said, 'and they weren't all fascists on the boat. Decio Anzani is on the missing list.'

Even the apolitical Serafina was aghast. 'You mean Mr Anzani from the Italian League of the Rights of Man? The man who gave talks at the library? What in God's name was he doing on the ship?'

The man shrugged, 'I don't know. But he's on the list.'

Fortunata's shoulders sagged. 'Decio worked so hard to get anti-fascists out of Italy,' she said. 'He was a good man . . . He fought evil . . .' She began to sob. Serafina, who was shocked beyond measure at the sight of Fortunata breaking down, put a tentative arm around her stepmother's shoulder. 'We must see the list, Fortunata,' she said, determinedly. 'We must get hold of the list.'

As she spoke, a murmur ran through the crowd. They looked up. At the far end of the room a young Italian had climbed on to a table, waving a piece of paper. 'They've given me the list!' he shouted in Italian. 'Shut up, everyone, and I'll read it out!'

He began to read, his youthful voice confident and clear. 'List of Enemy Aliens missing presumed dead after the sinking of the *Arandora Star* on the second of July, nineteen hundred and forty . . . Ready?' The crowd would not be silent. People in the corridor, unable to hear, shouted angrily. Some wept openly, others pressed their hands over their ears, irrationally refusing to listen to the news they had come specifically to hear. The young man began to read, running a careful finger down the list, to ensure he included every name.

'Abazzio, Pino. Abazzio, Giovanni. Alberoni, Pietro. Altofonte, Giuseppe—' The room had fallen silent. The enormity of the tragedy had begun to descend on the Italians. Some began to pray quietly, heads bowed.

'Anzani, Decio. Albanesi, Davido. Albanesi, Eduardo . . .' From somewhere towards the front of the crowd, they heard a piercing scream. There was a sudden flurry of movement. The boy on the table looked up. '*Madonna!*' he shouted, 'it's Eddie's mum – Signora Albanese – she's fainted! Get her out of here!' The crowd parted as the prostrate figure of an old lady in black was helped towards the door. Serafina found herself clutching Fortunata's hand very tightly. She felt the answering pressure from Fortunata, as they exchanged a brief, frightened glance. The youth began to read from the list again. The crowd began to sway and groan as names were recognised, and anger and grief rose to the surface.

'Bagheria Antonio. Belliniano, Massimo.'

'He's got to the Bs—' Fortunata said unnecessarily, her grip tightening. Even as she spoke, they heard, as if in a dream, the name they had dreaded hearing: 'Bianchi, Paolo.' For a second, Serafina felt the floor tremble, as if the centre of gravity had suddenly moved. It was to be their tragedy after all, not just something that was happening to other people. A terrible cold clamminess began to invade her body. She stood listening as the dreadful roll call of the dead and the missing was read. Paolo. He was gone. That animalistic grace, the ready laugh, the hedonistic enjoyment of life, the strong figure, handsome in his waiter's suit, that strange, sensuous mouth – these had been the stuff of his life, what had made him a living, breathing man. Gone, all gone. Fortunata was staring ahead of her, expressionless. How on earth, thought Serafina, could they tell poor, silly, pregnant Antonia that her husband was dead?

The boy's voice was becoming hoarse. He was having to shout above the increasing noise of the crowds, the sobbing of the women, the praying, the anger. More and more names, more friends. The nice boy who worked at the piano makers. The brothers from the fish restaurant. Old Baldelli.

Above their heads, the voice of the youth reading his list continued, for the most part expressionless, but every now and then breaking and cracking, as the boy came across a name he recognised. Time passed, an eternity. Still he read. The heat had become intense, and behind her, Serafina could feel the cool breeze of someone fanning himself with a sheet of paper. Next to her, an old man wept, standing upright, as if at attention. She could feel Fortunata tremble as the boy on the table continued his grim self-appointed task. Then there it was. He had said it, it must be so: 'Florio, Giuseppe.' Papa was dead. He was dead. A terrible vision appeared before her, opening up like a black flower – Papa floundering in an inky sea, Papa, his arm waving, calling "Nata! Maria! *Aiutame!* Help me! Maria, where are you . . .?' She felt the blackness engulf her and she staggered, only to be pulled up by the strong hand of Fortunata. She isn't weeping, Serafina thought irrationally, why is she so calm? Then she remembered. Of course, Fortunata did not love Papa. She had wept for Decio Anzani, but she had no tears for Papa. The two women stood apart, separate in their shock and disbelief, the world spinning wildly at odds with everything they knew: dislocated, sense- less, mad.

Then Fortunata turned to Serafina, distraught, and clutched at her. 'He's nearly got to the Ls. Serafina – he's nearly—'

'I know.' Serafina was biting her lip. She could taste blood. Roberto Lucente. All thoughts of her father disappeared. If the beautiful Roberto was dead, then there was no God. In her mind's eye she saw Roberto, standing as if in a blazing light, his eyes gleaming with the passion of his deeply held convictions, his sculpted face like a knight of old, heroic, unspeakably exciting, the embodiment of everything that was good in the world, the embodiment of life. If Roberto now lay on the sea bed in a cold and watery grave, Serafina swore that she would abandon the Church. She would smash the little Madonna from Nemi. She would burn her rosary. Rob- erto must not die.

It seemed that she stopped breathing. She heard the hoarse voice say 'Lucente, Joseph. LoBianco, Arturo . . .' Faintly she heard Fortunata murmur, 'Joe . . . Do you hear, 'Fina? Joe is missing, but not Roberto. Roberto is not missing.' With a sob, Serafina allowed herself to be hugged by her stepmother, so weakened by relief that she was unaware that this was the first time the two women had embraced for many years. Laughing a little through their tears, they rejoiced together.

'Thank God!' Serafina whispered, and silently begged for- giveness for her earlier moment of doubt. She would go to

Mass tonight, and she would kneel before the statue of Our Lady of Mount Carmel. She would light a candle for poor, dead Papa, another for Paolo, and another for dear Joe Lucente. But in her heart she would give thanks that Roberto, at least, had been saved.

They stayed locked in their desperate embrace, swaying together, oblivious of the crowd around them. Then, suddenly feeling foolish, Serafina pulled away. Fortunata seemed to be in some kind of a trance, a strange, shocked expression on her face, tearless and white.

'Giuseppe—' she was saying, 'Paolo. Joe. Decio.'

'Come on, Fortunata.' Serafina tugged at her sleeve. 'We must get home. The girls – they're waiting for news, remember?' This reminder of her daughters seemed to revive Fortunata. Obediently she followed Serafina, edging through the crowds, the inexorable voice still reading the names that no one wanted to hear, his audience spellbound with shock.

They were walking silently through the fading afternoon light, past the piles of sandbags, the shop windows crisscrossed with tape. The streets were quiet; the rush hour had not yet begun, and this corner of the city had a sad, deserted look. Neither spoke. There seemed to be nothing to say. Only as they turned into Grape Street did Fortunata hesitate.

'I don't know how to tell them,' she said. Her lips were quivering. 'Do I tell them together? Should I talk to Antonia on her own? What about Mamma—'

Serafina took her arm. 'Fortunata, you're not to think about it – you'll just make it harder.' She was firm. 'We'll go in and we'll tell them. Together.'

Yet even as she pushed open the front door, Serafina could sense that something had happened within. Claudia was standing in the hall, holding on to the banister, her face the colour of chalk.

'What is it? What's happened?' Serafina rushed to her sister. 'Claudia! Speak to me!'

Claudia stared beyond Serafina, to her mother. 'He's dead,' she said in a small, quavering voice, 'Roberto.'

'No, *cara mia*.' Fortunata kissed her youngest daughter with a strange vehemence. 'Roberto is not dead. Come into the front room, and,' to Serafina, 'call Antonia, 'Fina, please.' Fortunata was back in control. She pushed Claudia through the door into the parlour. 'We'll have a cup of tea.' She stood on the threshold, immobile. Serafina, hearing a gasp, hurried back down the hall from the kitchen, to see what had silenced her stepmother. Standing by the fireplace, smoking a cigarette, was Paolo.

'*Buona sera*, Mamma.' He tried to smile with his usual confidence, but failed. The hand holding the cigarette was trembling. 'Hello, Serafina.'

Fortunata sank into an armchair, Claudia at her feet. Lucia was sitting in her usual chair opposite, wringing her hands together and murmuring to herself in Italian. Serafina wondered briefly if Nonna had finally gone mad, but then the old woman raised her eyes and said, ' 'Tonia's making tea. Paolo's come home, as you see. He's had a bath. I told him to say nothing, Fortunata, until you got home. But he says Roberto is dead. Drowned.'

'No, he isn't!' flashed Serafina. She felt the world tremble again, and fall away, a great chasm opening up before her. *Madonna mia*. No. Not Roberto. She had a sudden clear vision of him laughing, pushing that lock of hair out of his eyes. Eyes full of pain and confusion. Roberto. Dead. She was still in the doorway, staring at the tall figure leaning against the mantelpiece. Surely this was a ghost? 'We've come from the Embassy – Roberto's name wasn't on the missing persons list.'

'I can explain that,' the ghost said, his strange eyes fixed on Serafina. 'Was Giuseppe's name on the list?'

Serafina began to think that after all it was she who was losing her senses. Here was Paolo, magically in the front room, and they were having this stupid conversation about lists! 'Yes, Papa is missing—'

'No he isn't.' Paolo sighed, and threw the remains of his cigarette into the empty grate. 'Your father's alive. I last saw him in a place called Warth Mills. He told me that if I contacted you before he did I was to tell you that he loved you very much.' He turned to where Fortunata sat staring up at him. 'He told me to tell you not to worry, he'll survive. He said to tell you that.' Oddly, Fortunata gave a little laugh.

Serafina's heart sank, as she heard Antonia coming down the hall, with a rattling tea tray. More madness. Tea at a time like this! She stood aside as Antonia, her face alive with barely suppressed joy, appeared.

'Here I am with the tea!' she said brightly. 'Isn't it wonderful, Mamma? Paolo's back, as you can see. I'm sure the others will be back soon—' Claudia had buried her face in her mother's skirts and was crying silently, only the convulsive movements of her thin shoulders giving her away. Fortunata reached down and carefully smoothed a curl on her daughter's damp cheek.

'Come in and pour the tea, 'Tonia,' she said calmly. ''Fina, go and sit down. You're exhausted.' Serafina obeyed, heading on shaking legs for the old horsehair settee. Fortunata turned back to Paolo, unsmiling. 'Tell us what happened, Paolo. Only tell us quickly. I understand that you are exhausted, that terrible things have happened. But we are tired too.' Her voice was very low, but perfectly audible in the silence. 'Are you on the run?'

'Well – I suppose—'

'Did they release you? Give you back your papers?'

'No. I've come all the way from Scotland – yesterday, it was. Yesterday morning I hitch-hiked on the A8 and got to Glasgow. Then I persuaded a lorry driver that I was a crew member from the ship—'

Fortunata shook her head angrily. 'No! Start at the beginning, tell us everything. We have to be told everything.' She took the cup of tea proffered by Antonia and placed it on the arm of her chair where it remained undrunk. The rest of the teacups were distributed. Paolo drank his tea in one gulp, and then lit another cigarette. The women watched him, hypnotised. He sighed, seemingly reluctant to begin.

'You want me to start from when we were arrested?' He looked at his wife for a moment. Antonia replaced the tea cosy on the teapot, grasped Paolo's free hand for a second and kissed it passionately, then went meekly over to join Serafina on the sofa, settling down with her legs tucked up under her skirts, like a small child waiting for a story.

'Just start,' said Fortunata.

'We were taken to a school. Some kind of registration, I suppose. Then we were all put on coaches.'

'Were you together? You and Roberto and Giuseppe?'

Paolo nodded. '. . . And Roberto's brother Joe. We sat together on the back seat of the coach. We were taken to Kempton Park – the racecourse.'

The women stared at him, open-mouthed. It was difficult to believe that they could have been taken to such a place – so normal, so absolutely nothing to do with the war. But Paolo's face was serious. 'It was pretty bad there – very crowded, everyone asking questions, no one getting any answers. We slept in the stables.' He inhaled on his cigarette, drawing the smoke far down into his lungs. He stared ahead, remembering. 'The food was grim – bread and the occasional sausage. Some men tried to kill themselves. The German Jews – they thought their number was up – started crying, like a bunch of kids.'

'Just tell us what happened to you, Paolo,' Fortunata said evenly, still stroking Claudia's hair.

'There was even a priest there. He got permission to hold a Mass in the grandstand. It was a Sunday.' His brow furrowed, as if what he was remembering did not make sense. 'The priest had made a cross – it was two boards tied together with a towel ... A few days later we were told we were going to another camp.'

'All of you?'

'Yes, the four of us were still together. We were handed over to a military escort – Scots Guards, they were. We had to march from the racecourse to the station. We went along a leafy lane. It was lined with Grenadiers, all with rifles and fixed bayonets. They looked at us—' His eyes grew hard. 'I've never seen men look like that before.'

'They thought you were the enemy,' said Serafina, her voice not sounding like her own. Paolo's eyes fixed on her for a moment, then he looked away.

'Yes,' he said, 'that's what they thought. Your father – Giuseppe – he had tears in his eyes.' He paused for a moment, remembering. 'We were crammed on to a train, heading north. Some time before dawn the train stopped at a station – I didn't see the name of it. We were marched through the countryside. We almost had to carry Giuseppe.'

Serafina saw Fortunata's eyes fill with tears. She stared at her stepmother, surprised, as Paolo continued. 'We went to some deserted warehouses. This was Warth Mills. We were all sent to a huge hall. There were four army captains. We had to strip naked. They took our watches, crucifixes,' he held out a bare hand, 'even my wedding ring, 'Tonia. It's gone.' Serafina sipped her tea. Paolo was talking still, recounting the terrible nights in the warehouse – the rats, the stench from the latrines, the hunger and the fear. A great tiredness weighed Serafina down. This had been a very long day. Her entire body ached with fatigue. But she must concentrate, she must know what happened.

'They read out a list of names,' Paolo was saying, 'and Roberto's name was on it. We were sure that he was going to be shipped out somewhere – that was the rumour. Then they suddenly said that everyone whose name wasn't on the list had to collect their luggage and prepare to leave at dawn. So we knew then – it was us being shipped out. That's when they changed places.'

'Roberto and your papa. Giuseppe was already collapsing – he was ill. He would never have survived another journey. So Roberto offered to swap places with him. It was easily done – lots of people did it. No one at the camp realised what was going on,' his voice was bitter, 'we were just a bunch of greasy wops to them – they couldn't tell us apart, they said. Made jokes about frying chips in our hair. Called us gigolos and queers.' He was silent for a moment, his face taut. 'So, Roberto just said his name was Giuseppe Florio at roll call – and that was that. Roberto told your father he was glad to do it – anyway, he wanted to go with his brother. They didn't want to be separated.' Claudia was sitting stiffly upright now, her face still very white, listening.

'So we left. It was raining. Pouring. We were all drenched. We were put on a train to Liverpool. We had to march to the docks, and then they put us on the ship. I didn't know its name then, it was just a ship. But when we got inside, we ended up in what looked like a restaurant, on the promenade deck. There were beautiful mirrors on the walls, with gold frames. I thought it must have been a cruise ship, commandeered for the war.' He threw away his cigarette and immediately lit another. He was talking rapidly now, his eyes on the floor, one hand occasionally running distractedly through his hair, still damp from his recent bath. 'We could hear some of the Germans – they were in the ballroom singing Nazi songs, very rowdy. They sent a squad along to tell them to take the flag down – they'd hung a swastika on the wall – but they refused. I was watching from the doorway. They just refused, and the squad went away.' Paolo seemed to have forgotten where he was. The words tumbled from his lips, a horrible torrent, unstoppable, ugly, because they knew what the end of the story would be. They knew that Paolo was telling them about the last hours of the *Arandora Star*.

'The ship sailed around midnight. Roberto managed to find a passageway behind the ballroom, and he went off exploring. When he came back he said he'd been to the forward section of the ship. There were more Italians there. No one knew where we were going. By the middle of the night Joe was seasick – he had to keep going outside.' He paused, staring into space. 'It was a terrible night. We slept under some trestle tables in the restaurant. One man – an Italian from Scotland – kept shouting in his sleep. We had to wake him up in the end.'

'How many of you were there?'

Paolo shrugged. 'I don't know. I would say several hundred.' He pulled out another cigarette, and lit it. 'Then, about seven in the morning there was an awful crash, a huge crash. We all knew at once it was a torpedo. It was completely dark. I shouted to Roberto. He answered me, but he was in a terrible state – Joe had been sleeping near the wall and one of the big mirrors had crashed on to him. He was cut to ribbons. Roberto was trying to pick bits of glass off him . . .' Paolo was close to tears. 'Joe didn't speak. I think he must have been unconscious. I'm not sure about what happened next—' he sucked his cheeks in, making a supreme effort not to break down. 'There were terrible screams in the darkness, and people shouting – in German, in Italian – it was chaos. Someone said we had to get to the boat deck. I told Roberto, but he wouldn't come, he wouldn't leave Joe.' He stared at Claudia, challenging. 'It was stupid – Joe was going to die anyway. Maybe he was already dead.'

Claudia suddenly slumped back. 'You bastard,' she said. 'What are you saying? You left them there?'

Antonia leapt to her feet. 'Don't call my husband a bastard!' she screamed. 'Don't you dare call my husband a bastard!' Serafina pulled Antonia roughly back on to the sofa. Yes he is, she thought, he is a bastard. She thought her head would explode.

'Shut up, both of you!' thundered Fortunata, and the two sisters were instantly silent. 'Carry on, Paolo.'

'I put on a lifejacket. I felt my way out on to the deck but there were people running about in a panic. There was no order anywhere. The soldiers were all still at their posts – no one had told them to abandon ship. So I thought perhaps it wasn't that serious. I headed back towards the restaurant. I was going to help Roberto get Joe on deck,' a tear glistened in his eye, 'but then the ship gave a terrible lurch and everything was tilted, things were sliding about—' he dashed the tear away. 'I knew I had to get off the ship. I went back on deck. I could hear someone with a loudhailer, telling everyone not to panic, that there was plenty of time. A group of old men – I recognised a couple from the *co-operativo* – were kneeling and praying on the deck. I tried to get them to go into the lifeboats, but they just wouldn't listen.' Paolo's body sagged. To Serafina he seemed suddenly small, pathetic, dwarfed by the magnitude of what he was trying to describe. 'I looked at my watch. Half an hour had already gone by since the torpedo had hit us. All the lifeboats had gone. Someone told me to jump, and told me to watch out for the lifejacket – you can break your neck in a cork lifejacket . . . I jumped.' He began to shiver. 'I was sucked under at first. I thought I'd had it. Then I came up again and started swimming away from the ship. There were lifeboats all around me but they were over-loaded. Men were hanging on to planks, home-made rafts, oil drums – anything. Then the ship began to go. It was like a dream—' Paolo's face reflected the horror of that vision. 'I can still see it – little figures rolling down the deck – the Captain and some officers were still on the bridge – it just suddenly tipped up and began to disappear—' He started to sob. The women sat immobile, gazing at him, gripped by his unspeakable story, unable to move. He brushed his hand across his eyes, determined somehow to finish. 'The sea was boiling and bubbling. Bits of the ship were flying about. The sea was black – we were all covered in thick oil. No one spoke. There was an awful silence after the ship went down. I suppose we were all shocked. I climbed on to a sort of makeshift raft with two other Italians already on it. There wasn't really enough room for me, but they let me on. Then we heard singing. It was the men in one of the lifeboats, they were singing "It's a Lovely Day Tomorrow" – I suppose to keep their spirits up.'

His reddened eyes stared into the distance. 'Bodies kept

bobbing up. Funny – they looked very peaceful. We paddled away from where the ship went down. We were all freezing – the water was like ice. I kept hanging on, but men were drowning all around me. Funny how quiet it was. You'd see someone you knew, and you'd shout at them across the water – then a few minutes later you'd look again, and they'd be gone . . . too tired to hang on any longer. You know Federico Viazzani?' They all nodded dumbly. 'I watched him go. He was hanging on to a lifeboat – it was too crowded to get into – he just slipped under the water.'

Serafina remembered seeing Signora Viazzani on the day of the wedding, in church. It all seemed such a long time ago. Federico! There was a terrible irony in his drowning – for he had been part of the crew of one of the little boats helping to ferry men from Dunkirk in June. Federico, who had spent most of his life as an illiterate failure, had briefly been a hero. Poor Signora Viazzani. Now both her sons were dead. Serafina stole a glance at Fortunata. For hadn't the Viazzani brothers been her suitors once? Serafina was sure Nonna had told her this. Fortunata's face was expressionless.

'There was a plane,' Paolo said. 'We shouted but it went away. Then another one appeared – a Sunderland, they said it was. It dropped a bag into the water, with provisions. The ship's motor launch picked it up, and then they shouted a message – "Keep your chins up – help coming". It wasn't so bad then. We knew we would be rescued.' Paolo's body sagged. He was reaching the end of his story. 'It was a destroyer – the *St Laurent*. A launch came and picked us up. The sailors cut the lifejackets off the dead men in the water so the bodies would sink. I don't remember the next bit – I ended up on deck – we were some of the first to be taken on board. Someone massaged my legs and gave me a cigarette and a mug of rum. Someone asked if I was crew or prisoner. I said prisoner. We were all herded together on deck, then some of us were taken below – someone gave me a pair of trousers and a navy sweater. I was lucky – I even had a shower, and got myself cleaned up. Some of the prisoners were still covered in oil when we docked at Greenock, and they had slept on deck covered in a blanket.' Paolo was shivering violently now. He groped for a cigarette but the packet was empty. Antonia got up and led him to her place on the sofa. She searched in her handbag, found a cigarette, lit it, and placed it between his trembling fingers. There was a lengthy silence, while the women absorbed Paolo's story. Finally it was Lucia, forgotten in the corner, who spoke, her voice very Italian.

'I don't understand,' she said, 'how did you get home?'

Paolo exhaled a long stream of white smoke with a shuddering sigh. 'We were marched to a warehouse, with an army escort, through the streets of Greenock. People stared at us – I don't know what they thought. I saw a woman weeping. We were sent to the top floor of the warehouse.' A frown crossed his brow. 'I don't understand it, really. They didn't take a roll call. Nobody seemed to be in charge. I went looking for a toilet – no one stopped me, so when I found a staircase I went down it. Then I pushed open a door and I was on a road – a main road.' He looked at Fortunata, as if for approval. 'I didn't think twice. No one had stopped me – no one had noticed me. I just started walking. I got a lift with a lorry driver. He'd heard about the *Arandora Star*, so I told him I was part of the crew. I was wearing a sailor's jumper, so he believed me.'

'You came straight here?' Fortunata asked coolly.

Paolo nodded. 'I just wanted to tell you what happened to Roberto, and that Giuseppe wasn't on the ship.'

Fortunata nodded. She looked calmly at her son-in-law. 'I'm grateful.' Her gaze shifted to her daughter, who sat at Paolo's feet. She sighed. 'Now,' she said wearily, 'you must go to the police station and give yourself up.'

'No, Mamma!' Antonia gave a terrible wail, from the depths of her being. 'No, Mamma!'

It was Serafina who intervened. 'You can't mean it, Fortunata!' She got up and went over to Paolo, as if her physical presence could act as a shield between her trembling brother-in-law and her stepmother. 'Paolo's been through hell. He isn't a criminal. He's done nothing—'

Fortunata's mouth was set in a firm line. 'I know that. But by coming back here he has endangered our entire family – Papa, you, the girls . . . me.'

'We can keep him here!' Antonia sobbed. 'We can hide him—' Claudia went over and hugged her sister silently. Paolo was still staring into the empty fireplace, his face blank, awaiting the decision on his fate.

'We can't hide him, 'Tonia,' Fortunata was saying. 'Can't you understand? Paolo's on their list of members of the *fascio*. We'd all be arrested, we'd all be branded traitors and sent back to Italy. Is that what you want?'

Serafina hugged the agonised Paolo to her breast in a sudden convulsive outburst of emotion, and glared at Fortunata over his shoulder. 'This is your son-in-law, Fortunata!' she said urgently, pleading now. 'Paolo is family. Imagine if it had been Roberto who had come back. Would you go to the police then? Are you sure this isn't really about your politics and not about morals at all?'

Fortunata stared at her, pained. 'There's nothing I can do, 'Fina. Paolo will be caught anyway. They'll be looking for him now—' Paolo clutched Serafina in a desperate crushing hold, almost suffocating her.

'Look, Mamma—' Serafina, who had never addressed Fortunata as mother, was at her most desperate; she knew she was fighting not only for Paolo, but for her two sobbing, frightened sisters, whose world was collapsing with such rapidity. 'Mamma, think of 'Tonia – Paolo is the father of her child. Do you want him in prison when the baby's born? So the baby always thinks of his papa as a criminal?'

Fortunata looked weary, suddenly made haggard. 'In the eyes of the British he is already a criminal,' she said. 'I'm sorry. I have to act for all of us, with Papa away. I must do what's best for everyone. I'm sorry, Paolo.'

Fortunata slipped from the room. Serafina heard her in the hall, her delicate feet tapping down the lino floor, and then the sound of the front door opening, closing, and the footsteps dying away down the street. Only then did Serafina realise that Fortunata had not uttered one expression of joy at the news that her husband was, after all, alive. 'You bitch . . .' Serafina murmured. Paolo, his head buried in Serafina's neck, sobbed violently. Gently, she stroked his hair, murmuring words of comfort to him, as if he were a child. She did not see, behind her, the face of Lucia, staring up at them both from her armchair, suddenly registering their desperate embrace with a look of terrible realisation.

CHAPTER SEVEN

1941

FORTUNATA WAS UTTERLY exhausted. She could not remember the last time she had enjoyed a night of uninterrupted sleep. Through the shortening autumn days, the
strange, lonely Christmas and into the new year of 1941, the
bombs fell. London had been transformed. Piles of rubble
were heaped everywhere. Families had disappeared. The smell
of leaking gas and exploded sewers hung in the air, foul and
suffocating. Buses were scarce, trains erratic. Letters didn't
arrive. Everything had changed; only the incessant rumble of
the Luftwaffe overhead stayed constant, passing across the
night sky with a grim regularity. Somehow people managed
to maintain a routine, struggling to work, producing meals,
looking after children – only now they had additional tasks,
as wardens, bomb clearance workers, good neighbours, fire-
men, nurses – all the new roles occasioned by the interminable
air raids.

In the Florio house in Grape Street, things had changed
irrevocably, and the war was not entirely responsible. Lucia
had become helpless, seemingly rendered dumb by some
strange unnamed despair. She sat immobile in the front room
for long periods, fingering her rosary and murmuring in
Italian. Her only excursions were to St Peter's, and even there
she seemed to find no comfort, emerging from the confessional with the same tired expression of despair she had worn
on entering. Her deteriorating health meant that Fortunata's
free time at home was occupied with caring for her mother.
Not that she had much free time; since the gown shop where
she had worked for so long had been demolished by an
incendiary bomb, Fortunata now worked in a munitions factory in Finsbury Park, alongside Claudia.

She would often reflect on the irony of this; now women

had all the earning power Fortunata had spent fruitless years fighting for, now they had a certain independence. Employers actively sought them, nurseries were supplied for their children, old people suddenly approved of this new emancipation. Women had finally begun to gain some equality in the workplace, and all because men had decided to go to war! Fortunata worked on an assembly line with a team of cheerful women, all of whom had evacuated children, or missing husbands. She could not help the occasional wry smile at the thought that these new friends had seemed so recently to be her enemies. In the factory no one cared where you came from. The women were united by the war, indifferent to nationality, class or politics – as Fortunata had found out when she made inquiries about union membership at the factory.

'Oh, we all belong to the union,' a co-worker told her brightly, 'but it's not really very active. I mean, we all want the same thing, don't we? There's a war on!' So she and Claudia had joined the union and regularly attended meetings, but it was clear that disagreements with management were being put aside for the duration of the war, and the meetings were hardly more than a cup of tea and a chat before returning to the serious business of the War Effort.

Claudia, numbed by the death of her beloved Roberto, had retreated, white-faced and silent, into her work. She went to and from the factory like a dazed robot, hardly communicating. The neighbours had begun to regard her strangely, asking themselves if Roberto's unjust and untimely death had not turned the Florio girl slightly mad. This view was enhanced by reports that one night Claudia had been found by a kindly ARP warden standing in the middle of Saffron Hill, wide-eyed and laughing, while around her the explosive hell of a full-bodied air raid was howling and raging.

Antonia had lost the baby she was carrying, shortly after Paolo had been taken away. She had retreated into a desperate cheeriness, never revealing her suffering, and filled the days by caring for Nonna Lucia, keeping her supplied with endless cups of tea. She never mentioned her husband. She had never asked about him, not since the police had arrived and taken him away. It had been Serafina who had clung to Paolo, sobbing, and begging the uncomfortable policeman for mercy. Antonia devoted herself to caring for Lucia as though she were a baby, spending hours reading to her patiently, or simply sitting silently with her in the gloom of the front room with its blackout curtains permanently in place. Paolo seemed no longer to exist for her, although the wedding photograph had stayed on the sideboard in the front room, and Antonia had made no attempt to remove it. Only Claudia seemed to have noticed the appearance of the photograph in its wooden frame, placed there by Fortunata as a reminder of happier times. She would hold it and examine it closely, staring at each figure in the group in turn: she and Roberto, gazing at each other, laughing; Antonia caught as she looked demurely downwards at the slight curve of her belly under the silk of her wedding dress, Fortunata's steadfast look straight into the lens, her long neck and piled-up hair giving a youthful, inquiring look, as she stood behind Giuseppe and Lucia hunched into two chairs on the church steps. Paolo had moved as the lens shutter clicked, and was a strangely blurred image, one hand outstretched in an odd, conciliatory gesture, his mouth open, as if he were laughing, standing slightly separate from his bride. Only Serafina was missing from the photograph – managing, as always, to dominate even when absent, Fortunata thought.

She was standing by the fireplace, patiently waiting for her mother to finish her cup of tea, and avoiding looking at the photograph. Best not to think of the past, she told herself sternly, as her thoughts strayed to Roberto ... It was the future that mattered – the baby, the girls, Mamma – and, of course, Serafina. Fortunata was responsible for them all.

Lucia had drained her cup, and handed it back to her daughter, grateful. 'You're a sweet girl, Fortunata,' she said in a low voice. '*Grazie tanto*. Where are the girls?'

'Claudia is still at work,' Fortunata's voice was bright, 'and 'Tonia is asleep upstairs. 'Fina is still at the studio.' She swayed slightly in the firelight, and placed the cup and saucer on the mantelpiece, 'Can I get you more tea?'

Lucia shook her old, grey head. 'No. No more tea. Read me Giuseppe's letter again.' Fortunata sighed, this would be the third time in as many hours. Obediently, she took the creased brown envelope from behind the carriage clock on the mantelpiece, and took out her husband's letter. 'It doesn't tell us anything,' she said, wearily. 'It's been censored so heavily it hardly makes any sense.'

Lucia waved a hand, irritably. 'I know. But I need to know he's alive. Everyone else is dead — or as good as dead. Roberto's gone, Paolo's gone, Eduardo seems to have disappeared — there is only Giuseppe left.'

'I know, Mamma.' Fortunata tried to keep the irritation out of her voice. She began to read the letter, omitting the first few lines, which complained that Giuseppe had not heard from his family. Fortunata and the girls had sent letters, food parcels, even a sweater, and he had obviously received none of them. It was pointless worrying Mamma still further. Better to let her believe that Giuseppe at least knew what was going on at home.

'Onchan, Isle of Man, January 3rd. My Dear Family, I hope all is well. I kiss you all, and think of you all the time. Did you receive my last letter?'

Fortunata peered at Giuseppe's spidery handwriting. Most of the letter was written in Italian, since he had always found English difficult; and he had always struggled with writing, persuading Fortunata or Serafina to write any correspondence. Consequently his letters from the internment camp were jumbled, illegible, and sometimes incoherent.

'Life is still difficult, because we don't know what is happening. It is my turn to cook this week. I don't know how to make cabbage taste good, like your mamma.' Lucia smiled contentedly at this compliment. 'The weather is very bad. We are on the east coast of the island, and the wind seems always to be blowing. Christmas was difficult, but we have survived it. Enrico, who is in the house with me, has a wonderful tenor voice, and he cheered me and Bill and Tony with cards and bits of opera. We have a camp choir and some musicians, and there was a Christmas concert. I thought of you all as I listened to the music.'

Fortunata paused, trying to imagine Giuseppe at a music concert. Perhaps the camp would change her husband into something other than the simple road worker she had so foolishly married in an excess of duty all those years ago. She returned to the letter, criss-crossed with black inky blocks where a censor had deleted whole paragraphs, as well as odd words.

'Our main problem is boredom. I have been attending English classes, organised by some of the men in the camp who are professors. We are reading poems by Wordsworth and Byron. Enrico and Bill are very keen on football, and have joined the camp team. They play teams from other camps. Tony is only eighteen. He gets very depressed.' (There was a long censored piece at this point). 'I miss you all. Have you heard from—' Fortunata coughed, to cover her mistake, for Giuseppe had been asking about Roberto, Joe and Paolo. No point in reminding Mamma.

'You should take a shot of brandy for that throat,' said Lucia.

'That's the end of the letter.' Fortunata returned it to its envelope and then to its place on the mantelpiece. She crossed over to the window. Beyond the net curtains and the black drapes, the sky was already darkening, even though it was only four o'clock. She gazed upwards, at the enormous full moon hanging over the roofs of the houses opposite. 'A bomber's moon . . .' she murmured, wearily.

'What did you say?'

'Nothing, Mamma.' She drew the curtains across, blocking out the persistent glow she had seen somewhere in the direction of St Paul's Cathedral. That huge fire from the previous night's raid was still burning. There was something too seductive about this new night sky over London, she decided, as she checked to make sure that no tell-tale chinks of light were filtering through to the outside. On the few occasions she had lingered too long staring upwards during a raid, she had been mesmerised by the strange beauty of the falling shells, sparkling brilliantly in the blackness, the criss-crossing bands of the searchlights, the white-green glow of the incendiary bombs hissing down into the deserted streets.

Lucia interrupted her thoughts. 'Will you write to Giuseppe tonight?' she asked. 'Will you ask him if he would like me to knit him a scarf? I've finished the gloves for Claudia, I can start a scarf . . .'

'Yes, Mamma,' said Fortunata, not really listening. She retrieved the teacup and headed towards the kitchen, listening on the way in the hall for sounds from upstairs. Antonia was evidently still asleep. Settling into her chair by the stove, Fortunata allowed herself the luxury of thinking about Joe

O'Connell. She wondered what he was doing at this moment. Her face softened as she imagined him thumping the table passionately at a Council meeting, his freckled face creased in anger as he confronted some war office bureaucrat about provision of shelters, lack of fire hydrants, or accommodation for refugees. Dear Joe. She had not really seen him to talk to for over a week, although she had glimpsed him emerging from the Council offices two days previously, as she trudged past, on her way to the Underground. He had been talking to some solemn-faced men in expensive-looking overcoats, but he had seen her. They had exchanged the briefest of glances, and he had slowly raised his hand. She leaned back in her chair, smiling sadly at the memory. She would probably have to make do with that encounter to get her through the next few weeks. There was little chance of seeing Joe, not for a while; for Serafina's baby was already overdue . . .

The wailing rise and fall of the siren woke Fortunata earlier than usual that night. She struggled into her dressing-gown in the darkness, shaking the sleeping Claudia next to her. Shivering, they groped for their 'air-raid bags' and made for the landing, where Antonia, clutching a pile of blankets, was calling.

'Nonna! Come on, it's the alert, Nonna!' Behind Lucia's bedroom door, they could hear protestations.

'I'm not coming! It's too cold! I'd rather die in my bed!'

The siren died away, leaving only the sound of an old woman grumbling for a moment. Then, as they all stood listening, they heard the awful, uneven throb of bombers passing over Clerkenwell.

'Mamma! *Subito!*' Fortunata pushed open the door, angrily. 'I won't let you stay here, so either you come quietly, or we'll drag you downstairs. Where's 'Fina?' She had suddenly realised that Serafina was not one of the shadowy shapes on the landing. They flinched, as they heard the first crump of a bomb finding its target. Lucia appeared in the doorway.

'Hurry up, Nonna!' They clattered downstairs fearfully to their shelter in the cupboard under the stairs. Serafina was waiting for them in the hall, a strange bulky figure in a long nightdress.

'I know this is a bad time,' she said to no one in particular, 'but I think I'm in labour.'

Another bang outside, louder this time, caused them all to rush for cover, crushing together through the narrow cupboard door. A few moments of chaos ensued, as they struggled to their positions in the blackness. Then Fortunata turned on the torch she kept in her bag, and they were all illumined, faces strangely yellow, in the glow. Lucia was huddled down on the mattress at the back of the cupboard space, where the angle of the stairs above was at its lowest. Antonia leaned over and gently covered her with a blanket. Lucia smiled at her granddaughter in the gloom, grateful for the comfort offered by Antonia's nervous grin, helping to ward off the awful terror of the stifling cupboard and the hellish sounds now raining down on them from the sky.

Fortunata peered at Serafina in the darkness. She was leaning against the electricity meter, one hand clutching her back, her face twisted in pain. Fortunata crawled over to her. A terrible crunching noise halted her.

'Sounds like a close one,' said Claudia, busy with a flask and mugs. Fortunata reached Serafina's side, and shone the torch slightly more in her direction. Serafina's eyes were wide, and her lips were white and dry.

'How often are the pains?'

'Every couple of minutes,' said Serafina, suddenly gripped by a spasm which caused her to arch her back and groan. Fortunata put a tentative hand on her step-daughter's arm. She immediately felt the muscles tense beneath her fingers. 'Try to hang on . . .' she said, uselessly. 'We can't get you to a doctor just yet. Try to hang on 'til the raid is over.'

Above the noise of the bombs and the crashing down of distant buildings, they could hear a loud, insistent bell.

'Must be the bookies,' Claudia said, in her peculiarly calm and distant way '– their burglar alarm.'

'Oh God,' murmured Antonia, hugging her knees and quivering, 'the bombers are right on top of us!'

'Can I smell gas?' Fortunata asked them. They all sniffed, and then cowered as another bomb landed somewhere close by. Antonia was crying. 'The street's gone, I bet the whole street's gone . . .' She clutched at Serafina. 'I want to go out to a shelter, I don't feel safe here, the house is going to be hit, I know it is . . .'

'Don't be silly, 'Tonia,' Serafina was trying to sound stern, through the agony of another shooting pain in her lower back.

'You can't go, I need you here – the baby's coming.' She grabbed her sister's sleeve, pointedly ignoring Fortunata. For a moment Antonia seemed to calm down. She crawled back to peer at Lucia, quivering under the blanket, trying to sleep. Then there was a loud, dull thud above, the walls seemed to rock, and plaster dust began to trickle ominously from the stairs overhead.

'The house has been hit!' Antonia sobbed, 'we'll be trapped here!' As if to echo her words, they heard the terrible sound of splintering glass, and an awesome rumble began to shake the foundations.

'Not now!' Serafina glared at the other occupants of the makeshift shelter, all oddly powdered a dusty white in the torchlight. 'We won't die now! My baby's coming – it's coming! We won't die!' Antonia could not be appeased. She knelt, crying helplessly, in the darkness, rendered immobile, paralysed with terror. '*Mamma mia!* It hurts so much!' Serafina was panting. 'The baby is coming now, I feel it –' Fortunata crawled towards her again, and felt her knees suddenly warm and sticky. She shone her torch at the floor.

'Your waters have broken,' she told Serafina, 'we'll have to prepare for you to have the baby here.' Serafina looked at her coolly, and nodded. 'All right. I'm ready.' But still Antonia cried, inconsolable, panic-stricken.

'Stop it, 'Tonia! Pull yourself together and help me here – 'Fina's going to have her baby and you have to help – do you understand?' Fortunata tried shaking her, but it was no use; she had collapsed into a limp heap, her bones made soft with fear.

It was Serafina who thought of a way of distracting her. She leaned forward gingerly, and pulled at her sister's sleeve. ''Tonia,' she said, trying to keep the pain and fear out of her voice, ''Tonia, I need you to fetch something for me.'

Antonia looked up, her tear-blotched face curious. 'You mean me, go out into the house?' Serafina nodded. 'I left my little Madonna upstairs – you know the one from Nemi, the one I always kiss for luck? I've left it behind – it's on the little shelf in the kitchen—'

'I know where it is.' Antonia was wiping her eyes, gulping back the tears. 'You want me to fetch it for you?'

'Yes, please—' Serafina glanced at Fortunata, who had been about to object, 'and while you're in the kitchen, can you bring some towels from the airing cupboard?' Fortunata understood then. Serafina was right. The baby couldn't arrive like this, in a filthy cupboard on dust-covered blankets, with a hysterical, screaming girl in the way. 'I don't think I can have this baby without my little Madonna to look over me,' Serafina was telling her sister, persuasively. 'You remember how all you wanted when – when you lost the baby was to hang on to Papa's little dog statue? Well I feel the same about the Nemi Madonna. Can you fetch it?' Antonia looked over for a second at where her grandmother lay sleeping, and hesitated. 'She's fine,' Serafina said, gritting her teeth as she felt another spasm creeping up on her, 'I need you, Antonia – don't forget the towels!' and she flung herself backwards with a grunt of pain as the terrible pull of labour struck her body. Antonia pushed open the door and crawled out into the blackness.

'One, two, three, four . . .' Claudia was counting quietly to herself. 'They're still very close,' she told her mother, 'they must have targeted Clerkenwell this time.'

Fortunata was struggling in the dark to make Serafina more comfortable, and hardly heard. 'Get 'Fina some tea from the flask,' she commanded.

'I don't want tea,' said Serafina.

'It will help to calm you and the baby – Damn you Jerries!' replied Fortunata as another deafening crash heralded a bomb nearby. 'Why tonight of all nights?'

Claudia was pouring tea calmly into a tin mug. 'Perhaps the child is cursed,' she said.

Serafina struggled to sit up. 'What do you mean, Claudia?' she asked, suddenly afraid for the first time in that long, agonising, noisy night.

Fortunata glared at Claudia in the gloom. 'She doesn't mean anything. Be quiet, girl, if you can't be helpful.'

'No,' Serafina gripped a dusty pipe above her head and managed to sit up a little. 'I want it said.' Her eyes were deep black in the torchlight. 'You all have things to say, but you never say them. We never say what we mean in this family—' She broke off, as the pain returned. Silently, she gripped the pipe with white knuckles, swallowing the desire to scream, and grimly hung on, sweating, until the contraction had passed.

Claudia handed her the mug of tea. 'Perhaps God is punishing you,' she said, 'because you won't tell us who the baby's father is!'

'That's not true!' Fortunata stared at her daughter, aghast, 'we know who it is. It's just unfortunate that Eduardo was called back before—'

Serafina was still staring at Claudia. 'But why should God punish me?' she asked, ignoring Fortunata. 'I've confessed my sin, I've done penance. I've told the truth to God the Father and God the Son and the Blessed Virgin, so why should my child be cursed?' She felt a soft touch, like a butterfly, on one foot, then the other. It was Claudia's gentle fingers, soothingly massaging the soles of her feet. That lovely, slightly mad face smiled at her from the corner of the shelter, as above their heads an enormous crash signalled a door caving in somewhere.

'Because,' said Claudia, 'you are hurting us all. You are killing our family. Mamma is in agony – how will she tell Papa about you? What will he say when he finds you are not married? The war will be over soon, and Papa will be freed. How can we ever be a family again, like we were?'

'But it's not my fault!' Serafina, in spite of her pain, was enraged. 'What about Fortunata? She sent Paolo away, and now he's disappeared forever! She broke up the family, she left Antonia a widow – or as good as one. I haven't hurt anyone!'

Fortunata shook her, shouting above the crash of falling masonry, 'Shut up, 'Fina! Always going on about Paolo! Shut up and concentrate on the baby – can't you push? Aren't you ready to push?'

Serafina shook her head, 'No, not yet – I can't . . . Claudia, – don't say the baby is cursed, please don't say it, *per piacere* don't say it.'

Claudia cringed as a loud whistling in the sky and a silence culminated in an earth-shaking crump somewhere outside. 'Eduardo, Paolo –' she panted, crouched over the array of blankets and provisions in her corner, like a gypsy woman selling her wares, 'you always talk about them, you and Mamma. What about Roberto? Why do you never talk about Roberto?'

She was silenced by her mother, who delivered a brutal slap across her face. '*Basta!* No more! We won't talk about Roberto, you hear me? He was too good to live, he was an angel, a saint – I don't want to hear his name dragged into family quarrels—'

Serafina was smiling in the darkness. 'Poor Fortunata,' she said, 'how difficult this is for you! A true challenge to your so-called liberal attitudes!' She stopped again, as another pain and, almost simultaneously, another bomb, descended.

In the night, the cries of the victims buried under the rubble of a devastated Little Italy grew fainter, as the breath slowly left their bodies. But in the house in Grape Street, as the night sky became streaked with the grey of dawn, a louder cry could be heard, a strong and lusty cry, celebrating the renewal of life, as tenacious in this collapsing, chaotic world as the rosebay willowherb already sprouting in the rubble heaps of the city.

They sat, incongruously, on the horsehair sofa in the street, sipping hot sweet tea brought to them by a plump and kind WVS lady, comforting in her sensible tweed suit and felt hat.

'Just don't worry about anything for the moment,' she had said, without a hint of irony, as she took the teapot away. They could still hear the jangling bell of the ambulance taking Serafina and her newly born daughter to hospital. Claudia still shivered uncontrollably, and was spilling most of her tea. Silently, Fortunata took the mug away from her and placed it carefully on the pavement as if it were a piece of Dresden china. Claudia seemed not to notice. Fortunata hugged her daughter, once, hard, and then released her. Poor baby. She had suffered such awful grief with enormous heroism; but this last blow seemed too much. Fortunata rubbed her eyes and peered down the street, trying to make sense of the devastation. Several houses opposite theirs had disappeared, and the house next door had lost most of the front bedrooms, leaving Signor Vittorini's brass bed and ancient wardrobe obscenely exposed. Fortunata half noticed a stocking dangling from the tree outside their house, looking like an amputated leg. A water main had burst in Vine Street, and water was gushing along the road. Behind her, she could hear the faint crackle of flames. She remembered Joe O'Connell then, suddenly, and an evening many years ago, when she had talked to him about Dante's *Inferno*, and tried to describe to him the nightmarish visions of this hell that had haunted her since she had first read the book in her teens ... She had seen herself and Joe as Paolo and Francesca, doomed by their adulterous love to eternal hellfire ... Surely this was it, this was the hell she had pictured. Through her fatigue, she saw the dirt-streaked face of Anna Vittorini loom in front of her.

'I can't find the bleedin' cat,' Anna said loudly. 'Poor thing's hiding somewhere. How can we go and stay with Auntie Vi in Walthamstow if the cat's still here? Who'll feed him?'

'I'll feed him, Anna,' Fortunata said, dully. 'You go along and look after your mother. I'll feed the cat.'

Down the street she could see her own mother, Lucia, wandering about on the arm of a neighbour, shaking her head and making the sign of the cross, her lips moving ceaselessly. Fortunata sighed. Mamma would not go back into their own house, but kept insisting on a tour of inspection of the street. Whenever anyone consented to accompany her she would lead the way, loudly bemoaning the fate of her neighbours, their tragedy, their misfortune. It was as if this distance from the awfulness of events in the Vialli house was her only way of dealing with the devastation.

Fortunata sipped her tea, still dazed, and then willed herself to look at their own house. Incredibly the facade was intact, although all the windows had been blown out. The blackout curtains in the downstairs front room billowed forlornly into the street, and Fortunata briefly glimpsed the sideboard, still upright, with the wedding photo sitting exactly where it had been when she read Giuseppe's letter the previous night. Was it really only last night? She sighed again. So much could happen in a few hours, it didn't seem possible. People could be alive one minute, and pale and cold the next. People died, babies were born, houses fell down, cats went missing, tea was made ... She smiled at the idiocy of this thought. How extremely British I really am, she thought with some surprise, to be thinking of tea at a time like this ... Yet most of our suffering has been because we are Italian.

Detached, she watched a gang of small boys run excitedly down the street towards the bombed-out houses, only to be turned away by a weary policeman. They were searching for shrapnel to add to their collections of German trophies. Disgruntled, they trailed back towards the main road. 'Let's go down to the church,' Fortunata heard one of them say, 'maybe that's been bombed, and we won't have to go to Communion class any more!' She shuddered. Surely not the church as well . . . Better not to tell Mamma.

Swaying slightly, Fortunata got to her feet. Immediately the WVS woman was at her side. 'What is it, dear?' Fortunata smiled at her wearily. 'I'm all right, really. I just want to go in and have a look around – see what's damaged.' The other woman looked dubious, so Fortunata added persuasively, 'If you could keep an eye on my daughter here, and my mother, I'd be most grateful. I'm all right, really. I promise I won't wander off.'

'I don't know if they've made the house safe yet,' the woman said.

Claudia suddenly shifted and stared up at her mother. 'Did 'Fina go to bed with my husband?' she asked. 'Is that Roberto's daughter she had?'

The WVS lady shifted uncomfortably, nonplussed. Fortunata swallowed hard, 'Go with this lady, Claudia, and have some tea. You're exhausted.'

Obediently, Claudia stood up. 'Did she sleep with Roberto? I thought that baby looked like Roberto.'

Fortunata flashed a pleading glance at the WVS lady. 'Please take her for a cup of tea,' she said, 'I think she's upset.'

As she was led away, Claudia spoke conversationally to her uniformed companion. 'Adultery is a sin isn't it? The Bible says Thou shalt not commit adultery . . .'

Fortunata stepped gingerly over the broken heaps of bricks and shards of glass strewn on the pavement. The front gate was hanging drunkenly from one hinge. Carefully, she opened it and headed towards the front door. She was met there by a fireman.

'Sorry, love,' he said, 'it's not safe. I can't let you in.'

'But it's my house.'

He pressed his lips together, regretfully. 'I'm very sorry, love.'

Fortunata hesitated. 'Could you fetch something for me?'

'Depends where it is, love.'

'Oh, it's just through here—' She pointed in the direction of

172

the front room and the flapping curtains. 'There's a photograph on the sideboard – a wedding picture.'

'All right, I'll fetch it for you. Go to the window and I'll pass it through.'

She heard him go down the hall, crunching glass as he went, and she in turn trod her way carefully to the window. She saw the fireman enter the room, sidling past the upturned armchairs and smashed ornaments.

'Yes – that's it!' He came towards her and handed the photograph across. 'Thank you,' she said.

'Just a minute, love.' He was searching in his jacket pocket for something, and Fortunata waited patiently. 'Here – they took it off your daughter when they found her. She was holding it. I thought you might like it.'

It was the Nemi Madonna, streaked with soot, but still calm and smiling, its delicate plaster hands clasped together. Fortunata took it and turned numbly away. As she reached the gate she almost walked into a tall figure standing there, imposing, in a long dark coat.

'Fortunata – it's me—' He held her at arm's length, looking anxiously into her face. 'It's Joe. I came as soon as I heard that Grape Street had been hit.' She stared at him. 'Tell me what happened,' he said, 'tell me what I can do.' Fortunata was vaguely aware of Mrs Vittorini staring at her further down the street. She opened the gate, and walked blindly out.

'Just walk next to me,' she said. 'Just walk, don't touch me, Joe, or I'll go to pieces.' They began to walk slowly together down the middle of the street, through the steady stream of water still flooding over the cobblestones.

'Serafina had a daughter,' she said, carefully negotiating a pothole. 'She says she's going to call her Maria, after her mother.'

'Fortunata, dearest,' Joe was saying quietly, 'is anyone hurt?'

'Antonia died, Joe.' Fortunata avoided looking at him, still staring ahead. 'She went to fetch the Madonna for Serafina, and she was killed.' They had stopped. He gazed down at her, all the love and compassion he felt for this woman etched on his freckled face.

'I wish I could hold you,' he said. 'I wish I could take you away—'

She looked down at his feet, at his fine black leather shoes, now dusty and wet. 'Please, Joe,' she said. 'I can't bear it. I can't bear it. Here—' She handed him the little statue. He held it, puzzled.

'What do you want me to do with it?' he asked.

The little Madonna looked blandly at him, her gaze unclouded. Fortunata was turning away.

'I want you to take it to Serafina in hospital. I want you to tell her not to come back. She won't be welcome. The Council will help her find a place. I can't forgive her, she killed my 'Tonia. My 'Tonia's dead because of her. I know I'm being unreasonable –' Joe tried to demur – 'I know I'm asking you to do an awful, impossible thing. I know what Serafina thinks of you.' Fortunata laughed a little dry laugh. 'She hates you – like she hates me.'

Joe stumbled slightly in the gutter. 'Fortunata, I have to tell you – about Serafina—'

'Don't tell me anything more, please. My head is full of Serafina. Always her, always her getting in the way of everything, spoiling everything.'

'I have to tell you something.'

For the first time she stopped and looked up at him, her dark eyes still as beautiful as ever. 'Whatever it is, it's of no importance now. My daughter's dead. Antonia's dead.'

Joe drew in a breath, sharply. He turned his hat in his hand, uncharacteristically hesitant.

Before he could speak again, Fortunata touched his arm, gently. 'Please do this, Joe – for me. Take the damned Madonna and give it to that cursed girl. I hope it brings her joy.' Still clutching the family wedding photo to her breast, she left him, heading off towards her mother, and her one remaining daughter, her head held high, her shoulders square and determined.

CHAPTER EIGHT

1945

THE CHOIR OF St Peter's had completed the final glorious hymn, and people were beginning to shuffle out, excited at the prospect of celebrating the first day of peace. Fortunata watched Giuseppe, still on his knees, seemingly deep in prayer. How much older he seemed! and somehow smaller, greyer. She tried to remember the young man sitting in the kitchen in Grape Street sipping Benedictine all those years ago. He had been self-contained, almost heroic, made strong by suffering. Now Giuseppe seemed defeated, weakened by the years of internment. It was as if what had made him Giuseppe Florio had seeped away and left a flabby facsimile of her husband. He had never been an easy man to live with, but he had had a fire within him, something very volatile and Italian, and now that had died. That drooping grey head bent over the pew seemed to belong to a stranger.

She shifted slightly in her seat, wanting to leave. She was tired of returning the smiles of her neighbours as they moved slowly up the aisle to the exit. She wondered briefly if smiling was appropriate. How was she expected to look? Joyful at the return of her husband, happy that the war was finally over? Or downcast at the memory of Antonia and devastated by the death of her beloved Mamma Lucia last year? She was exhausted, that was all she knew, and she had a telephone call to make. And where was Claudia, who had promised to come to the Thanksgiving Mass with them but had disappeared after breakfast? This had not improved Giuseppe's mood. To him, it was further confirmation of the collapse of everything Italian. Disobedient daughters were somehow modern, British, alarming. But then like many of the older Italians, Giuseppe's powerful sense of identity had been badly shaken by the events of the war. He and men like him had considered

175

themselves to be 'good Italians', maintaining everything they held dear in what was to them a foreign land – but a land and people that had always been benevolent towards them. Now that had been destroyed forever. It had all been a lie. The British had never trusted them at all. Everything they had worked for had been destroyed, and they did not seem to have the energy to start again.

Fortunata gazed at the ceiling, hoping she looked soulful, in order to avoid Mrs Vittorini who was hovering nearby. She read the words above the gold arches slowly, mouthing them to herself, as if in prayer: *Tibi dabo claves regni caelorum* . . .' Mrs Vittorini moved on. The words meant, 'I will give you the keys to the kingdom of heaven.' Fortunata had been staring at those words every Sunday since she was a child. She sighed. Odd that they should seem so comforting, when she had long since abandoned Catholicism in favour of politics. Only duty and a sense of tradition kept Fortunata from refusing to attend Mass. It seemed easier just to go. Refusal would mean bitter arguments, the shock and disgust of her family, a betrayal of Bruno and Lucia, for whom the Church had been so important. There had been enough argument in the house since her husband's return. The news of Serafina's illegitimate child had been like a mortal blow to Giuseppe. It was the final collapse of every standard he had upheld, every strict rule he had brought with him across the sea from the village of Nemi. But his internment had perhaps given him a glimpse of his own mortality, a sense that he must make the most of whatever time was left to him. For after a few weeks' silent brooding on the matter, he announced that he had decided to forgive Serafina. After all, she had given birth to the last Florio, small consolation in view of the terrible sin she had committed, but consolation none the less. He would go and visit his outcast daughter. There would be a family reconciliation. But he had reckoned without the anger festering in his wife's heart.

Fortunata had remained adamant that she wanted nothing further to do with Serafina. On this one matter she remained defiant, full of her old spirit. She had told Giuseppe firmly that he could visit Serafina and her child, but he had no right to expect her to do the same. She had made up her mind. She never wanted to see Serafina, or her child, again. There had been terrible scenes, tears, bitterness, but Fortunata had won. Giuseppe went to visit his daughter alone, and she was not spoken of again in the Florio house. Fortunata had won that battle, but at some cost to her peace of mind. The worst moment had been when she had had to go and comfort Rosa Williams, shattered by the death of Eduardo, who had been killed somewhere in France. Every time she had looked at Rosa, stunned and tearful, clutching the dreaded telegram, she had been forced to think of Serafina, who must be equally devastated. She was probably weeping even now, alone somewhere, uncomforted, her hope of happiness with the gentle Eduardo gone forever. Fortunata lowered her eyes again, depressed. Giuseppe was not the only one feeling the weariness of defeat that day.

He chose that moment to look round at her. 'Help me get up,' he said. As she moved to help him, Father Joseph, himself an old man, came to her assistance. Together they got Giuseppe to his feet and leaning on his stick.

'Thank you, Father,' said Fortunata, exchanging a smile with the genial priest who seemed to have been present at all the key moments in her life. 'It's a wonderful day, isn't it?'

'Hard to believe it's really over,' he said, one arm still under Giuseppe's elbow as the three of them made their way slowly towards the main door. 'It's been a hard time for all of us. Now we must put it all behind us somehow. Get on with the present.' You mean with mass unemployment and slum housing, Fortunata thought, but decided against speaking. Giuseppe grunted, unwilling to participate in the small talk. Father Joseph shot a sideways glance at the man hobbling next to him. 'We have to try and keep alive the memory of those we lost,' he said softly, directing the words at Giuseppe, 'but we must get on with our lives.' Giuseppe had stopped, as if to argue. Any moment now, they'll start talking about Serafina, thought Fortunata. Desperate, she spoke before Giuseppe could.

'Father, I wonder if you would do me a great kindness.' The priest looked expectant. She hesitated and then plunged on. 'I – I wonder if you would mind waiting here with Giuseppe for a moment, while I nip over the road and make a telephone call? I wouldn't normally ask, only—'

'Of course, I'd be delighted,' said the old priest, smiling, 'Giuseppe and I have a lot to catch up on—'

He was interrupted. 'Who are you phoning?' asked Giuseppe crossly. Her eyes never seemed to quite meet his since he had come home from the Isle of Man.

'I thought perhaps Claudia might be over at the Besagnis'. I've got the number of their shop somewhere. I thought – I thought I'd try—'

'All right, all right.' Giuseppe sat down heavily in a nearby pew.

Fortunata relaxed, the danger over. 'Thank you, Father,' she said, and as she genuflected before the altar, she murmured ironically to herself, 'Father, forgive me, for I know not what I do . . .'

There was a queue outside the telephone box on Rosebery Avenue. Fortunata waited impatiently for a few moments, but the man speaking excitedly into the receiver seemed to have made contact with some long-lost relative and was feeding pennies endlessly into the slot. The woman in front of Fortunata turned and said, 'This is going to take all day! I got to phone my boy, he's been wounded and he's in hospital in Plymouth. I got to find out if he's all right . . .' Fortunata made sympathetic noises and backed away.

'Never mind, love,' said a woman in the queue behind Fortunata, 'at least there's no more Hitler.'

Fortunata turned to smile at her, 'And no more Mussolini,' she said, '– even better!' The queue began a lively discussion about the shooting of Italy's fascist leader by partisans. The man in the telephone kiosk continued to talk. This was hopeless. Time was ticking away and Giuseppe would be getting annoyed and anxious for his lunch. Everyone in London wanted to telephone someone, today of all days.

In desperation she headed away from the church, trying to remember where she could find another telephone. Although there was a slight drizzle, the streets were crowded and noisy, with Union Jacks hanging from the windows, and people decked out in red, white and blue. Someone somewhere was blowing on a trumpet, a bad version of 'Rule Britannia', and a passing car hooted in reply. In spite of the grey spring morning an air of nervous celebration pervaded Little Italy. Fortunata noted wryly that most of the people waving flags and singing were young. The old went quietly about their business as usual, unable to shake off their ambivalent feelings about the Allied victory which had cost them all dear. She stopped outside the bakery in Summer Street. Perhaps Mr Ruffoni would let her use the telephone at the back of the shop . . .

So intent was she on her plan that she failed to notice a small girl leaving the crowded shop as she entered. They cannoned into one another, and the child's string bag flew across the floor of the bakery.

'My tomatoes!' wailed the little girl, 'Mamma will be furious . . .' She raised a grubby anxious face to Fortunata. 'You've spoiled my tomatoes,' she said accusingly. 'Look, they're squashed. You'll have to pay for them.' Fortunata could not help smiling at the small angry figure standing with her hands on her hips in a parody of an Italian mamma. She ruffled the child's curls and gave her some pennies, noticing the brightness of her blue eyes. 'Here,' she said, 'tell your mamma it's all Mrs Florio's fault!' Leaving the child open-mouthed she pushed her way to the counter.

Fortunately it was Angela Ruffoni serving today. She and Fortunata had been at the same class at school. Pink-faced and busy, she glanced at Fortunata signalling to her, and merely shouted, 'Go ahead! It's out the back, in the passage. Leave the money in the tin.' Gratefully, Fortunata slipped under the counter-flap and hurried through to the back of the shop, where all was cool and dark. Trembling, she dialled the number. Let him be there, please let him be there . . .

He answered almost immediately, his formal councillor's tone giving way to that joyful lilt she loved so much, as he recognised her voice.

'I've only got a minute, Joe,' she said, foolishly smiling into the receiver.

'Can we meet today?' he asked, his voice low. Someone else must be in his office, she thought.

'I – I don't know, it'll be difficult to get away . . .'

'It's always difficult,' he said, making an unsuccessful attempt to sound lighthearted. 'Please try. How about two o'clock, Lyons Corner House, on Piccadilly?'

'It'll be chaos there today.'

'I know. That's why I chose it. We need a bit of chaos.'

She hesitated. 'Not two. Maybe three o'clock. I'll do my best—'

'I'll be waiting.'

'I may not be able—'

'I'll be waiting anyway.' There was a silence, only the buzzing of the telephone wire between them. Both were reluctant to say goodbye.

'Joe?' she said, after a moment.

'Yes?'

'Joe – if I don't come, it's not because I don't love you, it's not because I won't have tried—'

'I know.' There was silence again. Someone spoke to Joe and he answered, his voice muffled, his hand over the phone. Fortunata's heart ached for him.

'I have to go,' he said, 'Victory Parade from the Town Hall.'

'Me too.' She cradled the phone lovingly. One of the Ruffoni boys, his hair white with flour, passed her and grinned. Sometimes Fortunata had the uncomfortable feeling that everyone knew about Joe . . .

'I'll do my best, Joe,' she said, furtive, desperate, knowing he was about to put the phone down and this tenuous connection would cease, 'I really will. Goodbye.'

'I told you. I'll wait for you. Goodbye.' There was a click, then the dialling tone.

Distracted, Fortunata wandered out to the shop again. '*Grazie*, Angela,' she said flatly, handing her sixpence. 'I might as well have a loaf of bread while I'm here.'

'Just in time.' Angela passed her a floury white bloomer. 'We're shutting up the shop at twelve – going to the West End for the celebrations. You going?'

'I hope so, I really hope so.' Fortunata's tone was so fervent that Angela looked up from the till, surprised, as her old schoolfriend hurried from the shop.

Lunch came and went, and still Claudia had not come home. Fortunata washed the dishes at the kitchen sink, staring out at an early blooming geranium in a pot on the windowsill. Giuseppe read the paper in his chair by the stove.

'I think the sun's coming out,' Fortunata remarked, propping plates on the draining-board. 'There should be a good crowd in the West End. You should go and join in, Giuseppe. I'm sure Claudia will take you.'

He did not look up from his newspaper. 'Churchill's on the wireless at three,' he said. 'I want to listen to what he has to say. Anyway, Claudia isn't here.'

'I'm sure they'll rig up loudspeakers outside the Houses of Parliament,' Fortunata tried to keep her tone light. 'Surely they'll realise most of London will be there?'

Giuseppe looked at her. 'Exactly. Most of London. Not really the place for a suspected Italian fascist, is it?'

She crashed a saucepan crossly in the metal bowl. 'You'll be the only one taking that attitude. I know the Ruffonis are going. Angela told me they're going to close the bakery—'

The front door was heard to open and close again noisily. Claudia had come home. She burst into the kitchen, a lively young woman of twenty-one, her face bright with happiness. Behind her hovered a sheepish young man in a sailor's uniform.

Claudia crossed the room to kiss her father. 'Papa, Mamma – you remember George?'

'Of course. It's George Winston, isn't it?' Fortunata smiled kindly at him. Claudia had met him during a bombing raid a couple of years earlier, and they had conducted a spasmodic courtship, mainly by post. Giuseppe made a polite noise at George but did not get up. The memory of the day of his return from internment still rankled. He had hurried home, intent on seeing his beloved family, and had found instead this pasty-faced English boy on the doorstep, his arm round Claudia, behaving as though he owned the house. Giuseppe tried to avoid talking to him. He did not approve of his daughter seeing a non-Italian. It was further evidence of the demise of the old world he knew and loved.

'I'll make some tea,' Fortunata said, to cover the discomfort of Giuseppe's evident disapproval. She turned to fill the kettle. 'I'm afraid you missed lunch.'

'Where on earth did you get that flower at this time of year?' Giuseppe was asking his daughter, sounding irritable but unable to keep the light of paternal love from his eyes. Fortunata turned to look.

'It's an orchid,' said Claudia, proudly.

'I can see that.'

George shuffled and coughed in the doorway. 'I bought it for her, Mr Florio.'

'It's lovely, George,' said Fortunata. 'Why don't you sit down? Tea won't be long.'

'I wanted something simpler, really – like a rose. Something less exotic,' Claudia said. Then, 'We've got some news, Papa, Mamma.'

Fortunata, spooning tea into the teapot, said, 'Yes?' absently. She heard the rustle of Giuseppe's newspaper as he finally put it down.

'Me and George – we got married this morning. Finsbury Town Hall.'

There was an awful, extended silence, broken only by the hissing of the kettle on the hob.

Fortunata sank down into a chair at the kitchen table, trying to absorb Claudia's words. Married! Her mind flew back to that other wedding and she saw again the strong, romantic face of Roberto Lucente as he waltzed with his new bride. They had been the epitome of everything beautiful, everything hopeful ... She looked at George Winston, still standing anxiously near the door, as if feeling he might need to make a quick exit. He looked back at her, stolid, sandy-haired, dependable.

'I'm sorry, Mrs Florio,' he said, his strong Cockney accent emphasising somehow the difference between him and this very foreign family into which he had just married. 'We wanted you – and Mr Florio – to be there, but we was offered a vacancy at the registry office for this morning, and – well – what with it being the first day of peace, and us not wanting any delay ...' his voice trailed off. Claudia went over and linked her arm through his, possessive, happy.

'Well, Papa?' she said. Giuseppe had not moved in his chair. 'Aren't you going to wish us the best?'

'Giuseppe?' Fortunata's heart sank. She knew him too well to be surprised by what followed. His hands began to tremble. Claudia's smile faltered.

'How dare you! *Non so come abbia l'ardire!*' As usual, he reverted to Italian when upset. '*E con questo – questo sconosciuto!*' He spat the word out, 'with this nobody!'

'Papa!'

'*Zitto!* Shut up!' He was trying to rise from the chair, but his legs crumpled under him and he sat down again heavily.

Fortunata got up instead, intent on calming things. 'Well

182

it's done now,' she said briskly, going to kiss her daughter and then her new son-in-law. 'It's a pity you rushed it, but it's too late for complaints. Anyway –' she turned to Giuseppe, appealing – 'it's VE day, a wonderful, historic moment, even for pacifists like me. They couldn't have chosen a better day.'

With a yell of utter fury Giuseppe managed to pull himself upright, and he lunged across the room, his arm raised, ready to strike his daughter.

'No! No! Giuseppe! I won't let you!' Fortunata leapt in front of Claudia and caught the full force of her husband's hand on her face. Claudia began to scream as Giuseppe struggled to push Fortunata aside.

'Mamma! Stop him! Papa – please don't be angry—'

'Mr Florio – please try and calm down—' George, trying to help, only worsened things by attempting to put a restraining hand on his father-in-law.

'Hands off me, you son of a whore!' roared Giuseppe, his face now a raw purple, a vein throbbing in his temple. 'Get out of my house!'

'Mr Florio—'

'You heard me—' There was a brief, ridiculous struggle and then Giuseppe crashed to the floor with a scream of pain. 'My leg! My leg!'

This was too much for Claudia, who turned and ran out of the room, sobbing. They heard the clatter of her feet on the stairs. George went to help Fortunata get her husband back into his armchair from his prone position on the lino.

'Get off me! The humiliation!' Giuseppe's eyes were full of angry tears. Fortunata could have wept for him, this once strong and still proud man, made ridiculous. The kettle began to whistle hysterically.

'Don't take any notice of him, George!' she said quickly. 'Get hold of him under his arm there – that's right. Come on, Giuseppe. Help us a little.' Slowly they transferred him from the floor to his chair, where he sank, defeated. George stood to one side, his face white.

'Mr Florio—' he began loudly, over the incessant whistle. Fortunata stopped him with a wave of her hand.

'No, George,' she said. 'Turn that kettle off and then go up and see your wife.'

'He doesn't go upstairs in my house.' Giuseppe was still trembling.

'They're married, Giuseppe.' Fortunata rubbed her face, where her husband's hand had left an ugly mark.

George hesitated, looking at Fortunata for guidance. 'Are you sure?'

'I'm sure. Go.'

'I'm sorry. I'm very sorry.'

'Just go.'

He obeyed reluctantly, closing the door quietly behind him as he left. There was blessed silence. Fortunata knelt at Giuseppe's feet, trying to absorb the shock of Claudia's announcement. Married! How could she, at a time like this? She reached out to hold his hand, which he tried to pull away. But she hung on, determined. Finally, as George's footsteps were heard on the upstairs landing, she felt his fingers relax. He had lost.

She sighed, 'It's done, Giuseppe. We have to accept it.' His face was creased with pain. She touched his leg, concerned. 'Are you all right?'

'Mrs Claudia Winston!' His voice was laden with bitterness. 'Mrs Claudia Winston!'

'These things happen. George is her choice.'

'She should have consulted us. Like I did your parents.'

She put a hand up to his face, gentle. 'Times change.'

Giuseppe's fists clenched tight again. 'Yes, times change!' he said bitterly. 'People have forgotten where they come from! Have they no pride? Italy was a great nation before all this! How can people forget so quickly?'

How can *you* forget so quickly? Fortunata thought, you who left Italy because you were persecuted!

'People are ashamed,' she said quietly, 'they want to forget the war . . .'

'And you!' He rounded on her. 'You've changed! Hob-nobbing with those English women from the factory! They used to spit on you, remember? Dirty Eyties, they called us!'

'Not those particular women.' Her voice was weary. This was not a new argument.

'Women like them! Don't you understand? They only like you because they think you're becoming like them – one of the bloody English! You're becoming integrated!' He spat the word, furious.

184

She sighed. 'Giuseppe, our daughter's English. She was born here, that makes her English. I was born here. That makes me English. We can't choose what nationality we are. Neither can George Winston.'

Giuseppe closed his eyes, his face still anguished. 'But he isn't even Italian! He isn't even a little bit Italian!'

'I know.' Again, silence.

'. . . And he isn't Roberto.' There. It was said.

Fortunata studied her husband's face surreptitiously. And you, she thought, are not Joe.

'I know,' she said. Giuseppe was still a good-looking man, although his years of captivity had scored hard lines on his face, making him taut, grim. 'But sometimes . . . Well, sometimes perhaps you're not meant to have what seems perfect. Sometimes you have to make do with second best.' Giuseppe opened his eyes again and was watching her, unsmiling. She looked down, fearing she had said too much. 'Like Claudia's orchid,' she said.

'Yes?' He was still watching, still unhappy.

'She wanted a rose, didn't she? But she – she made do with something else.' This floor needs cleaning, she thought irrationally. She gulped, then carried on, her lips trembling a little. 'She made do with something else . . . and it was all right, wasn't it? The orchid was fine. It looked lovely.'

'But it wasn't the rose,' Giuseppe growled.

'No. No, it wasn't. But she was happy with it in the end, that's what I'm trying to say.'

'But you don't believe it.'

She pulled herself up suddenly, so that her face was level with his. 'This is silly,' she said. 'We've got to find a way to accept George. He isn't Roberto, but that isn't his fault. He loves her—'

Giuseppe made a sudden movement, and held her face, trapped, in his scarred workman's hands.

'And I love you,' he said gruffly, 'you know that? I still love you.' With that his lips were on hers, passionate, suffocating. She wanted to scream, to pull away, but she knew she must not. She made herself respond, her heart sinking. Normally she would push him off with a light laugh, a joke, and once again delay the moment when she would have to be his wife again. She had managed to keep him at arm's length since his return, but his patience was running out. It seemed the more she laughingly kept him at a distance, the more he wanted her. Now the shock and anger he felt about Claudia seemed to be emerging in a sudden surge of passion for his wife, and for Claudia's sake, she must keep him sweet. This after all, was Claudia's wedding day.

'Fortunata . . .' he murmured, almost tearful, his lips on her neck, 'Fortunata, I need you so much—'

She had to think quickly. She stroked his hair, thick, dark, now streaked with silver, and whispered, 'Giuseppe! Not now . . . We've got to talk about our daughter—'

He groaned and sank back in his chair, 'They'll go to Trafalgar Square soon,' he said, 'then we'll have the house to ourselves.'

She got to her feet, her face bright. 'Let's have some tea, shall we?' she said. 'Things always look better after a cup of tea . . .'

'They'll have to have the marriage blessed by a priest.'

'Yes of course. We'll talk to Father Joseph tomorrow. Will you call the children, or shall I?' She put four cups carefully on a tray. She would never be able to meet Joe now.

Tea was an uncomfortable affair – Claudia too bright, George almost dumb with anxiety. Giuseppe, back in a position of power, was gracious and monosyllabic. Fortunata's fingers trembled as she poured the tea. Desperately she tried to maintain a semblance of normalcy, chatting about the events of the past few days: the drama of Germany's final unconditional surrender, the sight of Mrs Vittorini, very drunk, dancing a jig in the street at midnight, the wonderful sense of relief in the air. George was busy pouring his new wife a second cup of tea when there was a choked sob and Fortunata ran from the room.

'Leave her,' said Giuseppe. 'It's all this upset. Can you blame her?' The two young people looked suitably downcast, 'She'll be all right.'

'Dear Joe,' she wrote, half-blinded by tears, 'this will never work. Never, never. I can't explain to you how impossible things are. Claudia has got married and G. is furious. I can't meet you this afternoon. I just can't. I know you're sitting there now, waiting for me. I wish I was dead. I wish he was

186

dead. Please know that I love you, but this is impossible, it's killing me. I know we've said this before, but this time it really has to be. Please don't try and contact me, it will only make things harder for both of us. I release you, Joe, even if you don't want to be free. One day you'll marry someone else. You were meant for marriage, and I can't give you that. I love you, so I'm letting you go. Whenever I see a rose, I'll think of you, the real thing. Yours, Fortunata.'

She was busy writing the address on the envelope when there was a tap on the door. Hastily she folded the letter, slipped it in the envelope and sealed it. She scrabbled for a stamp in her purse, stuck it on the letter hastily and then stuffed the letter in her bag.

'Come in!' she called, wiping her eyes. She looked at herself in the mirror and a white-faced ghost looked back.

'Mamma—' Claudia's reflection appeared next to hers. They were very alike, especially today, when Fortunata, made softer by her tears, looked more like her passive and gentle daughter.

They smiled at each other. 'Forgive me, Mamma,' Claudia whispered, 'I didn't mean to hurt you. It was just that I knew how Papa would be, I knew he would say no to the wedding if I told him—'

'You're forgiven,' Fortunata hugged her, moved.

'It's just that I love George so much, Mamma, I couldn't wait. I was so frightened Papa would forbid me to see him . . .' She smiled at her mother, elated. '. . . And now it's done! I'm so happy I could dance on the roof!'

Fortunata smiled back at her. She was doing the right thing. Her family needed her. Claudia needed a shield between her new husband and her obstinate, angry father, or else this marriage could not work, and then another generation of Florios would slide into bitter division and recrimination. She could not – would not – let that happen.

'I'm sorry for rushing out like that.' She squared her shoulders. 'I'm all right now.'

'Good. Because I thought we could all go to Trafalgar Square to celebrate.'

Fortunata stared at Claudia. She had just resigned herself to an afternoon of Winston Churchill and the unwanted attentions of her husband. 'But Giuseppe wants to stay in.'

'Not now. I've persuaded him that you need an outing. He grumbled on about his legs, but you know me – I can twist him round my little finger.'

'He's agreed to go?'

Claudia nodded. 'He's even prepared to go now, before the PM's speech. So – grab your hat, Mamma, we're going to dance in the streets!'

A waitress in a silver pointed hat, grumpy about working today, approached the table. 'Can I get you anything else, sir?' she asked, pointedly removing the empty teapot. Joe O'Connell looked up at her, surprised. He had been staring, lost in thought, at the picture on the wall opposite his table, a poor print of the Houses of Parliament.

'Sorry,' he said, 'more tea, please.'

The waitress retreated, murmuring to herself about people who chose to hang about in here all day, when others would very much like to be outside . . .

Joe's eyes returned to the picture. He had been asked if he would like to stand as the new Labour Party candidate in his borough, when the next elections were held. Even though things were not looking good for the Labour Party at the moment, it was a fairly safe seat, and the chances were that he would win it. He was well known locally because of his union work and his frequent outspoken speeches in favour of nationalisation. He was popular. But did he want it? he asked himself. On the one hand it was what he had always wanted: a chance to change things – *really* change things. But then again . . . He sighed, toying with his spoon in the sugar bowl. None of this meant anything without Fortunata. It was difficult to see where he could find extra reserves of energy to fight the Conservatives in Parliament, when his fight for Fortunata exhausted him so.

Another pot of tea was slammed ungraciously on the table. Joe watched the waitress go, amused, and then looked at his watch. Half-past three. Perhaps she would still come. He looked hopefully towards the door but was rewarded only with the sight of two very old ladies leaving. Through the windows dripping with condensation he could see a massive crush of people, wild with joy, directionless, many of them drunk, some from an excess of alcohol, some simply intoxicated by this new sense of freedom. The noise, too, was new and strange – the sound of laughter, car horns, singing, after what seemed like years of silence, darkness, whispers. Even inside Lyons, the normally prim waitresses were sporting paper hats and rosettes, and the customers were loud and excited, moving among the crowded tables, strangers talking to strangers, couples kissing, a group of children in one corner singing 'Pack Up Your Troubles' noisily, unchecked by their parents. The air was full of smoke and the atmosphere was muggy and warm. Outside the sun had decided to shine, and men were in their shirtsleeves, girls in their summer frocks for the first time that year, adding to the sense of celebration.

Joe watched them, sharing the enormous relief that the cursed, unhappy war was over. It had brought so much horror with it. He doubted if London would ever be the same, so much of it was in ruins. He poured himself another cup of tea, wondering why he didn't feel the urge to go and dance in the streets with everyone else (for Joe was naturally exuberant, and the first on the floor at any dance). Of course he knew the answer. The end of the war had meant the return of Giuseppe Florio, and the end of so many hours spent with Fortunata. Now they were lucky to snatch ten minutes together. Now the sense of shame and guilt within her had returned, and she seemed more Catholic, more alien, more inaccessible. With her husband interned, Fortunata had been able to forget that she was married. Now that small freedom was gone, and with the freedom of the world being celebrated all around him, Joe recognised sadly that he was just beginning his own captivity, lost forever to the pleasures of a normal life, a marriage, children; doomed instead to an obsession for a woman who was married to someone else.

There was a small commotion in the doorway, as a group entering the tea-room collided with a family leaving. Coming in were two soldiers arm-in-arm with a young woman in red, and behind them a small, glum-looking child eating an ice-cream.

'Teas all round!' yelled one of the soldiers, a thin red-faced young man with a fine down of pale hair on his chin and several pimples. He looked like a schoolboy in the wrong uniform.

'Come on! We're gasping for a cuppa!' the young woman

said with a tipsy giggle, her hat tilted too far over her forehead, a red feather at an alarming angle.

Joe pulled back out of sight, tense, staring, as the group settled themselves noisily into the window seat vacated by the family. He had recognised the young woman. It was Serafina Florio.

He peered carefully at her, unseen at his table in an alcove. Yes, it was definitely Serafina. He had not seen her since the day he had visited her in hospital, just after the birth of her daughter, when, under instructions from Fortunata, he had handed over the little Nemi Madonna and mumbled that she would no longer be welcome at the house in Grape Street.

She had not changed a great deal in the intervening years, except that perhaps her body was now slightly more voluptuous, her face fuller. She had lost that anxious, pleading look which had characterised her teenage years, and she was now confident, outgoing, vivacious. Looking now at that vibrant, laughing face, he remembered how she had looked in the hospital. He had handed her the little statuette, and she had looked at it for a long moment, as if puzzled, trying to piece together Joe's words. Then she had kissed the head of the statue and looked at him steadily.

'Did you tell her?' she asked. 'Did you tell Fortunata about us?'

He had shifted uncomfortably, remembering that encounter in Fleet Street, the terrible desire he had felt for her on that desperately hot summer night. 'There was nothing to tell.'

'No?' Still her eyes had not left his face. Then she had merely said, 'Goodbye, Mr O'Connell,' and had closed her eyes, dismissive. Joe had walked away, ashamed.

He looked at the little girl in the brown coat, licking her ice-cream solemnly, oblivious to the noise in the café. She had rubbed a space in the steamed-up window and was staring out at the crowds. This, then, must be that child. She must be five now.

Serafina was now teasing the other soldier who was older, thicker set, with a more cynical-looking face. She was waving a cigarette at him, then snatching it away, laughing, as he went to grab it. Finally he caught hold of her wrist, hard, and pushed his face near hers. Joe watched her red mouth curve into that knowing smile. Her moment of power had arrived.

The soldier leaned forward to kiss her, and Joe shuddered a little, trying to suppress a feeling of disgust. She was drunk, that was all ... and the scene reminded him too much of the way she had taunted and teased him. Serafina knew a lot about men, but it was calculated, lacking in fire. Unlike Fortunata ...

It was approaching four o'clock. He knew Fortunata would not come now. He signalled to the waitress for his bill, and as he did so, he caught the eye of Serafina's daughter, who had finished her ice-cream and was sitting looking around her, her hands resting placidly in her lap. She gazed at him solemnly from across the room, her eyes a surprising blue, and then she looked away, bored.

Joe hurried from the Corner House, unnerved by the unexpected sighting of Fortunata's step-daughter and her child, and strangely depressed by the memory of that small, sad face in the middle of all the celebrations.

He turned down Piccadilly, cursing his own inability to relish this day as others were. It was as if he was dogged by the past, unable to look forward, standing on the sidelines wistfully watching the pleasures of others, like a spectre at the feast.

The crush was almost overwhelming, even for a big man like Joe. For a while he was forced along the pavement by the sheer pressure of the crowd. Somewhere in the distance a band was playing. A horse reared and whinnied nearby and there was a great burst of laughter over some unseen joke somewhere across the packed street. Joe found himself finally on the edge of Trafalgar Square. He clung to a lampost for a moment, exhausted by his involuntary journey. The famous lions could hardly be seen, so many people were astride them, and swarming over the heaped sandbags round the pedestals. The fountains were full of people, screaming and laughing as they splashed in the shallows. Great flocks of pigeons swooped and turned overhead, encouraged to descend by the offer of crumbs from the crowd and then soaring upwards again, frightened by a passing omnibus into a flapping ascent over the tumult below. Snatches of conversation reached him.

'Good ol' Winnie! Good speech!'

'... and if you get orange drink down the front of that dress, I'll give you such a hiding—'

'Lost in the trenches somewhere, they never got a telegram—'

'I'll give them windows such a clean tomorrow . . .'

He grinned, caught up for a moment in the joy of the day, and then turned, deciding to try and tackle the Underground, even if it would be crowded. Perhaps not many would be going to Holborn from here.

Then he saw her, only a few feet away. She was helping Giuseppe, holding him up, helping him to a doorway out of the way of the crowds. Fortunata's surviving daughter was with them, and a young man in a sailor's uniform, holding his arm out protectively against the throng. Fortunata saw him at the same moment, and time stood still for an agonising split second. He opened his mouth as if to call her, and her eyes flashed – don't.

She turned away, bending over her husband, solicitous. He would never know how much effort that single movement cost her. When she looked up, the crowd had closed around Joe and he was gone.

'This is too much for me,' Giuseppe was saying, his face white and exhausted.

'I know. We need a nice cup of tea and a sit down,' Claudia said, soothing.

But Giuseppe shook his head. 'You and – er – George – you go on and enjoy yourselves,' he said, almost managing to smile at his new son-in-law. 'Fortunata and me, we'll go home now. We can get a nice cuppa there. We'll get a nice bit of peace and quiet after all this.' He was squeezing the flesh on Fortunata's upper arm, gentle, insistent. 'We're too old for much of this, aren't we, *cara*?'

Claudia made to demur, but he was insistent. 'You go and enjoy the crowds,' he said, almost pushing George out of the shop doorway, '. . . and don't hurry home!' he called after them, as they, too, were swallowed up by the crowd.

Fortunata was crying again. He put a solicitous arm round her shoulders. 'Come on, girl,' he said, encouraging. 'Don't go all silly on me! I know this bloody war's been terrible, but it's all over now. You'll be better once we get home . . .'

They helped each other down the crowded street towards the bus stop, the prematurely grey, wiry Italian and his weeping wife. As they passed a pillar box, she reached into her bag, pulled out a letter and shoved it through the slot. But before she had posted the letter, as her husband had turned his head for a moment, she had kissed the crumpled envelope with a desperate passion before thrusting it away.

'Come on,' the grey-haired Italian was saying, as they moved away through the crowds, 'come on, my dear. It's all over now . . .'

And away in the distance, the crowd began to sing, 'I'm going to get lit up when the lights go up in London . . .'

CHAPTER NINE

1951

SERAFINA STOOD ON the steps of St Peter's, pulling on her white gloves, unaware that anyone was watching her.

Across the street a large woman with grey hair swept back into a bun stood, hesitant, studying the slim, erect figure of the woman opposite. Surely it *was* Serafina. She would be in her mid-thirties now, but there was no mistaking that proud chin, that arrogant tilt of the head, as she adjusted her smart felt hat and squinted at the last rays of the gleaming July sun disappearing behind the buildings of Clerkenwell Road. Her hair was still very black, although now cut short and curled in the kind of feathery perm stylish women were wearing now. Rosa sighed. It was hard to equate the poise of this sophisticated businesswoman with the memory of that grim-faced little girl scrabbling under the table at King Bomba, almost thirty years ago. Suddenly their eyes met across the busy street. Rosa saw Serafina frown, and then almost immediately her face lit up with recognition.

'Rosa!' she called, and hurried down the steps and across the street, tutting impatiently at a cyclist who dithered in her path. She hugged the older woman warmly for a moment and then said, 'I can't believe it's you! What are you doing so far from Old Compton Street?'

Rosa gazed at Serafina's smiling face. She had not blossomed into a late beauty, as people had once hopefully predicted; but her face had filled out, and the attention she evidently gave to her appearance certainly paid off. She looked elegant and almost attractive in a slim pale green suit with a chiffon scarf at the neck. Rosa felt drab and uncomfortable in her old black dress and dreary coat.

'I'm about to go and visit Fortunata,' she said. Serafina's

face changed, and Rosa asked, surprised, 'Is something wrong? Surely you two aren't still quarrelling, after so many years?'

Serafina looked sheepish. 'Not exactly, Rosa. We just stay out of each other's way.'

'That's a great pity, Serafina. Fortunata loves you, you know.'

'How are you – that's much more important!' said Serafina. 'I haven't seen you for so long!'

'I came to the Festival of the Madonna del Carmine last week.'

Serafina's gaze shifted away from the intelligent penetrating eyes of the older woman. 'Oh, I couldn't go – too much work.'

'I met your daughter, though.'

'Oh, you met Maria?' Serafina laughed, not entirely comfortable. 'Your namesake. Her full name's Maria Rosa, you know.'

'Was she named after me, Serafina?'

There was a long silence, interrupted only by the rumble of the passing traffic. Finally Serafina raised her head. 'This isn't really the right place to talk,' she said, 'but it must be said. Firstly she's named after my own real mother, whose name was also Maria. But she is named after you as well, Rosa. Because I have fond memories of you – and – of Eduardo, of course.' Rosa's lips began to tremble. Serafina hesitated. 'I know what you are thinking. I know what Fortunata would like to think; but I'm sorry – Maria is not Eduardo's daughter. I'm very sorry.'

Rosa sighed. 'You're sure?'

Serafina gripped the other woman by the shoulder. 'Look at me, Rosa.' Again their eyes met, the distance between them now not so great. 'I know that when Eduardo was killed, everyone began to say the baby was his. It made things easier for my family, you see – made me almost respectable, like a widow. It would have been more simple for me to go along with it. I could have taken Eduardo's name, Maria would have got you for a grandmother, Fortunata would have been happy – but it wouldn't have been true.' She gazed into the distance, over Rosa's shoulder. 'So I chose to be honest – well as honest as I could be, without hurting anyone – and to tell them the truth – that Maria isn't Eduardo's child.

But I won't say who is – so I'm branded as a loose woman, and my daughter is called a bastard at school.'

Rosa felt suddenly sorry for this smart, sophisticated woman, searching in her handbag for a handkerchief, fighting back tears. Perhaps the suit and the little white gloves and the jaunty hat didn't matter so much after all. Much as she missed her beloved Eduardo, Rosa was at peace with herself and the world. Serafina very clearly was not. Dabbing at her eyes, Serafina said, 'I must go – I promised Claudia I would collect Maria straight after confession. She's giving her tea.'

'How is Claudia? Pretty as ever?'

Serafina laughed wryly. 'Pregnant as ever! She's expecting her fifth! I don't know how she can stand it.'

'Five babies! It's hard to believe . . .'

'I must go, Rosa.' Serafina kissed her hard, on both cheeks, and then smiled at her regretfully. 'I miss Eduardo still,' she said, 'I want you to know that. I'll always miss him. You must be proud he died a hero.'

'I would have preferred a live coward!' said Rosa, showing a spark of her old caustic humour. They smiled at each other, and parted.

Serafina turned into Laystall Street, where Claudia and her husband George lived in one of the blocks of council flats newly completed on the site of a bomb crater where a row of small shops had once stood. It was odd to think that they were living literally on top of where the Baldellis' fish and chip shop had served the whole of Little Italy. The flats were the envy of everyone who had not succeeded in being housed there, and Claudia was proud of the gleaming bathroom, the balcony where she could hang her endless piles of washing, the big windows overlooking the street. Serafina could not see the attraction.

'Why on earth would you want to sit on a balcony and look out at Laystall Street?' she would ask her sister, teasingly. 'It's not exactly a wonderful view, is it – the back of the printers and the newsagents!' As she climbed the four flights to her sister's front door, Serafina marvelled again, as she did so often, at Claudia's ability to produce children year after year, and her seemingly endless capacity to love them all – including any spare ones (like Maria) that might happen to come along. Claudia was lucky to have found George Winston, she mused. He was fairly dull, and his job as a furniture polisher would never make him rich, but he was easy-going and dependable. As long as he had his half ounce of ready-rubbed, the evening paper, and half-a-dozen children, he seemed happy enough. Of course he was nothing compared to Roberto. Serafina stopped on the landing, breathless, remembering Roberto. She could still see him flicking that lock of hair out of his eyes, looking at her, smiling that heart-stopping smile of his. Of course no one could compare to him. Poor Claudia had been half mad when he died, and it had been George – steady, earnest, affable – who had courted her back to sanity with dogged perseverance. As she rounded the corner, two small children hurtled past, giggling.

'Maria!' The little girl stopped and turned. Serafina never tired of gazing at her daughter, who was tiny and delicately pretty, with enormous blue eyes. She saw the child stiffen, her face transformed into a mask of politeness.

'Hello, Mamma. Zia Claudia asked me and Julie to get her some sugar. We're just going down to the corner shop.' Little Julie, Claudia's eldest daughter, came bounding back up the stairs, pleased to see her bountiful aunt.

'Hello, Auntie 'Fina!' she said, showing none of the restraint of her cousin, 'can we have thruppence for sweets?'

She ruffled her fair hair affectionately, 'Certainly not, you little scrounger!'

'Can I still go to the shops, Mum? Please?' Maria looked up at her, pleading. 'Can't you have a cup of tea with Zia Claudia 'til I get back?'

'You've got ten minutes,' Serafina warned, 'then you'll be in trouble if you're not ready to come home!' As they clattered downstairs, Serafina heard Julie ask, 'Why do you call her Zia? That's silly – it's not English. It's *Auntie* Claudia. This is England, after all.' Serafina smiled grimly to herself. How typical – they were all so ready to forget their Italian origins. Claudia had not even given her children Italian names, and they never spoke Italian at home. She supposed that George must have had some influence; he was not, after all, Italian, and it was different for Claudia – she saw herself as a Londoner, too, because this was where she had been born.

Serafina let herself into the narrow hall with her own key. She could hear the sound of children shouting, a radio playing a dance band tune, and Claudia calling crossly, 'George! I said there's a cup of tea here for you – it's getting cold!' George Winston appeared in the hallway and smiled in his usual friendly way at Serafina.

'Hello, Sis,' he said, 'been confessing your sins again? Keeping Old Father whatsit busy?' A small child clutched his trouser leg, solemn in pyjamas. He scooped the child up and placed her on his shoulders. 'There you are, Susan,' he said, 'now you are even taller than Auntie 'Fina in her best stilettos!' In the kitchen Claudia was presiding over several steaming saucepans, rocking a baby in one arm and stirring a pot with her free hand. The baby snuffled and burbled, suspended in a state somewhere between tears and sleep, resting on the enormous bulk of Claudia's pregnant belly. '*Ciao*, 'Fina!' They kissed on both cheeks, and Serafina took the baby from her sister and kissed it too, whereupon she received an enormous toothless smile of recognition.

'Hello, little Anna,' she murmured. Then addressing Claudia, 'Why is it I get a better reception from all your children than I do from my one and only offspring, even though I hardly see them from one week to the next, and I see *her* every day?'

George grinned at her from the kitchen table where he sat drinking tea, little Susan still perched on his shoulders. 'That's probably the answer,' he said, 'they don't see you often enough to remember what you're really like!'

Serafina threw the tea-cosy at him. 'Where's my other big girl?'

'Bath,' said Claudia, busy tasting the contents of one of her saucepans, 'go and see she hasn't drowned, 'Fina, there's an angel. Give the baby to George. I'll pour you some tea.'

She crossed the hallway and went down the passage to the bathroom. Opening the door she was greeted with cries and splashes from the steam-filled interior. '*Mamma mia!*' she cried laughing, 'it's like a steambath in here!' Claudia's other daughter, Frances, four years old, giggled at the sight of her glamorous aunt. Serafina busied herself shampooing her blonde curls vigorously then rinsing them with jugfuls of warm water straight from the tap – what luxury, after years of tin baths and heating up kettles! She helped the little girl get dry and into her night-dress, revelling in her soft warm body, pink from the bath, and her chubby affectionate face. Funny to have blonde children in the Florio family. But they took after their sandy-haired father, of course, and anyway, Serafina thought sadly to herself, they were not Florios. They were Winstons.

She ushered Frances into the kitchen, for a maternal inspection.

'Go and play with them in the living room for ten minutes, George,' Claudia instructed her husband, 'while I talk to my sister.'

Obediently, he herded the two girls out, carrying the baby in his arms. He could be heard ushering them across the hall, singing 'The Grand Old Duke of York' in a loud Cockney baritone.

Serafina sank into the vacated chair, and sipped at the mug of tea Claudia had deposited in front of her.

'Long day?' Claudia asked.

'Hellish. Two workers off sick, and the Income Tax man and the Immigration people on my back as usual.'

Claudia laughed. 'I should have your troubles! I'd swap a day running the factory for my two hours sewing frills on curtains every night.' Her voice held no tinge of jealousy in spite of her words.

'Can't you give up the sewing? You must be exhausted by the time the kids are in bed. It's ridiculous you sewing all evening. When do you rest?'

Claudia looked at her mildly through the steam emanating from a huge pot of boiling potatoes. 'I don't mind at all, honestly. George sits with me and reads the paper – reads out interesting bits to me while I work. It's quite nice, really.' She clamped a lid on to the pan. 'Anyway, we can't afford for me to stop, not on George's wages. I'm more worried about your evenings.'

'Mine?' Serafina was surprised.

'Sitting in that house every night – what on earth do you do once Maria's in bed?'

Serafina stirred her tea and shrugged. 'I watch the television set sometimes, or read. Or do some accounts. Usually I just nod off in my armchair, like Nonna Lucia used to do, God rest her soul.' She changed the subject, brightening. 'Did I tell you the news about the Mosconis?'

'The family you knew in Nemi? I heard that the brother

was coming over here to work for you. Papa told me. He's very proud of you, 'Fina, helping a *compaisano* like that.'

Serafina glowed, unaccustomed to praise or approval. 'Guido's already here. He arrived last week.'

Claudia looked at her sister, curious. 'What's he like? Good-looking?'

Serafina lowered her eyes, unusually sheepish. 'More handsome than I expected, yes. But then he was only six when I left Nemi.'

Claudia returned to stirring a pot of soup, smiling mischievously. 'Can you imagine Papa's face if you ended up married to this Mosconi!'

Serafina looked indignant. 'Claudia! He's only just got off the boat!'

Claudia tasted the soup and added some more salt. 'That didn't stop you putting him to work the moment he got here, did it?'

'I had to,' Serafina said, brisk. 'It's in his contract.'

Claudia grinned at her. 'And this new plan – the one to bring his sister over as well – is that in his contract?'

'Papa's nothing but an old gossip!' Serafina had gone pink. 'Violetta Mosconi was my best friend, and now she's a widow, all alone. Her husband and her two boys all died in the war . . . I'm sure I can find her some work to do in the workshop . . .'

With some relief she heard the front door slam, and the sound of voices in the hall. Julie raced into the room, slammed a bag of sugar on the table, and disappeared again, panting. Then Maria's youthful voice could be heard uniting with George in a rowdy chorus of 'Ten Green Bottles', punctuated by giggles and shrieks from Claudia's daughters.

'I must go, Claudia.' She stood up, reluctant to leave the contented atmosphere of the kitchen, cluttered and crowded as it was.

'You will come tomorrow, won't you, 'Fina?' Claudia's face was anxious. 'I promised Papa you would come. He's so looking forward to it.'

Serafina picked up her gloves. 'I shouldn't really be taking a Saturday off work . . . but I ought to see the Festival, I suppose.'

'You suppose!'

'. . . And I want to see how my statues look – I've got a couple of giant Britannias on show, and they're selling my busts of Shakespeare in one pavilion, and my little lion and unicorn copies somewhere else.'

'That settles it, then. You can pretend it's work.' Claudia came over and kissed her older sister with genuine affection. 'But we want you to come, 'Fina – not just for Papa – for everyone. It's sad, this family quarrel.'

Serafina shrugged. 'It's not of my making. Where's that child? She always hides when it's time to go home. She'd much rather be here playing with George and the girls than home with me – even though we have got the only television set in the whole of Little Italy!'

'*A domani!* See you in the morning – eight o'clock sharp.' Claudia chose to ignore Serafina's complaints about Maria, as usual. '. . . And remember, 'Fina, you must be on your best behaviour, for Papa's sake . . .'

It had been a difficult moment, but both women were better versed than most in how to deal with awkwardness: Fortunata through her endless committee work, Serafina through her unusual role as a female *padrone* of an immigrant workforce. They smiled politely at each other and said hello, almost as if they had spoken to each other only yesterday, instead of over ten years ago. Serafina had pushed Maria forward.

'Maria – this is your nonna,' she said.

Fortunata bent down in order to be on the same level as the child. She realised with a shock that she had seen Maria before, but she could not remember from when or where. She just knew that those startling blue eyes had looked into hers on some other day, in the past.

She had smiled at the wide-eyed little girl, and held her hand in her own gloved one. 'Hello, little Maria,' she said.

Maria had said nothing, gazing at her with a self-possession unusual in a child of – what was she? Fortunata wondered – she must be ten by now. She was evidently a child who had been obliged to grow up fast.

'You spilt my tomatoes,' she said, finally.

'I did?' Fortunata looked at her, surprised.

'Yes. In the baker's.' There was a long silence, while the child studied her grandmother. 'If you're my nonna,' she finally said, 'why have I not met you properly before?'

There was an embarrassed silence. 'Because,' Serafina finally

201

said, 'because we've all been very busy. Now come on, let's go and look for Nonno . . .'

They had struggled through the crowds at the turnstiles, and headed straight for the famous Skylon, where they had arranged to meet Giuseppe. It had been difficult to marshal the children through the milling crowds, and tempting for all of them to be distracted by the towering statues and strangely shaped buildings they passed. Now here they were, at exactly ten o'clock, as promised, joining the crowds at the fountains beneath the slender finger of Skylon. They had arranged this spot as a rendezvous, and now realised ruefully that this was a mistake. Everyone else at the Festival of Britain had also, it seemed, arranged to meet at Skylon.

'We'll never find them,' groaned Maria, anxious to begin exploring, 'can't we come back later?'

They had arranged to meet George's young brother Bill at this spot. Bill had a Ford Popular, and had been elected to transport Giuseppe and the wheelchair to the Festival, since the Underground would be impossibly crowded.

'There they are!' shouted Maria, and she and Julie ran off to greet their beloved grandfather.

'Sorry we're late, everyone,' Bill was apologetic, 'you'll never believe it – they put a ruddy great flight of steps next to the car-park!'

Fortunata laughed, grimly. 'You don't surprise me! A Festival of Britain only suitable for workers without industrial injuries.' Serafina pulled a face at her sister, as Fortunata bent over the wheelchair and kissed Giuseppe distractedly on the brow. Claudia nudged Serafina and frowned.

She was right, of course, Serafina thought. This was not a day for fighting. She moved forward and joined Fortunata by her father's side.

'*Buon giorno*, Papa,' she murmured, holding his face in her gloved hands and kissing him firmly on the lips. The contrast in the two embraces Giuseppe had received was not lost on the family.

'Serafina!' Giuseppe's face shone. '*Que bene!*' He looked round him at the gathering of the Florios, stroked little Maria's hair and smiled benignly. Serafina and Fortunata exchanged a look. They both understood the situation. They were here for Giuseppe, and therefore a truce was in operation.

'A cup of tea first,' George Winston decided. 'Everyone game?'

They headed off across the concourse in search of a tea-room, and found one overlooking the Thames, with an orchestra playing dance band tunes and a woman looking chilly in a satin cocktail dress singing nasally into a microphone. While George and Bill went to join the queue, the women settled Giuseppe at a table, and sat down themselves. Claudia's children sat in a well-behaved row in a window seat staring round-eyed at everything around them. Sheer wonder at the scale of the festival kept them uncharacteristically silent, as they gazed. Only Maria was restless, her confidence greater than the other children's. She hung around Fortunata's chair, wanting attention. Eventually Julie began to join in too.

'Please, Nanny,' Julie was pleading, 'can't we just have sixpence and go away? We'll come back and meet you here.'

'Certainly not!' came the reply, 'and I've told you before, Julie, do not call me Nanny – I am *not* a goat.' Maria and Julie giggled, not in the slightest bit intimidated by Fortunata's stern-sounding reprimand, for the twinkle in her eye was apparent.

Serafina, only half-listening to Claudia chatting, watched her daughter scamper from Fortunata's side and attach herself to the trouser-leg of Bill Winston, shouldering his way through the maze of tables to their place at the window, laden with tea things. Maria likes everyone in the world but me, Serafina thought sadly, not for the first time.

'Ridiculous idea!' Giuseppe was complaining, 'where are the waitresses?'

'This is a self-service,' George explained patiently, arranging the melamine cups, 'like America. No waitresses. Saves on the overheads.'

'Damn silly,' Giuseppe murmured, eyeing a plate of éclairs thoughtfully. He looked older than his sixty-six years, Serafina realised sadly. The increased weight he had acquired over the years spent in the wheelchair had given him a florid, unhealthy look, with podgy cheeks and a protruding stomach that bulged beneath his waistcoat.

Now completely white-haired, Giuseppe bore little resemblance to the strong and silent labourer Serafina remembered from her childhood. Pain had rendered Giuseppe peculiarly garrulous, and his voice, still heavily accented with the cadences of Nemi, could usually be heard running like a thread through other conversations, complaining and demanding. The wheelchair infuriated him, and the fact that he had to rely on his wife and daughters so much was a deep humiliation he found hard to bear. Sometimes it was difficult to remember just how cruel life had been to Giuseppe, robbing him of his mobility, his daughter, his nationality . . . Everyone tried to be kind, but the truth was that Giuseppe was difficult, demanding and depressing in equal measure. Today Giuseppe was doubly difficult. He had not wanted to go to the Festival on this day, because it was the anniversary of the death of a friend, he said. Serafina had asked who it was, and had only been told, 'Antonio . . . Tony.' Claudia had explained in a whisper that it was some boy who had killed himself in the internment camp all those years ago. He had been buried in Bedford, and every year Papa tried to persuade someone to drive him there to visit his grave. This year his demand had been overruled by the family's desire to visit the Festival, and Giuseppe was punishing Fortunata for this outrage. Somehow today, as every day, Fortunata coped uncomplainingly with this crippled hulk who found so many things wrong with the world; she was always there, somehow, silently doing his bidding.

Serafina studied her stepmother as she sipped her tea. Fortunata was still strikingly beautiful, the kind of woman who would always turn heads. She looked amazingly youthful, with only a few streaks of grey becomingly adorning her curls, and her figure still trim. Even in her rather dated red coat (slightly too long and too narrow, Serafina thought critically), Fortunata looked vivid and full of life. Sometimes people mistook her for Giuseppe's daughter and there would be, after the embarrassed explanations, genuine surprise. Serafina's thoughts were interrupted by Bill, whose cheerful and open face was smiling down at her.

'Can I take Maria with me, Serafina?'

She blinked up at him, surprised. 'Sorry – what did you say?'

'Bill said he'd take us to the funfair—'

'Did he?'

'Down the road, Auntie 'Fina,' Julie appealed to her, 'Battersea. Please. Uncle Bill says we can go, if you say yes.'

Serafina looked at Bill Winston. His smile disconcerted her. He was such an innocent – only twenty-two, and looked even younger. She shrugged. 'If you don't mind, Bill.'

Fortunata raised an eyebrow. 'All of them, Bill? On your own?'

'No,' George stood up, grinning. 'Me too!'

So the Florios were left to themselves, as the children trooped away in excited confusion with the Winston brothers. There was an uncomfortable silence, broken only by a long sigh of relief from Claudia, leaning back in her chair, exhausted by the complexity of arrangements for the children, and by the tension of this reunion between Fortunata and Serafina.

'Are you all right, Claudia?' Fortunata asked her daughter, anxiously.

'I'm fine, Mamma. Don't fuss.' Claudia smiled at her mother. 'I'm just enjoying the silence!'

Giuseppe leaned forward in his wheelchair. 'More tea, Fortunata.' It was an order, not a request. She pushed back her chair and stood up. 'I'll go back to the counter, then,' she said evenly. 'Anyone else want anything?'

'Why don't you go with her, 'Fina?' Claudia suggested, hopefully.

'I think Fortunata can manage to carry a tray on her own,' Serafina said, struggling to keep her tone light in front of her father.

Fortunata's eyes met hers. They were full of pain. 'Of course I'll be fine,' she said. 'You two go off and explore for a while. We'll meet you later. Giuseppe and I will be fine here with our tea . . .'

Unable to repress a small smirk of triumph, Serafina said, 'What a good idea! We'll leave the old fogies to their tea, shall we, Claudia?'

But Claudia shook her head. 'No, you go on, 'Fina. I just want to sit. The journey exhausted me.'

So it was Serafina alone who wandered around the Festival. Standing outside a glass building housing British-made garments, she came across her Britannia statues. A small admiring crowd had gathered around them, and she was gratified to see several people clutching the small plaster versions she had persuaded the organisers to sell.

205

Someone touched her elbow. 'Mrs Florio?' It was Mr Butcher, the tense little man who had liaised with her over the statues for the Festival. 'A great success, a great success.' He was smiling and nodding at her. 'You must be delighted with the results. Your Britannia is positively beautiful.'

'Thank you. She was modelled on my mother.'

'And she's here – your mother?' Another voice, shockingly familiar, joined in. Serafina was aware suddenly of another man who had been standing there next to Mr Butcher, silently admiring the statues.

'I'm sorry—' Mr Butcher was flustered. 'Allow me to introduce you – Mrs Serafina Florio, this is Mr Joseph O'Connell, the Honourable Member for—'

'We've met.' Serafina was forced to shake the hand of the tall grey-haired man now gazing down at her.

'Is she here? Your mother?' Joe O'Connell repeated, forcing Serafina to meet his eyes. She returned his look, angry. 'No, Mr O'Connell. My mother died many years ago, in Italy. This statue is based on how she looked when I was a little girl.'

'I see.' They remained staring at the statue, as if hoping it might suddenly spring to life and put an end to this unfortunate meeting.

Mr Butcher began to usher them inside the gleaming glass building. 'This way, Mr O'Connell, Mrs Florio . . .'

'*Mrs* Florio?' Joe looked at her quizzically.

'A courtesy title. I'm sure my mother has told you—' He shot her a sharp glance. 'I thought your mother was dead.' She blushed, furious with herself for the slip. How could she have called Fortunata her mother, after all these years – and to Joe O'Connell, of all people!

'You know who I mean,' she said, coldly. They had both stopped walking and stood in the foyer, ignoring the throng of visitors pushing past. Mr Butcher hovered, unwilling to intrude, but feeling responsible for his illustrious visitor.

'Mr O'Connell, if you would just come inside and meet some of the designers—'

Joe glanced impatiently in his direction. 'I'll join you in a minute, Frank. I've got some unfinished business here.' He took Serafina by the arm and led her to an empty corner. She did not protest, curious, in spite of herself, to hear what he had to say, this man she had hated since that fateful encounter over thirty years ago, on the day that she first set foot in Little Italy. She looked up at him, dispassionate. He was still a handsome man in spite of his years. It was difficult not to compare him with Giuseppe.

'How are you, Serafina? How's your little girl? Maria, isn't it?'

'Why should you care?' she responded coldly.

'You know the answer to that.' His voice, still with an Irish lilt to it, was equally curt. 'I ask because I care about Fortunata, and she cares about you – although God knows why.'

'You think she cares? We hadn't spoken to each other for ten years until today.'

'Is she here?' His face lit up.

Serafina felt an odd pang of envy for such a display of naked emotion. 'Yes. With my father.'

'Of course.' Joe's face fell. There was an uncomfortable silence, which Serafina perversely enjoyed. It was broken by Joe.

'You know,' he said, 'I was always jealous of you.' She could not help looking surprised. 'I mean it.' His bright blue eyes met hers, unwaveringly. 'I *am* jealous. She loved you so much, and you wouldn't give anything back. All because you're haunted by the ghost of a woman who died when you were five, and in the meantime – all I ever got were the crumbs. The rest she gave to you! You and your family!'

Serafina looked at him, puzzled. 'You couldn't be more wrong.' She was aware of Mr Butcher, agitated, in the background. 'I don't get anything from Fortunata. We don't have anything to do with each other.'

He shook his head, a sad smile hovering on his lips. 'That's where you're wrong, you see. She devotes *all* her time to you. It doesn't matter whether you're there or not. You've destroyed her, all of you, one way or another, in your narrow little Italian backwater, with your strict Italian rules about how things have to be.' He was beginning to raise his voice. People began to stare. 'This is London! This is England! You never let her be what she wanted to be! She always had to be what you wanted! Do you think she would stay with her husband if she was allowed to follow her feelings?'

Serafina gave a hard little laugh. 'You've got it all worked out, haven't you?'

He nodded. 'Yes, I have. She stays because she has some stupid idea in her head about family, about duty . . . and part of that is about believing that you and she can be friends again.'

'I don't believe you.'

Joe shrugged. 'Suit yourself. I can only tell you that I asked Fortunata to marry me a hundred times. I offered to pay for the divorce. If she couldn't get one, I said we'd live together – hang the scandal – I didn't care. I just wanted to be with her.'

'And she said no?' Serafina saw, perhaps for the first time, the anguish etched into the lines on Joe's face.

'She said no. And don't kid yourself. You know Fortunata – she's never cared about convention. She would come and live with me tomorrow if it weren't for you and the rest of your damn Italian family.'

'And what about –' Serafina waved an expressive hand, very Italian suddenly '. . . what about your position? Being an MP, all of that?'

He looked suddenly weary, older. 'I've told you. I don't care about all that. I'm prepared to risk it. But Fortunata said no, so the question never arose. I haven't spoken to her in years.'

Serafina gave him a small, cold, tight-lipped smile. 'Good. I'm glad to hear it, Mr O'Connell. You've made me a very happy woman.'

He did not smile. Instead, he said, very quietly, 'I wonder if you are mad.' There was a small moment of absolute stillness between them, suddenly broken by the arrival of Mr Butcher.

'Mrs Florio – do forgive me – I've a message for you.'

'For me?' Serafina looked at him, surprised.

'Yes – can you go at once to the perimeter car-park – the one behind the Festival Hall on York Road.'

Without thinking, she clutched Joe O'Connell's arm. 'Why – is something wrong?'

'I'm not sure – the message was from your mother – she didn't say—'

'My mother!'

'She said you're to go to entrance D, on York Road.'

She felt Joe O'Connell's muscles tense under her fingers, and she immediately snatched her hand away.

208

'Goodbye, Mr O'Connell. I've got to go.'

He pulled her back towards him, gripping her wrist, and fixing her with his vivid gaze.

'I'll come with you.'

She pulled away from him, violently, vaguely aware of Mr Butcher's puzzlement over this odd moment of intimacy between such an unlikely pair.

'You will not!' she snapped. 'Don't be ridiculous, Mr O'Connell!' She gave him one last, cold glance. 'Just think,' she said, 'how angry Fortunata would be if I arrived with *you*!'

He stopped in his tracks. Then after a moment his hands reached up to the lapel of his well-cut suit, and removed a red rosebud pinned to it. 'Here. Give this to Fortunata. Please.' She hesitated. He pushed the soft bud into her hand. 'Please!' Then he turned away, defeated.

Serafina hurried through the crowds, her face tense and anxious. What on earth could be the matter? It must be something important that had driven Fortunata to put out a message for her. She hardly heard the roar of machinery, the calls of children, the music of the dance bands, as she hurried across the concrete walkways towards York Road. Perhaps Papa had had a heart attack. Perhaps the children had had an accident at the funfair. She had read about the Big Wheel . . . surely Bill and George wouldn't allow the children to ride on that . . .?

''Fina! Over here!' It was Bill Winston, waving at her over the heads of the people; he had shinned half-way up one of the ornate lamp posts built specially for the Festival, and had spotted her elegant blue-feathered hat in the crowd. She hurried towards him, as he descended to ground level.

'What's happened, Bill? Something dreadful?'

He grinned, and took her arm. 'No, nothing dreadful, unless you count Claudia starting to give birth in the tea-room as dreadful! They've got her in an ambulance in the car-park, but I don't think they'll bother to take her to hospital – she's too far gone, I think.'

Serafina, struggling to keep up with Bill in her high heels, breathed a sigh of relief. 'Oh, thank God – something normal! I thought something awful had happened!'

Bill slowed down a little, in deference to her stilettos. 'Well

. . . it wasn't just the baby beginning to arrive . . . Fortunata looks like she's about to get herself arrested as well.'

'*Dio mio!* I can't go off for five minutes! What happened?' They were walking through a flower garden, a vibrant mass of red, white and blue flowers. The crowds had thinned to a trickle here, and the dance band music had faded into the distance.

Bill grinned at the memory. 'Need you ask? We met a crowd of demonstrators at the gate – some of them are friends of Fortunata's—'

Serafina tutted. 'Don't tell me – she got herself involved in an argument.'

Bill laughed. 'How did you guess?' They had reached the exit and were now heading towards York Road down a quiet alleyway. Serafina could hear raised voices. She sighed, cross. Fortunata just couldn't seem to stay away from trouble!

They rounded the corner into the car-park. Away across the expanse of cars, Serafina could see the small crowd of demonstrators, waving placards and shouting: 'Waste of money!' 'Feed the poor!' 'Stop the Festival!' She could see Fortunata agitated, arguing with them.

'No, Frank, Arthur – you're wrong! We need a morale booster, the country needs cheering up! It's money well spent—'

A man shouted, 'Fortunata Florio – class traitor!' Giuseppe had now joined his wife, waving his fist from his wheelchair. 'Don't you insult my wife!' he roared.

Serafina groaned and clutched Bill's arm. 'There'll be a riot!' she panted, struggling over the gravel, cursing her shoes.

Giuseppe was in full flow now. 'Traitors!' he was shouting hoarsely. 'You should be deported! This is a great country! You should be proud—'

Fortunata turned on him, furious. 'Shut up, Giuseppe! Shut up! I'm not saying this is a great country—'

The demonstrators jeered. 'Fortunata Florio, supporter of the British Establishment! Who'd have thought it?'

Giuseppe looked as though he might explode. 'My wife is proud to be British,' he boomed, 'and so should you be! Reds! Traitors!'

Fortunata stared at Giuseppe. 'You've changed your tune

haven't you? Since when have you given two hoots about the British?'

Serafina and Bill arrived at last. 'Come on, Papa,' Serafina panted, 'don't get upset.'

But Giuseppe was in full flow. 'We should show the world we're a great nation again!' he bellowed, 'and the Festival's doing just that, don't you see?'

'No I don't—' Fortunata began, but Giuseppe had begun singing 'There'll always be an England' in his deep, guttural broken accent, and the demonstrators began to laugh, applauding ironically.

'Bravo, grandad!' they called, 'Britannia rules the waves, eh?'

Fortunata's rage was palpable. She turned on her husband, eyes ablaze. 'You're just a stupid, ignorant immigrant!' she shouted, suddenly very Italian herself. 'What have you got to be grateful to the British for?'

The demonstrators cheered. Giuseppe continued to sing, loud, defiant. 'Come on, Fortunata!' one of the men holding a placard called, 'come and join us!'

Serafina leaned protectively over her father's wheelchair. 'Yes,' she said to her stepmother, 'why don't you?' They glared at each other amid the noise and the shouting, still at odds with each other, still enemies.

The moment was broken by the arrival of a small contingent of police who had come to move the demonstrators away from the car-park exit, which they proceeded to do with a certain ruthless efficiency. The crowd melted away, only a few stalwarts staying to tussle with the police. 'Hooray for the boys in blue!' Giuseppe called.

Fortunata gazed at him, despairing. 'They're probably the same ones that arrested you in 1941,' she said.

'I wonder how Claudia's getting on,' Bill Winston said in his mild voice. Everyone stared at him, guilty. They had forgotten Claudia, and the ambulance parked by the perimeter fence. 'Shall we go and see what's happening?' he suggested.

Shamefacedly, the Florios followed him, the fight forgotten.

A small knot of people hovered, agitated, outside the ambulance. Giuseppe wheeled himself disconsolately in decreasing circles on the gravel some distance away. Fortunata paced up and down between two cars, silent and furious. Maria and Julie chased each other noisily around the car-park attendant's kiosk. Claudia's other daughters sat in a bemused huddle with a kindly passer-by, in the shade of a small cherry tree, one of a neat row specially planted for the Festival on the edge of the car-park. George was nowhere to be seen.

'Must be in the ambulance with the doc,' said Bill. 'I'll go and have a peek – see what's going on.'

Serafina looked at Fortunata, a strange mixture of desperate fondness and anger welling up within her. Fortunata turned and saw her. 'Well—' she called, her voice acid. 'You missed most of the fun, as usual.' Giuseppe wheeled himself painfully towards his daughter, until he was irritably intercepted by Fortunata. 'Oh, stop making such heavy weather of it, Giuseppe —' and she pushed the chair across the gravel until they all met by the ambulance.

'Call this fun?' said Serafina, drily. The ambulance shuddered once, and then began to rock gently.

'When will it be over?' fretted Giuseppe. 'I want to go home!'

'Soon, soon, Papa.' Serafina kissed her father on the forehead and then looked up at Fortunata, her eyes challenging. 'Anyway, who's to say all the fun was to be had here?'

Fortunata looked back at her, dark eyes alarmed. 'What's that supposed to mean?'

Serafina shrugged. 'I met a friend of yours.'

'Who?' Giuseppe's voice was wavering, querulous. 'Who did you meet?'

Serafina's eyes fixed on Fortunata's. 'No one you know, Papa,' she said. 'A political friend of Fortunata's.'

'Pah! Don't talk politics to me!' her father grumbled from his wheelchair, mopping his brow. 'It's politics have ruined this family! Politics, politics, always politics!'

'Too true,' said Serafina. The ambulance doors opened, and Bill emerged, grinning.

'It's a boy!' he announced. 'They're going to call him George! George Robert Winston!'

'George Winston! *Bravissimo!*' crowed Giuseppe, smiling for once. '*Que bello!* A wonderful *British* name!' He glowered triumphantly at his wife.

Fortunata raised her eyes to the heavens. 'Rule Britannia!' she said, ironically.

But Serafina had not heard. She was staring at Bill Winston. 'George *Robert* did you say?'

He nodded, smiling. 'George Robert Winston.'

A tear trickled down Serafina's cheek. 'How could she? How could she do that to his memory . . .' She turned and walked towards Maria and Julie, still playing happily some distance away. As she went, she remembered the rosebud, hot and crushed in her gloved hand. She turned back for a moment, staring at her stepmother. Then she threw the button-hole in a nearby wastebin, in a large, expansive, Italian gesture, and walked on without a backward glance.

Fortunata watched her go, and then turned back to her husband, her face set like a stone.

CHAPTER TEN

1953

MARIA FLORIO HUNG out of the upstairs window of the house in Grape Street and marvelled at the abundance of flapping bunting, red, white and blue, zigzagging across the street from drainpipe to drainpipe. The house opposite had erected an enormous crown, hand-painted and made from cardboard boxes. It teetered precariously in the breeze, wobbling on the chimney pots. The cotton-wool glued around the base to represent ermine was disintegrating in the drizzle. But to Maria's twelve-year-old eyes it was exotic, beautiful, part of the immense fairytale that was the Coronation.

She didn't want to be Elizabeth particularly. So much to learn, and everyone staring at you. But Margaret! She longed to be Princess Margaret. She was so pretty and sophisticated, always wearing long gloves and net dresses and little feathered hats. Down in the street she could see old Mrs Vittorini organising the arrangement of the trestle tables being laid out for the party, aided by her eldest daughter Annunziata and her four children, all now young women in their thirties. In spite of the rain, Maria knew this would be a wonderful day. The only thing spoiling it was Nonno, who stayed upstairs in bed all the time, and breathed in a very peculiar manner. Whenever Maria and her mamma came to visit him, she was obliged to venture into the darkened room, trying not to smell the sickly smell in there, in order to kiss her grandfather's dry and papery cheek. It was always the same. He would pat her hand and sigh, then croak, 'The last of the Florios! The very last of the Florios!' – at which point his rheumy old eyes would fill with tears and Serafina would say, briskly, 'All right, Maria, run along and play now,' and Maria would hasten from the room, glad the ordeal was over.

Still, there were compensations. There was always Nonna smiling in the kitchen, managing somehow to produce sweets in spite of the continued rationing, and always ready to listen to Maria's chatter. These were the moments that Maria loved most. It seemed to her that those times, curled up in Nonno's armchair by the stove, were the only ones when she would talk and someone was actually listening. Much as she loved visiting Zia Claudia's chaotic flat in Laystall Street, the rooms were always full of noise – the clatter of pans in the kitchen, Uncle George singing along to the wireless, Zia Claudia shouting at the children, baby George screaming in his cot. And at home in the smart flat she lived in with Mamma, Maria played silently in her room with her expensive doll's house, and listened to Mamma on the telephone making business calls. Otherwise Guido Mosconi was there, hanging about in the immaculate lounge, making sheep's eyes at Serafina and unable to communicate with Maria in anything but pidgin English or incomprehensible Italian, spoken with such a strong accent that Maria could not understand more than the occasional word.

Guido seemed a nice enough man. Maria viewed the prospect of him as her papa with indifference. He smiled pleasantly at her whenever they met. He even brought her the occasional lollipop or comic when he came courting, self-conscious in his best suit and carrying flowers for Serafina. But to the romantic Maria he was not handsome enough, or noble enough, to be a real lover. He didn't look like Flash Gordon, or any of her other Saturday morning cinema heroes. And Mamma's face did not light up when she saw Guido, even though she put on her best dress when they went out together. This happened a lot, which was perhaps why to Maria the Laystall Street council flat and these cramped and cluttered rooms of Nonna's house seemed more like home to her than her mother's flat. For she spent most weekends staying either with Zia Claudia or Nonna, so that Mamma could go out dancing or to the pictures with Guido.

Maria knew that Nonna did not approve of this arrangement at all. But this was another reason why Maria loved her grandmother so: because Nonna relented and allowed Maria to stay with her, and she did this, as she said loudly and often, only because she loved Maria. The thought made Maria glow.

She was not a child who often felt very loved. When she passed the Eleven Plus and was sent to the Grammar School, she had become distanced from the world in which she had grown up, the world of St Peter's, and nuns, and the statue factory and the bustle of the Hill. She knew as well that Serafina's decision to send her daughter out of the community and thus away from the local Catholic school had not been received well. It had been seen as a betrayal. But Maria's mamma had defended her action with practical reasons: 'My Maria's got to get on in the world,' she had said, 'she's got to learn to be a businesswoman like her mother if she's going to run the company. And anyway,' she would add defensively, 'she still goes to Mass . . .'

All Maria knew was that the change had isolated her even more than her lack of a father had in earlier years. At the Grammar School it was best to keep quiet about life at home, if it was out of the ordinary. What mattered was having a similar perm to Janet Hughes', and getting to play in Susan Brodie's gang at playtime, and being invited to a popular girl's house for tea. None of these delights had so far come Maria's way. She seemed foreign and strange to most of her classmates, and had had to make do with one friend, a serious, thin girl with ugly glasses called Evelyn Woodhouse. They hid together in the art room whenever possible, making neat little pencil drawings of catkins or pansies, pretending not to mind that they did not quite fit in.

She leaned a little further out of the window, watching a man climbing up a ladder to attach a flag to a lamp post. Best not to think about school. The man saw her and waved. She waved back, not recognising him. But he was doubtless one of Nonno's old friends. They all seemed to know who she was. She would find herself suddenly being smiled at in the local streets by strangers. 'That's the Florio child,' they would say to each other, exchanging knowing looks, 'the one born in the air raid – you know . . .' They were always just a little too kind to her, a little too eager to make her feel as if she belonged, as if being not quite respectable did not matter. Only Nonna was honest with her; but then Nonna seemed to have no interest in the things other people thought were important. True, she cooked, cleaned and scrubbed like all the women on the Hill, but in every other respect she was not like the other Italian women. Perhaps that was why Maria loved her so, because they were both outsiders, both somehow different.

'Maria! If you lean out any further we'll be scraping you off the pavement.' Fortunata was in the doorway, looking cross.

'Come and look, Nonna, it's beautiful!'

Fortunata grinned and joined her at the windowsill. 'You'll crease your new dress, *topolina*,' she said. They looked out on to the street, happy in each other's company, the grey-haired woman and the gawky girl.

'Will Nonno miss the Coronation?' Maria asked.

Fortunata was studying a group of little boys who had made a Coronation coach out of their playcart. Little Stella Vittorini was being queen, standing astride and waving a stick regally.

'Just like her mother . . .' murmured Fortunata. 'I'm afraid Giuseppe is very ill,' she told her granddaughter quietly. 'He should have gone to the Italian Hospital, but he won't go.'

'But will he come and watch the Coronation on the television?' Maria persisted.

Fortunata shook her head. 'No, *cara*. He's not well enough.'

Maria fought the feeling of relief welling up inside her. She had dreaded the thought of everyone in the neighbourhood gathered in front of the television set in the front room, and the presence of that sick-smelling old man, wheezing and gasping, interfering with the pleasures of the day. She knew this was a sinful thought. I'll confess it on Sunday, she thought, pleased to have found something to confess. Usually she had to invent sins in the confessional.

'Come on,' said Fortunata, straightening up, 'we'd better go downstairs.'

'What time is Mamma coming?' Maria asked, as they tip-toed past Nonno's room.

Fortunata shrugged. 'She'll be here later, *cara*. She and Guido have gone to the railway station to meet Guido's sister. Didn't she tell you?'

Maria hopped down the stairs on one leg. 'Yes. The one who used to play with Mamma in Nemi. Violetta.'

'That's right.' Fortunata bustled past her into the kitchen

217

murmuring drily to herself, 'I presume your mother will allow this Violetta a few hours' rest before she sets her to work.'

But Maria had heard. 'I'm sure she'll let her watch the Coronation,' she assured her grandmother, solemn.

Fortunata, looked at her closely. 'Is that a twinkle I see in your eyes?' she asked.

Maria helped herself to a biscuit, ignoring the half-hearted slap Fortunata aimed at her hand. 'I know my mother's a slave driver,' she said, munching, 'but I think even she wouldn't think a few plaster poodles were more important than the Queen of England . . . Would she?' She and Fortunata laughed together, conspiratorially.

'Nearly time for the hoardes to arrive,' said Fortunata. 'Are you going to help me get the wine glasses out?'

They were busy arranging the glasses on to trays when George, Claudia and their children arrived, bringing, as usual, chaos and clamour with them. Fortunata hugged her daughter happily, always pleased when the Winstons came to visit, because they brought life to the narrow little house and lightened her heart a little. At least Claudia seemed happy enough. But then she never talked about Roberto, so who knew how she really felt?

George settled into Nonno's chair and got out his pipe. 'Settle down, girls!' he called, without much conviction. 'Any tea on the go, Fortunata?'

She swatted him with the local newspaper he had brought. 'Men!' she said crossly, 'they're all the same. Take the girls into the front room and warm up the television, Maria, there's a good girl.' In spite of her words she was putting the kettle on. 'Claudia, go and say hello to your papa, I'll take the baby.' Her daughter headed obediently for the stairs and Maria herded the Winston girls out into the hall.

George looked at his mother-in-law thoughtfully as he lit his pipe. 'You all right, 'Nata?' he asked. 'You look really tired.'

She gave him a weary smile, jiggling baby George a little in her arms. 'I am,' she said '. . . and don't call me 'Nata – how many more times?'

'How's Giuseppe?'

She clattered some teacups on the draining-board. 'Not good, George. Not good.'

'Do you want me to talk to him again? About going into hospital?'

'There's no point. He just won't go.' Someone was knocking at the front door. She heard Maria run to answer it. 'Bother. They're arriving already.'

Fortunata was transformed into a bustling mamma, as if the previous conversation had not occurred. 'It's bound to be the Rossis, they're always early. George –' her voice was imperious, 'see to the wine while I go and take their coats,' and she was gone.

George sighed, shook his head and levered himself slowly out of the chair. Italians. They were a peculiar lot. Whistling 'How Much is that Doggy in the Window?' to himself, he began to open the chianti.

The flickering picture showed a young woman, head bowed, surrounded by clergy. Richard Dimbleby was intoning his commentary, ponderous and portentous. The occupants of the room squinted at the screen, engrossed. Claudia put her head round the door and signalled to her mother, who was handing round plates of biscuits. Fortunata quietly joined Claudia in the hall.

'Sorry, Mamma,' said Claudia, 'but I think you should go and see Papa. He seems worse to me, and he's asking for you. I think we should get the doctor . . .'

The sound of angelic singing emanated from the television.

Fortunata looked thoughtfully at her daughter's anxious face. 'Don't let's do anything hasty,' she said. 'He's had bad turns before. You go in and watch the television. I'll go on up.'

'But what about the Coronation?' Claudia asked.

Fortunata was already mounting the stairs. 'I may be forced to accept 'Fina's gift of a television set for the Coronation,' she said, 'but I don't actually have to watch it as well. I'm anti-royalist, remember? I may not be in the Communist Party any more, but old habits die hard.'

'Don't go in there and say that!' Claudia laughed, indicating the occupants of the front room, 'they'll lynch you! Here—' she tossed a newspaper into her mother's hand. 'Maybe Papa would like to hear what's going on in Clerkenwell. And Mamma – call me if you need me.' After a last anxious look at

219

her mother, she disappeared into the front room from where Fortunata could hear the 'oohs' and 'aahs' of the assembled children as they watched the fairytale princess being transformed into a queen.

She climbed the stairs slowly, delaying for a moment the sight of her sick husband. She knew he was dying. The doctor had told her so. She paused outside the bedroom door, trying to prepare herself. But it was no use. She knew that she would never be prepared for the sight of the man with whom she had spent most of her life fading away in the gloom of that bedroom, expiring in the marital bed. She pushed open the door and entered, trying not to recoil from the smell of decay and death. Giuseppe's breathing was very loud and laboured. She stood for a moment out of sight, listening. Each breath started as a strange bubbling noise and was then drawn up through his diseased lungs in an extended groan, held for a long moment in heart-stopping silence, and then exhaled in the longest and saddest sigh she had ever heard. She went quietly over to the bedside, and sat in the chair pulled up there by Claudia. Giuseppe's eyes were closed, every muscle on his face concentrated on the effort of breathing. She touched his hand lightly and his eyelids flickered open.

With an enormous effort, he spoke. 'Fortunata . . .' he whispered, his mouth slack, a small trail of saliva on his chin. 'Fortunata . . .'

She leaned forward, her face softened by concern. 'Don't try and speak. It's all right.' For a while he drifted away again. Faintly Fortunata could hear the voice of Richard Dimbleby followed by a cacophony of trumpets. The room was dark, with just a small shaft of light falling on the bed from a chink in the curtains. Fortunata looked around her. She had never liked this room. It had been her parents' room before, an impenetrable sanctum into which she had rarely ventured. She had always felt like an intruder, sleeping in here after Lucia's death. Even the furniture, dark and gleaming from many years of pointless but determined polishing, had been her mother's.

Outside, someone was talking about the procession. 'He was the Queen's Champion, that chap carrying the flag. They said his family goes back to William the Conqueror. Now

220

there's British for you! I thought Dimbleby was going to burst into tears . . .'

She got up quietly and went over to the window, peeking through the narrow gap in the curtains. There was some activity in the street now. The Vittorini women were covering the tables with crepe paper, and laying out plates. The Coronation must be over, and the street party about to begin. She saw Serafina coming up the street with Guido Mosconi carrying a suitcase, and a thin young woman in black. This must be Violetta, from Nemi. As the three of them headed towards the Florio house, there was a moment when Serafina, laughing at something Guido had said, looked up and saw her stepmother. Both women's eyes slid away. Fortunata stepped back from the window.

'*Cara* . . .' It was Giuseppe, conscious again. He beckoned to her with a feeble hand.

Fortunata crossed back to the bed and resumed her seat. 'Don't try and talk,' she said soothingly. 'Just rest.'

'Has it happened?' he asked, his voice an unrecognisable croak. 'The Coronation?'

'Yes, it's happened. She's Queen now.'

He smiled feebly. 'It's a good thing . . .' he murmured. 'And Everest – did they do it? Did they get to the top?'

She had already told him the news about Hillary. 'Yes, they did it.'

His eyes closed again. 'This is a great year for Britain,' he mouthed '. . . proves we're the best nation on earth . . .'

Fortunata prudently chose to remain silent. This was not the moment to berate Giuseppe for his misguided patriotism. 'Shall I call Doctor Lusardi?' she asked.

'No, no . . .' For a moment she thought he had stopped breathing altogether. But then his chest heaved, and he exhaled loudly. 'I want to tell you something, Fortunata.'

For a moment the old, irritable Fortunata was there. 'Oh, don't – please,' she said quickly, 'not confessions, Giuseppe. I couldn't stand it. Save your strength.'

He eyed her bleakly. 'What for? Here—' He made a convulsive movement, and then collapsed back, distressingly agonised, 'Help me sit up—'

'Giuseppe, don't!'

'I want to – help me, woman, don't argue!'

221

She managed to pull him up a little, and to prop another pillow behind his head, so that he was at least not completely prone.

'There,' she said, smiling and upset, 'you got your own way!'

'You remember Viazzani? Antonio Viazzani?'

'The gambler? Of course I remember him. His brother wanted to marry me, you know. Federico Viazzani. He was at Dunkirk. Didn't he go down on the *Arandora Star*?'

Giuseppe shook his head, fretful, wheezing. Fortunata took his hand again. Down in the street she could hear the children shouting. The street party had begun.

'Antonio . . .' he said, 'Antonio Viazzani.'

'He died, Giuseppe. He was stabbed in Brighton. Something to do with those gangs.'

He shook his head again. A tremor disfigured his lower lip. 'I'm a murderer, Fortunata. I'm a killer.'

'Don't upset yourself,' she said, puzzled and alarmed.

A sheen of sweat had appeared on Giuseppe's forehead. But he turned in the bed, grasping her hand more strongly. 'I had him killed.' His voice was nothing more than a whisper. 'He insulted you. Called you a whore. It was the Festival of Our Lady. Antonia and Claudia were only babies . . .' Fortunata could feel the heat rising in her face, as Giuseppe's terrible, agonised whispering continued. 'It must have been in twenty-four. I couldn't find you, you'd disappeared and I met the Viazzanis. Antonio said you were with another man. I had to fight him, but I lost . . . I lost, Fortunata.'

She stared at him, trying not to remember. 'Don't, Giuseppe,' she said, 'don't. It doesn't matter.'

But still the whisper went on. 'I paid someone,' he murmured. He pulled her, suddenly, sharply by the wrist, so that her face was very close to his. 'I paid someone to kill him. In Brighton, while I was away.' She tried not to flinch from the foul, sick breath on her face.

'Don't be silly, Giuseppe,' she said, 'you're tired. Try and sleep.'

He still held her there, his breathing stertorous, desperate with the effort of all this talking. 'God punished me,' he whispered, 'God pushed me under that machinery. He took away my legs.'

222

'It was an accident.'

He shook his head. 'No. And why was Antonia taken from us? I killed Antonio, so He killed Antonia. Don't you see? God was telling me . . .'

She pulled away, appalled and saddened. He was wandering, fading. 'Try to sleep,' she said softly.

Obedient, he fell back, wearied by his memories. His eyes closed. His breathing reverted to an unsteady but less noisy rhythm. Downstairs, the children were running about, laughing noisily. Fortunata wondered irritably why George and Claudia didn't control them more . . . The front door slammed, and she heard Frances and Julie quarrelling on the doorstep.

'You're too little to play with us.'

'I'm not!'

'She is, isn't she, Maria? Tell her, go on!'

Fortunata heard Maria's voice, placatory. 'This is a game for everyone, Julie. No one's too little for Pass the Parcel . . .' Their voices faded, merging with others in the street. Then Fortunata heard Serafina's voice, sharp, admonishing Guido Mosconi.

'Don't be silly, Guido! I just have to nip back to the factory and check the boys have put the ovens out. You stay here with Violetta. Claudia will look after you. Don't fuss!' She heard Serafina's high heels clipping briskly away down the pavement, and the murmured complaint of Guido in his guttural peasant's dialect.

She opened the newspaper quietly, flicking a glance at Giuseppe. He seemed to be sleeping more peacefully now, in this new semi-upright position, his mouth slack, his breathing less laboured.

She turned the pages of the paper, bored by endless pictures of the Royal Family. It was all so ludicrous. Why were all these Italians out in the street celebrating the crowning of a British queen? She had been in favour of the Festival of Britain – God knows, morale had needed boosting badly then. But this – another crazy display of British chauvinism. And the cost! Far better to have spent the money on the unemployed . . .

Her eye was caught by a photograph, and her hands, which had been turning the pages irritably, were stilled. It was ridiculous. He still had a devastating effect on her, and she was an old woman ... It was a picture of Joe O'Connell, seated with various dignitaries at some official dinner. She stared at his face, reduced to a mass of tiny dots. His prominence as an MP – and an outspoken one at that – meant that she never escaped him. His face seemed to be everywhere, always jarring her into a shocked reaction, even after more than half a lifetime of knowing that face, and loving it. Trembling, she read the caption: 'Member for Islington South speaks out against racketeers'. He never gave up, never stopped railing against injustice. She stared at his face, ashamed. He had given his life to politics, while she had made do with her family. But she knew even as the thought occurred that this was not important. What mattered was that neither of them had ever been happy apart.

Her eyes skimmed the accompanying article. Joe had been making a speech about the number of racketeers infiltrating England from Europe, profiting from man's misfortune. Below the text there was a row of small, blurred photographs, supposedly of men he had cited as examples. One, Fortunata noticed, was an Italian. She peered more closely at the photograph. She should really get spectacles, she thought; she could hardly read the caption. Slowly, she made it out: 'Paolo Ponti, a businessman visiting London, accused of profiting dishonestly from the post-Korean-war boom in Italy.' She looked again at the photograph. There was something about that mouth ...

Giuseppe stirred and snorted, his brow troubled. Fortunata touched his hand gently. Giuseppe would soon die. This was difficult for her to comprehend. She smiled to herself, sadly. Ten years ago she had longed for Giuseppe to die. Twenty years ago. Thirty. But now that his death was imminent, she could afford a pang of enormous affection for this man who had suffered so much at her side. She stroked his grey hair away from the damp brow. He had come to this country battered by bad fortune, hopeful of a new start but he had only encountered more misfortune, the first being to fall in love with Fortunata. Then the accident, internment, the horror of war, the death of his beloved Antonia, the sacrifice of Roberto Lucente ...

Fortunata suddenly sat bolt upright with a little gasp. She

snatched the newspaper up again. That photograph. She stared at it. 'Paolo Ponti, a businessman.' It was Paolo. Paolo Bianchi. That same cynical curve to the mouth, that same arrogant stare. Paolo Bianchi!

Fortunata realised with a small shock that she had stood up. Her heart was banging in her ribs. Slowly she went over to the old oak dresser opposite the bed. On it were some photographs, framed, standing amid the dusty clutter of hairbrushes, combs and medicines. She picked one up. It was the wedding of her two daughters, both beautiful, both smiling. But Paolo – he was a blur, impregnable, unclear. She put the photograph down, in a daze, and picked up another, this time a formal studio portrait of Serafina and Maria, taken when Maria was nine. Mother and daughter gazed directly out, their faces disarmingly dissimilar. Only their broad foreheads and strong bones indicated that they might be related. Fortunata touched the glass-covered cheek of her granddaughter. She had always harboured a suspicion that Maria was actually Paolo Bianchi's child. She had been almost certain that a secret liaison had taken place between Serafina and Paolo. The night of Paolo's arrest after his escape from the *Arandora Star* had, for Fortunata, merely been confirmation of what she had already surmised, after observing the secret glances, shared smiles of two people who believe that no one suspects them of having an affair. This, Fortunata thought wryly, was a situation with which she was all too familiar herself.

It also explained Serafina's refusal to name the father of her child. She had slept with her sister's husband: the ultimate betrayal. Fortunata returned the photograph to its place on the dresser. Who was she to make judgements? Slowly she went back to her chair. Serafina's conduct was no longer the issue. Growing within Fortunata was a fear, a terrible sense of impending trouble. It was not simply the inevitable death of her husband, labouring feverishly to stay alive as she sat there distractedly stroking his hand. It was a new fear, one of some new and terrible turn of fate to afflict this cursed family. For if Paolo was alive, then what was to stop him coming back? And if he came back to claim Serafina, what would prevent him from claiming the child that was probably his?

In the streets within the triangle of Old Little Italy, the sounds

225

of celebration had replaced the usual rumble of traffic. Almost every residential street was holding a party. At one end of Herbal Hill outside the Coach and Horses, a jazz band was playing, the sound of its trumpet and saxophone clashing discordantly over the rooftops with the more traditional songs being played by Romano's band outside the Fire Station on Farringdon Road. Everywhere bunting hung and Union Jacks were draped.

Serafina was making her way slowly back to Grape Street, from the factory, distracted every few yards by a new sight or a familiar face calling a greeting. Today, she thought ironically, she could have been almost perfectly happy. Guido had asked her to marry him. Violetta had arrived from Nemi. England had a new queen. A new era was beginning, a fresh start. She pulled up the collar of her smart fur coat and sighed. Papa was dying. That was the trouble with new beginnings, they inevitably meant loss as well as gain. Poor Papa. It was impossible for her to imagine existence without Papa. It was good that Guido and Violetta were here, it was like a circle being completed, somehow, a circle that embraced both a small village outside Rome and a scruffy district in London. Serafina smiled regretfully to herself. The trouble was she didn't fit into either place. Perhaps her destiny lay somewhere in the middle, somewhere else in that circle . . .

''Fina! 'Fina!' She spun round, confused. The voice, hoarse, urgent, was exactly the same as a voice from her past. A man stood there, elegant in a well-cut black woollen coat and black hat. She stared at him. He inhaled slowly on a cigarette and stared back at her. She noticed inconsequentially that he was wearing black leather gloves.

'Paolo,' she said. 'It is. Paolo.'

She stepped up to him, peering at the face which had been half-hidden under the brim of his hat. She felt an old, forgotten sensation, a weakness assailing her bones. The same dark intense eyes looked into hers. The same irresistible mouth curled into a smile, as Paolo enjoyed the sensation he had provoked within her. He always knew what he did to her.

He put his hand under her chin. She felt the softness of those leather-clad fingers. 'I told you I'd come back,' he said.

Behind them, a drunken chain of revellers burst out of a pub, singing and shouting, dancing in a long, ragged conga line. As they danced with the kind of abandon that only emerges after many hours of protracted celebration, some of them grinned and shouted at the prosperous-looking couple kissing in the doorway of the bakery, half-hidden by a flapping Union Jack.

But then the crocodile of swaying dancers was halted by a more dramatic distraction, as a child broke through the chain, scattering drunks as she ran urgently on. It was Maria Florio, coat flying, face white, racing towards the church.

'What is it, Maria?' shouted one of the conga line. 'Where's the fire?'

'It's Nonno!' Her voice was carried back to them as she turned the corner, 'I'm going to fetch a priest!'

The conga line quietly disintegrated, as the revellers, suddenly sober, crossed themselves, murmured, and then began to wander away, suddenly sheepish, deflated. And in the shop doorway, lost to life, death, the crowning of queens, everything, the lovers were still clasped together in a lascivious embrace.

CHAPTER ELEVEN

1953

SERAFINA HURRIED UP the stairs to the Winstons' flat, quietly cursing. She had spent too long at Papa's grave, and now Maria would be upset that her mother was late, today of all days.

Slightly out of breath, she let herself in. As usual, all was bedlam. Baby George was sitting in the hall, banging some saucepan lids with evident relish. Anna could be heard screaming with fury at some sibling injustice in the bathroom.

'Sorry, everyone!' Serafina yelled above the din.

Claudia appeared in the kitchen doorway, looking harassed. 'Thank God!' she said, 'I'll go mad if I have to pin that child's headdress on again. She's in our bedroom.'

Serafina found Maria wincing under the heavy hands of her Uncle George, as he tried vainly to secure a small white bonnet on to her curls with hairpins.

'Oh, George! I don't think hairdressing's your style, is it?' They kissed each other on both cheeks in a proper Italian greeting. George was learning to be an Italian. '*Ciao, cara,*' Serafina kissed her daughter, who had raised a dutiful cheek, but with no warmth or enthusiasm. 'Let me see – stand up!' Obediently Maria got to her feet and twirled around to show off her outfit, a copy of the regional dress of Lazio that Serafina had had made for her.

'*Bellissima!*' She and George admired the ensemble. 'Don't worry about the bonnet,' she told her daughter, 'we'll fix it just before it's time to go.'

Maria ran out to find her cousins while Serafina took her place at the dressing-table, pulling off her gloves.

'Where have you been?' George asked. 'She was getting upset. Thought you weren't coming to the procession. You know she's only doing this because you want her to.'

Serafina rooted in her handbag for a lipstick. 'As if I'd miss it! I was at the cemetery. Procession Day was always special to Papa. I just thought I should go there first – to the grave.'

Claudia had come in, carrying a basket of washing, which she proceeded to drape over a clothes-horse by the window. 'You go there too often,' she said, shaking out one of George's shirts. 'You're always there.'

Serafina, intent on applying red lipstick to her mouth, paused and looked at her sister in the mirror. 'He's all I've got,' she said simply, and then returned her attention to her lips. Claudia came over and hugged her, impulsive. They smiled at each others' reflections.

'I miss him too, you know,' Claudia said, 'we all do.' Not all of us. Not Fortunata, Serafina thought. George left the room, still unused to the way the Florios expressed emotion so physically.

'I'll be sorting out the pushchair,' he said, closing the door behind him, so that the eternal noise of the children was suddenly mercifully muted.

Claudia examined her sister's face in the mirror. 'Black suits you,' she said.

Serafina looked down at her expensive suit. 'It should do,' she said, 'this outfit cost the equivalent of two weeks' profit at the factory!'

Claudia was still studying her face. 'You're looking fabulous, 'Fina,' she said.

'I'm too plump to be fabulous.' Serafina powdered her nose, complacent.

'Nonsense. Anyway I was talking about that look on your face. You've got a real sparkle these days.' She studied her successful sister without envy. 'What is it? Have you finally said yes to that poor love-sick idiot who trails you around?'

Serafina laughed, nervous. 'Of course not. I'm very fond of Guido, but—'

'But what? You need a husband. He's a good man, a hard worker. Why not say yes? You know he'll look after you and Maria.' *You mean make do with second best – try and forget the one real passion in your life and marry a dull, adoring clod, like you did . . .* Serafina's eyes slid away, although her voice still had an amused ring to it. 'Listen, *sorella mia*, when I need advice on a husband, I promise you'll be the first person I ask! But until that day — why don't you just let me be the family *zitellona*—'

Claudia laughed. 'You — an old maid? I don't think so, 'Fina. Not you. There's too much of a gleam in your eye for that.'

Serafina shrugged, nonchalant, as she got to her feet, her make-up renewed. 'Well don't hold your breath waiting to be *comare* at my wedding to Guido Mosconi!' She turned, changing the subject. 'You're not going to the procession in that outfit, are you?'

Claudia looked down at her dowdy blouse, an old cast-off of Serafina's. 'I'll be all right,' she said. 'It's not that warm out there. I'll put my black raincoat on over the top. No one will see.'

George was calling from the hall, where he had marshalled the children: Maria in her regional costume, face set, still clutching the recalcitrant bonnet, Julie excited in her white communion dress, Frances and Anna waving small Italian flags and baby George, solemn in a green, red and white bobble hat knitted specially for the occasion.

Serafina paused in the doorway, giving her sister a speculative look as she shrugged into her rainmac. Serafina sighed. How could this overworked, middle-aged looking woman be her little sister? She was only twenty-nine, but she looked forty. Claudia caught her look and understood.

'We're just different, 'Fina,' she said gently, 'George, the kids — they mean everything to me. You're the glamorous one, the career woman. You don't need children or a home — they don't matter to you like work does.' Claudia followed Serafina into the hall and put a protective arm round Maria's stiff, cross shoulders. 'Tell the truth, 'Fina,' she grinned, 'what would you rather have — this delectable child who I seem to remember belongs to you — or a new plaster mould for a giant statue of the Pope?' They all laughed as they left the flat, but there was an underlying note of tension in the laughter; and Maria caught her mother's sideways look down at her, the coldness in her eye, and thought — yes, she would definitely rather have the statue . . .

Fortunata watched the procession wend its way along Hatton Garden towards St Peter's. It seemed a thin and half-hearted occasion, compared to the excitement and spectacle she remembered before the war. But then this corner of London had been proud of itself, vibrant, self-sufficient. Fascism had changed all that. Now people seemed almost ashamed to be Italian, and reluctant to appear publicly to celebrate their origins. Young people had actually refused to help prepare for the *festa* to be held that afternoon, and had disappeared for the day, defiant. Fortunata shook her head, half-smiling to herself. Such rebellion! They were indulging in the kind of anarchy she had longed to embrace as a young woman, but had been firmly prevented from doing so by the weight of tradition pressing on her shoulders. She was not sure, even now, if these angry young people were doing the right thing. Was it so difficult to acknowledge one's origins these days? Wasn't the war supposed to have been fought so that every race and nationality could be free?

She watched a group of middle-aged men march past, erect and sombre. These were the *Alpini* – those who were willing to march in the procession – men who had done their military service in some distant Alpine regiment. They sported perky pointed hats with a long feather pointing upwards, and as they marched, the feathers bobbed in unison. Some people in the crowd cheered and clapped. Fortunata wondered how many *Alpini* had stayed at home today, mindful of the fact that their *Associazione* had had its headquarters in the building of the *fascio*, in Greek Street, before the war. Many felt that it was best to forget former allegiances in view of Italy's shameful role in the war. Others were still defiant, refusing to be ashamed of the party of which they had once proudly been a part. The community was fractured now, vulnerable, uneasy.

Now the children were passing, in their brightly coloured felt bodices and embroidered skirts, each carrying a basket of flowers supplied by Buonavita, the florist. Fortunata peered, looking for her granddaughter. Maria was bringing up the rear of the group, unsmiling, staring steadily ahead. Fortunata's heart went out to her. This had been Serafina's idea, insisting that Maria take part in the procession, not seeming to understand Maria's reluctance. Fortunata understood. For a gawky twelve-year-old, unfamiliar with the other children and unable to speak fluent Italian (in spite of the *doposcuola* classes to which her mother sent her), this procession was dreary and embarrassing.

Maria passed without seeing her grandmother, still elegant in a veiled hat and black coat. Like her step-daughter, mourning suited Fortunata. The dark fabric emphasised her slenderness, and the veil hid the fine lines around her eyes. Her hair was still black, but now cut very short, complementing the fine bones of her face. At last, Fortunata was free to rid herself of that heavy burden of hair she had so resented as a young woman, and her new hairstyle gave her an off-beat, slightly eccentric stylishness that became her.

In spite of her age, Fortunata still drew admiring glances from the men of the Hill, who had always been impressed by her fighting spirit as well as her beauty. The death of her husband seemed not to have diminished either. In fact there were several grey-haired widowers in the crowd who eyed her with more than a little speculation.

Behind the girls in national dress, half-a-dozen young men were carrying a statue of Santa Lucia. Fortunata crossed herself automatically. This was her mamma's saint passing by . . .

She turned away, struggling to suppress tears. Slowly she headed towards St Peter's, walking parallel with Santa Lucia, whose benign plaster features smiled and bobbed over the heads of the crowd. The procession became harder to bear every year. It seemed that there was always someone missing, another name to add to the list of friends and loved ones who had died. Fortunata had spent the morning looking out for her old friend Rosa. They met every year outside Terroni's just as the procession was due to start. This year Fortunata had waited in vain. She told herself that Rosa had missed the bus, or had got caught up in the crowds at the Underground; but in her heart of hearts she had known that Rosa was dead. Finally, a passing acquaintance from the local Labour Party ward meetings confirmed her fears. Ironically, Rosa had died in March, on the same day as Joseph Stalin, alone in her dusty, book-strewn flat; alone with the memories of her long-dead English husband and her handsome, diffident son Eduardo, who had nearly been Serafina's redemption. Fortunata sighed. Although she was not someone who needed the comfort of routine, she felt more than a little shaken by this latest blow. She and Rosa had been together at the procession for so long . . . She remembered suddenly Rosa's face, taut and guilty, saying, 'He's here, Fortunata! He's on the Hill!'

She slowed her pace a little, remembering, her eyes clouded. She had become Joe's lover on Procession Day. She had cuckolded her husband, she had committed a mortal sin on the day when her people went out on to the streets to celebrate their church and their community. She had selected that day to renounce both . . . and she did not regret it. Perhaps that was the most terrible sin of all . . . Santa Lucia caught her eye, faintly reproving, above the heads of the onlookers. Sorry, Mamma, Fortunata said silently, I'm sorry I failed you . . .

The procession was slowing down, as they reached St Peter's. Ahead, Fortunata heard the familiar gasps of joy from children, as the fluttering of doves' wings signalled the climax, and softly coloured petals rained down from above.

Fortunata hesitated, not feeling able to enter the church, suddenly. She had been thinking longingly of the sins she had committed. How could she kneel at the feet of Our Lady and do penance, when her heart yearned to repeat that sin? She hung back as the crowd pressed forward, anxious to enter the magnificent gates of their church. She would go to confession tomorrow, for her dead mamma's sake. Now she would pull herself together, and return to the real world. She would go to Claudia's in Laystall Street and put the kettle on and wait for her family to come back from the procession. She would prepare herself for one of her rare and uncomfortable encounters with Serafina. She would struggle, as usual, to find some common ground, some bland, safe topic of discussion; and she would no doubt fail, as she always did, defeated by Serafina's icy demeanour; intimidated by her stiffness and distance; hurt by her barbed comments.

Serafina, she knew, would have visited Giuseppe's grave today, and she would make sure that her stepmother knew of the visit, staring at her with hard, accusing eyes as she spoke. Fortunata shuddered. It was almost as if Serafina knew her secret, knew of her infidelity, her betrayal of her marriage vows . . .

She did not know how long she sat there, on the low wall opposite the side entrance of the church, on Back Hill, dreaming, lost in her memories. All she knew was that suddenly the doors flew open and people began to emerge into the uncertain sunshine. Father Joseph, very old now, hovered on the threshold, chatting to a group of visiting dignitaries, some with heavy gold chains of office across their chests. He saw Fortunata across the road and waved at her. The men with him looked curiously in her direction, and, as she raised her hand to return the greeting, the smile of recognition on her face froze. For standing behind the old priest was the unmistakable figure of Joe O'Connell. For a blinding moment their eyes met. Still so blue, so direct, she thought, trance-like. Then he had shifted his gaze, and had turned and spoken to someone next to him, in a deliberate movement. Fortunata watched, her bones rigid, as the group moved away up Back Hill. A slim young woman with a blonde perm and a perky hat laughed at something Joe said, a hand on his arm, her face upturned, smiling at him. Fortunata watched, wanting to weep. Why had he come back to haunt her, today of all days, when she felt so vulnerable?

In an angry movement she stood up, turned and walked away in the opposite direction. It was over. It was for the best. Joe had never sought her out, even though he must know Giuseppe was dead; it had been in the local paper – and anyway, mutual political acquaintances who had known of Fortunata's widowhood – and possibly of her affair with Joe as well – would have told him. It was over. It was for the best. Her family would never have accepted Joe. He might as well come from another planet. And Serafina! It would finish them for good, would terminate forever the pathetic remnants of their relationship. No. It was over. It was for the best.

She had not gone to Laystall Street. Some instinct drew her back to the old studio, to the place where it had all begun. She turned into the courtyard and stood looking at the huge double wooden doors, painted bright green. Above them, a smart sign proclaimed 'Florio, Manufacturers of Quality Plaster Goods, Est. 1931' in black and gold. Fortunata allowed herself a wry smile. In spite of her repeated claims to be the family preserver of history and all things Italian, Serafina seemed to have no qualms about expunging poor old Bruno Vialli from his rightful place in the scheme of things. It had been, after all, *his* studio, *his* plaster moulds, that had set Serafina up for life. Poor Papa, Fortunata thought. All that back-breaking work you did to keep Mamma and me from starving – all gone.

The sun was shining with a vengeance now, and this July

Sunday had become hot, oppressive. There was a chair in the yard, left no doubt by one of Serafina's apprentices, taking his tea-break in the sunshine. Fortunata sank into it, tired. She would just rest a while here in the sun, and try to push those memories away . . .

'This is crazy,' she whispered, with a nervous laugh, feeling weak with anticipation.

His lips caressed her neck. 'I know,' he said softly, 'it is crazy. But it's right, isn't it? To come back here?'

His hands, those soft, seductive hands, were trailing across her back, light as the touch of a bird's wing. She turned suddenly, unable to wait, not caring if it was right or not, and sought his mouth. Feverishly he unbuttoned her blouse, feeling for her breasts, his breath coming in short, frantic gasps. She pulled him away, giving a little snort of impatience, and reached around to undo her brassiere, tugging her blouse off and revealing the whiteness of her flesh. He had taken off his shirt, and he fell on her greedily, pushing her back, crashing their bodies against the bench. She threw her head back, lost in the moment.

He raised his head and looked at her. 'Over there,' he said, 'the corner . . .'

'No,' she said, pulling his head back to her breasts, laughing a little to herself at the sensation of his mouth against her skin, 'no. Here. Stay here . . .'

Fortunata dozed quietly in the sun, feeling its warmth on her cheeks, and she smiled to herself, bathing in her memories. For they were all she had left. Tomorrow she must confess . . .

He had pushed her skirt up roughly and his hands were pulling at her underclothes, urgent, angry. She tried to move his hands away, to help him, but he would not let her, tearing at her clothes, pushing her legs open, entering her roughly, desperately. 'This is what you wanted, isn't it?' he muttered. She laughed again, carried beyond the boundaries of how she should respond, able only to receive him and think of nothing else. 'Yes, yes . . .' she breathed, as they moved together, 'this is what I wanted,' as he pushed her harder against the bench, until she thought her back would snap, as he moved further and further within her, until her legs wrapped around his in a movement of total abandon and she let out a cry, at the moment they shuddered together, muscles stretched, her eyes open in surprise, staring into his.

It was over. He was still inside her, his weight against her, his body wet against her breasts. Sweat trickled down her neck. He licked at it and then raised his head and looked into her eyes.

'You're a crazy woman, Serafina,' he said. 'But I could never resist you, you know that.'

She pushed him away, reluctant, feeling him slip away from inside her. She had wanted to keep him there forever. But she must be strong. His head rested, exhausted, on her breasts. She looked down at him, pleased, powerful, and then straightened up. 'Pass me my blouse, Paolo,' she said, 'we must get back . . . and you've torn my knicker elastic!'

Fortunata opened her eyes and tried to shake off her lethargy. She must not sit here dozing in the sun like some old peasant woman. Slowly she got up. She was moving out of the yard, her mind returning to the day and to the approaching *festa*, when she heard the sound of a man's laugh coming from the studio. She hesitated. Some of Serafina's workers must be putting in some overtime – and on Procession Sunday! Indignantly, Fortunata turned and headed towards the door. It was too much, this dogged pursuit of money. She would tell them off. Today of all days, they should not be working. The man laughed again, a throaty, confident sound.

Angry now, Fortunata pushed open the door, and paused on the threshold. Standing together in the shadows, clearly pulling back from an embrace, were a man and a woman. The woman was Serafina.

'I'm sorry—' Fortunata murmured, confused. If that idiot Guido Mosconi wanted to court Serafina in the dusty corners of the studio, it was their business, not hers. But then the man stepped forward, his face suddenly lit by the shaft of light from the skylight window above. Fortunata's gasp fluttered round the room and then settled in the plaster dust. She clutched the door for support.

'So you *have* come back,' she said.

'Fortunata.' Paolo smiled, that full, soft, selfish smile she remembered so well. The face of her dead daughter – poor, weak Antonia – spun into her consciousness, and for a moment she wanted to rush forward and hug him, this vivid reminder of her child, the man 'Tonia had fallen in love with, for better of worse. But then she shook the impulse away. She understood exactly what it was she had interrupted.

'Why did you have to come back?' she asked. 'I hoped you were dead.'

Paolo Bianchi's eyes narrowed. 'Sorry to disappoint you, mother-in-law. They don't kill people for belonging to the wrong political party, you know.'

Fortunata could feel her legs trembling. 'It depends,' she said, 'on what they did in the name of that political party, doesn't it?'

'Oh, for God's sake!' Serafina interrupted angrily, coming forward into the light and placing a proprietorial hand on Paolo's arm. 'This is hardly the time or the place for a debate on the rights and wrongs of fascism!' Her face was flushed, her normally perfect curls in disarray. 'I'm sorry you had to find out like this,' she went on, not sounding in the least bit sorry, 'but we were going to tell everyone.' She looked up at Paolo, her face soft.

Fortunata could not help feeling a small *frisson* of shock. She had never seen Serafina look like this; the hard protective shell she had built so carefully around herself as a woman seemed to have crumbled, revealing suddenly the vulnerable child beneath.

'Didn't you ever wonder what had happened to me after you turned me in to the police?' Paolo was asking her, angry. 'Didn't you care? You wrecked my life and all you can say is that you hoped I was dead!'

Fortunata was not listening. She was gaping at her step-daughter. She felt as though she had just been punched hard in the gut.

'You two—' she whispered, her lips dry. 'You two—' For a split second Serafina's eyes lowered in a moment of shame, but then she looked up again, defiant. 'You were seeing each other – you were sleeping together – back then, weren't you? Before the arrests?' Serafina said nothing, her face steely. 'Weren't you?' Fortunata persisted.

'Yes, we were.' Paolo put his arm round Serafina. 'We were. If I hadn't got 'Tonia pregnant, things might have turned out very differently . . .'

Serafina made a slight, nervous movement. 'Paolo,' she said, softly. 'Why don't you wait for me outside?'

'But I don't want—'

'Please,' her voice was urgent, pleading. 'Please!'

He relented, pushing angrily past Fortunata in the doorway. Then he turned suddenly, his face very close to hers. 'I'll tell you one thing,' he said, his mouth taut, 'I'm taking 'Fina back with me to Italy. We're both free agents. We're getting married. Then we're going home!' and he was gone, the slam of the door disturbing the plaster dust, which flew up into the shaft of light, a million tiny dancing white particles.

Serafina turned away from her stepmother, nervous. She picked up an unpainted statuette of the Virgin, a copy of the one she had brought from Nemi, and fingered it as she spoke. 'It's true,' she said, 'I'm going to marry Paolo. I'm going back to Italy.'

Fortunata had to ask. 'And little Maria? You'd take her away from – from everything she knows and loves and transplant her in Italy? You think she'd like that? You'd uproot her so that you can have what you want?'

Serafina shrugged, her eyes never leaving the little statue, her fingers examining it as if it were the most precious thing on earth. 'It's up to Maria,' she said, her voice cool. 'If she chooses to come to Italy, I'm sure we can accommodate her. But perhaps–' Serafina looked up at last, an odd expression on her face '–perhaps she'll choose to stay in England.' A pause. 'She's half-English, after all.'

Fortunata was still holding on to the doorframe, trembling. Serafina was going to reveal her secret at last.

'So . . .' she said, careful. 'So – Paolo isn't Maria's father. It was Eduardo after all?'

Serafina laughed a little, twisting the statuette in her hands, rubbing at an invisible mark on it. 'Do you think I only slept with two men in my life, Fortunata?' She smiled, a small secret smile.

'Don't play with me,' Fortunata said.

Serafina slapped the little statue down on the bench. Part of its base flew off and tinkled to the floor. 'Actually,' she said, 'that wasn't quite accurate – about Maria being half-English.' She retrieved her handbag from the bench, and stared at her stepmother. She was about to deliver her exit line, and she wanted the timing to be perfect. 'I'm not prepared to name names,' she said, 'that would be too cruel. But have a good look at Maria when you get back to Laystall Street. Has it ever occurred to you that she could be Irish?'

She threw a bunch of keys at her stepmother, who caught them, unthinking, automatic. 'Here,' Serafina said, 'lock up for me, will you?'

And she was gone, closing the door behind her, leaving Fortunata alone. Paolo was waiting outside in the sunshine, lounging in the chair that Fortunata had vacated. He looked up at Serafina and smiled, that same sensual, wry smile that had seduced her so long ago. Her heart turned over.

'*Va bene?*' he asked, standing up and taking her arm.

She reached up and kissed him. '*Si,*' she said, '*va bene,*' and together they walked slowly away, across the cobbled yard. Paolo drew her protectively closer as she shivered in spite of the sunshine. This had been her moment of triumph. Why, then, did she feel so desolate?

The sun was sinking away behind the grey rooftops of Clerkenwell, and the people of Little Italy danced in the streets, as they had done every year on that day for all their lifetimes and beyond. In the dark and silent studio Fortunata sat, motionless, cradling the last statuette of Our Lady. All the others she had smashed, and they lay at her feet, pathetic fragments of hand, robe, face, foot, gleaming white in the darkness.

Behind her the door creaked open. She did not turn.

'Fortunata.' That voice. That wonderful sing-song voice calling her name, making it sound beautiful. She gave a little cry and got up. It really was Joe, standing in the doorway, the lamp outside lighting up his grey-red hair like a bright halo. Joe, like a ghost, standing there, uncertain, full of love, his bright eyes fixed upon her.

Slowly she rose up, still clutching the little Madonna, and moved across to him. 'Joe,' she said, 'Joe.' She wanted to say so much, to ask so much. Was it true? Had Serafina managed to despoil the one true and beautiful thing in her life? Joe looked down at her, his love for her etched into every line on

239

his strong, still freckled Irish face, and suddenly it did not matter. Whatever Serafina had done, whatever weakness in Joe she had exploited – none of it mattered. For he was here, and he still loved her. She took another step towards him, almost timid. 'I – I've missed you, Joe,' she said simply.

He pulled her to him and kissed her, a kiss so full of pain and pent-up longing that she made a hurt sound. Then he lifted her up (for she was still as small and light as she had always been) and sat her on the workbench where they had made love another lifetime ago, and he talked to her. He told her of the long nights he had spent alone, the years of misery, watching her trapped in a loveless marriage, carrying out the duties of a good Italian wife and mother. He described the endless hours of work into which he had plunged in a desperate effort to erase their affair from his mind. He told her of the night he had stood, unseen, in the shadows of Grape Street, drunk and in despair beneath her bedroom window, torturing himself with visions of her in the arms of her husband; and of the terrible moments of cold fear at the thought of never holding her again, never loving her again, of dying alone somewhere, still thinking of her . . .

Mercifully, as he spoke, the name of Serafina never crossed his lips. She made a decision then. She would never tell him of the terrible claim Serafina had made, nor of her unworthy suspicions that it was all true, that Maria was indeed the child of Serafina Florio and Joe O'Connell. She smiled at him, strong in the knowledge that she loved him too much to cast a shadow over this reconciliation.

'And now–' Joe hugged her gently and stood back a little as if wanting to see her clearly and completely– 'now I must ask you—'

'Joe—'

'No. Hear me out, Fortunata. I've stayed away because I wanted you to feel you had a suitable period of mourning. No–' he held up his hand as she tried to speak– 'I know what you're going to say . . .' She subsided, elated and frightened all at once, as Joe brushed a distracted hand through his hair, looking for all the world like a self-conscious schoolboy, and ploughed on. 'I know I should have waited longer. You Italians like to observe certain proprieties . . .' His voice shook a little, 'Oh, but Fortunata I couldn't wait any longer. I've waited so long ... We both have ... and when I saw you outside the church, standing exactly where I found you all those years ago at another procession – you remember? It was like fate. Kismet. I couldn't just leave without seeing you. And now I have – well – I can't wait any longer. Lord knows how much time we have left. So – will you marry me, Fortunata Vialli? Can we forget all about the Florios and the damn war and Italy and everything, and just do what we should have done thirty years ago?' The tension in his face was too much for her. Her eyes filled with tears. 'Will you marry me, Fortunata? Will you marry me soon?'

'Oh, Joe.' She pulled him to her again, and rested her head on his shoulder. His arms went round her, hugging her tight until she could barely breathe. 'Joe,' she whispered, 'I can't wish away my life as Fortunata Florio. If there hadn't been Giuseppe, there wouldn't have been Antonia, or Claudia, or Maria, or Julie ... and the little ones – Frances, Susan, Anna, baby George – how could I wish them away?' She pulled back and gazed up at him. Gently he lifted the veil from her hat and saw how close she was to weeping. 'Even Giuseppe Florio himself. Even Serafina,' she whispered. 'I am a Florio, Joe, as well as a Vialli.' She lifted a gloved finger and traced the straight, anxious line of his mouth. A glimmer appeared through the tears. 'However,' she said, 'there's absolutely nothing to stop me becoming an O'Connell as well now, is there?'

With a great triumphant shout of joy, Joe lifted her up, twirled her around until she was breathless, and then kissed her until she had to pummel at his chest, laughing, gasping, begging him to stop.

And on a small shelf high above the workbench, half hidden by the paint pots and the jars of varnish, the little Nemi Madonna watched the reunited lovers, her faded face impassive, her brow clear and her eye as cool as ever.

CHAPTER TWELVE

1956

'THE SHADOW HOME SECRETARY wants another drink.'
Maria emerged from the crush of party guests in the
hall to the relative quiet of the kitchen, carrying some
empty bottles of wine. She smiled at Fortunata, pink-cheeked
and excited by the proximity of so many eminent people
crammed into the little Grape Street house. Her grandmother,
pulling a tray of sausage rolls out of the oven, was laughing at
a lady Labour Councillor's joke, and she straightened up at
the sound of Maria's voice, her face glowing. The two women
pretending to help her in the kitchen, one the Councillor, the
other the wife of the Honourable Member for Bradford, both
nibbled on their purloined sausage rolls and admired, as usual,
the charm and character of Fortunata O'Connell, who seemed
to have everything: an adoring husband, a devoted surrogate
daughter, a quick wit, intelligence, and a lovely face as an
unfair extra bonus. In political terms she played a relatively
minor role compared to her husband, working as secretary of
her local Labour ward. But her personality and history made
her a popular figure, much in demand behind the scenes,
constantly invited on to committees or asked to speak at
meetings. Added to which, she contributed articles to the
Italian newspaper *La Voce* and worked regularly for the Rev-
olutionary Socialist League, writing articles for their publi-
cation, *Socialist Fight*, happy to be once again involved in the
hurly-burly of editorial debate, always a feature of political
publications. She seemed to function in happy chaos, always
surrounded by the paraphernalia of her work: heaps of leaflets,
piles of reference books, the telephone constantly ringing, the
house always full of visitors. Yet she was never harassed,
always laughing, bubbling with enjoyment, as if eager to fill
every minute and make up for time she had lost.

'Here—' she was throwing a corkscrew across the room to Maria, 'but don't let him have the bottle – he might end up singing "La Marseillaise" like he did at that House of Commons do . . .'

Maria began opening a bottle of Frascati. 'Well, we're all supposed to love the French at the moment, aren't we? They're our allies.'

The MP's wife snorted. 'That would have been small comfort if Israel had decided to declare war!'

Fortunata groaned, shovelling the sausage rolls unceremoniously on to a dinner plate. 'I thought we made a pact – no talk of Suez, not tonight! We'll have a political debate raging in the front room for the rest of the night if the men hear you! You know what Joe's like.'

'No – what *is* he like? Tell us, Mrs O'Connell!' He was in the doorway, grinning at her. She felt the same small flutter that always descended on her at the sight of him.

Maria, still opening bottles, and the two women, arranging glasses half-heartedly on a tray, were all still for a moment, feeling the intense bond between these two, a palpable thread joining them across the room.

'Joe O'Connell is like a dog with a bone when it comes to politics,' Fortunata said, laughing at him, the moment dissipated. 'Once he's got some topic between his teeth, he never lets go.'

He stepped into the room, as always, seeming too tall for such an enclosed space, filling it with his broad shoulders and his bright hair, stooping slightly as if he feared his head might hit the ceiling. He put an arm round her waist, proprietorial, teasing.

'She's a terrible harridan, this woman,' he said to no one in particular, leaning across her to steal a sausage roll. 'You'd think she'd let up on a man's birthday . . . Just a quick five minutes on the blockade, or a couple of opinions on the trouble in Budapest—'

'Absolutely not!' She handed him the plate of sausage rolls, her voice firm. 'Bland topics only. Sir Anthony Eden's rest cure – now there's a safe bet. You'll all be agreeing that you wish him well, but not too well.'

Joe laughed, heading for the door. 'I'll bet you ten bob that lot in there could manage a punch-up or two even if the only question was how many medals we'll win in the Olympic Games!' He paused for a moment and looked at her. 'You will be coming to talk to us soon, won't you? I don't want you stuck out here all night like a skivvy. Hugh wants to talk to you and Edith hasn't even met you yet.'

'I'll be along,' she said soothingly, 'and you might just regret it. You know how I feel about Suez – I can't guarantee I'll behave myself in front of your powerful friends.'

'Good!' He grinned at her again and disappeared, holding the plate of sausage rolls aloft as he struggled down the hall through the noisy crush of guests all calling greetings to him and slapping him on the back.

'Rosemary – can you take these? And Peggy?' Fortunata sent the women away with trays of food and more glasses, and then went to sit down at the kitchen table. Maria, who had been heading towards the hall with her two opened bottles of wine, paused at the sight of Fortunata, wincing with pain, lowering herself carefully on to a chair.

'Nonna – are you all right?' Her blue eyes registered concern.

Fortunata waved her away. 'I'm fine. Just a touch of indigestion—' She bit her lip but managed a smile. 'Joe isn't the only one who's sixty, you know,' she said, 'we're getting a bit creaky, *topolina*, that's all. I'll just make myself a quick cuppa and I'll be fine. You go in with that wine, or there'll be a revolution in there!'

'Don't say that in front of Janos,' Maria called over her shoulder, 'he'll be setting up a barricade outside the house if anyone mentions revolution!'

Fortunata smiled to herself, rubbing her stomach gently, where the pain was. Maria had a severe crush on Janos, the serious-faced young Hungarian who was Fortunata's current lame duck. He was lodging rent-free in the spare room, a refugee from Budapest, a young activist in the recent uprising. Fortunata had insisted on offering him shelter. It was the least she could do to expunge her guilt and fury at this latest Soviet outrage. Like many ex-members of the Communist Party, she felt irrationally responsible for these new outbreaks of repression. Having Janos, pale-faced and silent, under her roof was the only action she could take. Joe, of course, had been happy to accommodate this desperate, unhappy young man. And Maria? Well, she was sixteen, and the Hungarian lodger with his high cheekbones, his dark eyes and his brooding silence was irresistible to a romantic sixteen-year-old girl. Still, Fortunata pondered, her interest in Janos had at least meant that Maria had destroyed her collection of Pat Boone pictures. Fortunata thought Pat Boone a singularly dull young man, whereas Janos Fekete had charisma. He was exotic.

The subject of her thoughts wandered into the room, slightly drunk, holding an empty wine glass. He came over and pulled out a chair next to Fortunata and slumped down in it, morose.

Fortunata patted his hand. 'I know, I know,' she said soothingly. Actually, she thought, she did *not* know. Janos spoke no English, and no Italian, and she spoke no Hungarian. Communication took place sketchily, by means of elaborate mimes and gestures, grimaces and barely understood monosyllables. Fortunata had no idea what thoughts were running through that young mind, what horrors he had seen, what memories haunted him as he sat there, twirling his glass around, silent. All she knew was that her heart went out to him. He was like Maria, abandoned in the world, without parents. Fortunata's own happiness, which had come to her so late in life, had given her the freedom to open up her heart and her home to all comers. At last she felt she could live the carefree, unconventional existence she had always longed for . . .

The sound of new voices in the hall and the slam of the front door interrupted her thoughts. She smiled wryly to herself. Had she been thinking about freedom at the very moment when her suffocating brood of sulking grandchildren had been gathering on the doorstep? Janos looked at her, regretful. 'Julie,' he said. 'Frances. Susan. Anna. George.'

'I know,' she said, getting to her feet slowly, suppressing again the twinge of pain that stabbed at her side. '*La famiglia . . .*'

Claudia put her head round the door first. 'Can we come in?' she called. 'Sorry we're late, only Frances wanted to wear her red dress at the last moment, so we had to wait while she changed . . .' She came into the kitchen, her collection of solemn-faced offspring behind her. 'George has gone into the front room – to talk to the men.'

245

Fortunata kissed her daughter. 'There are women in there too,' she said, her tone ironic. 'You forget. This is no longer an Italian house.'

Claudia shuddered, mock-horrified. 'Nonna Lucia would turn in her grave if she could hear you! Right – where's the wine?' Fortunata gestured to Janos, standing politely to attention by the stove, and he obediently went to fetch a glass.

'A handsome boy, that one,' said Claudia thoughtfully, watching him go. 'I hope you're keeping an eye on him. Maria's growing up fast. Oh, do stop hanging about in the doorway, you lot!' Claudia turned irritably to her children, suddenly very Italian, and ushered them inside. They stood in a row, staring at Nonna Fortunata, intimidated by the party and the sight of so many unfamiliar faces in the front room. She smiled at them kindly, wishing she could feel more affection for this sandy-haired, pale-faced brood.

Julie, the oldest and most self-confident at ten, stepped forward. 'Can I get George a drink of orange, Nonna?'

'Of course you can.' She watched them as they clustered round the sink – nine-year-old Frances, petulant in her best red dress, Susan whining as usual, Anna silent and fearful, peering from under a scruffy fringe; and George, the baby at five, with a permanent cold, but blessed with the easy grin and relaxed personality of his father. As always Fortunata wondered why these children somehow meant less to her than Maria. After all, it was Maria she had every reason to dislike. Not only was she the daughter of Serafina, but there was the question of her father . . .

'Fortunata?' Janos was at her side, looking at her, concerned.

'I'm fine, really.' She smiled at him. He understood suffering. Sad, really. He was too young to understand so much . . . 'Give Claudia a drink, Janos.' She looked at her daughter, so Italian, with those dark eyes and black curls tinged with grey and felt a wave of weary affection for her. Poor Claudia, who would be so offended by her mother's pity, if she had been aware of it. It was ironic really, that Fortunata had managed to produce a child that was the antithesis of everything she believed in. Claudia was a traditional wife and mother, subservient to her family, caught up in the daily drudgery of cooking, washing, cleaning, and seemingly contented with her lot. It never failed to amaze and depress her mother in equal measure. Added to which – the final blow – she shared her husband's politics. They were both staunch Conservatives, which made their visits to Grape Street tense occasions, with everyone on their best behaviour, anxious not to offend. Today, with the front room crowded with members of the opposition, Labour Party workers and trades union officials, the visit would be a true test of the Winstons' tolerance.

Fortunata moved across the kitchen and hugged her daughter, impulsively. Claudia was a good soul. She would do nothing to offend her mamma because she was a dutiful Italian daughter above all else . . .

'What was that for?' asked Claudia, surprised by the unexpected show of affection.

'Just for being here,' said Fortunata, simply. 'Come on, let's go and find Joe.'

'I can't go in there!' Claudia hung back, 'it's full of important people!'

'Not as important as you,' said Fortunata, taking her daughter's arm, firm. 'Come along!'

The noise in the front room had reached a deafening level. Above the cacophony of voices Fortunata could hear the strident sounds of a trumpet. She struggled through the crush to the window where, sure enough, Maria was presiding happily over the radiogram, sorting through a pile of jazz records.

'Maria!' she called, 'it's too loud – turn it down!' Maria grinned, but obeyed. 'Fuddy-duddy!' she said.

'I just don't want the Leader of the Opposition to have no voice in the Commons tomorrow because he's been shouting over Louis Armstrong.'

Maria had stopped listening, her eyes searching the throng of party guests for someone. Fortunata understood. 'He's in the kitchen,' she said, teasing, 'babysitting for your cousins.' Maria had the grace to blush. Then she noticed Claudia, hovering behind her mother, cowed by the famous faces around her.

'Hello, Zia Claudia!' Maria kissed her aunt fondly but hastily, moving away in search of Janos. She was sure tonight was the night. She knew Janos was attracted to her. Young as she

247

was, she recognised the signals, and the thought of what might happen made her heart pound, her cheeks pink. But her path was blocked by Joe O'Connell.

'My entire Italian family in one place at one time!' he said. 'This must be a record.' His eyes met Fortunata's, full of happiness. Maria was determinedly elbowing past him.

'Not for long, Joe!' she said. 'I've got to go and see my cousins in the kitchen—'

'And a certain Hungarian, perhaps?' asked Joe, innocent. Maria grinned back at him and stuck out her tongue cheekily. They liked each other very much, these two, Fortunata thought. It never ceased to make her feel both contented and yet anxious at the same time. Surely so much happiness could not last?

Maria turned back, remembering something. 'Father Joseph's here,' she said. 'I let him in a few minutes ago. He's over on the sofa, talking to some bishop or other.'

'Father Joseph!' Claudia was amazed. 'He must be about a hundred!'

'Never one to miss a good party, a priest,' remarked Joe, 'and he has known your family forever, it seems.'

Maria heard this as she struggled through the throng. She turned back and called, 'I think he's getting a bit senile – when I answered the door he said, "Oh – you're the O'Connell child, aren't you?" He often calls me that, you know!' She laughed and was gone, amused by the old priest's remark. Fortunata's eyes met Joe's for a split second. Then she turned to Claudia.

'Come on!' she said brightly. 'Let's go and make sure he's not terrorising the bishop,' and she ushered her daughter away, leaving her husband alone for a moment by the window, staring after her. Then he, too was drawn away back into the crowd, and after a moment or two his laughter could be heard, the same carefree sound that had captivated his wife so long ago, echoing around the room above the sound of party conversation and the clinking of glasses.

Maria found Janos cornered by the sink, hemmed in by the Winston children. He didn't seem to mind. He had baby George perched on the draining-board and was pulling funny faces and making him giggle.

'Janos is nice,' Julie announced to her cousin. 'He looks like a prince.'

'Are you going to marry him?' Susan asked. 'Will you have a dress like Princess Grace's?'

'Can I be a bridesmaid?' asked Frances, her lower lip already in a pout, expecting a negative response. 'I want to be a bridesmaid!'

Maria settled them round the kitchen table, thankful for once that Janos could not understand English. 'I'm not going to get married,' she said cheerily, 'I'm going to be the first lady Prime Minister!'

'But you have to get married,' Baby George squeaked from the draining-board, 'you're a girl!'

'. . . And Father Patrick says it's a holy state,' said Anna.

'A holy estate,' Frances corrected her, prim, munching on a fairy cake.

'What's that?' asked Susan.

Frances didn't know. She changed the subject quickly. 'Why don't you go to the Catholic school, like us?' she asked her cousin, disapprovingly. 'How can you be a Catholic and not go to the Catholic school?'

'It's possible,' Maria said, grimly. But only just, she thought. Her school years had not been happy ones. She had never got over the feeling that she was somehow the outsider, but, looking back, perhaps it was a good thing, she decided. For of all the girls in that smart, snobbish oh-so-English establishment, only Maria Florio and her solemn bespectacled friend Evelyn had passed all their exams with flying colours and now looked set to enter university. Perhaps all those painful, lonely lunch hours spent studying together, excluded from the tight-knit cliques of popular girls, had meant something after all . . .

Her thoughts were interrupted by baby George. 'Where's your mum?' he demanded. 'I want Nonna!'

'Nonna's not Maria's mum, silly!' said Julie. 'She's Maria's granny, just like she's your granny.'

'Where is your mum?' Frances asked Maria, interested. Maria turned to lift George down, her face not visible to her cousins. Janos watched her, aware of the change in the atmosphere.

She deposited George on the floor. 'In Italy. She married

another Italian and went to Rome,' she said. She began to run water into the sink, filling the bowl. 'I'd better wash some glasses.'

'Why didn't you go to Rome with your mum?' Frances persisted.

Maria turned and looked at her cousins, all gazing at her, their brown eyes expectant. 'Because I didn't want to,' she said simply, 'I didn't want to.'

There was a small silence while the children digested this, puzzled. Not to want to be with your mother! To the Winston children, whose mother was a constant presence, a constant reassurance, this was unthinkable, impossible.

'But surely—' began Julie.

Janos suddenly moved, breaking the moment. 'Cake,' he said, pushing another fairy cake under George's wrinkling nose, 'cake!' The girls giggled and squealed as he dabbed some chocolate icing on the little boy's nose and threatened to do the same to them, with exaggerated movements and loud snarling noises. Maria looked at him, grateful. Sometimes you just didn't need words . . .

The party finally ended at one o'clock in the morning. Maria had already gone upstairs to bed as Joe waved goodbye to the last guests on the doorstep. He turned back inside the house to find Janos hesitating, tea towel in hand, in the hall.

'Fortunata . . .' said Janos, tentative, indicating the kitchen.

Joe put a hand on his shoulder. 'Thanks, Janos. You've been great. You go off to bed—' he pointed upstairs, miming. 'Sleep. I'll finish off.' He took the tea towel.

'Fortunata . . .' said Janos again, still hovering.

'In the kitchen. Yes. Goodnight now!' Janos went slowly upstairs, watching Joe's receding back, his face anxious.

Fortunata was not in the kitchen. Joe looked around, puzzled. Trays of wine glasses, washed and standing neatly in rows, covered the kitchen table. A crate of empty wine bottles stood by the back door. The remaining food had all been put away, and the kitchen looked almost normal. Only Fortunata was not there. He was about to turn and go upstairs when he heard a faint muffled sound from the back yard. He opened the door and stepped outside, shivering a little as the autumn night air replaced the warmth of the kitchen.

'Fortunata!' he said, his voice full of concern, 'what are you doing out here? You'll catch your death, you daft eejit!' She was sitting perched on the low window sill, beside the pots of dead geraniums, her head bowed. He realised with a shock that she was crying.

'Fortunata . . .' he said again, his voice softer now, 'whatever is the matter?' She raised her face to his, her eyes red with tears. 'Nothing,' she said, 'nothing. It doesn't matter.'

He came and sat next to her. For a moment there was silence. Then a cat yowled somewhere in the dark alleyways of Clerkenwell, and there was the distant clatter of a dustbin lid. Fortunata sniffed a little.

Joe sighed. 'That was one hell of a party you gave me, Mrs O'Connell. I want to thank you.'

'You don't have to thank me.' Her voice was low, muffled.

He didn't turn or touch her. Instead he continued staring into the gloom of the back yard, dimly lit by the light from the kitchen. In spite of all the window boxes and the trellis for the ivy, there was no disguising the fact that this was the yard of a small, no-nonsense working-class house: a yard where women had worked the mangle, where men had polished their boots, where a thousand bedsheets had been hung on the line to dry. It was the right house for them, Joe thought, even if the ghosts of dead Italians seemed always to haunt the place. Giuseppe Florio. Lucia and Bruno Vialli. Poor sad Antonia. The Luchente brothers, Joe and Roberto . . . Rosa and Eduardo. And Serafina . . . although of course she was not dead . . .

He shifted slightly, still not looking at his wife. 'You know, Fortunata,' he said quietly, 'when we finally got married, we promised something to each other. Do you remember?'

She nodded. 'I remember.' Her voice sounded tired. 'No secrets. We promised never to have secrets.'

'We did. So why are you out here crying and swearing to me that nothing's wrong, if we have no secrets?'

'But is it true, Joe?' She turned from him, distressed, the tears welling up again. 'Do you not have a secret? Something you have never told me?'

He laughed gently. 'God, woman! How can you think that? I've shared everything with you – everything!'

251

She stood up suddenly, with a choking sob. 'I want to believe you! I really do!'

Joe stared at her. 'Fortunata—' he was puzzled, afraid. 'I have no secrets, I swear to you, I have no secrets.'

She turned to him, her face full of anger.

'And Serafina! What about her? What about you and Serafina?'

In the room upstairs, Maria froze in her bed, in the dark, listening to their voices in the yard. What further sin of her mother's was to be revealed now?

'Me – and – Serafina?' Joe was gaping at Fortunata, aghast.

She stared at him steadily. There. It was said. She felt stronger now. She could face this. She must face this. 'I want to know,' she said, 'I want to know what happened between you two. I know something did.'

'How did you know?' He couldn't help asking, amazed. 'How do you know?'

'Serafina, of course. You think she would keep something like that a secret from me? It was her great moment of triumph! Her final victory!' She looked at him, angry now, her voice bitter. 'I just hope she was worth it.'

Joe was slumped back against the window, his large frame blocking out the light. In front of him Fortunata stood erect, waiting to hear confirmation of what she dreaded hearing.

'It's true, isn't it?' she whispered.

Joe looked up. Even against the light she could see how white he was, how pained.

'Is that what you believe?' he asked.

'Just answer the question, Joe.'

They stared at each other. They had been so close, so united, and now a chasm yawned between them and the moment had come to discover whether that gap could ever be bridged again. The moment stretched into an eternity. Then Joe began to speak, conjuring up the night he would have preferred to forget. He was holding Fortunata's hand now, rubbing it as if to keep it warm.

'It was in June, wasn't it . . .' he was saying, 'when the internment started . . . I remember how hot it was.'

'And Serafina?' Fortunata persisted, unable now to stop.

The air between them trembled as he struggled with the words. 'I met Serafina by accident, in a pub off Fleet Street.'

Joe's voice was uncharacteristically low. Fortunata had to strain to catch the words. 'She was looking for news of Giuseppe . . .'

'No.' Fortunata interrupted, her voice bitter. 'She was looking for news of Paolo. Her sister's husband.'

Joe stared ahead of him, remembering, a frown crossing his brow. 'Those were crazy, crazy times. Everyone was half-mad.' He looked at his wife. 'And me more than most. I hadn't seen you for so long. So long!' he said, angry at the memory. 'I thought it was over, and yet I had been so sure, you know. Sure you were the one for me. Sure we would be married some day.' She felt the pressure on her hand as Joe squeezed it. He was finding this difficult, she realised with some surprise, the man to whom words always came so easily. 'And then Serafina appeared,' he said, 'like a ghost out of my past. I looked at her, in the middle of all that chaos, all that madness – and I saw you.'

Fortunata's hand was still in his, as she listened. She stared at those two hands joined together, and wondered if her happiness was about to be taken from her forever.

'I know she looks nothing like you,' Joe was saying, 'but just then – with her black curls and her big dark eyes—'

'She looked lovely then,' Fortunata remembered, rueful, without malice. 'She bloomed that summer. Some people thrive on misfortune.'

Joe sighed. There was a silence, as they both remembered those times.

'Go on,' she said gently, wondering why she was so anxious to hear the words that might destroy her marriage.

Joe took a deep breath. The grip on her hand tightened. 'I must tell you the truth,' he said, anguished, 'I don't want to keep anything back . . .'

'Good,' she said evenly, 'I'm ready to hear it.'

'We sat in the pub together. People kept buying me drinks – it was after a union meeting – the printers . . . I was drunk by ten o'clock.' He stole a glance at Fortunata, but her face revealed nothing. 'I was often drunk in those days,' he said, bitterly. 'I was half-mad with loneliness and fear. Then along comes Serafina Florio, a little bit of Italy, looking like a forbidden fruit and, by God, looking like she could offer a man some comfort in his hour of need . . .' Joe bit his lip. 'I was drunk, Fortunata, she – well – she wanted to—'

'You mean she offered herself to you?'

She waited for the answer, knowing already what it would be. 'Yes. She flirted with me, and she made it clear what she was after. She gazed at me with those big dark eyes and she leaned into me, and she touched me . . . and I was drunk.'

There was a silence. Finally Fortunata spoke. 'So it is true,' she said. 'Maria is your child.'

There was a moment when time hung suspended, when the night seemed to pause, crackling with tension, waiting for life to move on. Then suddenly, incredibly, Joe burst out laughing.

'Fortunata!' he gasped, gazing in wonder at her taut and incredulous expression. 'Is that what you've been thinking all this time? That me and Serafina – that Maria – oh, that's so daft it could only be Irish! You're a true O'Connell after all!' And he swung her round and deposited a kiss on her lips and then hugged her tight, almost crushing her. 'You idiot! You damned idiot!'

Upstairs, Maria felt the tension flowing out of her body like honey. Years of unnamed worry seemed to seep from her bones. She felt weak with relief. It was going to be all right, after all . . .

Joe was still hugging his wife. He held her until she stopped trembling, and then he kissed the top of her head and looked at her tenderly. 'God,' he said, 'is that really what you thought?'

'You seemed so ashamed,' she whispered, her heart flooded with relief, the world set to rights again.

'I *was* ashamed,' he said. 'Don't you see? I still am! Because I was tempted, Fortunata. That's the terrible thing. In spite of knowing Serafina, knowing what a scheming little witch she's always been, what a manipulating—' his voice shook, the thought unfinished. 'I wanted her that night.'

'But you said no.'

'I said no. But it was a hell of a struggle I had with myself, I can tell you. A hell of a struggle.'

Fortunata looked at him. 'But you said no.'

Joe stared at the ground, the memory of that night still able to make him shudder. 'It was like – in the middle of all that ugliness; the war, the terrible mess we were all in – someone comes along and offers you something exotic, exciting—'

'An orchid,' said Fortunata.

Joe looked at her, surprised. 'Yes, I suppose so. An orchid.'

Fortunata thought for a moment. Serafina's face came to her – the face of a child, tear-stained and exhausted, a child holding out a small statue and calling '*Guarda! Santa Maria! Guarda!*' Poor Serafina. 'Don't call her a witch,' she told Joe. 'She was never evil. Just unhappy. It doesn't matter what she tried to do. Only that you refused her.'

'But I was tempted and now I'm ashamed.'

Fortunata stood on tiptoe and held his face in her hands. 'Don't be,' she whispered. 'I've never loved you as much as I do now.' Her lips touched his, gently, and in the silence of the early morning, Joe O'Connell felt all the ghosts tiptoe away.

'Now let's have a last clear up and go to bed,' Fortunata was saying, suddenly brisk again, 'and a last check that Janos isn't prowling the landing intent on seducing my grand-daughter!'

Maria heard that last remark and smiled to herself, turning over finally to go to sleep. She had decided. Even if Janos were to appear miraculously at her bedroom door this very moment, she would send him away. Sex was a certain kind of power, she realised, but she didn't want that kind. It didn't last. She would set her sights on higher things . . .

As Fortunata followed her beloved Joe back into the house, she felt again the stab of pain in her side, a cruel reminder of the demands of time. No secrets, they had promised each other. She sighed. Tomorrow. She would tell him tomorrow.

Upstairs in the small back bedroom, Maria smiled and stirred in her sleep, dreaming of the day when she would take up her seat in Parliament . . .

CHAPTER THIRTEEN

1963

T HE BLACK LIMOUSINE turned quietly into the main
     drive of the North London cemetery, and slid to a
     halt.

'Wait here,' she told the driver, reaching for her umbrella,
for it was raining. She should have known. A British funeral,
a dank autumn day, the leaves whipped by the wind into
sombre little piles around the gravestones; of course it would
rain. She struggled out of the car, an overweight middle-aged
woman in an expensive black fur coat and a large-brimmed
black hat which threatened to blow away as she unfurled her
umbrella. The mourners were already gathered around the
open grave at the far end of the cemetery. She squinted a
little to see if she could recognise anyone, but the driving
rain had turned the entire dismal landscape into a blur, with
indistinct figures in black standing motionless within it,
heads bowed, either in prayer or against the wind, she
couldn't be sure.

Someone hurried past her, another late mourner, an old
woman in a moth-eaten navy overcoat and a headscarf. The
two women exchanged looks, curious, but neither recognised
the other. Slowly she followed the old woman towards the
grave. She felt numb – whether from the cold or from the
overwhelming significance of the day she did not know. She
went on tiptoe in her absurdly high heels and stood discreetly
under a dripping laburnum, almost out of sight.

She did not recognise the priest droning the words of the
service. He was young and red-faced, with a Birmingham
accent and no sense of drama. He might as well have been
reading a shopping list, she thought to herself, amused.

'Serafina! Serafina!' The drumming of the rain on her umbrella meant that she did not hear the voice at first. But

standing next to her, shivering, her face blotched with tears, was Claudia. 'Is it really you?' she was asking, her voice breaking with emotion. 'You really came! George said you wouldn't – but I knew! I knew you would!' The two women embraced under Serafina's umbrella, their faces streaked with a mixture of rain and tears, one plump with the sheen of wealth about her, the other thin and faded, old before her time.

By the graveside, Joe O'Connell looked up and saw. Involuntarily he reached out for Maria, standing next to him, her head bowed, her face blank with grief. She clasped his hand comfortingly, imagining only that the priest's prayers were having an unexpected effect on him, not seeing what he saw through the driving rain.

Now the coffin was being lowered into the ground. Many of the mourners could not hear the priest's words above the drumming of the rain, but they dutifully crossed themselves whenever he did, shuddering under their umbrellas, chilled and sad. The priest had paused now, and was looking expectantly at Joe. Maria nudged him; he seemed transfixed by Claudia, hugging someone on the other side of the grave.

'Joe–' she whispered, 'Joe! The rose!' and he suddenly came to himself with a little shake, and stepped forward. In his hand he held a red rose, drooping now, rain-sodden. He held out his arm stiffly and dropped the rose on to the coffin.

His eyes lifted and fixed on the woman in the fur coat opposite. Other mourners followed his gaze, and a murmur filtered through the crowd. Joe stepped back, reaching blindly through his tears for Maria. Serafina now stepped forward, her eyes hidden by the broad brim of her hat, but her chin jutting defiantly. She bent down and picked up a handful of sodden earth, heedless of her elegant black kid gloves. She paused for a moment and looked across at Joe O'Connell. For a moment it seemed that she might hurl it at the man opposite her. The mourners – those who knew her – held their breath. He was holding Maria close to him as they both wept, his head turned away, hers hidden, neither aware of Serafina. Pressing her lips together, her fingers tightened round the earth in her hand, squeezing it into a glutinous lump. She hurled the mud on to the coffin, where it landed with a small audible thud. Still they did not look up, both engrossed in

257

their own grief, Maria's head buried in the front of Joe's overcoat. Serafina turned away, robbed of her moment, and Claudia stepped up, crying copiously. She threw some lilies down into the grave. The sky darkened and there was a distant rumble of thunder. Now the sound of the rain thrumming through the drenched branches of oaks competed with the collective sobbing of the mourners. The priest clasped his hands: it was over. People began to turn away, murmuring to each other in little mournful clusters under the heavy sky.

Serafina found herself suddenly surrounded by familiar faces from her past, excited by her sudden appearance, emotional after the funeral. George Winston, never one to be intimidated by his sister-in-law, ducked under the dripping trees to hug her, his face a mixture of emotions.

'Good to see you, sis,' he said, gruffly. 'Just wish it had been different circumstances . . .'

The Winston children were there, all barely recognisable – four sulky-looking teenage girls decked out in cheap-looking fashions, and a surly, gum-chewing twelve-year-old boy, his expression unfathomable behind a very long fringe; this, she realised, must be baby George. They clustered around this rather large but expensive-looking stranger who was their Zia Serafina, visiting from Rome. But they were disappointed by what they saw. For a black sheep, she looked decidedly dull. However she was 'family' and they had learned the importance of this institution. Consequently they stood grouped self-consciously around her, like an adolescent guard of honour, while Italians who remembered Serafina from Grape Street and the statue factory, from the war and the terrible days of the *Arandora Star* tragedy, rushed up to kiss her or clasp her hands, exclaiming emotionally about the sadness of the day.

It was all rather gratifying really, this display of welcome, thought Serafina, kissing what seemed like the hundredth damp cheek. It was the kind of homecoming she had always imagined for herself. Only the key players in her imaginary drama were missing – either dead, or disinterested.

The old lady in the headscarf was standing in front of her, eyes rheumy with tears. 'I didn't realise who you were,' she said, her voice quavering, 'I never thought I'd see you again . . . My prize pupil . . .' It was Miss Perkins from the Italian school, Serafina realised, amazed. Still alive after all this time! It really was like a ghost appearing from the past. 'My prize pupil,' she was repeating, clutching Serafina's arm, trembling in an excess of emotion. '—Well, apart from Fortunata, of course. I was so proud of you both ...' Serafina forced a smile. Always to be compared to Fortunata and found wanting! She looked over Miss Perkins' head to the straggle of mourners heading slowly towards the car-park. Through the rain she could make out the tall figure of Joe O'Connell, helping Maria towards the exit.

Bitterly she turned back to the group of Italians clustered around her, a hurt smile on her lips.

She had not intended to return to the house in Grape Street. It held too many painful memories for her. But she had offered the Vittorinis, her old neighbours, a lift home in her hired limousine, and as the large car nosed its way through the streets of Clerkenwell, Serafina realised that she had placed herself in an awkward position. Anna Vittorini (now Anna Nero) had already mentioned Joe's open invitation to all the mourners to return to what was now, incredibly, called 'the O'Connell house', after the funeral. It was going to be impossible for Serafina to avoid attending, since that was where the car was taking them. Anna questioned her excitedly about her life in Rome, and she responded politely, automatically, her eyes drinking in the wet grey streets she knew so well. There were the gates of St Peter's, closed against the noise of the traffic on the Clerkenwell Road. She closed her eyes for a moment, emotional, imagining the silence within its cool, pale walls, and the statue of the Madonna del Carmine, standing where it had always stood, the face of the virgin still impassive, revealing nothing ... There was the bakery on Summers Street, where she had spent so many precious pennies as a child on the pastries of which she was so fond ... and now they were turning into Grape Street. Serafina stiffened. It looked almost exactly as it had when she and Paolo had left it so dramatically almost eight years ago. Anna looked at her curiously.

'You all right?' she asked.

'I'm fine,' Serafina said, her voice bleak. Anna patted her hand.

259

'We'll all miss her,' she said. 'She was a wonderful woman.' The car drew to a halt outside the red front door, as instructed. 'She would have been so glad you came, 'Fina.'

Serafina could barely repress a laugh as she descended from the car, drawing her fur coat around her. If only they knew! She did not even know if she would be allowed over the threshold of what had been, after all, her father's house . . .

'We're just nipping next door a minute,' said Anna, herding her family in the direction of the neighbouring house. 'We're helping with the food – got to collect the vol-au-vents. You go on in . . .'

And they were gone, clattering and chattering as they went, a busy, self-confident Italian family. Serafina stared after them. How uncomplicated their lives seemed! Yet, like the Florios, they had lived through the litany of tragedies that had befallen the Italian community. Carlo Vittorini had been an illiterate peasant when he had arrived in England. He and his family had struggled to learn English, had learned the catering trade, had endured crippling hard work and isolation, and now there was a modest string of cafés in east London bearing the name Vittorini. The family had suffered internment, they had lost a brother on the *Arandora Star*, they had endured the same bitter political divisions within their own ranks as other families had. Yet here they were, still together, absolutely and unquestioningly united.

Why? Serafina asked herself, not for the first time. Why not us?

Suddenly the front door of number seven opened, and Joe O'Connell stood there. They stared at each other, startled.

'Oh,' he said. 'Serafina.' He hesitated for a split second, and then stood politely to one side. 'You had better come in.'

'Have you told Maria I'm here?' she asked him.

He nodded. 'We've been expecting you.'

She was standing on the front doorstep now. She looked coldly at the tall, stooping figure holding the door open for her, his face a mixture of confused emotions. 'I've come to take Maria home with me,' she said.

'Home?'

'To Italy.'

There was a beat, as Joe digested this. Then he said, 'She's in the kitchen. I'm sure you can remember the way,' and he stepped past her into the chilly street, reaching into his pocket with a trembling hand for his pipe.

Serafina entered the house. The hall was full of people she did not know, although some of the faces, she was sure, had looked out at her from the pages of Italian newspapers. Politicians, she realised; friends of Joe's, come to pay their respects. She eyed them coldly. She still loathed politics. They had brought her nothing but grief.

She struggled through to the kitchen, but could see no sign of Maria. Finally, the young priest who had conducted Fortunata's funeral directed her upstairs. Maria had gone to lie down, exhausted by the day.

Serafina hesitated on the upstairs landing. She crossed to the door leading to the small back bedroom where she had slept as a girl, after her father's marriage to Fortunata. She tapped on the door.

'Maria?'

There was no answer. She was about to turn away and try the front bedroom when the door opened, and her daughter stood there, her face blotched and angry.

'You came, then,' Maria said. 'Joe said you would. You'd better come in.'

Serafina entered, tense but curious. Maria went over to the bed, flopped on it and reached for a packet of cigarettes. She offered them to Serafina who shook her head. 'I don't, thanks.' Maria lay back against the pillows and lit her cigarette, staring at Serafina, silent. Serafina looked around her.

'It's very different. The room. From when I slept here.' Maria did not reply, inhaling a great gulp of smoke noisily, her body rigid on the bed. Serafina went to the window and looked out. 'The back yard looks just the same.'

'What did you expect?' Maria's tone was deceptively light. 'A swimming pool? Conservatory?' She sat up suddenly, pulling her feet underneath her so that she was cross-legged, upright. 'Look,' she said, 'this is not a good time. Just say what you've got to say and get it over with. Then you can go back to Italy and get on with your life, and I can get on with mine.'

Serafina moved away from the window, distressed, unable to think of the right thing to say. This was not the reunion she had imagined.

'Did you get the birthday present I sent you?' she asked, prevaricating.

'Yes. I wrote and thanked you, if you remember.'

'But you're not wearing it.'

Maria shook her head. 'Sorry. Crucifixes are just not my thing. But thanks for the thought.'

'I had it blessed by the Pope,' said Serafina, trying not to sound hurt.

'I know you did. Look – Mamma–' Maria had difficulty with the word, 'I'm just not a chip off the old block. I'm sorry.'

Serafina turned on her, stung into spite at last. 'I don't know how you can say that when you don't even know who the old block is.'

Maria sighed. 'Not that old chestnut again! The mystery father! How Victorian you can be sometimes! Do you think I care who my father is? I honestly couldn't give a damn.'

Serafina returned to the window. The Vittorinis were filing through the back yard, carrying trayloads of food. Anna looked up, saw Serafina and smiled, but the face that stared down at her from the upstairs window was expressionless. 'You would be surprised if I told you,' Serafina said to her daughter. 'You would be very surprised.'

'Stop it!' Maria burst out, 'stop it! I don't want to hear your confessions. Save it for the priest. I've lived this long not knowing and now it doesn't matter any more.'

'No?' Serafina looked at the hunched figure on the bed. It was difficult for her to feel love for Maria. It was like looking at a stranger. 'So why are you so upset?'

With a sound of frustration Maria stood up, stubbing her cigarette out ferociously in the ashtray she had been holding. 'For God's sake!' she exclaimed, 'how can you be so stupid? Fortunata's dead, Mamma – dead! I've just buried her – the woman who meant everything to me – my darling nonna – she's dead, and you ask me why I'm upset!' She began to pace the room, distraught. '—And as for my father I couldn't give a damn who he is. Roberto, Paolo, Eduardo – they're just names to me, a lot of Italian names. Joe O'Connell's been more of a father to me than anyone – as far as I'm concerned, he is my father.'

Maria would never know how much her words stung. She

had found the only vulnerable spot in the suit of armour Serafina had constructed for herself over the years. For Maria had confirmed her mother's worst fears, she had spoken out loud those nameless thoughts Serafina had struggled to suppress for so long: she had lost Maria to the two people she hated most. Maria had declared herself. For her, the mother she had lost and the father she had never known had been replaced long ago by Fortunata and Joe. Even in death Fortunata had won!

'Listen, Maria,' Serafina tried to keep her voice even. She crossed the room and steeled herself to put an arm round her daughter's rigid shoulders. Serafina had never been demonstrative. 'Listen. I came back to London to take you home with me.'

Maria was too shocked to break free from Serafina's stiff embrace. She stared at her mother, unnerved by the similarity of the face looking back at her to her own.

'You mean – go to Rome?'

Serafina spoke rapidly. 'I've discussed it with Paolo and he's in full agreement. We have a beautiful *palazzo*, you know – a fountain, gardens. It's hard to believe we're so close to the Vatican. You would love it, Maria – you could have a whole wing to yourself, and invite friends round – and then you and I could go shopping together. You could come with me to the Paris collections every year – I always go – and then every spring we go to the Mamounia in Marrakesh – you'll love it . . .' Her voice trailed away, silenced at last by the look of absolute incredulity on Maria's face.

'You mean it!' Maria said, amazed, 'you really are serious!'

'Of course I am.' Serafina released her daughter, somehow aware that her moment of fantasy was over. 'You could continue your studies at university . . . Paolo will pay the fees . . .'

Maria was staring at her, her face softened by understanding. 'Mamma . . .' she whispered, sadly, 'you're lonely, aren't you? In your *palazzo*. With – with that man you thought you wanted.'

Serafina attempted to laugh, but the sound was horrifyingly closer to a sob. 'Paolo? I hardly see him. He's a businessman. He works very hard—'

Maria's face hardened again. 'I know what he is.' She bent

to find another cigarette. 'Let's not talk about him. Let's talk about you. Have you had enough of Italy, is that it? Are you homesick for London?'

'No, of course not!'

Maria was searching for her lighter. 'You want to take me back to Rome with you – a girl from London who can hardly speak Italian, who doesn't even go to Mass – someone you never liked very much but who happens to be your daughter!'

Serafina's eyes suddenly, amazingly, filled with tears. 'How can you say that?' she asked, lowering her head so that her face was hidden. 'I may not have been a very good mother to you, Maria, but I care about you! I do!' She scrabbled in her handbag for a handkerchief. 'I know I've made mistakes in the past–' she dabbed at her face with a tissue– 'but I want to put things right – I want to make a fresh start! You and me – in Italy, where we belong!'

There was silence for a moment, broken only by Serafina's sniffing. Then suddenly there was a knock on the door, and it opened, revealing a tall, pale young man with long hair. He looked at Maria, then at Serafina, then back to Maria, his hand still on the doorknob.

'You all right?' he asked Maria.

'I'm fine,' she said. 'Come in, Janos. I want you to meet my mother.'

'Ah.' For a second he hesitated. It was evident that he had heard all about Serafina Florio. He stepped forward, his hand outstretched, polite.

'How do you do?' he said, shaking her hand.

'This is my friend, Janos Fekete,' Maria said. 'He lives here.'

'I see.' He was good-looking in a dramatic kind of way, with high Slavonic cheekbones and dark eyes. In fact, she thought to herself, he could almost be Roberto . . .

He smiled at her. 'I'm not an Italian, I'm afraid,' he said, inconsequentially. Then, to Maria, 'I'll come back later—'

'Wait, Janos,' she said, 'don't go. My mother was just leaving.' Maria was standing next to the young man now. They both looked at Serafina, their faces full of youth and optimism. 'I can't come to Rome with you,' Maria said to her mother. 'I know it's hard for you to understand. But I have to stay here. You forget who brought me up. Fortunata taught me there's a battle to be fought here.'

Serafina made a small sound of annoyance. 'You mean politics? What nonsense! Women got the vote years ago, and socialism's a thing of the past.'

Janos merely smiled. Maria shook her head. 'You're wrong,' she said. 'Women have got a hell of a long way to go. And as for socialism – don't you read the papers? The Tories are in deep trouble!' For a crazy moment time seemed to spin backwards, and Serafina was seeing Fortunata, face alight, declaiming. 'The government's about to collapse! Macmillan's going to resign any day—'

'Christine Keeler's finished him!' Janos cut in, enthusiastic, his accent an odd mixture of Hungarian and Cockney. '—And we've got a new leader! Things are about to happen for the Labour Party!'

Serafina made an angry noise and headed for the door. There was no point in this. The girl had been brainwashed by Fortunata and Joe O'Connell.

'No, wait, Mamma – I haven't finished.' Maria's voice was gentle now. 'I want you to understand.' Serafina paused at the door, listening. 'I can't leave London,' her daughter was saying, 'I can't possibly go and live in Italy. I'm just not an Italian, Mamma. I belong here, in Little Italy. I've got this really strong feeling about the place – not just this house –' she waved her arm at the room, in a very Italian gesture – 'but Clerkenwell – all of it. I belong here, with the half-breeds and the immigrants and the mixed races, because that's what I am – whoever my father is! Don't you understand? I'm very sorry, but that's the way it is.' She went over to her mother and kissed her gently on the cheek. 'And that,' she said, 'is for Fortunata. Because I know she would want us to be friends.'

Without another word Serafina hurried from the room. She heard the door close behind her, and as she stood for a moment in the darkness of the landing, she heard the quiet whispering voices of Maria and Janos, friends comforting each other on this bleak day.

Joe was standing at the bottom of the stairs, almost oblivious of the mourners shaking his hand, murmuring condolences. He turned as Serafina descended. They stood for a moment in the hall, two enemies.

Then Serafina spoke. 'She wants to stay,' she said.

She saw Joe's body relax with relief, his fists unclench. He thought for a moment. What should I do now, Fortunata? he asked silently. He knew the answer.

'Come and have a drink, Serafina,' he said, politely. 'Stay a while. There are people here who want to talk to you. Guido Mosconi is in the front room, with his new wife. Did you know he got married? Not long after you left . . . and his sister Violetta, and your old foreman, Pino . . .'

Serafina shuddered. 'Please,' she said, 'I don't want to see anyone. I'm leaving. You've got what you wanted – you've destroyed me, broken up my family, stolen my daughter. You and Fortunata – you won in the end.'

'But there was never a war! Not even a battle!' Joe was suddenly angry. He straightened up, towering over her, looking as she had always remembered, charismatic and powerful. 'Serafina, how can you?' he asked, frustrated. 'When will you realise it's all of your own making – all of it! You're surrounded by people who care about you, and you just push them away. You hurt the people who love you. You hurt Fortunata terribly—'

She made an impatient movement towards the door. 'I don't want to hear this—' she said.

He grabbed her arm. 'But you *will* listen,' he hissed. People in the crowded hall were beginning to stare and mutter, sidling away, embarrassed. Joe ignored them. 'You told Fortunata that you and I – that Maria could have been my child. Why did you do that?' She struggled to free herself, but his strong hand held her firmly, refusing to release her. 'Why, Serafina?'

'Because – it was almost true!' she whispered, her face red, shocked by this confrontation. 'You played the gentleman because you were drunk – but I know men – and I know what you wanted! So I told Fortunata – because the thought is father to the deed, and you *wanted* me . . .'

Her eyes flashed at him. He held her still, staring sadly at her. Those beautiful, dark Italian eyes were all that remained of the girl he remembered. It was difficult to look at this plump, middle-aged woman and try to recapture the desire he had felt for her on that muggy summer night so long ago. Abruptly he released his hold. She stood there, rubbing her wrist, a small smile on her lips, remembering.

'You're right,' he said quietly, 'I was tempted.'

She was startled. 'You admit it!' she said triumphantly.

'Yes,' he said, 'I admit it and I told Fortunata, and she understood. Because she knew I loved her. I'm sorry, Serafina.'

'Don't be sorry for me!' she flashed. 'I don't need your pity.'

'I know it's hard for you to comprehend,' he said, as if she had not spoken, 'but we've all found a way to forgive you, we've all found our own ways to understand you – me, Fortunata, Maria . . .'

Brusquely she moved the last few steps to the front door. 'We have nothing more to say to each other,' she said, a distinct quaver in her voice. 'I came to take Maria back to Italy with me. She won't come. End of story. I won't trouble you again.' She turned, but her exit line was ruined by the arrival of a teenage girl wearing rather too much make-up and a very short black dress, its colour the only concession to the occasion.

'Zia Serafina!' she cried theatrically, pushing herself forward and planting a kiss on either cheek, leaving a peach-coloured stain. 'You remember me? I'm one of your nieces! Surely you're not leaving?'

Serafina looked at her dubiously. Claudia's children all had an awful sameness, a terrible, British unexotic quality. 'Susan?' she said tentatively.

Joe grinned, amused. 'This is Frances.'

'Ah. Frances. Why on earth didn't your mother call you Francesca? Why you all had to have these namby-pamby English names is beyond me!' Her voice was querulous as she pulled on her gloves, preparing to leave, upset and disorientated. Frances was beaming in front of her, oblivious to the atmosphere.

'You sounded just like Nonno Giuseppe then!'

Joe opened the front door, thankful the visit was over. But Frances still stood before her aunt, blocking her exit, her face suddenly serious. 'I heard what you said,' her voice was tense, 'about Maria not wanting to go to Italy.' She took a step closer to Serafina, urgent. 'Well – wouldn't I do instead? I'd like to go. I'd be good.' The speech became a desperate babble. 'I'm learning Italian at *doposcuola* . . . and I was

267

runner-up in the Miss Emigrante competition at Finsbury Town Hall in the summer, so I'm sort of Italian . . . and I always go on the picnic with the Mazzini-Garibaldi people – the *scampagnata* . . . Last year I even went with the Scalabrini fathers . . . I'm very Italian, Zia Serafina! Please take me with you, I'd love to live in your house in Rome . . .'

Serafina looked at her cynically. So much for family. Even gentle Claudia had managed to produce this grasping, greedy little teenager with an eye on the main chance. She patted her niece's arm coldly. 'I don't think so, Frances,' she said. 'You stay here with your own mother. Make the most of her, she's all you've got – the only person who will ever really love you. I should know. I lost my mamma when I was five.' And without a word of farewell she was gone.

'And that,' said Joe ruefully, 'is the root of all your sadness, Serafina.'

But the door had slammed and she was gone. Frances headed back to the kitchen, disconsolate.

Maria had come quietly down the stairs, followed by Janos.

Joe turned and found her there. He held out his arms and she went to him. They hugged each other, both overcome. He kissed the top of her head.

'Thank you,' he said finally, 'thank you for saying you would stay.'

She looked up at him fondly. 'There was no question,' she said.

Janos joined them, his face anxious. 'Your mother has a nice name,' he said to Maria, trying to defuse the atmosphere, 'very musical, very Italian. Why was she called that?'

Maria put her arm through his. 'I don't know, Janos. I don't know why my mother is called Serafina. It's something to do with the angels. Perhaps she was an angelic baby.'

'Serafina Florio,' Janos said thoughtfully, 'angel flower. What a beautiful name.'

'It's sad,' Joe said, 'how sad to have such a lovely lilting joy of a name. For she's the unhappiest woman I know.'

'And Fortunata,' Janos said, warming to the subject, 'What does that mean?'

Joe smiled a wry, sad smile. 'It means the fortunate one.'

'It should have been me,' said Maria, her face bright with

tears, linking her other arm through Joe's. 'I should have been called Fortunata. Because I'm the fortunate one.' And smiling up at the two men, she pulled them towards the kitchen. 'Come on!' she said, 'Fortunata would never forgive us – a whole hour has passed and not one political debate has taken place! Now then, Joe, about the Irish question . . .' Laughing, warmed by the memory of Fortunata, the three friends joined the other mourners.

JOURNEY'S END

Italy 1989

L AKE ALBANO, FRANCES thought irritably, was about as exciting as watching paint dry. She was sitting on the low wall of the English college villa garden, gazing at the hazy waters below. Behind her, the whoops and shouts of the Swiss Guards in the swimming pool interrupted the low hum of Mass being said on the terrace. Frances, slowly fanning herself with a wide-brimmed straw hat, was faintly aware that she made an attractive picture in her pale pink Jean Muir linen shift and matching pink sandals. She might be almost forty, she thought, rather pleased, but she was still attracting more admiring glances from the Swiss Guards than the two eager adolescent girls who were missing Mass in the hope of a flirtation by the poolside.

'Get him to take your photo!' Frances heard one of the girls shout to the other (the Guards appeared to speak no English, so discretion was not required).

The Swiss Guards, with sidelong glances at Frances, were diving from the boards at the far end of the pool and emerging further up, slicking the water out of their eyes and grinning. Frances allowed herself a quick glance and a tolerant smile in the direction of the splashing and whooping. It was difficult to believe that these short-haired brutes were the custodians of the Pope. Father Andrew had explained that they used the English college pool because if they wanted to swim in the pool at Castel Gandolfo they had to be disinfected first. This was because the Pope also used the pool and must be protected from infection. It was easier for the Guards to jump on a *motocicletta* and take the winding road to the English college villa, where Father Andrew welcomed them and there was the possibility (only slight) of a flirtation with a bored English-woman.

Far below, a small military plane was swooping over the misty waters of the lake. Frances could make out a canoe slowly manoeuvring round the opposite bank, where heavy trees hung over the water; the canoe suddenly disappeared beneath the overhanging curve of a branch and re-emerged a moment later from behind the next tree. How cool it must be, she thought, down over there under the branches. She hoped that Mass was almost over, so that they could go and have some lunch – somewhere cool and quiet in the hills, or perhaps down by the lake.

Beyond the washing lines (rows of Marks and Spencer towels, Laura Ashley summer frocks, children's white socks) the group of English people were murmuring in Latin, their faces set in expressions of concentration, lines furrowing their foreheads. Frances sighed. Bloody Catholics. Zia Serafina was just visible, her great bulk compressed into a wooden chair with carved arms, her eyes were tightly closed and her mouth hung open. The constant movement of her shoulders, glimpsed as a striped beach towel swayed in a current of air, puzzled Frances for a moment. Oh, but of course. Serafina would be playing with her rosary. Silly old woman. For the hundredth time, Frances wondered whether she could get to the end of this holiday without throttling her aunt, or at the very least having a massive screaming fit.

She had never imagined for a moment that an old woman could be quite such a burden, nor had she, until they arrived in Rome, realised how important her status as a single (i.e., free) woman was to her. Thank God her own parents were fairly self-sufficient, and she wouldn't have to be saddled with dealing with them for years on end. Her only consolation was that Zia Serafina was paying for this trip, and Frances needed to get away from England. Her last bout of freelance work, as assistant producer on a wildlife series, had ended in disaster. David had told his wife about Frances, there had been a terrible scene, and of course David had ended up promising the wife that he wouldn't see Frances again. Funny how they always went back to the wives, no matter how often they had told you how miserably unhappy they were. Anyway, that meant no more work with that particular company again, and the prospect of a jobless summer until the new series of *The Small Hours* started up in the autumn.

To save face, Frances had needed to get away somewhere. She had been cultivating her Italian aunt for some years now, and at last it seemed that the charming newsy letters and the remembered birthdays had paid off: the invitation could not have come at a better time. Serafina had of course invited her own daughter Maria first, but some obscure family quarrel apparently meant that Maria had refused; so Frances had nobly stepped in and offered to go, if her aunt wanted. After all, Serafina was an old woman. She probably didn't have a lot of time left; and Frances had been able to say to David's friends, 'There's a possibility of a big Italian drama co-production coming up with Jack Bond next year . . . I'm going to Rome for the summer to check out likely co-financers.' This wasn't exactly a lie. She intended to get on the phone to some of the big independents before she went home, so that she could present Jack Bond with some solid-sounding information over a drink sometime – if the Italian drama came off, she might well be offered work on it . . . and then of course there was also the added possible perk of a mention in Serafina's will . . .

'Signora?' One of the Swiss Guards was standing in front of her, dripping, a small towel round his shoulders. He was holding a camera.

'He wants you to take a photo,' a nervous English voice said. It was one of the teenage girls, pink and excited. Frances noticed how fleshy her upper arms were. She would be over-weight at twenty unless someone intervened.

'Why don't you take it for him?' Frances asked, amused.

'No, it's my camera – I want a photo of him with me and my friend. I think he wants you to take it.' The guard was holding the camera out and grinning suggestively. He said something in German.

'Sorry, I'm useless with cameras,' Frances shook her head at the man, and smiled. 'Anyway, Mass is finishing – hadn't you better go and find your parents?' The girl's face dropped, and she turned away. The Guard remained motionless, still smiling.

'He's still got your camera!' Frances called to the girl. Flushing, the girl came back, snatched the camera and stumbled away behind the washing lines towards the emerging group of people. The Guard stayed where he was, and repeated what he had said in German.

Frances smiled at him evenly. 'Fuck off,' she said. With a snort of laughter, he went back towards the pool, where his companions were watching, grinning.

Frances turned and stared again out towards the lake. She thought about their visit to the Vatican the previous day, where she and Serafina had had an audience with the Pope, arranged by Father Andrew. Frances wondered idly if anyone had ever made a documentary about it. Probably cameras weren't allowed in. A pity. The spectacle had been breathtaking: row upon row of groaning and singing penitents, rising and falling in a great swoon before their emissary to the Lord.

There had been a huge crowd of young Hungarians, all mysteriously wearing yellow bandannas which they had waved in the air like a flock of fluttering canaries. There had been a crowd of statuesque women from the Cameroons, wearing tribal robes in blue, embroidered all over with the Pope's face, picked out in white chain stitch, white satin stitch . . . Frances wondered for how many years these women had been sewing, sewing on the other side of the world, in readiness for this moment. The Gospel singers from Pennsylvania in red and black choir robes had stood up and sung 'America the Beautiful', their voices soaring round the vaults of the great modern auditorium, ringing with patriotic fervour and a passionate religiosity. But the Poles – they were the most fevered, the most ecstatic. When the Pope had appeared, flanked by his Swiss Guards and Vatican Secret Police in well-cut Armani suits, a great sigh had flown up to the rafters from the Poles; and when the Pope had raised his hand and nodded, a Solidarity song had been sung, echoing around the great space above their heads, deep and wearisome.

The Pope, a minute figure leaning wearily in his throne, head resting on one hand, way below them on the distant stage, had acknowledged the song with a slight incline of his head – somehow more poignant than a great and grand gesture.

Even Frances, who frowned on Catholicism's more high-flown moments of drama, recognised the power of this scene. For a moment she, like her Aunt Serafina, had found herself clutching her neighbour's hand with a passion. But when the speeches began her chair had seemed intolerably uncomfortable, the heat returned, oppressive and insistent, the groaning nuns in the row behind once more irritated her.

The Pope murmured something, and a young priest stood and told the congregation in English that their artefacts would now be blessed. Serafina was rustling about in her capacious handbag. Frances glanced across, irritated. She must be looking for her rosary – but surely she was already holding it . . . To her surprise, she saw Serafina's gnarled hands retrieve a small bundle, wrapped in a linen handkerchief. As the praying and murmuring of responses quickened around them, Frances watched in fascination, as the linen was pushed aside to reveal a small statue of the Virgin Mary, faded pinks and blues. Serafina was caressing it, and praying, the sweat beading on her forehead underneath the expensive silk headscarf. Frances put out a hand to touch the statue, but had been amazed to feel her aunt brusquely push her away. Frances lowered her head, as if in prayer, to get a better look at the figure her aunt was holding so tightly. She couldn't make it out. She certainly hadn't bought it in the Vatican shop earlier – Frances had actually paid for all the cheap rosaries and Pope plates her aunt had bought there. How extraordinary, she thought; her aunt must have brought the statue with her from home. It didn't look anything special – just your average Virgin Mary statue.

She shrugged, mentally. Catholics. They moved in mysterious ways their wonders to perform, and she no longer understood their ways at all. Nor did she want to. However, that evening in the bar of the hotel, she had asked her aunt about the statue.

'*Domani*,' Serafina had replied, wearily. 'I'll tell you about it tomorrow . . .'

Tomorrow is here, thought Frances. I'll make her tell me over lunch. The movement beyond the washing line indicated that Mass was indeed over. A thin man in large khaki shorts was remonstrating with the two girls, sheepish now, heads downcast. The Swiss Guards splashed on regardless. Frances peered beyond the washing for a glimpse of Zia Serafina. Damn. She was disappearing inside the villa with Father Andrew, no doubt for more mumblings and rosary-fingering.

Frances stood up and threaded her way through the gardens and through the washing towards the house. Stepping on to the verandah, she could hear Serafina murmuring '. . . *Ora pro nobis, Sancta Maria Virgio Mater Dei . . .'* Peering into the gloom beyond, she could sense her aunt's great bulk hunched over, Father Andrew standing above her, his face bland, a priest on duty. He looked up, saw Frances on the verandah, and motioned to her to wait with a little wave of his hand. Petulantly, she sat down, making sure her sigh of impatience was audible.

'Francesca, I'm ready for lunch now.' I'll bet you are, you great whale. Frances stood up, forcing a smile on to her lips.

'Come along, Zia 'Fina, let's go and find somewhere cool.'

Father Andrew, following them out into the glaring sun of the courtyard where their hired car sat baking and unprotected, mopped his brow and repeated thoughtfully, 'Lunch . . . somewhere cool . . . I know!' – a sudden inspiration – 'There's a marvellous little restaurant a few kilometres away from here, right in the middle of the woods, they make the most marvellous pasta dishes using mushrooms picked fresh by the locals – a bit pricey, but worth it.'

'Thank you, Father, I'm sure we'll find it,' said Frances, unlocking the car door for her aunt. But Serafina hesitated, swaying in the heat, pink-faced, distressed.

'I'm sorry, Frances. I don't think I can face the drive. Not in this heat.' Frances' face fell, the prospect of lunch fading.

'Come on, Zia Serafina, I'll drive slowly, I promise.'

Serafina hesitated, mopping her brow. 'I don't know . . .'

Frances turned to the priest, determined. 'Where did you say it was, Father? Up the hill or down?'

'Down, down – and then left when you get to a little road sign saying Via Campanata – past the group of villas on the right. Ristorante Funghi Campani – tell the chef Father Andrew sent you. I recommend the house wine – the white – one of the best in the region and quite reasonable—'

'Sounds wonderful, doesn't it Auntie . . .?'

Frances waited, her hand on the car door handle, for her aunt to decide. Serafina stared at her, seemingly lost in thought. Then she gave a little shake, as if waking up. 'No, no . . .' she said, irritable. 'It's far too hot. I need to sit quietly somewhere . . .'

'We could rustle you up an omelette here,' Father Andrew said, helpfully. Frances glared at him.

Serafina had already turned back to the quiet shade of the

villa. 'You go, Frances,' she said. 'Here –' reaching in her bag and thrusting a wad of notes at her niece– 'my treat.'

Frances looked at the money. It was far too much. 'Are you sure?'

'I'm sure.' Serafina was heading back, leaning on Father Andrew, her face distorted by the effort of walking. She suddenly seemed very old.

Frances opened the car door, feeling a blast of hot air from the interior. She could not help a parallel wave of relief washing over her.

'Thanks, Auntie . . . I'll be back soon, I promise, and after lunch you can be telling me about that funny little Madonna you were holding in the Vatican yesterday . . .'

'She won't be back until this evening,' muttered Serafina under the noise of the car engine starting up. 'Selfish bitch . . .' Father Andrew patted her hand and was silent. The car began to edge its way down the hill, out of the drive.

The sun was moving slowly upwards in a cloudless sky. Serafina sat in the shade of the verandah, only her feet sticking out from the shadows, the sun warming her toes. She felt better after the omelette. Father Andrew had brought her a cup of tea, and she took a gulp of it now, to help her swallow her tablets. She had several hours before Frances would reappear, irritable from her uphill drive in the heat.

She fanned herself with the prayer sheet from that morning's Mass. The sun had moved to her ankles. She shifted slightly, enjoying the warmth seeping through her support stockings. Just the smell of the Roman countryside made her happy, the dry aroma of dusty plants and pebbles, baking in the heat. It reminded her of the hot cobblestones of Grape Street in those sunny idyllic days before the war . . .

She thought about Antonia and Claudia, and smiled a little to herself, remembering their beauty . . . How jealous of them she had been . . . She closed her eyes. Not any more. Poor 'Tonia – died so young, buried under the collapsed kitchen wall, her eyes wide open, her arm outstretched, holding the Nemi Madonna, as if to say, see, Serafina, I did what you wanted, I always did what you wanted . . .

Had 'Tonia known about Paolo? Serafina wondered. Probably not. Paolo was such a coward, he had never confessed to his young pregnant wife that he was having an affair with her sister. And 'Tonia had been too in love with him to suspect anything. She opened her eyes, remembering. Above her, a small plane swooped across the lake towards Castel Gandolfo. She squirmed slightly in her chair, remembering that day in the factory. She had seduced him, she could not deny it to herself. She had teased him, provoked him, brushing herself against him when no one was watching, gazing at him provocatively over the teacups when the family met for Sunday tea at Grape Street, leaning over him just a little too intimately to show him a photograph, insisting on dancing with her brother-in-law at parties. Poor innocent Antonia, so engrossed in her own pregnant radiance, had never noticed . . . and it had been so easy. Paolo had not resisted for long. There is always something irresistible about forbidden fruit, Serafina thought grimly. That, after all, was why she had married Paolo herself.

Funny, she could hardly remember him as he had been when she last saw him, in his coffin, a fifty-year-old stranger. She had looked at that dead face and felt no emotion, trying in vain to recall what it was about Paolo that she had wanted in the first place.

She heaved herself up a little in the sun lounger. The sun had been creeping hotly up her legs, in an unsettling parody of an exploring hand, oddly sexual. She fanned herself again. How had she survived this constant heat, as a little girl in Nemi? It was unbearable. She searched in her handbag and found a handkerchief with which to mop her brow. She peered along the verandah. It was dark and deserted. A pity, she could have done with another cup of tea. She leaned back again, staring unseeingly at the green blur of trees on the opposite side of the lake.

An image of Roberto suddenly appeared, unbidden, below her. Roberto, with those frank eyes, that disarming habit of flicking his hair out of his eyes, that perfect profile . . . Seducing Roberto had been harder. It had taken longer. In fact she was still not sure that she had seduced Roberto. Perhaps that was how she liked to see it, to avoid facing up to how she had really felt about him. Roberto Lucente . . . She groaned slightly, to herself, clutching the damp handkerchief. Roberto, Roberto . . . There had always been something between them, some unnamed bond they struggled against, disguising it with indifference, whole afternoons spent not meeting each other's gaze. Even when they had first met, at the dance in the library, Serafina realised, he had avoided her on purpose, as if he sensed danger there, something he did not want to touch, to defile himself with.

A trickle of perspiration began to move down behind her ear. She had wanted him so desperately. How much of it had really been the calculated revenge plan she had concocted to punish Fortunata, and how much of it was – dare she even think of it? – something like love?

She swatted irritably at the sweat on her neck. It didn't matter now. Roberto was long dead, and he had served his purpose. He had weakened, he had performed the unspeakable – good, true, noble, perfect Roberto had taken his fiancée's sister to the little upstairs room in Grape Street, he had slowly removed the dress, the slip, the stockings, the undergarments, and he had trembled at the sight of her, naked and unashamed on the narrow bed. And not just once . . . not just once. Serafina realised that the dampness on her cheek was not caused by the heat, after all. It was a tear, trickling slowly down her face. She dabbed at it. Stupid old woman. It was all so long ago, like someone else's life, so distant it hardly mattered now.

One or other of those two was Maria's father – she had no idea which. Some days, when Maria had been angry as a child, and her mouth tightened in fury at some action of her mother's, Serafina's heart had contracted and she had seen those full, cruel lips of Paolo's. Then Maria would laugh, or brush her hair back impatiently, or suddenly turn and face her mother with eyes as clear and true as Roberto's, and Serafina had been thrown into confusion again. But did it really matter? She smiled to herself again, peace restored. She had done what she had set out to do. She had proved to herself that she was the only real Florio child, she had usurped those pretty, silly sisters in the only way she knew. She had done it all for Papa. And she had quietly and privately punished Fortunata for the moment of marital infidelity that a small, confused child had witnessed from her perch on the roof of the studio, through the skylight . . .

Unbidden, Fortunata's face came to her through the blur

of her memories, that glazed, ecstatic, perfect face, frozen at the moment of orgasm, staring up at the dusty skylight. Had she seen the scared, shocked face peering back down at her through a shaft of light? Serafina would never know.

Strange, she thought, how moments of carelessness, of abandon, get fixed, static, begin to matter, to take on immense importance, and eventually have a monstrous new life of their own . . .

She looked at her watch. Frances would be here soon. Then, after prayers, they would go down the mountain for dinner, and over dinner, Serafina would tell her niece more of her story — not all, of course, but some. She would select the bits that did not make her seem too cruel, too calculating. She was human, after all. She wanted to be well remembered after she was gone. Even by Maria, her angry, absent daughter.

She smiled again, relaxed now the memories had receded. She had never managed to persuade Maria to come to Italy, but she had succeeded in getting Frances to come, and she would be able to give Frances the gift to deliver to Maria, the most precious gift she could pass on. She groped in her handbag, and pulled out the little statue, and the letter addressed to Maria. She turned the faded Madonna in her hands, and smiled.

And tomorrow . . . Tomorrow she would go back to Nemi again . . . Tomorrow she would try to recapture just for a moment those days of precious innocence, before the world tipped suddenly sideways and catapulted her into a foreign land . . . *Ma sono Italiana!* she reminded herself, *sono Italiana!* I am Italian! Her eyes closed for what was to be the last time, and a final tear trickled down that wrinkled, faded cheek.

EPILOGUE

London 1990

T HE WOMAN ENTERED the cemetery alone, carrying a bright bunch of daffodils. She walked purposefully, her head up, towards a particular corner shaded by laburnums.

She paused for a moment before a large stone angel, its wings unfurled over a marble stone, and read the inscription:

'Qui nella pace del Signore riposano le anime amate di Bruno Vialli 1865–1932, e di sua sposa Lucia 1867–1943'

Next to the angel, a more modest headstone carried the names of 'Giuseppe Florio, *marito devoto e padre affettuoso*' and 'Antonia Florio, *sua figlia, 1923–41. Dobbiamo amare la vita, ma non temere la morte, perche l'una e l'altra sono doni di Dio.*' The woman leaned over, translating the Italian words carefully, murmuring them to herself. 'We should love life and not fear death, for they are both the gift of God . . .'

She paused there a moment, and then moved on to the next grave. Kneeling, she removed some fading roses from the urn standing by the headstone, replacing them with the daffodils. Lovingly, she reached out and touched the grey stone, her fingers tracing the words:

'Fortunata Lucia O'Connell 1895–1963. Joseph Sean O'Connell 1895–1985, Member of Parliament for Islington 1949–51 and 1964–1970.'

She reached into her bag and pulled out a small, faded statuette. Carefully she stood it in front of the headstone, next to the flowers. The cool, clear eyes of the little Madonna gazed out at the world, expressionless. Her blue cape with the stars was streaked with age, the golden rose at her feet was chipped, and the delicate fingers holding the rosary were almost worn away. For a moment time seemed to hang suspended. A breeze rustled through the trees and somewhere a thrush began to sing. The woman hesitated a moment, staring at the statue. Then, slowly, she reached out and retrieved it. Getting to her feet she looked at the grave once more. '*Ciao, Nonna,*' she whispered. And, turning away, she walked briskly to the cemetery gate, where a man waited for her, impatient, stamping his feet to keep out the sharp spring chill.

'You didn't leave the statue?' he said, his accent slightly odd, with a foreign, sing-song quality to it.

She shook her head. 'I couldn't. I don't know why. It just didn't feel right. Too final, somehow – as though I was making something come to an end.' She looked down at the Madonna still in her hand. 'And of course there isn't an end. Serafina may be dead and buried in Nemi, but there must be something of her in me, somewhere, and in our children.'

The man put an arm round her, reassuring. 'Only the good bits, Maria, only the good bits.'

She smiled at him. 'Life goes on – I suppose that's what I'm saying.'

She put the little statue carefully back in her handbag, and together they walked back towards the taxi. Several young faces peered excitedly from the back window, through a disorganised pile of luggage.

'I think she should be on display somewhere in our new home,' the woman was saying.

He laughed, teasing. 'They'll love you in Budapest, my darling – they love a bit of passionate Catholicism.'

'This has nothing to do with religion,' she said, crossly. Her voice floated back across the silent cemetery, across the grey headstones and the bright splashes of colour where crocuses grew. 'We'll put the Madonna somewhere where she can keep an eye on us – and on our children . . . and maybe even our children's children . . .'

Her voice faded away. The cemetery returned to its silent seclusion, peaceful in the spring sunshine. And somewhere across the sea, above a lake in a small Italian village near Rome, the ghost of an Italian woman heard her words and smiled.

LILIE FERRARI

Angelface

London, in the 1950s. The streets of Soho are bustling, cosmopolitan and lively. But inside the Imperial Café, the Peretti family is face to face with its Sicilian enemies, who have come to call in a debt of honour incurred back in the old country.

Marionetta Peretti, although bound by the duties of an Italian daughter, despises the cowardice and caution of her family. She fights against the corruption caused by the Moruzzi brothers, whose implacable hold over the people of Soho has caused so much misery.

But it is Marionetta herself who is forced to make the harshest payments: a sacrifice of her love, her freedom, and finally herself . . .

Read on for a preview of ANGELFACE, a dramatic story of classic enmity by Lilie Ferrari, out now from Michael Joseph

CHAPTER ONE

1947

A pigeon, pecking hopefully on the pavement, turned its head sideways, its tiny eye gleaming, and watched the girl in the window.

'Marionetta! Wake up, girl! Three teas and two ham sandwiches over by the window!'

Francesca Peretti, frail and bad-tempered, was glowering at her daughter from her perch at the sink piled with dirty dishes. The café was full to overflowing, and people clamoured for attention at the counter.

Marionetta, who had been leaning in the doorway gazing wistfully out at the crowds hurrying by, returned to earth with a jolt. The old man at the corner table watched her, his face thoughtful as he stirred his tea.

'Sorry, Mamma,' she said, penitent, turning back into the steamy interior of the Imperial Café. The last thing she wanted to do was upset her mother, so pale and ill. Pushing back an unruly curl of black hair, she hastened to the counter where her father Tomasso was frantically buttering a mountain of sliced white bread.

'Two spam, three cheese and tomato!' he yelled, too preoccupied with the orders to reprimand his daydreaming daughter; but his wife was still frowning at the sink, her damp, reddened hands on her hips.

'More customers than we've had all summer, and she's

staring out of the window!' Francesca muttered, cross. 'And where's Antonio, for heaven's sake?'

Her younger son Mario, arriving at the counter with a trayload of dirty teacups, grinned at her.

'Don't you dare,' she said, smiling in spite of herself, 'Don't you dare sing at me . . .'

But it was too late. Mario had his arm round his mother's bony shoulders, his cheek next to hers. 'You've got to accent-uate the positive,' he crooned. 'Elim-inate the negative . . .' Customers turned and listened, as they always did when Mario sang, and Marionetta paused by the window table, proud, listening too.

'He ought to be on the radio,' someone at the table said.

'That voice — like an angel,' Marionetta heard one of the regulars remark. She turned to him wryly as Mario's voice soared. 'Latch on to the affirmative, don't mess with Mr In-between . . .'

'He may sound like an angel,' she said, mopping the table briskly, 'pity he doesn't behave like one!' But she stopped to listen again. The old man in the corner smiled to himself. What a picture she made, slender in her black waitress's dress, standing there listening to her brother sing. She reminded him of another girl, another time, another place . . .

Mario finished his song with a flourish and a mock bow, and was applauded by his admirers at the counter and hugged by his relenting mother. At sixteen, Marionetta mused, he still had the baby-faced charm of a boy rather than the aquiline, manly good looks of his older brother, the missing Antonio.

As if on cue, the tall figure of Antonio appeared from behind her and whisked away the cloth she was using to wipe the tables.

'Tony!' she protested. 'I was —'

'Sssh!' He was already scrubbing away at a table his sister had just cleaned, much to the bemusement of the family of four seated around it, trying to eat their fruit cake in peace. 'Mamma won't notice I've been away . . .'

And sure enough, Francesca chose that moment to look up from her sink of steaming crockery and saw Antonio industriously cleaning. 'There you are!' she called. 'Good boy, Antonio, you can finish early.'

'Mamma!' Marionetta was indignant. 'I've been here since six this morning . . .'

'And so you should be.' Her mother's voice was brisk, brooking no argument. 'Your place is here, learning the work. Antonio's a man, he has other business.'

Antonio smirked at his sister. Angrily, she snatched the cloth from his hands and turned to another table, as Antonio sauntered to the counter and disappeared out into the back of the café to collect his coat.

'More tea, Nonno?' she asked. She was standing at the table in the corner, where the old man sat smoking a cigarette and coughing. He scowled at his grand-daughter, in an effort to hide the flood of affection that he had been feeling for her, and the mixed emotions he had experienced when he remembered that other girl, who looked so much like Marionetta, but who had long since gone.

'Filthy English drink,' he said, spluttering in between gulps at his cigarette. 'Coffee – proper coffee.'

Marionetta looked down at him, despairing. 'Nonno, you know I can't. Mamma has forbidden coffee. She says it'll kill you.'

The old man coughed some more. 'I'm seventy-one,' he said. 'Time to die.'

'Nonsense!' Marionetta swept his cup away. 'I'll get you more tea.'

Up at the counter, her father, his mountain of sandwiches

almost complete, glanced over at the old man in the corner, irritated. 'Why does he have to come here today of all days?' The question, although directed at Marionetta, did not require an answer. 'Our busiest day and he takes up a whole table.'

'It's still his café, Papa,' Marionetta reminded her father gently, 'and he wanted to be part of today – you know, part of the celebrations.'

'Why?' Tomasso handed her a plate of bread and butter. 'Table Four. Your grandfather hates the Royal Family. He's an old fascist.'

'He just pretends to be,' Marionetta said, handing the plate to Mario, who was passing. 'Table Four ... You know he wouldn't have missed today for anything ...'

The door of the café crashed shut as the family who had been by the window left. The queue at the counter had diminished, and for a moment the café seemed almost quiet.

'There!' Marionetta poured another cup of tea for her grandfather. 'The rush is over now.' She poured a cup for herself and went over to join the old man, who was lighting another cigarette.

'Nonno!' She was despairing. 'You shouldn't, not with your chest –'

'Don't nag, girl, you sound just like your mother.' He was secretly pleased that she had brought her tea over to sit with him. He had a definite soft spot for Marionetta, even though she was a girl.

She was leaning back in her chair, exhausted after a long day, her eyes closed, and he was able to study her face surreptitiously. Yes, she had exactly the same fine bones as Giulietta had had, the same arched brows and full mouth, the same habit of biting her lower lip when she was angry ...

'Have I got a smudge on my nose?' Marionetta was looking at him wide-eyed.

He leaned across and touched her cheek. 'Just a bit of jam,' he said gruffly.

'What a day!' Marionetta sipped at her tea. 'It's been wonderful, hasn't it? I just wish I could have got away and seen the coach . . .'

Princess Elizabeth had married Lieutenant Philip Mountbatten that day, and the streets of London were packed with people who had come to see the procession to Westminster Abbey. Even the sharp November chill had not dampened the spirits of Londoners who desperately needed cheering up after a long and dreary war. The cafés of Soho were doing splendid business, and the Imperial Café, situated in the middle of Old Compton Street, had benefited from those weary procession-goers who had wandered away from the crowds on Charing Cross Road and Tottenham Court Road in search of a sandwich and a cup of tea.

The Peretti family had not worked so hard since before the war. Even on VE day, the café had not been so crowded. Marionetta surveyed the floor of the café glumly: the paper flowers, the discarded flags, the squashed crumbs and the stained lino. It would be her job tonight to mop the floor and render it spotless before she was allowed to turn off the lights and take her weary body home to the family's cramped flat in St James's Residences. Princess Elizabeth and the glamour of the day seemed very far removed from the back-breaking hours she had spent that day in the café. She sighed.

Her grandfather caught the sigh and misunderstood its origin. 'I know,' he said conspiratorially, following her eyes. 'That lino – *orribile* – dreadful. The old wooden boards – they were fine. Just a quick sweep and a good scrub once a week, that was all the floor needed then . . .'

Marionetta smiled at him ruefully. She patted his wrinkled old hand. 'You're not very happy about Papa's changes, are you, Nonno?' She stirred her tea wearily, looking round at the place she knew better than the living-room at home. Papa had painted the walls blue, the paintwork white, and Mamma had made bright red curtains for the windows. It was all very patriotic, to go with the café's new name. But a change in the colour scheme could not change for Marionetta the dreadful, grinding boredom of day after day spent serving snacks to the people of Soho. She knew every stain in the sink, every crack in the lino, every cup on the groaning shelves behind Mamma's sink. And to increase her frustration, she also knew that *out there* on the streets of Soho, there was a teeming, exciting bohemian world, full of eccentrics, women of the night, artists, poets, painters, madmen! They passed by the windows of the café early in the morning as they emerged from their mysterious late-night activities, they reappeared on the streets late in the afternoon, bleary-eyed from sleep, and she glimpsed them as exotic shadows late at night, flitting past in the gloom, intent on lives that seemed so much more exciting than her own.

Occasionally they would actually come into the Imperial for a late-night cup of coffee or an early-morning bacon sandwich, and Marionetta would stare at them, transfixed, until her mother nudged her crossly and told her to stop daydreaming. Sometimes Papa would hurriedly cross to the door as they entered and murmur something apologetic and ask them to leave.

'Why?' Marionetta would ask, angry. 'They can pay like everyone else!'

'Your mother doesn't want their kind in here,' Papa would say, nervous, refusing to give further explanations. But Marionetta knew who these people were, she had not lived in Soho all her life for nothing. These were the pimps and the prostitutes, the people whose names appeared in the newspapers, who lived off 'immoral earnings' and made their money from sex. Marionetta, good Catholic girl that she was, knew that these were sinners, wicked souls beyond redemption. So why then did they inspire in her such envy, these women with their fox furs and glossy red lips, these men in their beautifully cut suits and their two-tone shoes? And why was theirs the only café that refused to serve these people and got away with it?

She stirred her tea thoughtfully. Perhaps it was because her family were Sicilians, she mused. After all, they seemed to be the only Sicilians for miles around. All their neighbours in St James's Residences came from Southern Italy, to be sure, but none from Sicily. The other Italian families in the tenement block where they lived were all *compaisani*, all shared friends and relatives from the same area. Only the Perettis were different, having no family along the passage or down the hall or even in Clerkenwell, London's 'Little Italy'. Marionetta knew that everyone feared Sicilians; they believed everyone from Sicily was in the Mafia. It was ridiculous – as if anyone could seriously imagine that Tomasso and his hard-working family, slaving away in this little café, could be anything other than hard-working immigrants trying to survive . . . Marionetta smiled grimly to herself. If anyone in her family was in the Mafia, she thought, they must be superhuman, because they all worked so hard and for such long hours that there was no time even for pleasure, let alone to join the Cosa Nostra . . .

Her thoughts were interrupted by the arrival of her brother at the table, his coat slung over his shoulders.

'Bye, sis,' he said, grinning. 'If I see the Princess I'll send her your regards, shall I?'

Their grandfather stirred and frowned. 'When my

Marionetta gets married,' he said, 'her wedding will be ten times more beautiful.'

'Nonno!' Marionetta laughed. 'I'm only seventeen!'

'Princess Elizabeth's only twenty-one.' Antonio's face was solemn, but he was nudging his sister, unseen by the old man. 'Only four years, Marionetta! Time's running out . . .'

She threw a napkin at him, cross. 'And I'll be a spinster for ever, stuck in this café all hours of the day and night!' she said, trying to sound good-humoured. 'Go and play with your silly friends and leave the women to do the work, as usual.'

Antonio headed towards the door, whistling, waving a careless goodbye in the general direction of the counter. '*Ciao*, Mamma!' he called to Francesca, and then he was gone, the door slamming shut behind him, making the bell dance and jangle as he went.

The old man frowned. 'Where's he going?' he asked.

Marionetta stood up stiffly, her tea finished. 'Who knows? Out with his policemen friends again, I expect.'

Her grandfather snorted derisively. Marionetta patted him on the shoulder as she retrieved his teacup. Antonio was going to join the police force, and this meant one less person to help in the café. For the old man Franco Peretti, it meant the death of a cherished dream that he had brought with him from Sicily – to start a business and hand it on to his son, and then to his first grandson. For Marionetta it merely meant the prospect of fewer helping hands and more hard work.

She glanced up as the doorbell jangled again. It was a huge party of procession-goers, elated and noisy, in search of a sandwich before moving on to a pub. Marionetta forced a welcoming smile. 'Good afternoon!' she said. 'There's a large table over by the window, and another one there by the counter . . .'

*

It was getting late. Marionetta felt as though her knees would buckle if one more customer came through the door. Her dark curls stuck damply to her forehead, and the rough material of her dress scratched at her skin in the heat from the stove. If only it was time to close! But it was still early, even though darkness had fallen outside and the flashing lights of Soho were illuminated; and still the customers came and went relentlessly. As the clock struck eight, Francesca Peretti wearily put on her coat and called for her younger son. It was time for her to go home and do the washing, and it was time for Mario to go to his singing lesson.

'Mamma, your collar's in a muddle.' Marionetta crossed the café and rearranged her mother's coat collar, trying to hide her concern at the worn face so close to hers. Impulsively, she kissed the faded cheek, and was shocked to feel her mother's flesh burn against her mouth. Francesca was feverish. She had probably been like this all day.

'What was that for?' her mother asked, surprised at the kiss.

Marionetta shrugged. 'No reason. Will you promise me something?'

Her mother raised an eyebrow, waiting. 'Will you promise me you'll sit and have a cup of tea and a rest before you start the washing, Mamma? You're exhausted . . .'

'*Come mai?*' Francesca was irritable, 'Whatever for? I'll just get to bed even later.' She shook Marionetta away. 'Are you coming too, Papa?' She asked as she headed for the door, pushing Mario ahead of her.

Marionetta's grandfather was still at his place in the corner, nodding sleepily over a small brandy. The old man shook his head, stubborn. 'I'll stay. It's early yet . . .'

Marionetta's mother made an irritated noise. 'And who's going to get you home if you feel tired before closing time?'

'I won't get tired! In fact I may even help Tomasso behind the counter for a bit.'

Marionetta grinned at her long-suffering father, busy frying potatoes at the stove. 'Papa would be very pleased to have extra help, wouldn't you, Papa?' she said, teasing, as Francesca and Mario left.

Tomasso pulled a face at her through the heat haze of the chip fat. 'Of course you can stay, Papa,' he said wearily, ladling the fried potatoes onto a plate. 'Why not?' He could not resist adding sarcastically, 'It's not as if I need the table.'

'Papa!' Before Marionetta could admonish her father, the door swung open again and Antonio appeared, flushed and excited.

'I just met Mamma and Mario.' He was breathless. 'I told them they'd better scarper.' He paused. 'There's going to be a raid,' he said loudly, 'over the road!'

His words had the desired sensational effect. Customers craned their necks to see and climbed on their chairs to peer over the net curtains at the windows, as the familiar sound of a police-car bell approached. Marionetta joined her brother at the window.

'Who's being raided?' she asked, excited.

'The Triple X Club – chap in CID said they're pulling in some tarts,' Antonio said importantly, revelling in what he thought was police jargon. Sure enough, two police cars had screeched to a halt outside the darkened windows of the building opposite the Imperial, and several uniformed men leaped out and rushed inside. A ripple of excitement ran through the crowd in the café, and a large man jostled Marionetta out of the way to get a better look.

Marionetta turned to her brother, frustrated. 'Take me out there, Tony, I want to see —'

'No, Marionetta, stay here.' Her father had heard and was calling from behind the counter.

But it was too late. Antonio, pleased that he had infected Marionetta with some of the excitement he felt himself, had ushered his sister out onto the pavement.

The night air was intoxicatingly cold, and for a moment the harshness of it took Marionetta's breath away. She moved to the edge of the pavement, her hand clutching Antonio's sleeve.

'Here they come,' he was saying grimly. 'God, what a collection!' The police were ushering out a handful of women, pushing them across the road towards Marionetta and her brother and into a Black Maria which had materialized outside the Imperial. As the women were shoved past and into the van, Marionetta caught a whiff of exotic perfume, and the softness of chiffon brushed her face as someone's trailing scarf blew in a wintry gust. The women were stiff and dignified, only their faces reflecting their anger. One of them stopped for a moment in front of Marionetta to retrieve a corsage of violets that had fallen from her jacket into the gutter. As she straightened up, she seemed to see for the first time the wide-eyed girl in her waitress's uniform standing shivering and excited on the pavement in front of her. She hesitated for a moment, then held out the flowers.

'Here,' she said, 'You might as well have these.'

For a moment it seemed that no one moved or spoke, then all at once Antonio was shouting, 'She doesn't want your flowers, you tart!', a policeman was shoving at the woman from behind, saying, 'Get in there, you!', and Marionetta, in a swift movement, had shaken off her brother's restraining arm and had taken the flowers from the woman, looking her straight in the eye.

'Thank you,' she said, her voice a little fearful but her face brave. 'Thank you very much.'

The moment was over. The doors of the van slammed shut, the police cars revved their engines and the convoy moved off. The small crowd that had gathered on the pavement began to move away. Her nose buried in the sweet-smelling flowers, Marionetta turned and saw that the Lee Fungs, the Chinese family occupying the rooms above the café, were moving away from their windows, from which they had been observing the arrests. Even Bella, the café cat, had re-emerged onto her place on the window-sill, satisfied that the fuss was over and she could resume her feline study of Soho night-life.

'Honestly, Marionetta!' Antonio's voice was pained. 'Fancy accepting flowers from a prostitute! What do you think Father Joseph would say?'

Marionetta looked at her brother thoughtfully. 'I hope,' she said, 'that he would remember the story of Jesus and Mary Magdalene.'

Antonio snorted. 'How typical of you to turn it all into some romantic fairytale!' He snatched the flowers from her. 'Those women are filthy, diseased whores, and if Mamma knew you'd accepted flowers from one of them –'

Determinedly, Marionetta prised the crushed violets from her brother's hand. 'Ah,' she said, 'but who's going to tell her? Surely not Tony Peretti, the boy who went off drinking with his friends the other night when his dear mamma thought he was at the Church boys' club?'

Their disagreement was halted by the arrival of a large, gleaming Bentley which drew up silently opposite them, outside the Triple X Club's doors.

Antonio nudged Marionetta, excited, all thought of the violets forgotten. 'It's the Moruzzis!' he breathed. 'I might have known they'd turn up when it's all over.' He gulped a little as a tall, well-dressed man with an eye-patch over one eye emerged from the car and glanced casually in their direction. Antonio pulled his sister towards the safety of the café. 'We'd better go in . . .'

But the man had turned away, indifferent, and was following his two companions into the club. Marionetta watched them go, intrigued, as always. The Moruzzis were the kings of Soho. They ran everything – the gambling, the vice, the prostitution. Their reputation was fearsome.

'Marionetta!' It was her father, at the door of the café, anxious. 'Get inside, you'll catch your death in that wind!' Slowly she went inside, still holding the violets, distracted by the sudden moment of excitement in an otherwise dreary day.

Immediately there were orders to take and tables to clear, and it wasn't until an hour later, as the last paying customer left and Tomasso wearily locked the door, that she was able to think about what had happened. Papa was sitting with Nonno and Antonio, drinking liqueur, when Marionetta, still clearing up at the sink, found the violets where she had discarded them on the draining-board. They were a little dry now, and a few were already fading. She pressed the soft petals to her cheek. How wonderful they felt, how soft and exotic . . . She filled a tumbler with water and sat the flowers in it, placing the glass on a small shelf in the back room near where her coat was hanging, so that she wouldn't forget to take them home.

Wearily she went back into the café. 'Silvia's coming to collect me at eleven, Papa,' she said, 'so can I leave the floor until the morning. . .?'

'Yes, yes!' Her father waved her away, impatient, engrossed in his conversation. 'So you're saying the Moruzzis are looking to expand their business?' He was addressing Antonio. Both he and Franco were leaning forward, intent.

Antonio was enjoying his role as temporary centre of attention. He shrugged. That's what my friends at West End Central tell me. They're saying that Barty Moruzzi has scared off some of the other pimps and so he's got more girls on his books than anyone else in the area. And that new club in Greek Street, the one that just opened — they're saying it's Carmelo Moruzzi's, even though it's in someone else's name . . .

'Carmelo's the one we just saw, isn't he?' Marionetta was interested. 'The one they call the Pirate, because of his eye-patch?'

'They're in a bit of trouble though,' Tony carried on talking to Tomasso as if his sister had not spoken. 'They had a handy contact in West End Central, and he's just gone down for three years on a corruption charge.'

Tomasso raised an eyebrow. 'A bent policeman?'

'Apparently. He used to meet Carmelo Moruzzi every Friday night in Soho Square and tell him what was going on. Then Moruzzi would hand him a brown envelope and they'd go their separate ways. Nice little arrangement.'

'Carmelo?' Marionetta persisted, 'Carmelo Moruzzi, the Pirate? The one we just saw? He paid a policeman to tell him things?'

'None of your business!' Her father was agitated. This was no conversation for a young girl. 'I thought you said Silvia was coming at eleven. I just heard the clock strike.'

'So if he's the Pirate,' Marionetta persisted, 'which one is Barty? Is he the one in the black hat?'

Tomasso exploded. 'The Moruzzis are nothing for you to concern yourself with!' he snapped. 'All you need to know is that they're evil men and they'd slit your throat without thinking twice about it.'

Well, in that case,' Marionetta continued, rendered more than usually brave by her earlier encounter with the prostitute, 'don't you think I ought to know who they are? So that I can avoid them?'

Her grandfather, who had been silent, chuckled a little to himself, although his face remained grim. 'She's right, Tomasso,' he said. 'Just like her grandmother, she's always right . . . You might as well tell her about the Moruzzis.'

'Why?' Tomasso was annoyed. 'It's just to feed her silly excited ideas about criminals. She'll only go home and have nightmares.'

Antonio, annoyed at having lost the dominant position in the discussion, slammed his glass down on the table. 'Oh, for heaven's sake, Marionetta,' he said, pouring himself another measure of liqueur, under the disapproving eye of his father, 'it's quite simple to tell them apart. There are three of them.'

'And their father,' put in Tomasso, not to be outdone. 'Don't forget the father. Alfonso, he's called.'

'Alfonso . . .' The old man stared into space, remembering. 'Alfonso Moruzzi . . .'

'But no one ever sees him these days,' Antonio explained to his sister, a little condescending. 'He's retired. It's the sons who run things. A, B and C.'

Marionetta looked puzzled. 'What do you mean?'

'Just what I say. That's their names. A, B and C. There's A, Attilio. He's the big boss, keeps himself to himself. Barty – he's the middle one, B – a nasty piece of work by all accounts. Got a broken nose. And then Carmelo – C – he's the one they call the Pirate, with the eye-patch.'

'And what do they do?'

'That's enough, Antonio!' Tomasso's voice was stern. 'She's only a girl.' The doorbell jingled, and Marionetta's friend Silvia came in, still wearing her cinema usherette's uniform.

'*Ciao*, everyone!' she said. 'Ready, Netta?'

Marionetta ran to fetch her coat and, after a second's hesitation, pulled the violets from their makeshift vase, shook them a little, and then pinned them to her coat. Defiant, she went back into the café. For a moment her brother looked at the drooping purple flowers, then at his sister. Then he grinned, admiring her stubbornness. He wouldn't say anything.

'Goodnight, Papa! Goodnight, Tony! Goodnight, Nonno!' And she was gone, happy to leave the stifling little café at last, and too eager to escape to notice that her grandfather had not answered. He was staring into space, his mind full of memories. The beautiful Giulietta, Alfonso Moruzzi . . .

And what Marionetta did not see either, in her haste to leave the café, was a tall figure crossing Old Compton Street from the Triple X Club. The man strolled across the road and entered the Imperial Café. The only witness in the street was Bella the cat, crouched on her perch outside, her yellow eyes staring. Only she heard the gasp of fear from the men inside the café, and only she saw the gloved hand turning the 'Open' sign on the door to 'Closed', as the man with the eye-patch came to visit the Perettis.

Marionetta and Silvia, arm-in-arm, took their time heading towards their respective homes in St James's Residences in nearby Brewer Street. Neither was in a great hurry to enter that grimy tenement with its stale odours of too many people trying to inhabit a small space. There was never any room for entertaining friends or sitting up late and chatting. There was always a brother or a sister waiting to get to bed, or a weary parent in the sitting-room. The only privacy the two friends ever had was this kind – late-night walks home through the dark streets of Soho, clutching each other and gazing, transfixed, at the evidence of other more sordid lives unfolding around them.

Yet, like most Soho residents, in spite of the night-time vice and its accompanying sense of continual danger, the two young women would not have dreamed of living anywhere else in London. This magical network of tiny streets was to them the best place on earth, hidden away between the department stores of Regent Street and the bookshops of Charing Cross Road, bounded north and south by the bustle of Oxford Street and the theatres of Shaftesbury Avenue. They loved the sights and smells of Soho, from the early-morning blocks of ice melting on the pavement outside its restaurants, to the last eccentric drinker being ejected from the pubs at closing time. They loved the smell of *petits pains au chocolat* wafting from Madame Valerie's, the traces of perfume hanging in the air outside nightclubs. Happy in this melting-pot of races and cultures, where you could buy your coffee beans from an Algerian on Old Compton Street, fresh pasta from Italians on Brewer Street, and suspiciously cheap nylons from spivs in the Berwick Street market, they were completely at home even when the daylight faded and the cafés closed for the night. That was when the second layer of Soho society came into its own – the gamblers, the prostitutes, the late-night revellers. Girls like Silvia and Marionetta were told time and time again by over-zealous parents about the dangers of this nether world. They were exhorted to 'hurry home after dark, don't stop for anyone, don't speak to anyone'; sensible advice, but for two young girls the lights and sounds of late-night Soho were as seductive as the more familiar daytime Soho they knew so well. Consequently these night-time walks home were laced with a heady combination of fear and fascination, and they did not hurry quite as eagerly as perhaps they ought to have done.

They were passing Isola Bella, the smart Italian restaurant, and as usual, they paused for a moment to wave at Lino, a young Italian waiter who always managed to be hovering near the door at the time they passed each evening.

Marionetta nudged her friend. 'See? He was blushing!'

Silvia giggled, pleased. 'Of course he wasn't!'

'He was, I tell you! He's got a soft spot for you, that one.'

Silvia looked wistfully at her friend. 'Don't be silly. You know all the boys are after you. I can't compete with your looks, Netta.'

Marionetta squeezed Silvia's arm, ignoring her flattery. She dreamed of having a strong face full of character, like Joan Crawford or Bette Davis. She hated it when she saw men become transfixed by her startling, doll-like prettiness, when she was trying to say something interesting. In any case, she rather envied Silvia her pert, rounded features and her peroxide blonde waves – she was so much more fashionable than Marionetta, who still had long girlish hair and an old-fashioned, soulful look.

'I'm telling you,' she insisted, tugging Silvia away from Isola Bella's imposing entrance, 'I've seen the way he looks at you – it's you he's after, not me . . .'

Her voice faded as they negotiated their way past a group of prostitutes chatting on the corner outside Delmonico's Wine Store.

'Did you see that fabulous fox fur?' Silvia wistfully turned back for another look. 'Silver-grey fox! It must have cost a fortune . . .'

'Don't even think about it.' Marionetta was firm. 'You know how she earned that fox fur?'

'Of course I do!' Silvia was rueful. 'But surely there must be easier ways . . .'

As if in reply, a couple suddenly emerged from a dark

doorway in front of them and headed towards the kerb, the man calling loudly for a taxi. The two girls stopped, breathless at the sight of so much glamour. The woman, a glossy red-head swathed in a satin stole, picked her way through the late-night debris of revellers with some disdain, revealing a delicate satin-tipped toe beneath her ballgown.

'They've been to the Pavilion Club,' Marionetta guessed under her breath. 'Upstairs there's a casino . . .'

'See?' whispered Silvia triumphantly. 'I bet *she* isn't a tart!'

Marionetta smiled wryly as the smart couple disappeared into a taxi. 'No? I don't expect she'd call herself that, but maybe she's no different to those women back there –'

'Wise words from one so young.'

The voice startled them both and they turned, shocked. An old man had been standing in the dark shadows of the entrance to the Pavilion Club, and he had heard what they said. As the two girls turned and their faces caught the light of the street-lamp, he drew in his breath sharply, as if he had seen a ghost.

Marionetta was indignant. Usually the late-night prowlers of Soho left them alone. 'Come on, Silvia,' she said, turning, 'I think we should leave.'

The old man stared at Marionetta, his face white with shock. Silvia's kind heart took over. She stepped forward, concerned. 'Are you all right?' she asked, ignoring Marionetta's hissed 'Silvia!'

'I don't know.' The man's voice was trembling, and he held on to a nearby window-ledge for support. Silvia grasped his elbow. 'I think we should take him home, Netta.'

Marionetta was appalled. 'Well, I don't! Papa would be furious! And your father would beat you! You know we're not supposed to talk to anyone —'

Silvia frowned at her, embarrassed by her words. 'Netta, can't you see?' she said. 'This man's a *compaisano* – he's an Italian, one of us!'

The old man seemed to recover. He pulled himself upright, suddenly indomitable, powerful. Marionetta noticed for the first time his expensive overcoat, the soft leather gloves, the aura of money about him. He looked at Marionetta closely. 'And who', he said, 'is your papa, exactly?'

'None of your business!' Marionetta's head was up, defiant. This man was not a *compaisano*, he was rich and arrogant and belonged to the other world of Soho, not theirs, with its downtrodden workers scraping along trying to make a living.

Silvia, however, evidently felt differently. Her father had brought her up to believe that other Italians were automatically accorded respect. And the older they were, the more polite a young girl like Silvia should be. 'Her papa is Tomasso Peretti,' she said, glowering at Marionetta.

The old man stepped forward a little, studying Marionetta's face, a gleam in his eye. 'What a coincidence,' he said quietly. 'Peretti. And your name?'

Marionetta looked back at him, fearful. There was an air of menace about this old man that filled her with foreboding, in spite of his mild expression.

'Her name', said Silvia determinedly, 'is Liliana, *signore*. But everyone calls her Marionetta. And mine –'

But the old man held up his hand imperiously. 'I do not want to know your name,' he said. He looked at Marionetta again. 'I want to be taken to your father.'

'The café will be closed. He works in a café. It will be closed . . .'

The old man waved a hand, and a black car nosed its

way down the street towards them. 'The café will not be closed,' he said, as the car pulled up alongside them. 'Your father will be expecting me. Get in. You can show me the way.'

Marionetta's heart pounded in her ribs. She was about to be abducted. Terrible tales of white slave traders sprang into her mind. This man was going to drug her, take her away, sell her to a sheikh. A swarthy-looking man had emerged from the car and was holding the rear door open, standing stiffly to attention, for all the world as though he were a chauffeur at Ascot rather than a thug in a dimly lit Soho street witnessing the abduction of a young girl.

'Call the police!' Marionetta called to Silvia as she was bundled into the car.

Silvia's white face peered in. 'What do I tell them?'

The old man laughed incongruously and smiled at Silvia as he settled himself into the soft leather upholstery. 'Exactly. What indeed? I tell you what,' he had closed the door of the car and was speaking to Silvia through the rolled-down window, 'why don't you give your friend here half an hour, and if she's not back in St James's Residences by then, *then* you can call the police.'

The car moved away, leaving Silvia open-mouthed on the pavement. Too angry and curious now to be frightened, Marionetta turned to her captor. 'How did you know where I lived?' she asked, amazed.

She could see his eyes watching her, lit by the neon of a passing striptease club. 'You're Italian, aren't you?' he asked, his voice casual. 'So if you're Italian it's ten to one you live in St James's, isn't it?'

'I don't gamble,' she said frostily.

He laughed again, a low, gentle laugh. 'You have a strong character,' he said mildly. 'I like that.'

'It's not yours to like or dislike,' Marionetta was saying,

angry. But the car had already arrived outside the Imperial and had come to a smooth halt. Marionetta stared out. The lights were still on inside, and she could just make out four figures sitting round the table where she had left her father, brother and grandfather such a short time before. Someone else was with them . . .

Angrily she pushed past the old man and climbed out of the car. 'Papa!' she called, rushing inside the café, setting the bell off into a loud clanging and sending the terrified cat under a table. 'Papa —' she stopped. The fourth man at the table was the Pirate, none other than the dreaded Carmelo Moruzzi. He looked at her, interested, and then at the old man who had followed her inside.

'Papa,' he said, 'We've been expecting you. Tomasso here has put the coffee on.'

Marionetta was aware of the faces of the men in her family – Antonio, Papa, Nonno – all staring at the old man, their expressions reflecting different emotions: Antonio's numb amazement, Tomasso's anger, and grandfather . . . Marionetta gazed at him. He had risen to his feet, trembling, anguished, a look on his face that she had never seen before. It was a look of absolute terror.

'Alfonso Moruzzi,' he said, his voice suddenly sounding tremulous and small in the silence of the empty café.

The other old man looked at him and smiled a cruel smile. 'Franco Peretti,' he said. 'It's been a long time.'

Time seemed to hang suspended as the two old men faced each other, one in his shabby jumper and worn trousers, the other in his immaculate camel-hair coat, turning a smart trilby in his gloved hands.

Finally Alfonso Moruzzi spoke. 'It's time, old friend,' he said.

Franco seemed to shrink. 'No . . .' His voice quavered. 'No, Alfonso, not yet . . .'

'I'm afraid the hour of reckoning has come.' Alfonso Moruzzi began to peel off his gloves, loosening each finger carefully. 'I have come to claim my debt.'

Franco sat down suddenly in his chair, his face a strange, waxy grey. Marionetta moved forward anxiously. 'Nonno!' she said. 'Nonno, let me help you –'

But her grandfather put up a quivering hand. 'No, Marionetta,' he said. He looked up suddenly at his adversary, his face full of venom. 'Do me one favour, Moruzzi,' he said, his voice determined.

The other man raised an eyebrow inquiringly.

'Let her go.'

'Marionetta?' Alfonso Moruzzi turned to look at her. The look of desire in his eyes made Marionetta shudder. It was obscene – he was an old man. 'She's very beautiful, your Marionetta.'

'Let her go!'

The old man shrugged. 'Very well. My driver will take her home.'

'I don't want to go in your filthy car!' Marionetta burst out, 'I want to stay here, I want to hear what this is all —'

'Do as you're told, Marionetta!' It was her father, speaking to her savagely, in a way that she had never heard before.

'But I don't want to —'

'Just go!'

She stood there for a moment, at a loss. Seated round the table were three of the people she loved most in the world, something terrible was about to happen to them, and she was going to be sent away! Alfonso Moruzzi nodded imperceptibly at his son, and Carmelo the Pirate got up and went silently to the door, holding it open for Marionetta. He inclined his head politely, his one eye fixed on her implacably. She had no choice. She turned stiffly and walked out on to the darkened street and into the waiting car. The driver closed the door and went round to the driving-seat. Quietly, he started up the car and edged his way out of Old Compton Street, taking her home.